DEADLY
JEWELS

ALSO BY JEANNETTE DE BEAUVOIR

Asylum

DEADLY JEWELS

JEANNETTE DE BEAUVOIR

MINOTAUR BOOKS

NEW YORK

DEADLY JEWELS. Copyright © 2016 by Jeannette de Beauvoir. All rights reserved. Printed in the United States of America. For information, address St. Martin's Press, 175 Fifth Avenue, New York, N.Y. 10010.

www.minotaurbooks.com

Library of Congress Cataloging-in-Publication Data

Names: de Beauvoir, Jeannette, author.
Title: Deadly jewels / Jeannette de Beauvoir.
Description: First Edition. | New York : Minotaur Books, 2016.
Identifiers: LCCN 2015044397| ISBN 9781250045409 (hardcover) | ISBN 9781466844049 (e-book)
Subjects: LCSH: Women detectives—Fiction. | BISAC: FICTION / Mystery & Detective / Women Sleuths. | GSAFD: Mystery fiction.
Classification: LCC PS3604.E1125 D43 2016 | DDC 813/.6—dc23
LC record available at http://lccn.loc.gov/2015044397

Our books may be purchased in bulk for promotional, educational, or business use. Please contact your local bookseller or the Macmillan Corporate and Premium Sales Department at 1-800-221-7945, extension 5442, or by e-mail at MacmillanSpecialMarkets@macmillan.com.

First Edition: March 2016

10 9 8 7 6 5 4 3 2 1

*For Assaf, who inspires me (more than he knows),
encourages me, and keeps me on track. And for Jacob and
Anastasia, who continue to teach me a lot about love.*

ACKNOWLEDGMENTS

As always, thanks to my very lovely first readers with their quick eyes, patience, and fabulous suggestions: Carem Bennett, Marion Hughes, Alicia Sovas, Dianne Kopser, Assaf Levavy, and Fred Biddle. I come to you with plot holes and inconsistencies and impossible situations, and you help me mend them all.

And to all of those who continue to open up the world of this amazing city to me, especially to my very dear friend Edward Franchuk, for giving me Saint-Jean-sur-Richelieu; I cannot wait to share those amazing fish and chips at Capitaine Pouf with you again! A nod also to the real-life François and those who, every day, show the world how very special Montréal is.

Thanks to Daniel Rosenbaum for his kind help with Avner, the diamond business, and proper manners, and to Richard and Poppy Quintal for help translating my "French" French into more appropriate language for Québec.

The people I work with are fabulous, and I'm grateful beyond words to them: my literary agent from the Philip G. Spitzer Agency, Lukas Ortiz, and my amazing team from St. Martin's/Minotaur,

Daniela Rapp, Lauren Jablonski, Lisa Davis, and Ken Diamond: Without you, there would be no book. Thanks also to publicity guru PJ Nunn from Breakthrough Promotions for helping me introduce Martine LeDuc to mystery readers everywhere.

DEADLY JEWELS

PROLOGUE

He really had to do something about the noise the girls were making. His wife was supposed to be resting.

"Right," he said, going down on his knees on the rug next to his giggling daughters. "Enough of that. A little c-c-c-care, if you don't m-m-mind."

The stutter coming back because he was so tired.

"Father!" Margaret, the younger one, holding a bloodred ruby to the center of her forehead. "Aren't I beautiful?"

"You are the most b-b-b-beautiful of all p-p-princesses," he said gravely. "But even princesses have to work, s-s-sometimes."

"They call jewels 'bijoux' in French," she said, showing off.

"Indeed they do."

Lilibet was trying on a tiara for size. "I've never seen this one before," she said. "Why do you keep them locked away, Papa? What's the point of having crown jewels if nobody's ever meant to see them?"

He took the tiara from her and reached for one of the hatboxes. "The p-p-p-point is that they're th-th-there," he said. "And we're meant to be taking these apart, not trying them on." Worry was making him abrupt.

"What does that mean, that they're there? It sounds like a riddle!" The king allowed himself a smile. "The crown jewels are only ever used at c-c-c-coronations. You'll wear them when you are c-c-c-crowned queen, someday, Lilibet." God willing, he thought. If the whole island isn't speaking German by then.

"When will I be queen, Father?"

A conversational turn he hadn't expected. "When I d-d-d-die, my dear. That's when you'll be queen. It's a long way off."

"I don't want to be queen if it means that you'll die!" It was a squeal.

"Everyone dies," said Margaret unexpectedly.

"But not our sp-sp-sp-spirit," he said. "And that's precisely why we need to attend to the task at hand. Every st-st-stone taken out of every setting." Remembering what his wife had told him about children needing encouragement, he added, "and you're almost there, cl-cl-clever girls that you are."

"In hatboxes?" Earlier in the day, his wife had been shocked at the idea. "You cannot be serious, surely!"

"We can hardly send them off with, 'Caution, royal jewels' on the shipping labels, my dear," he'd said mildly.

"But hatboxes!" She shook her head. "Needs must, I expect. They're an important symbol. Best to get on with it. Have the girls help you, it will just look like playtime together."

"Perhaps we're the ones p-p-playing," he said. "Worrying about jewels when Winston is sending s-s-s-securities and gold."

"Mr. Churchill doesn't understand the value of tradition."

"What Mr. Churchill understands, my d-d-d-dear," he said, "is the value of fighting on, no matter what."

A moment of silence. "It's going that badly, then." It wasn't a question.

She was too perceptive, he thought. "Yes." There was no reason to deny it. "If the securities and gold are safe in Canada, we'll be able to *pay to stay alive. Supplies. Perhaps s-s-s-ships. It's what Winston s-s-s-says."*

"Bertie!" she said, and then stopped, gathering herself together. "Bertie," she said again, more calmly this time. "They won't invade England, will they?"

"My dear," he said. "I'm very much afraid that's the plan."

Now he sat on the floor with his two daughters, prizing jewels from their settings and wrapping them and putting them in hatboxes. A king and two princesses in the lamplight, the jewels flashing with colored refracted light and, all the while, the dread gathering in his heart.

CHAPTER ONE

"I see we have a lot of Americans on this tour," said the man with the headset standing at the front of the bus. "Okay, let me ask you this: who here speaks French? Raise your hands? Only a few people? Do you all understand English? Everybody? Yes? Good, we can do the tour in one language, eh?"

I watched as he started distributing maps of the city to the other Gray Line passengers. While all of Canada is supposedly bilingual, Québec's first language is officially French, and here in Montréal there's always the question. Go into a shop, and they'll say, "Hello-bonjour," all in one breath, and wait to see how you respond. In which language flavor, so to speak.

But while tourists come in all shapes, sizes, and native tongues, most of the people sitting on the bus with me were part of a group that had just gotten off the cruise ship docked out on the waterfront, tremendous and a little overpowering on the St. Lawrence Seaway skyline. Americans, all of them.

The guide handed me my map with nothing more than an impersonal friendly smile, and I was glad: what I didn't need was to be recognized and have anything on the tour changed or adapted because I was there. I'm the *directrice de publicité*—the publicity director—for the city of Montréal, and the tourism people tend to be a little touchy about my treading on their perceived territory. Most of the time we're able to play well together, but it's a tenuous relationship with plenty of opportunities for faux pas and worse.

I try to take the Gray Line excursions at least once a year, both the half-day tour of Montréal that I was on now and the full-day expedition that goes to Québec City. It would be easy, in my job, to just sit in my office down in the Old City and handle problems, soothe ruffled feathers, solve perceived, potential, and real crises, and leave every day with a headache the size of Manitoba—and that isn't what I signed on for. Taking the sightseeing tour reminds me of all the reasons I'm really here. The history of my city, its diversity, its cultural riches, its urban pulse, its amazing cuisines, all of that gets touched on during these trips, and every single bit of it lifts my spirits.

I was born here and have spent most of my life in Montréal, and I still fall in love with this city over and over again at least a couple of times a year.

My ability to do my job flows directly from that love. Like any entity, human or geographic, Montréal has its detractors, and I'm here to protect it, to make sure that they don't hurt the city too much. It ends up being damage control a lot of the time. And when you consider the city, provincial, and federal politics that go on here . . . well, you understand why what I do is so vital.

And so headache-inducing.

The guide, who had identified himself in the usual Montréal manner ("My name is Frank, or François in French"), was now asking us to open our maps. "Yes, this way. No, the other side. There you are. Here is what we call *centre-ville, vieux-Montréal,* the *vieux port*: that's the downtown area, with Old Montréal and the Old Port, eh? As you can remark, it follows the great river, the Saint Lawrence. We will soon see that Montréal is still a working port as well as an historic one."

He folded his map and everyone around me struggled to do the same. If any of these people had seen their seventieth birthday in the past few years, it would have surprised me. Good for them for being out and about. "We are starting our tour today in front of the Sun-Life Building, where during the Second World War, the British crown jewels were stored for safekeeping. And now, if everyone is ready, we'll begin, eh?" He settled himself in his seat and started the engine, causing the floor beneath our feet to vibrate. The bus pulled slowly and a little ponderously out into Dorchester Square.

"Again, I wish to welcome you to Montréal," François was saying in English. I'm one of the city's francophones—well, seriously, with a name like Martine LeDuc, what would you expect?—and so I automatically mentally assigned him the French version of his name rather than the English one. "I will tell you a little about it now. There are sixty-five subways in the city. These are a very useful way to get around, especially in the winter, eh?" He had the native Canadian way of lilting the end of his sentences so that they sounded like questions, as if he were inviting agreement. It's actually a pretty sophisticated psychological technique; hard to disagree when agreement is almost forced upon you.

"You may have heard of our underground city, what we call the *ville souterraine*, or the *ville intérieure*, the internal city, and you can go and see it for yourself at the end of this tour. I can drop you off right at one of the entrances, it is not a problem. Much of that underground city is linked by the Métro system, eh? Some people can go from their apartment buildings directly into the city, so that in January they can go and get their coffee and newspaper without putting on a winter coat!"

There was, I recalled, an almost absolutely apocryphal story of a man leaving his high-rise through an underground passage, getting his coffee and paper, hopping onto the Métro, getting off in the financial district, walking through a few corridors, and taking an elevator up to his office, where he finally realized that he was still wearing his slippers. It's one of the stories that we love to tell the tourists, and apparently the tale was still evergreen. I think I'd first heard it at least a decade ago.

There was a titter of reaction to his remark, the bus made a few turns as he navigated some crowded streets, and then he continued. "Montréal is a large city. Our downtown population is one-point-seven million people, and we welcome fifty million visitors every year."

"Imagine that!" said the woman sitting behind me. "No wonder everyone speaks English!"

I grimaced, but in silence. Most of us *do* speak English, actually, but for rather different reasons than she assumed. Like much of eastern North America, Québec had its share of being tossed back and forth between French and British governments, both completely ignoring the indigenous populations, and both going to war at tediously regular intervals. But it was the wealth of the fur traders and the railroad that built the big mansions up on Mont-Royal, and those captains of industry all spoke English.

Over there, on the west side of the city, they still do.

"Look on the right and you can see a fast-food restaurant, with the chicken?" said Francois. "You see it there? This is a chain of restaurants we have here, it's called Saint Hubert. They've been around since the nineteen-forties, delivering rotisserie chicken in yellow cars. I want you to try some; it's very good."

Well, my stepkids would agree with that, anyway. Both Lukas and Claudia, who lived most of the time in a Boston suburb with their mother and visited us on a regular schedule, loved St. Hubert chicken. Mine, it seemed, never quite measured up to what the friendly fellow with the red crown had to offer.

"Here we have the rue Sainte-Catherine, Saint Catherine Street. It is the longest commercial street in Canada. . . ." And has changed a lot, I found myself thinking. There was a time when a good third of this very long street was given over to peep shows, topless bars, and streetwalkers. Prostitution is legal in Canada, but this was a little too in-your-face for a lot of the city to feel comfortable with. Sainte-Catherine cleaned up most of its act, but sometimes I wondered if the upscale chain stores that lined it now were such a big improvement.

Some people, Claudia among them, thought so. The moment my stepdaughter arrives for her bimonthly weekend with her father and me, she's off and running: La Baie, Eaton Center, Sainte-Catherine. Bright lights and the dopamine high of purchasing.

I roused myself. Daydreaming about my family wasn't a great way to spend this tour. "This is the *quartier chinois*, Chinatown," François was saying. "It is very small, just this one street. It is very good; I invite you to visit it while you are here. I enjoy to have ginger and lobster here, myself." I listened to the sentence structure with a smile: François was clearly more at home in French than in English.

He wasn't alone in that—a lot of people here don't speak any English at all. Or speak it with some resistance. Take, for example, my boss, the current corrupt mayor of a city that specializes in corrupt mayors. Actually, Jean-Luc Boulanger and I were generally at odds about everything *but* our shared language. He wanted the impossible: to be popular (his biggest and best dream is to have a street named after him), but also to line his pockets at the expense of everyday Montréalers, whom I try to represent before him. That never goes very well.

If it weren't Jean-Luc, it would be someone similar and possibly even worse: we seem incapable of electing a mayor who might actually put the city's well-being first. I remembered my husband, Ivan, remarking a mere two weeks after the election of my current boss's predecessor, "Well, he hasn't called in sick yet. That has to be a good sign."

We were heading down into the Old City now, with a half-hour stop so passengers could get a coffee, take photographs, and buy souvenirs at the myriad tiny shops lining the rue Saint Paul. We were also very near my office, and I considered whether I should leave the tour and go look at the pile of papers and e-mails no doubt awaiting me. Maybe.

"This is the basilica of Notre Dame," François announced. "It was an Irish-American architect who designed the church. He was a Protestant, but he converted to Catholicism just so that he could be buried here, it is so beautiful. And now we will all look at our watches to determine the time we will meet here again. If you are not here, we have to leave without you. The good news is that you can wait, and I will be by again at the same time tomorrow!"

A wave of obedient laughter, and then people began getting up, reaching for maps, sweaters, and handbags. I sat and waited. The basilica is in fact, to my mind at least, the most beautiful church in the world. It's where I go to Mass every Sunday. It also is the place where, last year, I was kidnapped, after a surreal chase that had me hiding (rather stupidly) in confessionals, under pews, and behind the high altar, all of it to no avail. For one horrible half hour, the church that usually felt like a piece of heaven had threatened to become my own personal hell.

Not that it was the church's fault, of course. Still, not all of my feelings about the Protestant architect's masterpiece are positive.

François was waiting and I realized I was the last passenger getting off the bus. "*Tu viens de Montréal?*" he asked, conversationally, and I nodded. "Yes, I live here. I like taking the tour," I said in French. "It reminds me of how much I love the city."

That got a smile, quicksilver and warm, and then he was shutting the door, closing up the bus. "Will you join me for a coffee?"

"Thanks, but no. I have—an errand. I'll be back on time, though, don't worry!"

"*Très bien.*" He was already turning away and clearly still had no idea who I was. That was a good thing. Another good thing was that I could get to City Hall in less than two minutes, check in with my deputy, Richard, and be back before the tourists had finished buying their cans of maple syrup and their postcards.

As it turned out, I never got back to François and his tour.

Richard texted me even as I was crossing the Old City's cobblestones, heading toward City Hall. "Mayor wants to see you."

I stopped, staring at my smartphone, annoyed. I'd let everyone know I couldn't be available until well after four o'clock: the Gray Line tour is comprehensive. I punched his single-digit code into my phone and snapped when he answered, "What is it that can't wait?"

"*Bonjour*, Martine," Richard said calmly.

I sighed. He was right: courtesy should always come first. "*Désolée*, Richard. But, seriously, what is it? I'm out all afternoon. That's what's on the calendar. That's what I told Chantal. Out all afternoon. That's what everyone was supposed to expect." And *respect*, too, but there's not a lot of *that* in city government.

"I know that you are out all afternoon. Chantal knows that you are out all afternoon. The mayor knows that you are out all afternoon, also, but for his part, he doesn't care."

I sighed. This wasn't a battle I was going to win. "Okay. *Bon, d'accord.* So, what disaster has occurred that needs me specifically? It's not something you can handle?" Wishful thinking, Martine.

"Perhaps it is; he was not kind enough to offer up that information." Richard is nothing if not smooth. "But—well, I think you want to come in. There is a buzz that I cannot identify going on in the building. Something is happening here."

I grimaced; this wasn't going to be pretty. Somebody caught with his hand in the cookie jar, no doubt; that's our usual scandal. Sexual peccadillos aren't as popular here as they are in our neighboring country to the south: we're French enough that we really don't care who sleeps with whom, as long as the job gets done. But graft and corruption? That's our daily bread and butter. And that of the newspapers, needless to say: a PR nightmare.

My nightmare.

"All right. Give me five minutes to tell François."

"François? Who is François?"

"If it doesn't sound too odd, he's the man with whom I was hoping to spend the afternoon," I said. "The Gray Line tour director. You really have no idea what it's about?"

"As to that," Richard said cheerfully, "we may be pleasantly surprised."

There was a little man in the little room, and he was worried.

"They got here from London all right," he said to Faith Spencer, his assistant, for the fourth or fifth time.

London to Scotland. That alone seemed enough of a miracle.

She shivered. "I don't even like to think about it." She was twisting her hands. "I can't believe there's not some other way. Some other place. What happens if they never come back?"

He looked at her sharply. "It's hardly up to us to question it. London knows what they're doing. The Prime Minister—"

"You really believe this comes from the Prime Minister?" She started shuffling papers on her desk, lining up the edges of the piles so that they were perfectly even.

He said, "It's not up to us to question who it came from."

"You know what it means. It means they think we're about to be invaded."

"It means nothing of the sort," he said, irritable because he agreed with her.

The crates were sitting under guard in the next room; that knowledge alone was enough to induce a heart attack. The king himself had dismantled the jewels, and had hidden them in hatboxes, much to the delight of his two daughters, Elizabeth Alexandra and Margaret Rose; the royal princesses had helped with the packing, and Princess Margaret had even left a saucy note attached to one of them. Her Royal Highness was known for her cheekiness, and Faith had thought it best to discreetly remove the paper.

"Is it true," she asked, "that they're not even insured?"

He looked at her sharply. "For heaven's sake, Faith. Who would insure them? For what amount? How do you insure the embodiment of eight hundred years of monarchy?"

She sighed. "I suppose you're right." Faith liked things clear. She liked everything organized and official and aboveboard. She liked her work accompanied by regular correspondence and excellent filing and predictable outcomes.

This project was none of those things.

The crates had come to Greenoch under heavy—but very discreet—security, and even now the HMS Emerald was sitting in the harbor, waiting for them to be added to its cargo.

The Emerald, Faith knew, had already started ferrying valuables across the Atlantic: back in September it had headed up a convoy from Plymouth to Halifax with gold—the first installment, as it were. Two million pounds sterling in gold. The mind boggled.

And now? Churchill had replaced Chamberlain as prime minister, and he gave the convoys a name: Operation Fish. He'd used the War Powers Act to confiscate securities ledged with the Bank of England and was sending them, along with the gold bullion, to pay for munitions.

Britain was isolated and embattled and the convoys were its lifeline.

The Royal Navy knew only that there was additional freight being *added, and sailors had been instructed to dress in tropical whites; there was a lot of guessing among the men as to why, and what their destination might be. The gold bullion that HMS Emerald was taking across the Atlantic to safety in Canada had already been loaded, openly enough; no one in Greenoch had any feelings about gold bullion one way or the other, and they had to pay for the convoys somehow.*

But the crown jewels? That was something else altogether.

CHAPTER TWO

Jean-Luc was lying in wait for me.

Chantal, our administrative assistant, lurked nervously in the corridor outside the office, looking, as always, as if she'd chosen her outfit somewhat randomly from a vintage-clothing shop, and not a great one at that. For all I knew, perhaps she had. "He is here," she said in a low voice.

"Who is here? And why are we whispering?"

She lowered her voice still more. "*Monsieur le maire.* He is waiting for you."

"Yes, I know, Richard already told me," I said briskly. "I just need to drop off—"

"*Non,*" she interrupted. "*Tu n'comprends pas.* He is *here*. In your office."

Well. That was a first. Whatever this was, it had to be serious. I wouldn't even have suspected that Jean-Luc knew where my office was located.

Not only was my boss in there, he was pacing like a harried hamster. The comparison was apt: he had plump cheeks that looked like pouches, coupled with a tendency to sniff the air. Trying to home in on possible illicit monetary sources, no doubt. "Madame LeDuc," he said as I opened the door. "What has kept you?"

I walked past him to put my purse on my desk. Standing behind it gave me high ground in terms of authority, something Jean-Luc never voluntarily gave up. I wondered why he'd been willing to do it this time. "I was working out of the office," I said.

"So I understand. That is the trouble. You're letting the biggest PR coup this city has ever experienced slip through your fingers!"

Did I mention his tendency to lapse into hyperbole? I should have. I assumed a serious expression. "What coup is that, monsieur?"

He wasn't going to give it away that easily. He pulled out one of my conference chairs and sat down, adjusting his ever-perfect suit coat and tie as he did. A well-dressed hamster, my boss. "I have called a meeting," he said importantly.

That was nothing new: the mayor liked meetings. Preferably long ones at upscale restaurants, with the city footing the bill. I didn't get invited to *those* very often. Mine were more of the let's-see-what-Martine-has-done-wrong-this-time variety, held in his office or at a convenient corridor for maximum spectator attention. "I see," I said cautiously.

"In one hour," he added, looking at his Rolex by way of illustration and urgency.

"And can you tell me what it is about, monsieur?" I was starting to feel testy with his drama. For this I gave up my afternoon with François and the Gray Line?

"Madame, all that you need to know is this. You must be there. Monsieur Rousseau must be there. And you must be prepared to launch a campaign that will bring the eyes of the world to Montréal!" Well, you can see how he got elected. Who isn't up for a little overstatement served fresh with their morning *café* and croissants? "I came here myself," he added importantly, "to be sure that you understand, and to see that you are on time."

That was a little unfair. I'm always on time. In fact, I'm usually the first to arrive for any appointment or meeting. Courtesy, one would think; yet actually it's because I like to be able to pick my geography. There's nothing worse than coming late to an awkward encounter and finding oneself sitting in the least comfortable seat. And with Jean-Luc, most encounters tend toward the awkward.

"I'll be there, monsieur," I said levelly.

"*Bon.*" He tapped his knees and lifted himself out of the seat, acting for all the world as though we'd just made an important decision. "My office. Four o'clock."

"I'll be there," I said again; but I said it to his back.

Chantal was hovering in my doorway in the wake of his departure. Jean-Luc always made her nervous. One of his predecessors had once sacked the entire secretarial and administrative staff at City Hall, and she remembered that. Of course the strikes and marches that followed hadn't been to *his* advantage. "Are we in trouble?" she asked, eyes wide.

"*Some*thing's going on," I said slowly. "I don't know what to think. Where's Richard?" Richard Rousseau was my deputy and always seemed to have his finger firmly on the pulse of City Hall. If anyone knew what this was about, it would be him. And if *he* didn't know . . .

"In his office, I think," said Chantal. "Shall I tell him to come in?"

"Would you?"

I turned and looked out the window behind my desk while I was waiting. If I hadn't wanted this job for the substance, I'd have wanted it for the view: City Hall sits on a rise in the Old City, and my window takes in the esplanade and the river, an ever-changing panorama of action. I could even see the cruise ship that the geriatric tour goers had debarked from, and I could imagine François's tour continuing: "These are silos and grain elevators: the island is manmade, using rock that was excavated from the Métro and the Underground City. They call this the Canal Lachine, does anyone know why? It is because when the French arrived here, they thought it was China, eh?"

Or something to that effect.

Behind me, Richard cleared his throat. Dressed impeccably—he was always dressed impeccably, always looked like he just stepped out of a magazine spread, elegant and at ease, even during that bad time last year when his new girlfriend was murdered and he was briefly on the list of suspects—and bemused. "Monsieur Boulanger is in good spirits," he said cautiously.

"So it would seem."

"It makes one nervous," Richard said.

"It does indeed," I agreed. "You don't know anything about this magnificent PR coup we're about to be orchestrating, I assume?"

He shook his head, sitting down in the chair that Jean-Luc had vacated and crossing one elegant leg over the other, flicking an imaginary bit of lint off his trousers. I swear this man should be gay. "I hear it's good news, for once." He smiled. "That makes for a change, anyway, doesn't it?"

"Boulanger's not exactly about change," I reminded him. Jean-Luc wanted everything exactly the same all the time, so that he wouldn't take the fall if any innovation failed. Change was bad; status quo was good.

Richard shrugged elegantly. "Perhaps he is now."

Richard and I were on time, but that turned out to be meaningless: everyone else was already there. Maybe the mayor had things he wanted to talk about with them before I came into the room.

"Ah, Madame LeDuc," Jean-Luc said as we entered. "Kind of you to join us." He was speaking English, and that underlined my earlier conclusion that this was indeed something different and, for once, positive: *monsieur le maire* doesn't do anger in English. If he were going to list failures, the numbering system he used would be French.

"I don't mean to interrupt," I said, taking in the table and the people sitting around it.

"It is nothing. Thank you for coming," the mayor said, gesturing a welcoming hand. Richard and I slipped into the only two vacant seats at the conference table. Richard was looking amused; he'd tell the story, later, and everyone would laugh.

Still, the fact that Jean-Luc was in a good mood had to be appreciated.

I looked around the room to see what—or who—had inspired this generosity of spirit. Three men, one woman, and I only knew one of them, Dr. Pierre LaTour, curator of Montréal's Pointe-à-Callière archaeological museum. When one considers that my job really involves knowing people, a lot of people, knowing only *one* of them? That alone was strange.

"You know *monsieur le docteur* LaTour, of course," said the mayor, and Pierre and I nodded to each other. "This is Mademoiselle Patricia Mason." Her name—which he managed to mangle—made it clear why we were all speaking English.

She smiled. "Hello." The other two men were, apparently, not to be introduced.

The mayor cleared his throat. "We have wonderful news," he informed me.

Okay. I settled my face into an I'm-waiting-to-hear-wonderful-news expression and shot another look at Richard. He gave a very Gallic shrug in response.

Patricia Mason was about ten years younger and about ten pounds heavier than I was, with neat black hair in a bob and glasses that kept sliding down on her nose; she used her left index finger to keep pushing them up.

"It's for my doctorate," she explained now, her voice earnest, her eyes eager behind the thick lenses. "I've been doing research in London and Scotland and here in Montréal for my dissertation, and the mayor thought that you might be interested in it. In what I've been studying, and what I think I'm about to find—um—what I'm going to confirm."

"I see." I was noncommittal, my interest level ratcheting down a notch. Doctoral research may be—*must* be, I suppose—intensely exciting for those involved in it, but my experience has been that long dissertation titles and pages of footnotes have little to do with anything related to public relations.

Museums, yes. My office? Not so much.

Patricia was undaunted by my lack of enthusiasm. "As you probably know, in Europe, World War Two displaced a lot of valuable items—art, jewelry, that sort of thing."

"Wasn't most of it stolen by the—er—Germans?" I asked. Like everyone else since the book and its subject had been made into a George Clooney movie, I knew about the Monuments Men.

She nodded. "Of course, but that's normal. Well, normal, no. I mean normal in terms of war. That's what occupying forces do, they steal stuff." She brushed it away with her hand, an annoying gnat of an idea. "But what's known, also, is that the United Kingdom was looking at what would happen if the British Isles were occupied, and so, very early on, they conducted a massive shipping effort, sending a lot of their treasures abroad."

"Gold," said the mayor, nodding. I could almost see it reflected in his eyes. He managed to restrain himself from licking his lips.

"Gold," Patricia agreed. "A whole lot of gold. Gold that they needed to pay for war expenses. Gold to pay for the American and Canadian convoys that were supplying Great Britain. The island would have starved, otherwise." The glasses had slipped a little and she pushed them up again. "It went on for months, this shipping stuff to North America in payment. It was called Operation

Fish—yeah, I know, but it really was called that, I'm not making this up. It was the largest movement of wealth in history." She looked around the room, her face positively glowing. "The treasure ships," she said softly.

Jean-Luc's eyes were predatory. "Treasure ships," he repeated.

"The first shipment," said Patricia, "was sent to Canada in 1939 on a British cruiser called the HMS *Emerald*—I'm not making *that* up, either—which docked at Halifax."

"Interesting," I said. I still had no idea where this was going, but I could suddenly see it clearly, what she was describing: rain sluicing down on the ships plowing through the North Atlantic waves, the holds filled with gold. Gold to pay for food and supplies. Gold to pay for the life of a besieged country.

She caught my eye and smiled. "Bear with me, Ms. LeDuc," she said. "It really *is* interesting, and the story gets better." A deep breath. "So, anyway, the gold was transferred off the cruiser in Halifax. There was a train waiting, and the next day it arrived here in Montréal. The gold spent the war in a specially designed underground vault three stories under the Sun-Life Building on Metcalfe Street. No one knew: it was all very hush-hush."

It was tickling something in my mind; I'd heard about that already. The combination of gold and Sun-Life (which, in the normal Montréal custom of using both French and English when possible, was called the *Edifice Sun-Life Building*) sounded familiar.

Or maybe it just felt that way because of the voraciousness of insurance companies.

Patricia shifted in her chair, pushing her glasses up on her nose. "Something else that no one knew, but that's been circulating as rumors in the war-history community, was that the British crown jewels were on that first ship, on the HMS *Emerald*, as well."

Okay. That was it. Not exactly stop-the-presses earthshaking news, since François of the Gray Line tours had already announced it as fact—and offhandedly at that—just that very morning. And I'd heard the rumor before, somewhere, sometime, I was pretty sure. Rumors came and went. But proof? I looked at Patricia Mason, doctoral student, and found her wavelength with a click. If there *were* proof positive, then we could work with that. I could see the press releases already, the headlines: MONTRÉAL PLAYS VITAL ROLE IN WORLD WAR TWO. MONTRÉAL SAVES THE ENGLISH CROWN. Even as a historic event, it was good PR.

Who was I kidding? It was *great* PR. I exchanged glances with Richard and he was nodding. "The crown jewels *definitely* spent the war in the basement of the Sun-Life Building," I repeated. "You have proof."

She nodded, then qualified her agreement. "I have a *line* on proving it," she said. "I'm at McGill, and so I have some resources, stuff that's open to scholars. Archives. Memories. And, of course, Doctor LaTour."

Pierre LaTour caught the metaphoric ball from her and cleared his throat. "Mademoiselle Mason is interested in what we're doing with the museum expansion in terms of the access that might be available as we're opening up some of the disused underground tunnels," he said.

Ah. I parsed his rather flowery language into museum expansion and tunnels. That, I knew about. The museum, which was primarily archaeological in focus, was engaged in a multimillion-dollar expansion slated to be finished in a few years—timed not coincidentally with the city's 375th anniversary. My office was already hard at work planning events in conjunction with the tourist board. There were milestones in the meantime, including excavating and opening up St. Ann's Market, the site of Canada's 1832 parliament.

But the largest and most ambitious part of the work was the

underground network that would be made available for the museum complex via the collector sewer that was all that remained, now, of the Little Saint-Pierre River.

Montréal isn't exactly a stranger to the underground. Its own underground or interior city, dreamed of in the urban-loving 1930s and gradually coming into being in the decades after the war, is one of the world's largest, offering food, shopping, transportation, and entertainment to a city that gets more snow every winter than does Moscow.

What the museum was doing, however, had nothing to do with shopping for high fashion or the occasional bite of fast food.

The Iroquois—the First-Nations tribe that called this area Hochelaga and lived here until Samuel de Champlain claimed it for France—no doubt used the Saint Pierre River. In 1611 Champlain wrote about the river, the wild strawberries and other fruit and nut trees that grew along its banks.

But when Montréal needed land, the river went underground. Literally.

"As you know," said Pierre, "we are undertaking an important project at the museum. The Little Saint-Pierre River, converted into a collector sewer, will be the backbone of the Montréal Archaeology and History Complex: a network connecting a unique collection of authentic archaeological and historic sites. The collector sewer, accessible along a distance of three hundred and fifty meters, is a magical place in itself, a dramatic and fascinating journey into the belly of our historic city. Aboveground, it will be transformed into urban gardens."

Patricia Mason was nodding eagerly. "Most of Montréal's rivers were buried in the late 1800s," she said. "Well, they had to be, they'd become open sewers, the city's reputation was terrible."

"A public-relations nightmare," murmured Richard.

She hadn't heard the undercurrent of amusement I'd caught in my deputy's voice. "Right? But then the William Collector, which diverted part of the Saint Pierre River, was built, and it was an amazing engineering feat for its time. So all the sewers went underground. And that's how Montréal grew, actually, because the villages around it couldn't afford to build sewers on their own, for themselves, so they became part of the city."

"Give up independence, get sanitation," Richard said. This time the irony was felt by everyone in the room, and the mayor gave him a hard look. Well, he would: all of those incorporated villages were now Jean-Luc's domain. He didn't really care how they got there, as long as he could make some money from them.

"I'm not sure that I understand what the sewers have to do with the crown jewels," I said. Someone had to get to the point. "If they were stored here, they were stored in the basement with the gold, isn't that the story?"

"It's more than a story," snapped Patricia. She took a second to compose herself, then said, carefully, "They really were here. That's not a rumor. That's true, and I'm going to prove it. But you're right about there being a rumor. The *rumor* is that some of them stayed here, they were stolen and smuggled out through the sewers."

She paused. "The rumor is that there are still British crown jewels here in Montréal somewhere. And I believe that *that's* true, too."

It was a gamble, and no one knew that better than Winston Churchill himself. The nation was taking a gamble on him, and he was taking a world-shattering gamble with its future.

"You're a bloody Cassandra," his friend Frederick Lindemann told him. "Nobody wants to hear what you have to say, and you're always right, which makes it all a damned sight worse."

"Not always," Winston grunted. "Was wrong about the war in Spain—thought they knew what they were doing. Was wrong about the king's abdication—still angry with him about it, in fact."

"You've been right about Germany all along," said Frederick. "And that's what bloody counts."

Was it?

He'd already started setting things in order. On the same day that Germany invaded Belgium and the Netherlands, he'd taken the prime minister's seat in the House of Commons Chamber for the first time and ruthlessly woke Britain from her appeasement. On this, the darkest of nights, he hoped he wasn't too late.

The British Expeditionary Force, long considered the finest fighting machine in the world, was standing alongside the French army. But everyone knew how poorly trained and equipped the French were. Still, the BEF would take care of things; they always did. Who could have known what would happen?

Now, he knew.

His aide had woken him at 7:30 on May 15, five days after he became prime minister. "Urgent telephone for you, sir. Monsieur Reynaud, the French president."

Paul Reynaud was hysterical. "We are defeated!" he screamed. "We have lost! Tout est perdu!"

Winston put down the telephone, took a deep breath, and wrote his first letter to the president of the United States. There was simply no time to lose: France was about to fall, and Britain was clearly going to be next. The Americans had to enter the war. "We expect to be attacked here ourselves, both from the air and by parachute and airborne troops in the near future," he wrote. "If necessary, we shall continue the war alone and are not afraid of that. But I trust you realize, Mr. President, that the voice and force of the United States may count for nothing if they are withheld too long."

"It's all about the Americans now," he told his wife. "We've got to get them involved. They have to see that it's the only course."

"It may not be in time," she said.

"I know. I know that."

The next day, he put legislation before the House of Commons that The Daily Telegraph *described as "the most sweeping constitutional measure ever placed," giving the government full powers over both property and persons in Britain. Defending it before the war cabinet, he was able, somehow, to find the right words: "It had hitherto been thought that a seaborne invasion of this country was an enterprise which the Germans could not hope to launch with any prospect of success for some considerable time. I think the events of the past few days and the grim possibilities of the next must cause us to modify our views."*

Days later, Boulogne fell, and Calais was under siege. The boys from the British Expeditionary Force were flooding the beach at Dunkirk, right up against the English Channel, and that had to be his first concern: getting them out. Getting them home. Keeping them alive.

They'd fought fiercely and well, they'd endured a nightmare crossing northern France, only to find themselves caught between the sea and Jerry, with nowhere to go, past exhaustion, wounds going septic, and no hope of escape.

British warships were unable to make it to the beach because of Dunkirk's shallow harbor. There was only one thing to do. "Get me everything," Winston told his aide. "Every Thames River sightseeing boat, every fishing boat, every yacht, everything that can cross the Channel, I want them over there, evacuating."

"Sir?"

He was impatient. "They can ferry men out to the warships. Let the call go out!"

It did, and the miracle of Dunkirk was that they responded, every last one of them. It still gave him chills, the bravery, the sacrifice, the instant and unequivocal support. Yachts, pleasure boats, yawls. Sailboats from a sailing school. Ferries, trawlers, sloops. Fishermen all up and down the coast battening their nets in preparation for hauling a different catch altogether onto their decks.

Anything that had a means of propulsion was called for—and everyone answered the call. All of them sailing straight into horror: Calais aflame, the Luftwaffe strafing the beaches and the harbor, boats exploding, and still there they were, going over again and again until all the boys were safe. That was who the British were, thought Winston. That was who was worth saving.

He didn't have time to waste. As soon as the "little boats" had performed their miracle, there was more to be done. Most of the men had been saved, but their fighting equipment was still littering the beach in France, being picked up and over by the Germans. Britain's munitions factories were already running day and night, but it would take months to replace what had been lost.

Britain didn't have months.

Two things had to be done: weapons, airplanes, and warships had to be purchased from the United States. And Britain's wealth—some of it in gold, but most of it in the form of securities—had to be kept out of German hands.

Winston had a plan that would take care of both.

CHAPTER THREE

Well, at least I could see why my boss was suddenly so interested in history. PR was one thing; finding buried treasure was, as the ad says, priceless.

And I could see something else, too: if he stayed involved, this could quickly get so far out of hand that we'd never recover. The feds would get involved. Great Britain would get involved. Well, those things were going to happen anyway; but it would be one thing for Richard and me to deal with it, and something else altogether to leave it to Jean-Luc. He would assume he could handle them the way he handled local politics, and *that* meant that it would all blow up, and blow up very quickly.

Talk about a PR nightmare. Treasure ships, indeed!

I took a deep breath and looked at the guys sitting silently across the table. "I know you know who I am," I said, choosing one of the two at random to address, "but it would be helpful if you could return the favor."

If he was upset by my sarcasm, it didn't show. "Yves-Robert Blouin," he said blandly. "Assistant commissioner and commanding officer, C Division, RMCP."

Oh, hell. Of course: the feds were already in on it. Who else *but* the Royal Canadian Mounted Police would be involved, if Patricia was right? That made all the sense in the world, and complicated the matter no end. I looked at the other man. "And you, monsieur?"

"Regional director, CBSA." He was apparently to remain nameless; and who cared, really? What mattered was that the feds were in on this in force, and in civvies as well: both the Royal Canadian Mounted Police and the Canada Border Services Agency have impressive uniforms for those in the organizations' higher echelons, but these two guys weren't wearing them.

"Well, this is all very interesting," I said, keeping my voice as level and uninterested as I could. "Mademoiselle Mason, if you could return with me and Monsieur Rousseau to our office, we can talk more about how far your research has gone, and how specifically we can be of assistance to you."

Jean-Luc was nodding. If someone else wanted to do the work, that was just fine with him, as long as he got the credit. And any errant crown jewels that happened to be lying around as well, of course. "You will keep me informed, *naturellement*, Madame LeDuc?"

I exchanged another glance with Richard. My initial thought had been right: this thing was going to get very out of control very quickly if we didn't do something. Jean-Luc might be enjoying the attention he was getting now, but this was going to turn into an interagency pissing match that he didn't have the ability or intelligence to foresee—and that he didn't have a chance of winning, though he'd gladly bleed the residents of his city dry in the attempt.

"This meeting is perhaps premature," I suggested. "*Messieurs*, gentlemen, my office will be happy to work with Mademoiselle Mason and McGill University on this matter. If I understand the situation correctly, no current crime is under investigation, yes? And as this is Montréal, even if there is a cold case to be reviewed, that surely falls to our *own* police force?" I looked hard at Jean-Luc and, miracle of miracles, he picked up on what I was talking about. "But of course it is our own police force that will do any investigation!" His voice was explosive, outraged. "That is a given."

"Should it lead to issues of interest to the national or international community, then of course *monsieur le maire* will be quick to inform you," I went on, and then turned to Patricia. "Mademoiselle Mason? Perhaps you would like to accompany us to our office now so that we can discuss specifics?"

She was still looking a little dazed, which was surprising: institutions of higher learning practice cutthroat politics, and she should have been accustomed to territorial disputes. "Well, yes, of course," she said uncertainly, looking back at Jean-Luc as though for direction.

He nodded, his fingers tapping a quick tattoo of sound on the edge of the conference table. "Please go ahead, mademoiselle," he said generously. "These gentlemen and I will continue our conversation." He'd found my path of navigation through the quicksand and was ready to follow it enthusiastically. Jean-Luc might have started out liking the federal attention, but once he realized how much they outweighed him—and how little they were impressed with his office—his survival instincts came to the fore. I could usually count on that.

Manipulation of my boss? *Mais oui.*

Once in the corridor, though, I rethought my invitation to go chat *chez moi*. The reality is that my office is located in a public building, and either of the gentlemen we'd left—or a host of other people—were liable to walk in on us at any moment. Interrupt us. Overhear us.

And this was something I'd rather keep control of, at least for as long as I could.

There were plenty of places in City Hall that, one could argue, were private, but I'd had a thought. Getting Patricia out of the building altogether seemed like the best possible solution to keeping the lid on her information, and there were only two other places in the city that I was absolutely, positively guaranteed were private. One of them was my apartment, and both Ivan and I have always been clear that it constitutes neutral territory. It's a place of refuge: he doesn't bring his work there, and neither do I. That left only one option.

"Have you ever," I asked Patricia Mason, "been to the Montréal Casino?"

Nothing exciting had ever happened to Alexander Craig.

His father had been a banker, and it was correctly assumed by everyone involved that the young Alex would be a banker as well. He didn't mind; in fact, he rather liked the work, the precision of it, its predictability. He was meticulous and correct, and the cloister-like en-claves of the Bank of England's Foreign Exchange Control in Thread-needle Street suited him to a T.

He was in his office every morning promptly at nine o'clock. He preferred milk, no sugar, in his tea when elevenses rolled around; and he went to the same restaurant for lunch every day precisely at one. There were no crises, no panics, not even any decisions of tremendous import to be made. Each day was like the one before it and the one that would follow, and Alex was comfortable with that.

His wife, Marjorie, knew little about his work and expected noth-ing more: it was always very hush-hush. "Boring, if we knew the half of it," she guessed, and spent most of her time tending to the needs of the couple's two daughters.

And then came the Friday when Alex Craig came home and did not have his usual whiskey at 6:00, did not have his usual exchange of banalities with his wife about his day, did not inquire into the menu for dinner. Instead, on this Friday, he told Marjorie to pack. "We're moving to Canada."

For the first time in his life, something intensely exciting was hap-pening to Alexander Craig.

He'd been plunged from his predictable stable routine into something fearful and exciting and historically significant, and didn't know whether to be pleased or dismayed by it. For Alex was preparing to supervise a special convoy, to cross the Atlantic with Britain's gold reserves as well as the vast wealth it possessed in negotiable dollar and foreign securities. Once there, he would act as the custodian of the foreign stocks and bonds privately owned by British citizens and corporations, securities that had been taken over by the government to fight the war.

They were preparing to move more wealth than had ever been moved in the history of the world. And he was the man in charge.

It was extraordinary, really. Who could ever have imagined?

He was going on ahead of the family, getting ready in a matter of days. That first evening he spent trying to design crates that would carry the securities—imagine, him, designing crates! And then packing hastily, leaving most of the moving up to his wife. "You need to take more," she said, worried. "You're not going to have much money out there."

A rather delicious irony, wasn't it?

First time he'd ever been to Scotland, and he wasn't seeing much of it now. Sheeting rain; if this was what it was like now, he wouldn't care to be here in winter. They could keep this weather, the Scots.

He didn't have to stay there very long, anyway. The gold and securities had already traveled from London and were under guard in Greenoch; he'd met the administrator, Faith Spencer, and she struck him as a woman who knew what she was about. They gave him a bed in the officers' quarters and he slept soundly.

For the last time in quite a while, if he'd but known it then.

They'd spent the night loading the Emerald, *and by the time Alex had breakfasted and dressed they were ready for him.*

Faith Spencer met him dockside, wearing a mac and carrying a clipboard. "2,229 boxes of gold bullion," she said, reading from a rain-soaked list, "and 500 boxes of securities, worth two hundred million pounds."

He stared at the ship for the first time. "Good God."

"There wasn't enough room," she said, apologetically. "The gold all fit in the ammunition lockers, that was fine, but we didn't know about all the securities. We've had to get them tucked in wherever we could."

That was an understatement. Crates were in all sorts of odd places, in the captain's day room, in the mess hall, everywhere. The captain himself, Francis Flynn, was unhappy about it. "No room to breathe," he grumbled. "Ah, Mr. Craig. These your babies, then?"

"It would seem so," Alex agreed, shaking the other man's hand.

"Well, we'll make a run for it," the captain said. "Have some help along the way"—he swept his hand out over the harbor where four other naval vessels were being readied to put to sea—"and good weather for the first day, anyroad. Hope you're comfortable on a vessel at sea, Mr. Craig."

"I don't know," Alex confessed, "I've never been to sea before."

"Really?" It seemed a novel and bizarre concept to the captain.

Alex shrugged. "I work in the City."

"Not now, you don't. Well, come on board, laddie, and make yourself at home."

Faith Spencer was sympathetic. "Good luck, Mr. Craig," she said. "I trust you will all arrive safely."

"Thank you, Mrs. Spencer."

He was remembering that conversation a day later as they rounded the tip of Northern Ireland. Safety? They didn't need Germans: they had the weather.

It was like sailing into a wall of water: a full gale blowing and mountainous waves hammering the vessel. Up one side of the wave and down the other. Up one side of the wave . . . Alex dashed for the railing again.

His City overcoat wasn't doing much for him in the North Atlantic cold, and he'd long ago thrown up anything that remained in his stomach. How long could this nightmare go on? Minutes moved like hours. If he were dashed over the side, he thought miserably, it would be an improvement.

Captain Flynn was equally unhappy, though for different reasons. "The destroyers are slowing us down," he complained on the third night.

"We need them," said the first officer. "They've got the asdic sonar, they can locate the U-boats."

"There won't be any need to locate them soon, we'll all know where they are, they'll be clustered around us," said the captain. "There's a gale blowing out there, and we're sitting ducks."

"What's the alternative, then?" asked Alex, who had no idea what they were talking about. He wondered if he looked as green as he felt.

The two other men conferred some more and then the captain turned to Alex. "We're going to send the convoy back," he said. "We'll move faster without the escort."

Oh, excellent, the man from the Bank of England thought. Moving even faster than this.

He wanted to die.

CHAPTER FOUR

We took the Métro's yellow line to the Jean-Drapeau station, named for one of Montréal's more beloved mayors (hence my own boss's craving to be memorialized in a similar manner; he harbors delusions that we all love *him*, too) and located out on the Sainte-Hélène Island. The station connects people to the La Ronde amusement park—now part of the Six Flags franchise—and to Montréal's casino, located in what was originally constructed as the French pavilion of the 1967 Expo, a sort of world's fair that did a lot for the city's economy back in the day.

Drapeau is credited with the establishment of the Métro itself, along with securing the city as the site for both Expo '67 and the 1976 Summer Olympics. Not a bad legacy, altogether. Jean-Luc, on the other hand, so far is credited with $500 lunches and $450,000 petty cash accounts.

Yeah, okay, they're about even.

Patricia was quiet for most of the ride, and my efforts at small talk got little response. She wasn't interested in the weather. She agreed unenthusiastically that the Métro was faster and quieter than other subway systems she'd been on. She didn't have a lot to say about McGill as an institution. I thought she might be miffed for my having cut her triumphant presentation short, but I wasn't about to bring the subject up in the crowded Métro car, even speaking English, so I kept babbling inanely about superficial topics. If my PR gig didn't work out someday, I could always try out for a tour guide position.

"Do you gamble?" Patricia asked, finally, having apparently decided that I wasn't going to talk about her research and getting tired of comments about the temperature.

"Gamble?" I repeated and laughed. "No, no, it's nothing like that. It's just that we can get some privacy out here."

Her eyebrows went up. "Privacy? In a casino?"

I smiled. "Wait and see."

The Montréal casino looks a lot like a spaceship—even now, over a half century after it was built, it looks futuristic; I can only imagine what visitors to Expo '67 thought of it. Inside, it's—well, it's a casino, where round-the-clock bright lights, a lack of windows, and the absence of timepieces encourage gamblers to stay for just one more hand, one more roll, one more drink. Some people call it preying on the weaknesses of others. Some people call it providing a service.

My husband, Ivan, calls it his workplace. He's the director of the casino, and its bright colored lights and smiling staff are the backdrop to his everyday professional life.

I didn't come out to the island often enough for the croupiers to know me by sight, but there's always someone watching through closed-circuit television in any gambling establishment, and we hadn't gotten very far before a smooth voice at my elbow stopped our progress. "Martine! How pleasant to see you."

I turned, a smile ready, and dutifully kissed one of Ivan's managers on the cheeks in greeting. "*Salut*, Jean-Yves. *Ça va?*"

"*Bien, bien*," he responded, looking past me to my companion.

A stellar friend, Jean-Yves, and a terrific manager, but one with the curiosity of a cat that hasn't yet embarked on any of its nine lives. "This is my friend, Patricia," I said in English before turning to her. "Patricia, this is Jean-Yves, who runs many parts of the casino."

They shook hands. Patricia was looking around her like a child visiting Disney World for the first time. "You are here for Mr. Petrinko?" Jean-Yves asked me in English.

"If he's not busy, I'd love to see him," I said. "But actually, Jean-Yves, I just wanted to use his office for a little while." My husband's office is the only place I know of that's absolutely, positively, no-questions-asked secure. Ivan makes sure of that on a daily basis.

"Of course. He is in the poker rooms, I believe. I will let him know that you are here, if you wish. There is no one in the office right now, you will be undisturbed." He inclined his head and looked at my companion. "Mademoiselle, pleased to have made your encounter."

"Thank you," said Patricia. She looked a little dazed.

I swiped my magnetic identification card at the door that didn't look like a door, and let us into the back corridors that shot through the building like rabbit runs, linking the prosaic undercurrent that enables the fairy-tale aspects of the casino to operate smoothly. Waiters passed us with carts of food, dishes protected by gleaming silver domes. Security officers gave us automatic sharp looks as we went by. A cleaner was rattling her trolley on the way to some spillage.

In Ivan's office, I closed the door behind us. Patricia was staring at the bank of screens on one wall, monitoring the myriad security cameras placed throughout the building. "This is fascinating," she said.

"This is big business," I told her. The bright colored lights, the mesmerizing tables, the seductive whispers, none of it did anything for me. There's no mystique to gambling as far as I'm concerned. I know that for some people it's an addiction akin to that of alcohol or drugs; but it's always seemed to me that the greater addiction is to money, the money to be made from all the world's addictions. It was an uneasy thought. "Come on, sit down. That sofa's more comfortable than it looks. Can I get you something? A coffee? A glass of wine?"

"Wine would be nice."

I pressed a button on the intercom and spoke to Ivan's new administrator. "Marie-Claire? *C'est* Martine."

"*Bonjour*," the box said.

"Will you ask Raoul to bring two glasses of Ivan's Côtes du Rhône to the office?"

"But of course."

I settled back into a chair and smiled at Patricia. "I'm sorry for all this," I said. "The secrecy, everything. You must be wondering what kind of crazy woman I am. And, forgive me—but you may not have thought of this—but there are a number of important political ramifications to your work. Consequences. Things that call for specialized treatment. And I'd rather take it slowly, think about the information you have and what we will release, when we will release it, that sort of thing. You saw that already there are many parties interested."

"The whole *world* should be interested," said Patricia vigorously, pushing her glasses up her nose. "Already, as it is, not many Canadians know about Operation Fish. I think that's terrible. It was one of the major coups of the war."

I thought that not many of us knew much about history, period, but that was beside the point.

Patricia was pursuing her thought. "Still, it's good for me, I guess. I mean, it's a guaranteed career, isn't it?" That would be the way she'd look at it, of course. "The thing is, I'm doing something significant, isn't that what everybody wants for their life? And after this, everyone will know about what happened, because this was part of it."

"What was part of it?"

She looked at me. "The jewels! The British-goddamned-crown-jewels. I mean, it's a lot more glamorous, isn't it? It's sexier to talk about jewels than about gold or plain old securities."

So she did know something about public relations. I checked myself: I'd been treating her like an *enfant terrible*, a prodigy who didn't know anything outside of her own limited field. She was smarter than that.

"It *is* sexier," I agreed. "It's a natural human impulse, to be fascinated by anything that expensive." Or that shiny, as the case may be.

"It's not just the expense," Patricia said. The glasses had slid down again and she pushed them back, her finger on the nosepiece. "It's—well, *everything*. Jewels are gorgeous all by themselves. Glittering, brilliant, glamorous, Audrey Hepburn and Queen Elizabeth all rolled into one, you know? And then there's the symbolism—you know, centuries of history."

There was a knock at the door, and Raoul came in with a tray. "Thank you," I said distractedly; Patricia kept talking. "Imagine if London had been invaded and occupied—like Paris. It's what everyone thought was going to happen, after all. Imagine Hitler posing with the British crown jewels, maybe even sitting on the throne, can you see it?" She pushed the glasses back up again. She stopped to think for a moment. "And *that* would have killed the English faster than any bomb."

I sipped my wine and thought about it, the little man and the glittering jewels that had inspired and defined an empire. "But hang on," I objected. "Letting them leave England—wasn't that taking a big risk? What if the convoy had been lost at sea? How could they trust people in another country to keep them safe?"

"But that's the genius of it," she said persuasively, the glasses sliding down again. "No one *knew*. The jewels were the last thing on anyone's mind. *Think* about it! London's getting bombed to bits and all you're going to be doing is wondering where the king decided to put the fucking crown jewels? I don't *think* so."

She finally sipped her wine. "Later on, during the war, there was this rumor circulating that the jewels were hidden in a cave somewhere in Wales. But no way: if England fell, Wales was going to fall, too. That wouldn't have made any difference. So they were here. They were here all the time."

"And still, in a sense, on British soil, with Canada being Commonwealth," I said slowly. "Still part of Great Britain, with whatever meanings people wanted to ascribe to that." She nodded. "Still in Great Britain," she said. "Just a lot safer."

"Okay. I'm convinced of the logic of it," I said. "But you said something about proof. And you also said something about some of them being stolen."

She nodded, her eyes steady over the rim of her glass.

I took a deep breath, let it out slowly. "I'm not going to pretend that there aren't any problems with what you're saying, but let's say for a moment that it's true. *If* it's true, why has it taken so long to find out? No offense to you, I'm sure that you're really good at what you do, but there've been a lot of researchers in Montréal since 1945. Historians, archaeologists, people like that. If there was something to find, surely they'd have found it by now."

"Only," said Patricia, "if they were looking in the right place."

"I can't feel my hands."

"Count yourself lucky, then. Haven't felt me toes since we left Scotland."

"Didn't feel mine even when we was in Scotland."

It had to be the North Atlantic, the lookout thought sourly. And on a bleeding light cruiser. Not built for these waters, innit? Should be doing the Mediterranean route, picking up them New Zealand and Australian and Indian troops from Cairo. But no: it had to be the bleeding North Atlantic.

The bleeding frigid *North Atlantic.*

There'd been storm warnings when they'd left port, but that wasn't enough to deter the Royal Navy and His Majesty Captain Flynn, no sir, guv'nor. Not a bit of it. And now here they was, in gray seas against a gray sky, the seas running higher since morning, and watching for U-boats that could blow them out of the water at any moment.

And not just them. A bleeding convoy, it was. H.M.S. Emerald, *Uncle Tom Cobley, and all.*

He could just about make out the shape of one of the escort ships to the west. Rain sluicing down since midmorning, hard, when the seas had started to kick up. Spotter plane left yesterday, more's the pity: there was no help now. With them submarines out there, making the ocean their playground, lurking under the water and the first you knew of it was when the torpedo hit.

And now a storm coming on. Didn't need no bleeding meteorological officer to tell him that: bin goin' to sea nine years, innit? Can tell the weather out yere sure as anybody else.

Couldn't hardly see the destroyer now anyway, and the speed well down, making them sitting ducks, if you asked him: sitting ducks for any prowling wolf packs. The animal imagery was pleasing in a depressing sort of way. Quick as you like, that was the way to cross the Atlantic safely. Not like this, jest waitin' fer a break in the weather and halfway across with nowhere to hide. Trust the captain with his life, he'd done it before an' he would again, guv'nor knew what he was doing. But still, feelin' like a sitting duck.

An' weather worsening all the time.

The lookout braced himself to light a cigarette, shielding the lighter from both weather and possible periscopes. Still, all in a day's work, innit? Convoy's got to get through, God and King, I vow to thee my country, all that.

Halfway to Halifax. God help them.

CHAPTER FIVE

"Why didn't you tell me you were coming out to the casino? We could've had dinner together." Ivan came up behind me as I stood at the kitchen sink, wrapping his arms around me and pushing back some of my dark hair to kiss my neck. Beside us, Bisou the cat cried plaintively for his dinner.

I finished rinsing the plate and stuck it into the dishwasher. "Didn't know I was going," I said. "It just worked out that way. Actually, I'd meant to spend the day with someone called François."

"François?" asked my husband, lifting one eyebrow.

I grinned. "He's a tour guide."

"Oh, right, you were doing the tourist thing today." He reached past me to grab an apple out of the wire three-tiered basket suspended next to the sink. Ivan is always hungry. Even when he's just eaten, he's hungry.

He says it has to do with the privation and pogroms suffered by his Jewish ancestors in Russia. The truth is that he's only ever visited Moscow on a college package tour that involved more vodka than history; his worst privations as a young adult had to do with not being able to find "pahking" in his native Boston.

Still, he can play the fiddler on the roof to perfection.

"Got sidetracked." I put the detergent into its little door, shut the dishwasher, pushed the requisite buttons. I turned to lean against the sink and face him. "Ivan, what do you know about the Second World War?"

"My people—"

"Don't even go there!" I poked at his chest. "I'm serious. I've been reading, this afternoon. And, um, talking to some people. Did you know that Canadian participation in the war has been seriously underplayed? One of the beaches at D-Day, Juno Beach, was exclusively Canadian. Plus, between 1939 and 1945, more than one million Canadian men and women served full-time in the armed services. Come on, I'll tell you about it."

I went into the living area and sat on the sofa; Ivan followed me, still polishing his apple on his suit jacket. "You've become a font of historical information today," he observed.

"Pretty, too," I said.

"That as well." He sat next to me. "Why this sudden interest in twentieth-century wars?"

I half turned to face him, drawing one of my legs up under me. "There's this woman, a doctoral candidate from McGill," I said. "She's stirring things up a little. The thing is, Ivan, she's found proof—well, she *says* she's found proof—that the British crown jewels were here. In Montréal. They were held in a vault under the *édifice Sun-Life* during the war."

He took a bite out of the apple and chewed reflectively. "Think I already heard that somewhere. Maybe in a magazine?"

"It's probably been a whole lot of places. It's no secret, it's actually part of the Gray Line tour narrative," I said. "Except that it's said so casually that you really don't have the time to reflect on it. You know, statistic this, statistic that, so forth. And anyway, you're right: for most people, it feels like ancient history."

Nothing but the sound of him biting into the apple, chewing, swallowing. "But?"

"But what?"

"I can feel it coming. There's another shoe due to fall at any moment. And don't give me that blank look, you're not that French, you know the idiom. Your English is better than my grandmother's."

"Everyone's English is better than your grandmother's."

"*Alors*?"

"Well, it's a bit of a long story, but essentially the Brits sent a lot of stuff here at the beginning of the war. They sent the country's gold reserve, and everyone's securities, too, private securities they'd confiscated. It wasn't just to keep them safe: they were payments, agreed between the governments to pay for convoys sent from Canada and the States to supply the British." I hesitated. "Believe it or not, it was something they called Operation Fish."

"Appropriate," my husband commented. "What about the crown jewels? Were they part of this fish thing?"

"They came with the second shipment," I said, picking my notes off the coffee table. "Complete secrecy, of course, they even had the crew put on tropical white uniforms to confuse any lurking German spies into thinking they were heading south—well, there were U-boats all over the North Atlantic. The *Emerald* survived a bad storm and docked in Halifax; the gold and jewels went on from there by train to Montréal."

"It would make a good movie," Ivan said. He runs the casino; he always has an instinct and eye out for entertainment.

"It did," I said tartly. "Something called *The Bullion Boys*, produced in the nineties by the BBC, has Liverpool dockworkers plotting to steal the gold before the *Emerald* sails."

He nodded approvingly. "Good premise."

"Why do I feel you're not taking any of this very seriously?"

Ivan sighed, stood, stretched, took his apple core into the kitchen, came back. "It's all fascinating, Martine, but I don't see the connection to Montréal's public relations in the twenty-first century." He headed up the open staircase that leads to our bedroom on the second level of the loft. "I'm going to change my clothes." For reasons best known to him, Ivan stays in his elegant work suits during dinner. It's a little like having a date, albeit one in which I have to still do the cleanup.

"There *is* a connection!" I yelled after him. "We saved their jewels for them!"

"Not exactly hot off the presses, that news." His voice was muffled; I imagined he was pulling a sweater over his face.

"But *proof* of it would be," I said. "And there may be more. In fact, there may be a *lot* more. This researcher—she's been hinting around at it, giving me bits and pieces, I think she's being cagey because I work for Jean-Luc. I don't think she trusts the government that much—"

"Amazing that anybody could feel that way," my husband interrupted drily, coming back into the room in a sweater and sweatpants.

"Sarcasm will get you nowhere," I told him. "She's feeling us out. Well, me, anyway. I got her away from Jean-Luc as quickly as I could."

"He isn't one to inspire confidence," Ivan agreed.

"And I do think there's a mystery here, Ivan. I think that maybe something happened back in 1939, and now we need to find out what it was. I think that—"

Ivan sat down on the coffee table, right across from me, his knees touching mine. "No," he said.

"You haven't even heard—"

"I've heard enough," he said. "Remember, I've heard that from you before. Something about the past having repercussions on the present. And the last time you got involved in anything mysterious, you came way too close to getting killed." He put a hand on my knee.

"I've gotten used to you, see," he said easily. "Don't want to have to break in a new model."

He was right: I had, in fact, come perilously close to getting myself killed when I'd decided to "assist the police with their inquiries" into some murders in Montréal the summer before. And my flippant "murders aren't good PR" hadn't gone over too well with my husband then, either. I reached out and touched his wrist. "This is completely different. If anything happened, it happened so long ago that nobody will care."

His eyebrows went up. "Right. Like investigating something that happened in the Duplessis years," he said, then raised his hands in surrender. "Okay, okay, I know that look. Just be careful. Your extracurricular activities make me nervous sometimes."

"You said it yourself. You just don't want the bother of shopping for a newer model."

"The shopping isn't the problem. The price tag is."

I swatted at him halfheartedly and we settled companionably down to our evening. After all, *Orphan Black* was on television.

It was the next day that we found the body.

They'd put a mattress on top of the securities crates in the captain's day room, and that was where Alex was sleeping.

If one could call it sleeping.

Every time the Emerald *pitched or rolled—and he had no idea which was which—he was dumped onto the floor. He considered simply putting the mattress down there, but there was scarcely room, and the space was needed frequently.*

Just as well: it got him on his feet in time to go and get sick again.

The gale blew on and the captain dismissed the destroyers. "I'm not leaving us sitting in the middle of the ocean, not with this kind of cargo," he told Alex. The convoy steamed eastward and they stood in the wheelhouse watching it go, seeing the lights disappear into the rain. "On our own, now," said Captain Flynn cheerfully.

Alex looked at him. "You sound elated," he said, curious.

"I am, laddie, I am. Best way to be, on our own. We'll show them a thing or two!" He turned to the officer of the deck. "Increase speed to twenty-two knots," he instructed.

"Twenty-two knots, aye, sir."

The captain was doing everything but rubbing his hands together in glee. "Now we'll show them what we've got."

And it must have worked, because the next day the gale died down and the sun came out. Alex felt like Noah when the dove returned with the branch: not only did he finally believe that he might actually live through the ordeal, he found that he now actually wanted to.

He mentioned it to Captain Flynn, and the other man smiled. "Sunday service tomorrow," he said. "Time to show your gratitude."

Alex grinned. They might well play darts and sing hymns, he thought; but he'd never seen anything like the men he met on the Emerald. "They signal action stations every time there's a U-boat in the vicinity," he wrote in a letter to his wife once the seas were calm enough for him to manage a pen. "Every time, no matter what a man is doing, he's at his battle station. Immediately. Quietly and without drama. We bankers could take a page from their book."

And so, quietly and without drama, the Emerald entered the harbor at Halifax, Nova Scotia. It was time to unload.

CHAPTER SIX

Patricia handed me the headlamp. "You attach it to your helmet," she said.

I looked at her dubiously. I already was wearing more foreign objects than I'd ever even *seen* on a single person: chest waders (now *there's* a fashion statement), climbing equipment, ropes slung casually over my shoulder, a tool belt with portable spotlights, and now a headlamp.

And none of it particularly light to wear or carry.

Patricia, on the other hand, seemed completely comfortable with the equipment. And the process. "What we do is, we mark it on Google Maps," she'd explained to me that morning when we met for coffee in the glass and chrome of Café Pavé, probably the last time in a while that we'd be bathed in light. "This way, just in case anything goes wrong . . ."

I looked at her sharply. "What's going to go wrong?"

"Nothing," she said and laughed as she pushed her glasses back up her nose. "It's just a precaution, don't worry."

Easier said than done. But it was my own fault; when she had started to describe the urban exploration that had brought her to the center of her dissertation, I'd held up my hand. "You mean there's something *still there*? Something from the forties?"

"Yes, of course."

"Why of course? And why hasn't anyone seen it? And *what* is it?"

"It wasn't always open," she said reasonably. "Urban explorers have been down in these tunnels before; you're right, they would have found anything there was to find. But the museum's expansion work diverted some of the waterways, and one of them broke through into these rooms I'm telling you about. The rooms are under Sun-Life and they've been sealed off, bricked up. I think the vault was probably in there."

"The vault's gone?"

"High-tech for its time," she said. "They probably sold it."

"So how do you know—?"

"Because it's a mess in there, and I didn't take time to look at everything because frankly I was a little spooked, but there were some empty crates. And there was a hatbox."

"A hatbox?" I wasn't getting the significance.

She leaned forward. "The story is that King George and his two daughters—one of them is Queen Elizabeth to us, by the way—took the jewels out of their settings and packed them into hatboxes. Diamonds and rubies and emeralds and God only knows what else—well, you see why I got excited."

"I see why you got excited."

"So when do you want to go?" She caught my look. "Well, *don't* you? Isn't that the point? You don't want your boss or those cops finding it first, and neither do I. Listen to me, this is perfect. I want the discovery to be mine, you want to keep this under wraps, so we both win. I need a witness to the discovery, and once you see what's at stake, you'll know how to handle the politics—which, frankly, is way beyond either my interest or ability."

"Uh-huh." I thought about it for a moment, rubbing my finger around the rim of my wineglass. The longer we waited, I thought, the more likely it was that it wouldn't be our secret. Someone else would find the underground rooms. The feds, or customs, or my boss would get involved; and Patricia was right—once that happened, the genie was out of the bottle. I'd rather be able to decide on the timing of its release myself. "Tomorrow."

"Sorry?"

"We'll do it tomorrow. Unless you have anything more—"

"No," she interrupted. "This is all I have."

I looked at her and thought, she's telling the truth. It was there if you looked for it, the gleam of obsession, the single-mindedness that's probably shared by crazy people and geniuses alike.

"All right," I said. "Tomorrow."

Which was how I was now finding myself wearing gear that I hadn't known existed, and listening to someone talking lightly about leaving a bread crumb trail in case things turned nasty.

What could be nasty, after all, about wading through sewers?

"We're not actually going to cross any active ones," she said, uncannily reading my mind. Or perhaps it was my expression. "It's just a precaution." Like leaving Google Maps open on her computer, I thought. This woman didn't leave much to chance.

We went down into the complex two blocks away from my apartment, which was also a little unsettling, down through a manhole that Patricia slid carefully back into place once we were through. "Put on your flashlight."

"It's on," I responded. "How did you figure this out?"

"What, getting around underground?"

"For want of a better description."

"This way." She touched my elbow and slipped past me. "Follow me." There was a pause. "How did I figure it out? I've always been into this."

"Wading through sewers?" I was skeptical. "What, did you have a particularly bad childhood?"

She laughed, and the sound echoed down the tunnel in front of us. "I guess you could call it recreational trespassing," she said. "I was studying history and I was particularly interested in urban history—how cities came to be, you know?"

I didn't, not really. "I don't know that I've ever given it a moment's thought."

"Most people don't. Watch your step, here: stay on the brick if you can, it's older."

"It's older? That's supposed to be reassuring?"

"The brick's better. It's more solid. They started working with concrete in the 1920s, but it cracks over time. Anyway, so I was interested, and I felt that a lot of historical significance of cities ended up buried, one way or another. So I started hanging out with this group of people, some students, some not, and we did all sorts of exploring. The Paris catacombs. The Neglinnaya River, which flows under Moscow. New York."

"Recreational trespassing," I said, nodding, thinking that it takes all sorts to make a world.

We were advancing slowly, and while it was certainly damp, it wasn't wet. Yet, I reminded myself darkly. There was the occasional sound of something skittering away, lightly, invisibly; rats, no doubt. The tunnel was large and wide, with an arched ceiling and so far mostly brick.

We were probably under my building right now.

"It shows you how much work went into all the stuff we take for granted," said Patricia earnestly, leading us forward. Her voice echoed around us. "Any city's infrastructure, you know, it's how they function, but it's mostly in places that people never see. And it's in layers, like an archeological dig. First, you see the utility networks, that's right under street level. Then, under that, there's centralized steam heating. At the lowest level is the water supply system."

I contemplated for a moment explaining to her why, after last summer, I wasn't quite ready to embrace the idea of exploring a steam tunnel, and decided against it. "Where are we now?" I asked instead.

She stopped and looked around her, the floodlight she carried swinging around crazily. "Place Royale, more or less," she said. "Anyway, it's all connected, isn't it? These tunnels were built in the nineteenth century, and yet any new building that goes up in a city will be relying on them. The past is never really past."

"Nice phrase." Not bad for marketing copy, either.

"True phrase. Come on, this way." Her goggles were keeping her glasses in place, I noticed. We were branching off the main tunnel and still moving north. A thought struck me and I stopped. "Aren't we supposed to be up closer to Dorchester Square?" I asked. That was, after all, where the Sun-Life Building still stood, on Metcalfe Street, even though Sun-Life itself was long gone; a whole list of corporate and noncorporate entities leased space in the building now. And it was a good distance from where we'd entered the tunnel, in the Old Port section of the city.

Not that it was all that meaningful: unlike other big cities, you can walk across Montréal in less than a day.

Patricia had stopped also and was waiting for me. "I can feel you thinking," she said. "Pity you can't walk at the same time."

"You're so funny. So answer the question."

"The *vault* was under Dorchester Square," she said patiently. "But the jewels were moved."

"How do you know?"

"Because I'm a researcher. That's what I do: I find out stuff like that. And I'm about to show you where they ended up," she said, a current of impatience moving through her voice. "There were documents in London, that's what started me on all this in the first place. Documents about them being afraid that Sun-Life was compromised. So, assuming that was right, ask yourself, Martine: who else had a decent vault at the time?"

"I don't know." I was feeling a little irritable at her pedantic approach. Maybe academia does that to people. "Banks?"

"Banks, sure. Good option. But also the Montréal Stock Exchange." She put up a hand. "Don't say it. They're downtown now, yeah, but they used to be—"

"—at the Centaur Theatre!" I couldn't help the interruption; *this* part of history, at least, I knew about. The Exchange was in a Beaux Arts–style building in the Old Port when, in 1969, the Front de Libération du Québec set off a bomb there (the Exchange apparently representing a bastion of Anglo-Canadian power), blowing out the northeast wall.

Now the Exchange lived in one of Montréal's highest modern buildings, and the English-language Centaur Theatre played where stocks were once exchanged. About five blocks from the Pointe-à-Callière museum, where the excavations were going on.

"Got it in one," said Patricia cheerfully. "Come on."

We proceeded in silence, which was fine with me: I really didn't want to hear any more about recreational trespassing, since we were pretty much doing the same thing now and the thought of possible professional consequences should we be caught had started wending its way through my brain. I could already hear Jean-Luc denying any knowledge of anything I happened to have done at any time. . . . I walked straight into Patricia's back. "Sorry."

"It's okay," she said. "Look, we have to climb here onto that shelf . . . see it?" She moved the spotlight to an opening that was about shoulder height and seemed very, very dark. Probably filled with rats, too. "I can boost you up," she said encouragingly.

Okay, so I might not be twenty-three myself, but I wasn't all that decrepit. "I'll manage," I said.

"Not in those waders," she said. "Come on. I'll boost you, then you can give me a hand up."

"All right." Even with her help, I struggled, and ended up on my stomach on what felt to be a very narrow ledge. "You're doing great," she said. "Now, just give me a hand."

She was up surprisingly quickly. Okay, so maybe there *is* something about being twenty-three.

We had to crouch to enter this tunnel, and as the light moved ahead of us I could see scurrying forms, shadows moving fast. I'd been right. We were right up against the river, after all, and the Old City has always had a rodent problem. I wasn't as concerned about them as I was about ending up on my knees if this thing got any smaller. I've never been particularly aware of being claustrophobic, but there's no time like the present to find out something new about oneself.

"Over here." It was clearly an accidental opening, without the fine brickwork that had been in evidence in all the other openings I'd seen so far, and I could see where high water had left debris drying around it; it hadn't happened all that long ago. Patricia pushed me. "Go on."

She'd been right; it opened up onto a room. I swept my flashlight around: the cluttered floor, now smelling rank; the walls that were perfectly dry above where the water had coursed through. A doorway into another room.

Crates, several of them, one or two completely falling apart, held together only by the sturdy iron reinforcements at all the corners. Stencil-stamped. I played my light over the labels: HOUSEHOLD GOODS.

"Here it is," she said, and I followed the beam of her spotlight to the faded circular hatbox beyond. Treasure, I thought. Even if nothing else ever comes of this, here is treasure. I imagined for a moment the two princesses, one now dead, the other elderly, giggling at the game their father had invented, wrapping up diamonds and sapphires and rubies. In the stillness of the underground, I could almost hear the echo of their laughter.

And then I played my own light beyond the crates and looked into the empty orbs of a skeleton's eyes.

Hans had told them he was from Holland.

Not many people really could grasp the difference in accents, not if they didn't speak either German or Dutch. And, in fact, he'd actually spent a summer in Amsterdam, back in 1933, so he could even throw in a word or two for color if necessary.

It never became necessary. They desperately needed people for the work crews, what with all able-bodied men signing up ever since it had become clear that Canada was following Britain into war.

Someone like Hans, with an official-looking exemption from military service, was a gift from the gods. No one ever commented on his name. No one ever commented on his accent. And this in spite of what they were all talking about, the only topic of conversation, it seemed: the war with Germany.

Hans talked about it, too. Rationing; everybody talked about rationing, and so he talked about rationing. They talked about the insanity of following a crazy clerk bent on world domination, and so he talked about the Leader in disparaging ways, too. But mostly he talked to the foreman about the rush job they were on, building this ultrasecret, ultrastrong vault under the Sun-Life Building in Dorchester Square.

"Peterson! Hey! You gonna marry those plans, or what, you keep staring at them like that?"

Hans forced himself to laugh. It was no laughing matter, though, and he was intensely aware of that, every day. He had a mission, and he was going to carry it out. For the Führer. For the day when Great Britain fell. For the day when Germany finally had the Lebensraum it deserved, the necessary space to give to the people who deserved it.

Here was what he knew: the British were sending something over by secret convoy. Whatever it was, it was going to be hidden here, in a vault in this place that he was helping build, and it was up to him to find out when, and what, and what could be done about whatever it was.

Hans frowned; he didn't like the vagueness of his orders. But they were orders, for all of that, even though he wasn't in uniform, even if he wasn't called by his rank anymore. He was a Dutch workman installing a vault under an insurance building in the heart of Montréal.

And he had his orders.

These people, they were all alike. All fat and contented with their lot. Not like what they'd all put Germany through after the war. His father . . . Hans could barely think about his father. A life savings of one hundred thousand marks, money put away, year after year, from his job as a steelworker. His mother's modest savings from household expenses, kept in a can, doled out for Hans and his young brother Gerhardt for special treats, the cinema, ice cream.

They'd survived that war, the Great War. Somehow, they'd survived it, the family reeling from deprivations, cold and hungry and depressed, Hans's father gone to fight the Tommies in the Ardennes. And then it was over, his father back from the front with a distant look in his eyes and a hacking cough that he never lost.

But he hadn't given up. He hadn't given up yet.

Not until the currency plummeted. It had taken a mere five months—five months!—in 1923, for that hundred thousand marks to not be enough to buy the family a loaf of bread. A loaf of bread! As long as the money had been there, there was a future.

Not anymore.

And so Hans's father took out his service revolver and killed his wife, killed Gerhardt, and killed himself. Hans had been away, on an overnight hiking trip with a friend. He came back to dried blood spattered across the rose-printed wallpaper of the family living room, to the stench of decaying bodies, to his life over.

He was only sixteen.

And all because of the powers, the French and the Belgians, the Americans and the Canadians and the British. They had killed his family as surely as if they'd held his father's gun in their dirty multinational hands.

But by 1923 Adolf Hitler had organized the SA, and there was a place for Hans in the new order. A decent place. A place with a future. And he embraced it with all of his heart.

"Peterson! Get a move on! Lorries here!"

Crates, heavy crates. Hans had volunteered to stay and help move whatever it was into the vault. The Royal Canadian Mounted Police had arrived yesterday, examining the square, the building, the cellars.

"Where does that tunnel go?"

"Into the sewer system, sir."

"Make sure it's blocked off."

"Right away, sir."

Hans watched as the RCMP corporal scurried to get the iron ordered. Good luck with that: all the country's iron was needed for the war effort. It would be a makeshift affair. That was good. And he'd be sure to be on the work crew. He'd be sure to have access.

Whatever this was, it was going to be important.

Drinking one night with the corporal—Maurice, his name was— beer and messy reminiscences. On the cop's part, not on Hans's. Finding secrets, that was what it was all about. Finding secrets that he could use. Finding secrets that would allow him to take a peek inside the mysterious crates loaded into the vault. There were rumors of all sorts of things, gold and riches beyond belief, because the Brits were running scared. It was only a matter of time before Germany could take the British Isles, and even the English knew it. Who knew what might be in those crates?

Hans was going to find out.

CHAPTER SEVEN

I think that maybe Patricia screamed. I know for certain that I did.

My spotlight went clattering to the floor, but she kept hers trained on the bones. A stronger woman than I was. I took a deep breath, picked mine up, shook it, and found that it wasn't going to work. *"Merde!"*

"Just use your headlamp," she said.

"That means I have to keep looking at it."

"Yes, well, there's that," she murmured distractedly. She was already pushing one of the crates aside, moving forward.

"Wait," I said. "What are you doing?"

"Looking at it."

I forced my gaze back to the skull, which had fallen back slightly from the rest of the body. Well, that would happen, wouldn't it? After a while, when the rodents had had their way with your body, and time had passed, there wouldn't be much reason for your head to stay attached anymore, would there?

The bones weren't the pristine white that one imagines when one thinks of skeletons—not that I've ever spent a lot of time thinking of skeletons, come to that—but browned and dirty and certainly not intact; some of the smaller bones were scattered around willy-nilly. "You didn't see this before?" I asked Patricia.

She shook her head and her headlamp swept a beam of light across the dark room. "No. I only got as far as the doorway. I saw the crates and the hatbox, and that there were a couple more rooms, but Dr. LaTour was with me and I didn't want to make a big deal of it yet. I wanted to think about the ramifications. He was the one who made me take it to the mayor."

"I see." I couldn't stop looking at the skeleton. I was never going to feel the same about Halloween again.

"Let's take a closer look." She moved past me, squatted beside the bones. "Martine."

"What?"

"Martine."

"What is it?" I couldn't tell if the pressure in her voice was a good or a bad thing. I pushed aside a rotting crate to make my way over to her. "Hang on, I'm coming. I mean, if you think that—" I broke off midsentence. Something very bright and very beautiful was in the middle of the bone collection. "No," I said.

"Yes," she breathed.

"They can't be," I said. "Not after all this time. Someone would have noticed them gone. Things like that don't just go missing. Someone would have known, there would have been a scandal." I was suddenly aware that I was babbling, and fell silent.

Patricia was squatting beside the bones, her floodlight directed at the tiny cluster of brilliant jewels that, even after all this time, glittered as though they were still affixed to a royal crown. As if they emitted a light of their own.

But I'd disturbed the skull, and my initial reaction of revulsion at touching it disappeared as I focused on what I was seeing now that it had rolled over.

A hole in the back of the skull, in a place where no hole should be.

We were still sitting beside the boxes ten minutes later, our goggles pushed back onto our foreheads, our feet inches from the skeleton. And I was getting tired of arguing. "I trusted you," said Patricia, and there was bitterness in her voice. "I trusted you to be my witness, not to ruin everything. I want to keep this my find, my information. You have no idea what will happen when academia gets hold of it."

"This person was *shot*, Patricia," I said for what felt like the thousandth time. "That's a crime. We have to have the police in."

"No! That will make it public."

I was losing patience. "They already know. They were at the meeting. They know you are on your way to proving the jewels were in Montréal, and they probably know you think some were stolen. Obviously you were right. They'll want to know why."

"But they don't know about this. About them being *here*."

I said, as reasonably as I could, "I know that your career is your first priority. But this person was *murdered*, don't you see? You could lose your big scoop; he lost his life. There's a matter of perspective here."

There was a long silence, and I could hear water dripping somewhere behind me. "But it was a long time ago," she said persuasively. "Don't you see? He was probably killed when the jewels were moved here from Dorchester Square. Sometime towards the end of the Second World War, for heaven's sake! No one's going to catch the murderer now."

She was probably correct, but that didn't make it right. "Okay," I said finally, biting my lip. "Here's a compromise. I know someone with the city police. He's—he's a bit of a black sheep over there. He does things differently. Let me get him here to look at it. I don't know at what point something becomes an archaeological find rather than a crime scene, but he'll know. And he'll be discreet."

"I don't want—"

"It's nonnegotiable, Patricia," I said, feeling the weight of my years and the lightness of hers. She sounded like a sullen two-year-old. "Someone has to see this. I'm offering you someone who won't call up the newspapers. I'd take it if I were you."

She was regretting getting me involved. She'd wanted me to be her own private PR person, ready to make her famous. I didn't really care.

There was another silence, and while Patricia was struggling with her inner petulant child, I looked at the skull again and wondered how long he—or she—had been lying here. Had the bright stones been in a pocket, with the fabric rotting away over time? Why hadn't whomever shot this person taken them?

Finally, I felt rather than saw her pushing her glasses back up her nose. "Okay," she said.

"Okay?"

"Just the one policeman."

"For now," I cautioned. "Really, Patricia, if Julian—that's the guy I'm talking about, Julian Fletcher—if he says it needs to be investigated, then there's nothing either of us will be able to do about it. There will have to be crime-scene techs, probably some cold-case detectives assigned, who knows? It will have to go through the whole police procedure. You have to be ready for that to happen."

"I see."

"Look, they're not going to call up the universities and alert the world. You still have the scoop. You were still the first to find this. It'll be your dissertation. But that doesn't mean it *belongs* to you." *Zut*, I'd heard about academics being territorial, but this was ridiculous. Perspective, people: perspective. I tried again. "This was somebody's *life*, Patricia."

Her headlamp swung in my direction. "You're right, of course," she said, so briskly that I found myself wondering why the sudden change of attitude. "Come on." And then she was turning around in the small space, turning away from the bones, crawling, putting out a hand to help me. "I have to keep perspective."

Not to mention reading minds, I thought. Hadn't I just been thinking about perspective?

The way back seemed longer than getting there, and I was conscious only of a prickling feeling at the back of my neck, as though someone were following us, watching us. Or maybe it was just because of what—of *who*—we were leaving behind, abandoning to the darkness. He'd been there already for decades, I thought: there was no need to worry about leaving him alone now. Yet it felt wrong, somehow, to take the light and the voices away, to leave him back there in the dark and the damp.

With the jewels.

"You and Dr. LaTour were the only people to see this?" I asked finally.

"They just got control of the stream that broke through," she said. "We were here two days ago, and Pierre has so much on his plate, he wasn't very interested. We left, but I'd seen the hatbox with the crates, and I knew. I came here from London to find it, and I found it."

There didn't seem to be anything to say to that, so I didn't say it. Patricia lapsed into silence, too, and it allowed me to think about contacting Julian. *Détective-lieutenant* Julian Fletcher, to give him his title and full name, both of which were meaningful: he had a decent rank within the city police force, and his surname was one of those echoed in the wealthiest enclaves of Montréal. Julian Fletcher, of the Westmount Fletchers.

Last year, I'd served as liaison between City Hall and the city police in the business of a string of murders that had happened over the summer, and while everybody in Montréal was pointing toward a vagrant serial sex murderer, Julian and I had uncovered something deeper and far more troubling. You'd think they'd have given us medals, but instead Julian stayed at his desk for two months of forced paper pushing and Jean-Luc made sure that I got to represent the city at every irrelevant and miserable event— nothing too small—throughout the city until his pea brain had moved on to something else.

Not without, of course, his having taken the credit for what we'd done.

I wondered how Julian would feel about my contacting him again. But he was a self-anointed outsider, both in his family and in the police force, and I had a feeling that this particular adventure might just appeal to him.

My boss? I was anticipating a different reaction altogether.

"So," Hans said, leaning on the bar, pretending to be far more drunk than he was, "what's in the shipment?"

"Hmm?" Maurice blinked blearily at him through the smoke.

"The shipment," Hans said. "Coming tomorrow. From Halifax."

Maurice shrugged. "Don't know, do I?" he asked. "Not privy to what them higher-ups is about, eh? I do what they tell me to do, and I collect my pay. Whose round?"

"Mine," said Hans, even though it wasn't. He held up his hand to the bartender. "But what I'm thinking," he said, as the man refilled their glasses, "is that if you had to, you could find out what's in that shipment."

"Cheers," Maurice said and downed a third of the whiskey. "Whew! What was that you said?"

Hans took a deep breath. Gott grant me patience, he thought. "This shipment from Halifax," he said. "If you wanted to find out what's in it, you could. If you really wanted to."

"Yeah, probably could, eh? But why would I want to?"

The perfect opening. "I can give you three good reasons," he said.

"Eh? What's that?" Another blink through the smoke, another swallow of whiskey. "What're you on about, then?"

"They have names," said Hans. "Monique, and Adele, and Ethel." Maurice was staring at him openmouthed. "Here," he said. "Enough of that. How'd you know?"

"You told me," Hans said, adding under his breath, "you imbecile." Maurice was still uncomprehending. "Whose round?" he demanded, finishing his drink in one fast swallow.

Hans's hand came down fast and clamped on Maurice's wrist. "Listen to me," he said, his voice low. "You told me about them. And about Felicity, who's expecting your first baby. Felicity wouldn't want to know about them. And they probably wouldn't like to know about each other. Would they?" He paused. "Me, I don't know where you find the time. But I've got plenty of time and I know what to do with it if you don't help me."

Maurice seemed to have gotten very sober very fast. "What do you want me to do?"

"Not much," Hans said, lessening the pressure on the other man's wrist, but not letting go altogether. "All I want to know is what's in the shipment."

"That's all?"

"That's all," Hans said reassuringly. He squeezed Maurice's wrist one last time and let it go. "For now."

CHAPTER EIGHT

Julian returned my call just as I was getting ready to go home, packing up my briefcase. "So they're letting you out to play again? Never thought I'd see the day."

"Don't ask, don't tell," I said. "How are you, Julian?"

"*Comme ci, comme ça*," he said. "So-so."

"You don't actually need to translate for me," I pointed out. Montréal is a city divided, and the Fletchers are most *definitely* on the Anglophone side of the line. The *wealthy* anglophone side. LeDuc is just as aggressively francophone, though the nuns had made sure that I grew up perfectly bilingual. It wasn't strictly necessary—French is Québec's official language—but there were still, amazingly, people in the city who spoke no French at all, legal language or not. On the other hand, in my professional capacity, I'd have welcomed knowing far more languages than I did.

"Just showing off," Julian was saying.

"Impressive."

"It is, isn't it? I rather thought so, too. So how can I help our fair city's even fairer *directrice de publicité*?"

I hesitated. "Julian, if I show you something, what's your obligation for passing it along? Do you have to tell anybody about it?"

"If it's a crime, then I have to."

"It's a crime," I said. "But it could be—archaeological."

He gave a snort of laughter. "Don't tell me you've found a body!"

"Well, what used to be one," I conceded. "And unless this particular person was the patient of someone who did some nifty trepanning, he was shot."

"Trepanning?"

"Drilling a hole in the skull," I said. "Medieval medicine."

He chose to ignore that. "It's a he?"

I shrugged, then realized he couldn't see me. "I'm guessing. Could be anybody: it's just bones."

He whistled. "LeDuc, how *do* you get yourself involved in these things? All right. Where is this mysterious body?"

I shifted uncomfortably in my office chair. "Well, see, that's the thing. I can't tell you. I need to show you. And *just* you, at least for now. I promised somebody."

"Well," he commented, "this ought to be good. I'm sufficiently intrigued. Tomorrow do you?"

"Sure," I said, wondering what I'd tell my staff about yet another absence. Hell, it was Friday, let them think what they wanted.

"Lunch," said Julian. He never meets unless it is over food, a passion he has in common with my husband.

I'd known it was coming. "Jardin Nelson," I responded, naming one of the restaurants on the Place Jacques-Cartier. At least it got him into the Old City.

"Haven't had *pouding chômeur* in a while," he said, naming one of the restaurant's specialty dishes, a maple pudding cake.

"How did you know they have it?"

"I'm not a detective for nothing."

I grinned, finished packing up, and headed home.

I hadn't been inside for two seconds when the apartment erupted. First the sound of shrieking, then a door slamming and an adolescent girl's voice: "I *hate* you!"

I put my briefcase on the hall table, slipped out of my shoes and jacket. "Ivan?"

He was in the kitchen area, in the act of sipping some wine, and looking sheepish. "The kids are here," he said.

"I *had* managed to deduce that fact." I went over to kiss him. "Aren't they a day early?" Ivan's children, Claudia and Lukas, stayed with us for a month in the summer and every other weekend during the school year. Weekend: meaning arrivals on Fridays, departures on Sundays. Or so one might think.

"I forgot," my husband confessed. "We'd agreed to a long weekend ages ago—well, at least two months, anyway—but I didn't mark it on the calendar. First thing I knew was when they called me from the airport."

I walked past him, pulled the cork from the bottle of Côtes du Rhône on the counter, and poured myself a glass. Ivan had wisely already started; from the sound of things, we were both going to need it. "Well, that's all right, I don't mind, but what are we doing with them tomorrow?" Another burst of earthshaking noise. "And what's Claudia slamming doors about?" Good thing our new place was in an old piano factory, I thought: it could withstand years of abuse, including even the dramatic tantrums of an adolescent girl.

"What's she *ever* slamming doors about? Cheers," said Ivan, touching his glass to mine. "I'm cooking goulash," he added, a little unnecessarily: he's a great cook, but finds himself unable to produce anything without using every pot and pan we own. I loved our new loft-style apartment. I loved it especially because it had a dishwasher. "I think that Lukas threatened to tell somebody named Brittany that she has a crush on somebody named James."

"Why should Claudia care who Brittany has a crush on?"

"Funny woman," Ivan said. "I should be the one worried about who she has crushes on. I'm telling Lukas to mind his own business, when the truth is that I'd rather be pumping him for information." He stirred something thick and red on the stove. "I guess I need to come to terms with not being the only man in her life forever."

"You're already not the only man in her life," I pointed out. "She lives with a stepfather, don't forget."

"Right to the heart," said Ivan, miming a heart attack. "You're cruel."

"Not half as cruel as I'll be tomorrow when you ask me to leave work early so I can keep an eye on them, and I say no."

"You haven't even heard my persuasive arguments yet. I've been practicing for hours."

"Answer's still no. I've got a date after lunch."

"Not with the tour guide again?"

I smiled. "No. An old flame."

He got it at once. "You said you were going to be careful."

"And I am. Don't you see? That's why I called Julian." Well, that—and the little matter of a murder.

Don't ask, don't tell.

"So," said Lukas during dinner, "What are we doing this weekend?"

Lukas is a planner. He's the only ten-year-old I know who keeps a diary with dates and appointments. He measures out his time, not in coffee spoons, but in squares on the page. Something, I understood, about trying to restore order to a life that must have, at least occasionally, felt chaotic.

Though I had to say that the kids handled having two homes with more aplomb than I probably would have managed at their ages—or perhaps even at any age. The good side to the split-home deal was that they had four adults who loved and cared for them. The downside, of course, was that two of those adults lived in a Boston suburb and the other two lived in Montréal.

Ivan and Margery, his ex, may have had their differences, but they coparented together pretty well. Claudia was five and Lukas three when Ivan moved to Montréal, so neither of the kids really remembered a life that didn't involve regular airplane trips and having different bedrooms in different places—different *countries*, even. Margery had remarried before Ivan; I came into the kids' lives two years on, and spent one pretty horrible year getting grief from them ("Mom doesn't cut the bread that way!") before they started seeing me as part of the landscape.

For myself, I'd never wanted children. My own mother instilled enough guilt and grief into me to last for several generations, and my father had been perennially absent from my life, an academic with an obsession that kept him far from Montréal.

I used that as an excuse, of course; the truth was that I felt way too self-centered to be a good parent. I loved my life. I loved my work. I loved my weekends spent in cafés, strolling the streets of the Plateau, where I lived back then (or, in winter, the thoroughfares of the Underground City), going out with friends, reading a good book. I loved all the indulgences I permitted myself, the luxury of time being my own, the ability to take off at a moment's notice for Toronto or New York.

I didn't know when we first met that Ivan had children, and once I learned of their existence, I was already too far gone in love with him for it to make much difference. Now, I couldn't imagine my life without them—though, of course, I had them in the relatively small doses we'd arranged in custody hearings.

Now I looked blankly across the table at my husband. He would just *love* me to do something with the kids tomorrow rather than spend the day with Julian, whom he associated with my nearly getting killed last year.

Not that any of that was Julian's fault, mind you; but our brains work in mysterious ways and make illogical associations. "We'd planned to go to the Insectarium on Saturday," I reminded them.

"Ewww," said Claudia.

Lukas whipped out his notebook, sat with pen poised. "What time?"

I glanced at Ivan again, but he wasn't in the mood to help. "It's the *dégustation*," I said. "I don't know what time they do it, I'll have to check the Web site."

"Oh, even more ewww," said Claudia. "I'm not eating any bugs."

"They'll crawl around inside you!" Lukas told her, delighted.

"Stop it! Ohmygod Lukas you're not funny! Make him stop it!"

"You'll feel their creepy-crawly little feet and wings coming back up your throat!"

"That's enough, Lukas," Ivan said mildly. "And, Claudia, the insects are very dead and some of them are actually delicious. You'd be surprised. Some taste just like chocolate."

"I'm going to be sick," Claudia promised.

"Then go to the bathroom," I said.

"Ohmygod, not *now*, Belle-Maman! I'm going to be sick *Saturday*. If I even have to *see* anyone eating bugs! That's dis-*gust*-ing!"

"You don't have to eat the insects if you don't want to," I said. "You *do* have to eat your goulash now, though."

"It's too spicy. You know I don't like it too spicy, and you do it anyway. You hate me!"

"I made the goulash, Claudia," Ivan said.

She leapt to her feet. "Then you *both* hate me! That's fine—I hate you, too!"

Another slamming door.

Lukas spoke into the silence of her wake. "So," he said, pen poised, "what time on Saturday?"

Maurice met him at the port, where the ships docked.

"Our ship didn't come in here," he said unnecessarily. "Docked in Halifax, sent the cargo on by train. Arriving two thirty today."

"Yes," said Hans encouragingly. "I do understand that."

Maurice pulled a packet of cigarettes from his pocket and shielded the lighter with his hands. Hans waited for the first inhale-exhale. "Well?"

"Well," Maurice said. "Came from England. Or Scotland, guess it's not the same thing, eh?"

Hans wanted to shake him. "Apparently not. And?"

Another quick puff and he dropped the cigarette and ground it under his heel. "And it's the Brits sending everything that's anything over here to keep it safe from the Nazis when they invade," he said. "Sorry, I know they're in your country, too, eh? Anyway, the Brits got the drop on 'em. Sent it all over here. There's gold. There's securities, though damned if I know what them are."

"I see," said Hans, thinking about it.

Maurice grinned. "Saved best for last, eh?"

"What do you mean?"

"What I'm hearing," said Maurice, "is that they've got the royal crown jewels in with it all."

Hans stared at him. "The crown?"

Maurice shrugged. "I dunno what it means. Crown, crowns, who knows what these people wear? But that's it. I got you what you want." He glanced nervously at Hans. "We're even, right?"

Hans was watching a freighter being unloaded. "Yes," he said absently. "We're even." At least for the moment, he thought.

He had a message to send.

CHAPTER NINE

Late September, it was easy to get a table at Jardin Nelson. In the height of the summer season, there'd have been a twenty-minute wait. Worth it, mind you; but a wait nonetheless.

On the other hand, I had a feeling that Julian Fletcher never had to. Wait, that is. He's in his early thirties with the kind of crooked smile that women fall for, and everything about him whispers money. Even though he's a cop. Well, he was one of the Fletchers of Westmount long before he became a cop, and would remain one long after he retired from the force.

If the city police let him last until retirement.

He held my chair for me as I sat down. That was definitely a Fletcher thing. "Martine. You look well."

"As do you, Julian."

He handed me my menu. "So, why all the mystery?"

I closed it. I didn't need to look: apart from the two Breton *crêperies*, Jardin Nelson has the best crêpes in town. "Because the secret's not mine. Well, not really." I paused. "Well, maybe."

He nodded. "I like your decisiveness. It's becoming."

"Sarcasm always sat well on you, too."

We beamed at each other. The waiter came and we ordered, Julian glancing around, automatically checking the environment. That wasn't a Fletcher thing; that was a cop thing. "So what do you have for me?"

"Some remains down in one of the sewers. Well, a room off the sewers. It's a skeleton, actually, but parts of it are disarticulated." I was rather proud of that word: I'd just learned it that morning, sitting in my office and reading about how one determined the age of corpses. Lovely stuff.

"And it concerns me because . . . ?"

"A bullet hole in the skull," I said with my sweetest smile. "Don't you remember? Does that work for you?"

He whistled. "Does it ever."

The waiter came and brought us the bottle of wine Julian'd ordered, poured, and left again. "I'm glad it cheered you up," I said. "Me, I could have done without it."

"That's what you get when you muck about in sewers," said Julian cheerfully. "What got you mucking about, anyway? Wouldn't have thought it part of your job description."

"I am in a challenging and exciting line of work."

"Apparently so."

I took a deep breath. "Okay. *Voilà.* There's a doctoral student at McGill. Her name is Patricia Mason. She's been following up on the rumor about the British crown jewels being in Montréal for safe-keeping during the Second World War."

"Thought that was fact, not rumor."

"Depends on your source," I said, remembering François and the Gray Line tour narrative. To him, it was gospel, anyway. Probably everyone in the city who knew anything about it thought it gospel, too. I spared a moment of pity for the sad folks still championing the "cave in Wales" story. "Anyway, she's been spending a lot of time underground. She's been part of the team over at Pointe-à-Callière, opening up the underground rivers, but she's also been doing a lot on her own, pretty much sub rosa. She calls it recreational trespassing."

"Urban exploration," Julian said and nodded. "Have a couple of friends who're into it."

He would. They probably got around on skateboards, too. I was feeling old. "She found some documents—I think they were letters—in London saying that some of the jewels had been stolen, maybe replaced with imitations," I said. "She thinks that at the end of the war they were moved from the Sun-Life Building, and that's when some of them were stolen."

Our lunches arrived, and Julian continued to look at me, steadily, while plates were put in front of us. "No, *merci*, that's all for now," he said to the waiter.

I cleared my throat. "When they were still in London, the jewels had been taken out of their settings—I guess there's not much secrecy in packing a bunch of crowns and scepters and what-have-you—and apparently put into hatboxes. The hatboxes were put into mislabeled crates and sent over here along with the gold that was paying for convoys. When they were returned at the end of the war, they were in different packaging."

"Hatboxes didn't fit in the vault?"

I shrugged. "I don't know. But someone took away the hatboxes and the crates, and they turned up under another building—the old stock exchange."

"Which, presumably, also had a decent vault," said Julian, making the connection instantly.

I took a forkful of cheese and mushrooms simmered in béchamel and wrapped in a crêpe, chewed, and nodded. "Presumably so. Patricia got under the Exchange—well, it's that theater now."

"A very good theater."

"Just so. And she found—"

He held up a hand. "The suspense is killing me, so let me guess. The hatboxes."

"One of them. And the crates. And a skeleton with a bullet hole in its skull. And"—I took a deep breath—"some of the missing jewels, right where his pockets used to be."

He choked on his wine. "You're kidding."

"Never," I said, solemnly.

"But this is all just speculation. You have to look at the facts, and you don't know for a fact if any of the jewels went missing."

"Okay, you're right." I put up my hands in surrender. "Then someone else was running around with priceless jewels in hatboxes during the Second World War. City was probably full of them."

We sat for a while without saying anything. I took a couple of swallows of wine and scoffed most of my crêpe while Julian thought about it. Finally he put his napkin on the table. "Even if they knew," he said slowly, "no one was going to say anything."

I nodded. I'd already worked that out. "There would have been English opposition to sending the jewels across the ocean," I said. "It was a risky move. The North Atlantic was already full of U-boats. To have it proven that they'd have been safer, after all, in some lonely cave in Wales—well, it wouldn't have made anybody popular. And Britain after the war needed a rallying point. There had been so much damage, there was so much rebuilding to do. Everything was still scarce, and the king and queen took leadership roles in keeping things positive. They couldn't afford to admit that everything having to do with the royals wasn't perfect."

"So the guy with the bullet's the thief?"

I shrugged. "I don't know. Depends on who he was when he still was . . . him, I guess."

"Hmm." He signaled for the bill. "Is Miss Mason going to take us there?"

"*Bien sûr.* I'm pretty sure that I couldn't find my way again on my own, and it's creepy enough that I wouldn't want to. And anyway, it's really her find." I hesitated. "She'd like to keep it as quiet as possible, Julian. Her academic career is kind of hanging on it."

He gave me a look as he sorted through bills and coins. Obviously the success of Patricia's dissertation was way down on his list of priorities; but I'd given her my word, and I was going to at least try to keep some discretion in the proceedings. "I told her we'd meet at the theater at two."

"Then let's be off. And, you know, you need to get out more, Martine," he said. "Used to be you only *worked* in the Old City; now you live down here, eat down here, discover corpses down here . . ."

"Don't quit your day job," I said, and he grinned at me and we were on our way. On foot, fortunately: Julian had an Audi TT and an approach to driving that was guaranteed to turn your hair white. Always supposing, of course, that you survived the trip.

Patricia was hopping from one foot to the other when we arrived. I introduced them, and she kept looking around, still moving, not really seeming to be present. "What is the problem?" Julian asked her.

"Nothing." She shrugged and looked around again.

"Then let's go," I said, but he put a hand on my arm, stopping me. "Something's the matter," he said to her. "Is someone following you?"

She looked startled. "No," she said. "Yes. I don't know."

"Then let's take a walk," Julian said easily, as though nothing could be more natural on a fine Friday afternoon in September. "Where did you leave your gear?"

"At the museum," she said. "They let me store things there."

"Good. We'll head that way."

Three people walking together anywhere is awkward; three people navigating the narrow cobbled streets and alleyways of the Old City is ridiculous, and made carrying on a conversation together nearly impossible. Julian, however, seemed to find it quite comfortable. He engaged Patricia in talking about McGill and a mutual acquaintance there, and in the process he managed to walk behind us, beside us, even in front of us, walking backward and laughing at something she'd said. I thought he was completely out of his mind.

We reached the museum and he gave us a small formal half bow. "Ladies," said Julian. "Miss Mason—may I call you Patricia?"

She nodded, bemused.

"Great. Patricia is right. We've been followed. I'd like you to carry on into the museum and wait for me there. I'm anxious to see this body of yours, but I don't want us to bring anybody else along with us."

"This is your fault!" she hissed at me. "I didn't want to bring anybody in on this!"

"They didn't follow *us*, Patricia," I pointed out reasonably. "They followed you. You're the one who noticed them." I looked at Julian. "Who are they, anyway?"

"If you'll just do as I say," he responded without bothering to clear the exasperation from his voice, "we just might find out!"

We did as he said.

In the end, of course, he didn't find out. We sat and chatted with the woman staffing the museum's front desk about nothing for about twenty minutes before Julian showed up again, slightly pinker under the collar than usual. "We can go now," he said.

"Who was it?"

He shrugged. "Haven't a clue. He picked up the bus near the World Trade Center. Let's go."

"Didn't you follow him?"

He sighed. "Martine, right now it's more important for us to figure out whether or not there's actually anything to investigate here. If he wants more, he'll be back. We'll get a second chance. Let's go."

"But what if he wasn't alone? What if—"

"Do you want to show me this find of yours or not?" he demanded. "Let's *go!*"

We went.

Generaloberst Karl Schultz was staring out the window.

He wasn't staring at anything in particular; night had already fallen on Berlin, and all he could really see was his own reflection, the reflection of the lit chandelier behind him, and that of the younger man nervously fingering the captain's uniform cap he was holding.

He had good reason to be nervous.

"We have someone in Montréal?"

"Yes, Herr General."

"And he has access?" He hadn't moved from the window, hadn't turned to face the young officer.

"Yes, Herr General." The captain cleared his throat. "The vault is guarded round the clock by the Royal Canadian Mounted Police, but he's obtained access through one of the men on the rotation."

"His report?"

"That the first shipment arrived from Halifax last week. Crates with significant weight. Probably the gold." He paused, gestured uncomfortably; Karl could see the reflection of the movement in the dark window. "The rest is really nothing but rumors."

"Which say . . . ?"

"It seems almost too fantastic to repeat, Herr General."

"Be fantastic, Captain. Let yourself go." The voice was dry.

"Very well." He cleared his throat again. "My man reports rumors that the freight includes the—er—well, the British crown jewels." A pause. "Sir."

There was a long silence. The longcase clock by the door ticked loudly; a log in the fireplace fell, sizzling. "The British. Crown. Jewels."

"Yes, Herr General."

"Perhaps not as fantastic as you think, Captain." The younger man couldn't see him, but Karl was smiling. Everyone knew the convoys were there, and it was sheer bad luck that none had ever been caught as they made their limping way across the Atlantic.

But this . . . this might be even better than sending the English gold to the bottom of the sea. This could mean a lot of things.

It meant the Englanders were scared. As well they should be.

It meant there was an opportunity for a boot on the neck of the damned island.

"Get my aide," he said.

"Yes, Herr General."

The young soldier came in, snapped to attention. "Herr General?"

"Get me Reichsmarschall Göring on the telephone," said the general. "We have some very interesting news for him."

CHAPTER TEN

I stopped at a Provigo on the way home for some groceries; I shop differently when the kids are in town. Don't think for a moment that good behavior can't be elicited through a few well-placed bribes, including ones of an alimentary nature: it can. I'm living proof.

There was, naturally, bad news at home.

"I'm sorry," Ivan was saying. "I know it's not convenient, but there's really never a time that's convenient, is there?"

I stared at him. "I don't understand. You have to go to *Boston*?"

"Just for the day. I'll be back Sunday, well before the kids leave."

I felt bewildered. Ivan did, in fact, travel for his work, but the trips were usually planned quite a while in advance, and almost never at a time when Lukas and Claudia were in town; Margery was good at being flexible around our schedules. "Why? I don't understand."

"There's nothing to understand." He clearly didn't want to talk about it. "Margery needs to talk to me without the kids around."

"So she can call. She can Skype. She can come here sometime during the week. Why do you have to go now?" I was sounding petulant, and didn't like it. But, seriously? I was dealing with an ancient murder, someone tailing Patricia, Jean-Luc about to have a coronary if he didn't get to crow about all this, and now I was going to have to be in charge of entertaining Ivan's kids because Ivan decided to go to Boston and talk to his ex?

"It's not that long," Ivan said. "We were going to go to the Insectarium tomorrow anyway, you can just do it without me." He caught my look. "Unless you were planning on working," he said suddenly.

I felt defensive. "Part of the day, anyway," I said. "It's only because—"

"Sometimes," he interrupted, "once in a while, Martine, mine has to come first."

"That's completely unfair," I said. "I don't expect my stuff to always come first."

"No," he said. "You just have a hissy fit when it doesn't."

"I'm not having a hissy fit!" Here's a thought: if you have to scream it, then you probably are.

There was an exaggerated sigh behind me. "Oh, look," said Claudia. "The grown-ups are acting, like, real grown-up again."

Yeah. That helped a lot.

Even Lukas was in a bad mood. "We had to stay in Dad's office all afternoon," he informed me over the spaghetti dinner that I'd assembled hastily, banging the pots as much as possible to vent. "It was *bor*-ing."

"I'll bet it was," I agreed.

"Why do you have to go to Boston?" Claudia asked her father.

"I have something I need to do there," Ivan said. He wouldn't meet my eyes.

"Can I come with you? You can drop me off at Mom's house. That way I don't have to go eat bugs with Belle-Maman and Lukas." Lukas stuck his tongue out at her.

"No," said Ivan. "I'll be back Sunday. Your mother isn't expecting you until the usual time. She might not even be home."

"So what? I'm old enough to, like, stay alone in the house, you know."

"I'm sure you are. You're not coming."

"What kind of bugs do we eat at these things?" Lukas asked.

"I think they're called insects," I said, trying hard to stay engaged with him. It wasn't his fault I was angry with his father. "And I don't know which ones. I've never been to a *dégustation* before." I tried to rally some enthusiasm. "It'll be an adventure, won't it?"

Claudia scrunched her hands up under her oversize sweater sleeves, a gesture she'd taken to doing a lot lately. "Yuck. I've totes lost my appetite. Can I be excused?"

"Yes," I said and "No," said Ivan simultaneously. We glared at each other.

Later, as we were getting ready for bed, he tried being conciliatory. "I'm sorry. I didn't even ask you how things went today with Julian."

"Things went fine," I said shortly.

"So it's just an archaeological thing? Nothing for you to worry about?"

"Nothing for me to worry about." I snapped out my light.

The truth was that Julian hadn't quite known what to do with Patricia's find. "I guess someone should tell someone in London," he said. "But damned if I know who should tell whom."

"You mean about the murder?"

"About the theft," Patricia said unexpectedly. "Once the jewels were placed in the vault, that more or less ended the English participation in the process. Well, there were Bank of England people who went with it, but they didn't spend the whole war in Montréal. Anyone who had access to it was Canadian, so the thief must have been Canadian, too."

Julian shook his head, his headlamp moving as he did. "Not

necessarily," he said. "Anyway, it doesn't matter what nationality they were, if the killing was done here, it's ours, one of our *crimes contre les personnes*. But it's one hell of a cold case." A slight pause. "Still, we have people who like doing those."

"And you're going to bring them down here." Patricia's voice was flat: she knew already.

"I have to. This guy—and it's most probably a guy—was murdered in Montréal; we have a duty to investigate. And we've got to get London involved, which probably means first getting Ottawa involved." He sighed; Julian was no lover of governmental red tape. "This may be great news for your dissertation, but it's gonna cause a lot of sleepless nights for somebody, and a lot of work for the rest of us."

"Well, I'm not apologizing," she said. "It's still good for me, and it's good for you, too, Martine, right?"

I considered. What had sounded like the perfect PR coup— "Montréal Saves Crown Jewels from Hitler's Clutches"—was muddied a little with the emergence of this possible Montréaler who'd helped himself to some of said crown jewels. I wasn't really sure how to spin that into something useful. Not yet, anyway. "The jewels were in his pocket?" I asked Julian instead. He'd been squatting by the bones for the past ten minutes; he'd better have learned something. It seemed colder in the room than it had the day before.

"Not so much, I don't think," he said.

"What?"

"Well," he said reasonably, "someone shot him, probably right here, to get what he had. So why didn't they take it?"

"Maybe they did," I said. "Maybe there were more to begin with and they missed a couple." There were two stones, I could see now, winking in the light. I hadn't gotten close enough to count them before.

His light swung around to shine in my face and I put up a hand to shield my eyes from it. "Seriously? You think that somehow some-one killed this guy, went through his pockets, and *missed a couple?*"

"He swallowed them," Patricia said.

Julian nodded and the headlamp did its bobbing thing again. "That would be my bet," he said. "And not right in front of whom-ever shot him, either, or they'd have opened him up right here. He must have done it before."

I stared down at the bones and the sharp bright glitter they pro-tected. "What are they, anyway?"

"Diamonds," said Patricia. "Those are diamonds."

"There you go," Julian said comfortably. "A girl's best friend."

I didn't tell Ivan about the body. Not about the body, not about the diamonds, not about the thoughtful look on Julian's face when he talked about Patricia Mason being followed. Despite whatever our argument was kicking up between us, I didn't want to worry him.

On Saturday morning he left without our having said more than a handful of words to each other. Claudia was once again hiding in-side an oversize sweater and Lukas was giving her as much grief as possible. I suggested that we make crêpes at home before heading out to the Insectarium. "You know how to make crêpes?" asked Lukas. Apparently I hadn't done so in recent memory.

"I have mad skills," I informed him.

"Ohmygod I can't believe you just actually said mad skills," Claudia said dramatically.

Her reaction puzzled me. "I've heard you say it."

"Well, *yeah*"—she managed to draw the word out into at least three syllables—"but I'm not, like, *eighty years old.*"

Lovely. "Come on," I said, carrying on undaunted. "You can put Nutella on yours."

Nutella is one of those buy-the-kids'-affections foods, destined to please no matter what storms were raging. *Dieu merci*, it seemed to still work. Claudia even consented to help with the batter, while Lukas was soon, more or less, expertly flipping them out of the pan.

The Insectarium is in the eastern part of the city, part of a complex that also houses the botanical garden, with the Biodôme and the Planetarium not far away across the street. The whole of it is now called the *espace pour la vie*—area for life—and was constructed originally for the 1976 Montréal Olympic Games while incorporating the American pavilion as the Biodôme. I could almost hear François telling his passengers, "The safest games there ever were, since they were the first ones since Munich." Now transformed, the Biodôme was gutted twice by fire before it was decided that its moveable roof should cease moving.

I shared all these fun facts with Lukas and Claudia as we parked the car. They were remarkably underimpressed.

I saw him first as we were standing in line to buy our tickets. Claudia was already complaining that she could feel something crawling down her back. "I'm sure that some of them, like, get away."

"And they all want you," said Lukas, gleefully.

I was turning to tell Claudia that it was all in her mind when a middle-aged man, a belted black raincoat stretched across his considerable belly, caught my eye. In a city with a sizeable Orthodox and even Hasidic presence, it wasn't unusual to see a man in a yarmulke, but it was unusual for him to be staring so intently. Specifically, at us.

Orthodox Jewish men just don't stare at women.

"Did you know that if we were at the top of the stadium observatory and looked down on the Insectarium, we'd see it's in the shape of an insect?" Even as I was asking the question I was moving unobtrusively so that I was standing between the kids and the man in the black raincoat.

"Which one?" Lukas wanted to know.

"Which what?"

"Which insect, Belle-Maman! Which insect is it shaped like?"

"Do you know," I said, "I have no idea." I risked a glance back, part of me assuming that he'd have disappeared, or turned to chat with his own family group waiting in line, assuming that I was reading dark meanings into everyday occurrences.

No such luck. Still there, still staring, and my stomach tightened. Surely there was no danger here, not on a Saturday afternoon at a tourist attraction. The sun was shining; a child laughed nearby. I wished I could believe in the light.

I paid the entrance fee and the special tasting fee, and pulled the kids in far more quickly than they'd anticipated. "Ow, Belle-Maman, don't, like, grab me like that!" snapped Claudia.

"Get over here," I hissed, and both of them, surprised, obeyed. That was a first. We walked briskly through several rooms, not looking at the exhibitions, not looking at anything, my hands holding their forearms. I looked back once, and he was there, hurrying after us. Damn.

I pulled the kids into the first darkened room we came to, with lit glass display cases showing off wings, antennae, larvae. "Stay here. Do you hear me? Stay in this room, stay right on this spot, and don't leave. If someone tries to make you move, scream. As loud as you can."

I would have to remember that tone of voice: I'd never elicited such complete attention and acquiescence before. "What if they know the secret word?" asked Lukas.

Distracted, I repeated, "Secret word?"

Claudia tossed her hair over her shoulder. "You know, Belle-Maman, you told us a long time ago that if anyone, like, ever came and said that we should go with them because you were in the hospital, we should ask them for the secret word. And if they didn't know it, it meant you hadn't sent them after all."

I stared at her. So she'd actually listened? I'd instituted the secret word years ago. "I don't think I still remember it, Claudia."

A sigh. "It's aardvark," she said disdainfully.

"Aardvark," I repeated, nodding. "Good word. Good idea. Don't go with anyone who doesn't say 'aardvark.' But don't worry, it's not going to happen and in any case, I'll be right back."

Lukas's eyes were as huge and round as saucers. I put my arms around him and gave him a fierce hug. "Stay with your sister," I said. "I really will be right back, Lukas. I promise."

"Okay, Belle-Maman," he said in the tiniest voice.

"Take care of him," I said to Claudia, decided against hugging her, too, and slipped through the doorway.

The man in the black raincoat was rushing along now, his short legs pumping. I waited until he was almost in the doorway, and when he was about to pass me I stepped out in front of him. "*Bonjour, monsieur.* Is there something I can help you with?"

He reared back like a frightened horse. An overweight frightened horse. One hand went to his chest. "Ack. You almost killed me, there, with your '*bonjour, monsieur*'. What is it you're wanting? Hmm? Is it me to have a heart attack? This will make you happy?"

"I'm wanting," I said carefully, "to know why you're following me and my children."

He produced a handkerchief and mopped his forehead. "Your children, no, I don't need to follow them. But you, yes, you I am following. You are of great interest to me. You, I need to learn more about."

"Really? And why is that?"

He looked at me, surprised. "Why," he said, "because of the diamonds, of course!"

The fat man was laughing.

Everyone in the room exchanged nervous smiles. When Hermann Göring was amused, it usually seemed to mean that someone was in

trouble. Sometimes, very bad trouble. "I thought we'd have a time of
*it, convincing the English that we're serious about invasion," he said,
*wiping a tear from the corner of his eye, still laughing. "They're the
ones convincing me!"

"But, Herr Reichsmarschall—"

He waved the incipient objection away. "I know what I've said,"
*he said. "And I stand by it. We won't need a ground invasion. We'll
take the damned island by air."

"The Luftwaffe will always reign supreme, Herr Reichsmarschall,"
one of his aides said.

The laughter faded. "If I need a sycophant, Horst, I'll tell you to
speak," he said.

"Yes, Herr Reichsmarschall."

The fat man regained his good humor. "But if this is correct—and
*I believe my general—then what an opportunity for a delightful trick
to play on the Englanders!"

"A trick, Herr Reichsmarschall?"

He rubbed his hands together. "Indeed. They're so afraid of us
*they've sent their precious crown jewels, the pride of the empire, across
*the sea, out of reach! Obviously—and rightly—they believe in inva-
*sion." He chuckled. "The scenario's perfect, gentlemen. We take over
*England, and when we make them claim them from Canada, poof!
They're not all there." He paused. "Or, better still, they're not all real!"

"If it can be done, Herr Reichsmarschall . . ."

He turned on the group. "I don't want to hear anybody talking
*about problems! It can be done! It will be done! I will not stand for
negativity here!"

"Jawohl, Herr Reichsmarschall!" *Everyone had stiffened in their
chairs.

"We will locate these jewels and we will do what we want with
them and we will break the backs of the damned Englanders!"

"Jawohl, Herr Reichsmarschall!"

The fat man was smiling again—that was how most of his victims remembered him. "So. We will take care of the Englanders' jewels. But not a word of this to the Führer! Not yet! It will be a pleasant surprise for him."

"Jawohl, *Herr Reichsmarschall.*"

CHAPTER ELEVEN

We were sitting in a restaurant whose name I couldn't readily dissect from all the writing on the sheet glass advertising special *plats du jour* and urging customers to *apporter* their own wine. Claudia and Lukas were sitting at a table nearby, eating ice cream and pretending that they didn't know me.

And I was talking with the man from the Insectarium: Avner Kaspi.

"You have to understand, perhaps you do not, that the diamond trade, it runs in families, it is passed from father to son as a birthright," Avner was saying. That we were already on a first-name basis indicated probably nothing more than my complete shock when we'd met; but after ten minutes with the man, I felt I'd known him for years. "There is my son Lev, a fine young man, a real mensch, if you were not already married I would recommend him to you. He will do well in the diamond trade he gets from his father once he stops this thinking that he belongs in school forever—what did I do wrong there?—and starts looking for the right girl."

"I see," I said faintly. I actually saw nothing.

"Ah, but you are not here to talk about my son or his matrimonial

plans, or perhaps I should say lack thereof," said Avner. "I understand. You're like mine wife Naomi. 'Avner, get to the point,' she is
always telling me, but it's not so easy to do, is it, when there's a long
story to tell?"

"Why don't," I said carefully, "you start at the beginning?"

"This is a good question. You are a smart woman, I could tell that
right away about you. So this is where I will start. I will start at the
darkest time in Europe's history, I will start as the war began."

"Your family—" I started to say, and then broke off. "I'm sorry.
That's none of my business. Go on, please."

"But it is your business, Martine LeDuc! This is why I have
looked for you, to find a time to talk. Yesterday I look for you, but
could not find you, all day I wait near City Hall to see you, but the
directrice de publicité is somewhere else, so they tell me, always she
is somewhere else, and I cannot see her."

Light dawned. "Were you following me yesterday? Or Patricia?"

He frowned. "No. I go home to my Naomi and I say, 'Ach, I cannot find her, this Martine LeDuc person.'"

It was just an idea. "Go on," I said again.

"Yes. So my father, he was in the diamond trade, of course, I tell
you this is how it works, we pass it on so it all stays in the family. If
there is no son, God forbid, there is a nephew always, a son-in-law,
someone. It's part of our history, yes? Diamond trade routes follow
the Diaspora, so this trade, it is particularly suited to Jewish enterprise." He smiled. "And since these diamonds were a relatively rare
and new commodity in Europe, we find a niche there. You see how
it is? You are following me?"

"Yes," I said. "Faint but pursuing."

"So my father, him, he is in Antwerp, in Belgium. It is a big center for the diamonds, Antwerp. And he is doing very well, thank
God: there is always food on the table. There were bad things hap-

pening, yes; there was reason to fear. But still they stayed there, in Antwerp. Still they think they can ride out this storm. Until 1939."

I didn't have to ask what had happened in 1939.

Avner was unemotional. "My father and his wife, this is his first wife I speak of now, they were sent to a transit camp, and then he went on to Buchenwald. We think his wife, she was sent to Ravensbrück, maybe much later. Who can say? My father, he survived. Everything they made him do, everything he endured, and he came out. His wife, she did not."

He paused, and there was an awkward silence. I had no idea what to say.

"So after the war, my father, he returned to Antwerp, to take up again the diamond trade. And things, they went very well for him then. He found my mother, and married her, and I was born. It was all good."

A happy ending for someone, at least. "I'm glad," I said awkwardly, inadequately.

He smiled. "You do not have to be embarrassed," he said. "This is the past of which I speak now. But the past is never completely gone, do you not find this is so?"

"Especially lately," I said.

"Yes. I see that you know what I am going to speak of next." He took a deep breath. "My father, he who is in the diamond trade, he teaches me the diamond trade. From a small boy I learn it. I know what there is to know." He glanced at me. "My son, Lev, he is in the business, when he is not in classes at McGill. And my son, he has changed the business for me. Grading systems and something he calls e-commerce, and e-mail. Currency exchanges." He shook his head. "He is very smart, my Lev."

I had a time limitation—i.e., how long Lukas and Claudia were going to be willing to sit still. "What happened, Avner?"

"Ach, well you might ask. So here we are. And my family, we are not all of us happy with life in Antwerp. My brother, he does *aliyah*, you understand this? Goes to live in Israel. He thinks he can be a better Jew in Israel. Me, I think, you take who you are with you. And I meet a girl, a nice Jewish girl, I wish that my son Lev would meet such a nice Jewish girl like this one, only mine, mine Naomi, I married. And she is the daughter of such an important rabbi in this city called Montréal! A very famous rabbi, he is. So this is where I come, for my father-in-law, he wants to have his daughter close, and who can blame him? He tells her to live in Montréal, so we live in Montréal."

I tried to imagine telling Claudia and her future husband where they should live, but gave up. "How did you meet her?"

"Sorry?"

"Your wife," I said. "How did you meet her?"

"Ah. Yes. This is also a story. Mine wife, she was in Antwerp for a doctor who practices there." He glanced at me. "She stays for some time to get better. In a special hospital, you understand? After the war, there are many not right in the head, you know this? And she was not right in the head, no, but she is always right in the heart, and that is where it counts. She takes pills now, they help her."

"I'm sorry," I said. "It's really none of my business."

"So I move to Montréal," Avner was saying. "And I bring with me my diamond trade, and there are more Jews here who do it, too, so I am happy to find that I fit right in."

I cleared my throat. "Avner, I'm not seeing the connection between—"

He interrupted. "Three years ago, my father died. It is no surprise; he was a very old man. A *very* old man," he emphasized, looking at me as though I'd been about to accuse him of murdering his father. "And I take mine wife Naomi and mine son Lev and we go to Antwerp to sit *shiva* with my family. You understand this?"

"It's like a wake, isn't it?" I said cautiously. "Only it lasts longer. Days?"

"Days," he confirmed, nodding. "So we are in Antwerp, and I am remembering how to speak the language, because I have not spoken it in many years, here it is only French and English and Yiddish, you see."

I nodded.

"And so I am speaking Flemish again, and my aunt, she who also endured and survived the Shoah, she is giving me my father's possessions, that she says he wanted me to have. It is boxes and boxes. Too much to deal with. Too much sorrow, too many memories, too many people to see. So we have the boxes sent to Montréal and we stay for two weeks in Antwerp and then we return home. And you are thinking, I know you are thinking, that this is the end of my father's story, but no! It is not. Because finally when I look at my father's papers, I find out things. He wrote of the camp where he was, of Buchenwald, and I must force myself to read it, because I do not want to know."

"I can understand that."

"But as much as I do not want to know, I want to know. It is a very confusing feeling. So I read it all. He is writing this after he has returned to Antwerp, after the camp is liberated, you understand: he is writing of his memories. And he is writing of what he did for work when he is in the camp."

I sat very still. Behind me, Lukas's laughter.

"The Nazis, they found him very interesting, my father. They like that he knows about diamonds." He took a deep breath. "And here it is, now I tell you this thing. They find him especially, my father, they look for him and find him and bring him on purpose to Buchenwald, because he works with white sapphires, and special garnets, and can make from them what looks like diamonds, cut just so, even an expert might think they are diamonds."

It felt inevitable. "They knew that the crown jewels were here," I said. It was the only place this could possibly be going, and at the same time I couldn't see how.

Avner nodded. "Very quick, you are. Would that Lev could find such a nice girl—Jewish, though, of course—as quick as you are. Yes. And here is the thought. The English hide their jewels, and the Nazis, they take them. Not all of them, just some of them. They think these diamonds, they hold magical powers, some of them. For centuries they hold the power of kings, king after king, some people, they believe that this builds the power, that it gets bigger. And Hitler, everyone knows, he thinks highly of such things. Very interested, he is, in tales of mine people, of kabbalic mysticism. He believes that these jewels will bring him the greatest power of all." He leaned forward and lowered his voice. "He will be able to make nature itself bend to his will."

"Then why replace them with anything?" I asked. "Why not just steal them outright?"

"This is another very good question, Martine LeDuc. You do not maybe have a little Jewish sister, a younger one maybe, one we can introduce to my son Lev? They will steal the diamonds, yes, but replace them with clever fakes, fakes that my father makes for them from white sapphires at Buchenwald. And why, you ask. Well, I will tell you the why. It is because they believe that they will take England. It is a matter of time only. And when the English call for their magical crown jewels, they will be shown to be paste, to be nothing, just as the English, they are nothing. This is the plan."

"How did they learn the jewels were in Montréal? It was supposed to be a secret."

He lifted his shoulders in a very Gallic gesture; he'd lived in Montréal long enough to pick that up, anyway. Or maybe they shrugged like that in Antwerp. "Who can say? This, I do not know. Except that secrets very often are not secrets at all. People, they are very bad at keeping secrets, and the more time passes, the more it is possible to share them around."

I nodded. *"C'est vrai,"* I said. "Okay. So you read about what your father did, and you probably wanted to learn more about it, since here you were, living in Montréal yourself. How did you find out about . . ."

". . . the diamonds under the theater?" he asked. "Because my Lev, he is a genius with a computer, have I told you this? Always doing this with the computer, that with the computer. Me, I know nothing about this, but mine son Lev, he does. It is what he studies."

"At McGill," I said, light dawning.

He nodded. "At McGill, where he meets this girl—she is not as smart as you, I think, and she is not a Jewish girl, but mine boy Lev, he likes her."

"Patricia Mason," I said, and swore. *"Bordel,* I don't believe it." There are four major universities in Montréal, two of them English-speaking. What were the chances of the diamond merchant's son and the doctoral student fetching up in the same place? "What kind of coincidence is that?"

"The world, it is smaller than you think, and only in movies do they say, 'I do not believe in coincidences,'" said Avner. "There is a word for coincidence in all the languages I know. And so it does exist. She has not told him everything, but she has told him what she has found. I think that if you identify your skeleton, Martine LeDuc, you will find someone who worked for the Nazis."

"So who killed him?"

He shrugged again. "This, also, I do not know. There is very much I do not know. What I know, only, is diamonds. About diamonds, I know everything. And I would like very much to see the other diamonds. I think they are the real ones that my father made copies of. The one I have seen, it is perfect, it is like his drawings that I have seen."

"Hang on," I said. "What do you mean, the other diamonds?"

He looked at me blandly. "Besides the one that Miss Mason has shown me already, of course," he said. "The one from the room under the theater."

"Yes," I said faintly. "Of course."

It wasn't the way he would have chosen to fight the war, living this double life. He loved the Wehrmacht uniforms, everything correct and commanding respect when a soldier walked into a room; and he could have been more than just a soldier, too. Hans was sure of it. He could have become an officer, had ribbons on his chest; everyone would know that the boy whose father had killed his family had risen high, far above his beginnings, his tragedy, know that he had become a real man.

Instead, he was forced to live far away from anyone he knew, pretend to be someone he wasn't, fight a war without a gun. It was dispiriting.

He had very little contact with anyone from the Fatherland. That might have helped, Hans told himself. Hear someone speaking German—any German, any accent, it wouldn't matter. Making jokes that only another German would understand. Talk with people from the Party, hear the Party gossip.

Instead, he had Kurt.

Kurt was stationed in New York City. He sometimes sent coded messages—Hans had taken the requisite course in codes and cyphers— and sometimes came up to Montréal himself. Even though he longed for German companionship, Hans preferred Kurt's communiqués to Kurt's actual presence: there was nothing about Montréal that the other man couldn't find to criticize. It was too cold; it was too hot. The French was incomprehensible; Kurt had been in Paris and considered himself a connoisseur of all things French. The food was good enough to feed to the dogs. The women were all too thin. And so on.

New York, on the other hand, was the center of Kurt's universe. He was, of course, a good Party member, a staunch Nazi, and he knew that the depravities of the United States of America were its ultimate weakness—but that knowledge never kept him from exploring and enjoying those depravities to the fullest. "Times Square, you should see Times Square," he said to Hans as they strolled along the river in Montréal's quiet residential section called Anjou. "The women there— not very proper, not very careful, completely edible!"

"What do you have for me today?"

Kurt turned away from the water and looked at Hans, his eyes narrowed. "You're very eager," he observed.

"I am eager to do my duty for the Fatherland," Hans said. "Sometimes it feels—"

"Ah, yes, I see what you are saying." He turned and resumed the walk, his hands clasped behind his back. Hans told people it was his brother who was visiting. "You wish that you had more excitement here. You wish that you could make a difference for the Führer. I can sympathize. It must be terrible, stuck in a provincial backwater like this."

"I do my duty," said Hans stiffly, wishing he could just push Kurt into the river. There were rapids in the St. Lawrence, fast water that, with a little luck, could take him all the way out to sea. It was not an unpleasant thought.

"That's what I like to hear," said Kurt. "Bear your frustrations for the Fatherland, Peterson. This is your war, right here." He couldn't help but snigger as he looked around. Anjou was blue-collar and unkempt, not like downtown; Hans suspected that Kurt had selected it on purpose. Unworthy thoughts of my superior, he reminded himself, but thought them anyway.

"Is there news?" he asked diffidently. Kurt would prolong this as long as he could.

"There is always news," Kurt responded. "Tell me, is there a

decent restaurant in this city, or do I have to take the train back right away?"

Hans started to defend Montréal, then thought better of it. "Nothing to your standards," he said. The sooner Kurt was out of his hair, the better.

"Thought not," said the other. He was looking with ill-disguised disgust at a woman walking toward them on the towpath. Waiting for her to pass, he said, "Everyone's pleased that we know where the royal jewels are," he said. "There's a lot of interest from Berlin."

"Am I to do anything about them?" A little action would be nice.

"Not for the moment." He shook his head. "Me, I'd think they'd be after the securities. But that's not the case. They have a plan. And it's not for us to question it!" He scowled at Hans as if he'd done just that.

"Jawohl," said Hans neutrally.

"So you are to wait," said Kurt with some relish. "Wait until you hear from me. Make yourself part of the community." He glanced over. "Your cover is still good?"

"It's still good."

"All right." He grinned. "I think I will take the early train down after all. There's a show at Radio City Music Hall tonight I don't want to miss."

CHAPTER TWELVE

By the time we got home, I was fuming. I'd tried calling Patricia several times on her mobile, but it went straight to voice mail. So did Julian's. So did Ivan's. Nobody, it seemed, wanted to talk to me.

Claudia was clamoring about having dinner in the Underground City, and as she hadn't made our trip to the Insectarium an actual disaster, I was inclined to agree. I'm not crazy about the Underground City as a destination, mind you: it's really just a shopping mall that spreads its tentacles all over, connected by corridors and, of course, the Métro; but it is certainly popular and, in the winter, extremely useful.

There'd been various attempts over the years to make it more attractive to those seeking culture along with their fashion and fast food, and of course there was Québec's "one percent" rule: any building constructed for public use has to put aside one percent of said building for the arts. So there's always an attempt. The corridors connect some cultural venues, of course—the museum of contemporary art, some theaters, a tremendous movie house—but, by and large, it's a mall.

Still, there's a lot to be said for it. Underground, you can eat, drink, visit bookstores and pharmacies, pay your taxes at one of the government offices, book a trip at a travel agency, buy your dinner wine at one of the *societé des alcools du Québec* outlets, and of course shop, shop, shop.

The reality is that most Montréalers use it as a means to an end: the Underground City is a commuter's dream. No rain, no snow, no traffic. Weekdays they're all there, morning and evening, walking briskly to and from their workplaces downtown, grabbing the Métro, stopping occasionally for a quick coffee.

But it was the bright lights, the window displays, the fashion, and the relative safety of the mall environment that drew Claudia and other adolescents like moths to a flame.

It was a particularly fine day and so we eschewed the Métro and walked up the hill to the Eaton entrance. "I need to go to La Baie," Claudia was babbling. "And to Ailes de la Mode, and to . . ." Her eyes were glittering, and I shook my head. Nothing like offering a fix to an addict.

We did a little shopping and a lot of looking around and finally found ourselves in one of the lower-level food courts, eating hamburgers and fries. Ivan, who was on an organic-foods-only kick, would have been horrified, but the kids were ecstatic and I felt they'd earned it. Ivan was never away when they were with us, and they must have been feeling it.

"Belle-Maman? Belle-Maman!"

Distracted, I focused back on the kids. "What is it?"

"Can we look around?"

"Did you finish eating?" Lukas had; he inhaled food, and his intake was prodigious. Claudia picked delicately at hers and had clearly eaten everything she planned to eat. "All right. Check back with me in fifteen minutes."

"Fifteen *minutes!*" It was a wail.

"All right. Twenty. Let me see your phones."

"Lukas has his."

"Twenty minutes," I said again, and they were gone.

So what should I worry about first? The fact that Patricia had clearly grabbed one of the diamonds and hadn't bothered mentioning it to me, or the question marks that surrounded Ivan's sudden need to see Margery?

How fortunate that I had a plethora of things to choose from that I could feel anxious about.

What was Patricia's game, anyway? She presented as so straightforward, the graduate student with the great ideas, pushing her glasses up her nose and talking about history as though she'd lived it. Was she becoming obsessed? I'd considered it, but at the end of the day I'd have said not: I've met some obsessed people in my life, and Patricia was more grounded than that.

But why steal a diamond? Why show it to Avner? Why go completely off the reservation when she'd promised to work with me? She didn't trust me, hadn't trusted me since I'd brought Julian in. But she'd taken the diamond before that.

And then there was Ivan. My mind approached that one more delicately. Margery had been sick last year; what if it hadn't been the cut-and-dried situation, the successful surgery she'd told us it was? What if it were something far more serious? How could the kids lose their mother?

The cold feeling in my stomach was intensifying. I took a deep breath, shook my head as though to banish the images, and consciously moved my thoughts off the subject. Patricia: there was a puzzle that was less emotional. Why would she have taken one of the diamonds? Did she think they were going to disappear, that for some reason the government was going to bury them in red tape and international relations; did she feel she needed to save one to prove that they existed? Or did she just want it?

And was it really accidental that she'd run into Avner's son Lev at McGill?

I took a deep breath. Ivan would have to wait, but Patricia? Her, I could do something about. I punched her contact icon on my mobile and when the voice mail clicked on, I left a terse message. "Contact me as soon as you get this message, or I'm going to the police."

How cliché can you get?

Julian, when I finally spoke to him, was more sanguine. "I'm not especially surprised," he said.

I frowned. I was curled on the sofa, Claudia and Lukas having taken their various packages to their bedrooms, both clearly tired. I'd just poured a glass of wine when Julian returned my call. "You're not surprised?"

"She's emotionally involved," he said. "She's got a lot at stake here."

"So that means it's okay to steal a crown jewel? I just left her a message threatening to call the police, but, gosh, apparently the police don't care."

"Didn't say I didn't care, just said I wasn't surprised," Julian said. "My, you're prickly tonight."

I took a swallow of wine. "Sorry, Julian. Bad day. So tell me—what's your take on Patricia? And do you even know where she is?"

"I think that she's probably getting the diamond assessed," he said. "It's certainly the first thing I'd do."

"Too late. She's already done that." And I told him about Avner of the black raincoat. "He says she met his son, who's some kind of computer genius but apparently lacking in the marriage department, at McGill, and asked Avner to look at the diamond."

"What did he say?"

What *had* he said? He'd talked about the Koh-i-Noor, the most famous of all the diamonds. About the replacements for the jewels that King John had supposedly lost when crossing the Wash at Sutton Bridge. And then he'd told me about the curse.

"Of course there's a curse," said Julian, delighted. "Tell me, tell me!"

"Let me see if I remember," I said. "I wasn't taking notes." Another swallow of wine. "So first you have to understand what we're talking about here. They're not all actually jewels, though a lot of them are. All sorts of jewels, not just diamonds, though that's what we're dealing with here. When you say the crown jewels, you're actually referring to anything that's used or worn or even is just present at a coronation. So there are scepters and swords and all that sort of thing, too." I paused. "Valuable objects that can allegedly pick up—influences—along the way."

"Influences," said Julian.

"That's where Hitler came in," I said. "See, it's all about a certain tradition, isn't it? And there were all these treasures accumulating over the decades in the royal coffers, and everything was lovely in the garden until Cromwell arrived."

"Cromwell?" He was sounding bewildered. That was fine; I'd felt bewildered, too, between Avner's version of history and what I'd looked up since I'd gotten home.

"The English Civil War," I said. "You know, the antimonarchy mob. Didn't you do English history at school? King Charles was executed in—oh, sixteen-something, I can't remember. And all the royal gold was melted down. The jewels themselves—the gemstones, you know?—they got taken out of their settings and sold. Cromwell was determined that anything that was a symbol of royalty and kingship should be completely eradicated."

"So none of the current crown jewels are older than the 1600s," said Julian.

"None of the ones that came from England," I said. "They

acquired older pieces from other countries, but essentially that's correct. And that's where the curse comes in."

"Go on."

I settled myself even more snugly into the sofa. "So there was this tiara," I said. "All diamonds—it came from France. It was put into the collection—it was stored at Westminster then, not the Tower of London—and the first thing that happens is that it's getting cleaned, and the person doing it gets cut and dies."

"Every curse has to start somewhere," Julian observed.

"And a little infection will kickstart it," I agreed. "No one talked about a curse, though, until the tiara started stacking up bodies. Over time, mind you. Decades. In the twentieth century, the jewels were out for Elizabeth II's coronation, and one of her ladies-in-waiting, who apparently handled the tiara, died within the week. Of course, she already had emphysema, but curses don't care about that."

"And you think the diamonds that Patricia found are from this tiara?"

"Avner thinks so. He's seen one of them, remember, and he's a guy who really knows his diamonds. So, yeah, we probably have the cursed jewels here."

"Well, whoever got shot down there no doubt agrees," said Julian.

"About him, Julian—"

"Yeah?"

"Well, what's the plan? Are you going to launch an investigation? Get forensics and crime-scene people down there?"

"Probably not," he said. "I had a talk this morning with the boss, and he's less than impressed. He only wants to catch killers if they're alive so they can have a spectacularly expensive trial and go to prison. It's about notches on the bedstead. Um—metaphorically speaking, of course."

"Of course," I agreed. "He'd probably be thrilled to arrest Patricia, though."

"Not giving him the option. I'm going to find her first, get the diamond back. That's a headache for other people, by the way. The moment I talked about the crown jewels his eyes glazed over. Way above our pay grade. But Ottawa's going to have to get involved."

"I thought they might." And I was going to have to explain all this to Jean-Luc on Monday. I wasn't exactly looking forward to that. "Do you know where she is?"

"Not at this actual moment. But I'm going to find her tomorrow and see if we can lift this curse."

I put down the wineglass. "I'd rather like a word with her then, too."

The evening wound down, and the later it got, the more depressed I felt. Ivan didn't call. I checked my phone to make sure the battery hadn't run down. I thought about calling him, and didn't.

Ivan didn't call, but Julian did: he called me back just as I was getting ready to go to sleep. "You know that curse?" asked Julian. "It worked."

"What are you talking about?"

"It's Patricia Mason," he responded. "She's dead."

The sign over the main gate said it all. JEDEM DAS SEINE, *which, loosely translated, meant that if you were here, you were getting what you deserved.*

But nobody deserved what they got at Buchenwald.

It went operational in 1937 and was the first camp to be liberated by United States troops in 1945. There was a lot of time in between. A lot of time, and a lot of bodies.

But not Elias Kaspi's body. Not if he could help it.

There was a large oak tree in the center of the camp, Goethe's Oak it was called, funny thing it seemed, to be naming trees. They say he wrote Faust *right there, under that tree, and what a thought, a deal with the devil in a place that, if you believed in hell, was right here, right now.*

Elias didn't like looking at the tree. He'd made his own deal with the devil.

Someone had to live, he told himself. And he'd been given the opportunity. To live on. To someday leave this place.

Ruth hadn't been given the opportunity; they'd been separated, and the officials who'd requested Elias didn't request that his wife come along with. He didn't know where Ruth was. He didn't know if she was alive or dead, in Belgium or Germany, in another camp or had escaped, God willing, fleeing down a road and then, perhaps, strafed by the Luftwaffe. He'd seen that happen enough on the roads around Antwerp.

He couldn't think about Ruth. Not now. At night, in his bunk in the long barracks he shared with forty other equally emaciated men, after the obligatory head count and nibbling on the bread he'd saved from the morning's rations; then he thought about her. But during the day he had work to do. Work that was keeping him alive.

Who would have thought that his trade, his gesheft, *was what in the end would have saved him?*

A diamond merchant. A man who knew diamonds, intimately, who lived and breathed diamonds. Who had generations of diamond trade singing in his blood. Who knew, in fact, everything that there was to know about diamonds.

Because Elias didn't only sell diamonds. Elias could cut them, too.

Who would have thought?

His brother Herman had emigrated to Eretz Israel in 1930 along with a large group of Jews from the low countries, Jews who established an important diamond industry in Palestine, bringing their technical skills and commercial connections with them.

At first, Elias had gone with Herman. It seemed like an exciting plan, something daring, to go to this place of their ancestors, to live in the strange heat shimmering off the desert. He was young, and eager, and had worked hard with Herman in Netanyah for three years. But it was not his home, this strange hot country, and in the end Elias returned to Antwerp to marry Ruth and take up his father's business, taking care of shteyns *there.*

But Herman had helped make Palestine into the gem diamond center of the world, and the Nazis knew all about him. And because of Herman, they knew about Elias.

So they hadn't put Elias into one of the trains that nobody was talking about yet, that the world learned about later. They had been polite. They had knocked on his door. It was only when he'd refused to go with them that they had shown their true colors. And by then it was too late.

Still, here at Buchenwald, there was a chance of survival. They gave Elias a workshop and two apprentices. They paid him in camp money. And they had something very specific in mind.

"These photographs," the camp commander had said when Elias first arrived. "Look at these photographs."

They were crowns and scepters, tiaras and necklaces. "Very nice," Elias said. He didn't know what they expected of him.

"The diamonds," the commandant said. "Do you know what diamonds these are?"

They were big stones, what his father used to call mame-zitsers. *Elias looked again and shook his head. "Crown jewels," he said, that much was obvious. Whose? The Nazis were plundering so many countries, who knew?*

"It doesn't matter." He was brusque. "Can you imitate them?"

"What?" Elias was bewildered. "These are diamonds. They—"

A swift backhand across his cheek. "Enough! Do not play with me! It is my understanding that there are other gems that can be cut to have the same appearance. Am I incorrect?"

*Light was dawning and with it, hope. "You are not incorrect,"
Elias said. "There are some gems, yes, yes. It can be done. Yellow sapphires . . . there's a special garnet . . ."*

*"We will procure what you need," the commandant said. "You will
create copies of these jewels."*

"Yes," said Elias. And lived.

*The work was wretched, and the conditions even more so. Every
morning he awoke to more death, more pain, more despair. Sometimes one or more of the men in his barracks had died next to him in
the night. There were beatings; there was solitary confinement. There
was so little to eat that men dropped around him of starvation; and
Elias himself finally stopped dreaming of the Sabbath dinners that
Ruth used to put on the table.*

And then there were the singing trees.

*Buchenwald, he knew, meant "beech forest," a beautiful name for
such a terrible place. And there were trees, a whole grove of them,
where Goethe used to walk with his love. It was in these trees that
Commandant Koch hung prisoners from the wrists, their arms behind
them; the singing that he spoke of was their screams. They echoed inside Elias's head, those screams, even when he wasn't hearing them.
He was sure that they would never leave.*

They never did leave. But, one day, Elias finally did.

CHAPTER THIRTEEN

My husband is Jewish, though he sees it as belonging to a tribe rather than practicing a religion. Me, on the other hand, I'm as Catholic as they come, despite many reservations about how my church sometimes practices its faith. Margery, the kids' mother, occasionally attends a Unitarian-Universalist meetinghouse, but doesn't manifest a lot of enthusiasm for any organized religion.

So when Ivan and I got married, I took the kids' religious training firmly in hand. I don't care if, as thoughtful adults, they turn their backs on the church. I just want to give them something on which to turn their backs . . . or even, perhaps, not.

So Sunday mornings when they're in residence, our apartment is alive with protest. "I don't want to go!" howled Claudia from behind her closed door.

"Ten minutes, Claudia, and you are coming whether you want to or not."

Lukas sat at the kitchen table, carefully noting the day's schedule in his planner. "What time's Dad getting in?"

"I have no idea," I told him distractedly.

"What if he comes when we're at church?"

"I seriously doubt that he'll take that as a rejection, Lukas." After a sleepless night—we call it a *nuit blanche*, a white night—I probably wasn't at my best. "Sorry. I didn't mean to snap at you."

"I think someone should be here when he comes," he said.

"It'll be fine, Lukas, I promise." I raised my voice. "Claudia!"

"I'm not going!"

"You are if you ever want to see the Underground City again." I'd agreed to another visit this afternoon, mostly so she could think overnight about spending forty dollars of her saved allowance on a skirt she'd seen yesterday. I was hoping she'd decide against it: it seemed like a lot of money, and Claudia wasn't finished growing yet. But it was her decision.

"That's blackmail!"

"It is indeed."

"I hate you, Belle-Maman!"

Tiredness won out. "Get in line."

Jean-Luc Boulanger, my esteemed boss, was going to be at the front of that particular line. Not only had I excluded him from the excitement of working with a McGill researcher about to uncover a triumphant moment for the city—hello, street named Boulanger Avenue—I'd managed to allow her to steal an international treasure and get killed in the bargain. To my boss, that was as good as wielding the weapon myself.

I roused myself from the dread: sufficient unto the day, so forth. I managed to coerce the kids into relatively clean clothes, make Claudia take off half her makeup, and get them and myself to the basilica with about two minutes to spare before the 9:30 A.M. Mass. An accomplishment.

What I wanted, right then, more than anything else, was the feeling I get in this church. I was seriously shocked about Patricia—and starting to be seriously afraid, as well. I might not believe a story about a cursed set of diamonds, but something had reached out from the past to claim her, and until I knew what and why, there was a decent risk of it happening to someone else.

So I wanted to sit in this place that I loved above all others in a city that I love with all my heart. You'd think that after what happened last year the basilica would have bad associations, but it didn't: the weekly and occasionally daily comfort I derived from being here hadn't changed. Being in the basilica is like being already in heaven, its tall walls interrupted only by stained-glass windows, the blue of the soaring reredos behind the altar, the thousands of candles lighting up the darkened corners of the side chapels . . . it had always been, for me, a place of peace and comfort. My Happy Place, you might say. And I needed very badly to take Patricia here with me, in my heart and my mind.

She had, of course, been murdered.

"Shot," said Julian, "through the head."

Eerily familiar. I didn't need to close my eyes to see the heap of bones in the sealed room beneath the theater, the hole in the skull where no hole should be.

Julian was bringing in the troops. He couldn't, after all, keep a modern murder to himself. "My boss isn't very pleased to have gotten plunged into it after all, but it's not like I was keeping the secret for weeks. I'd only met her the day before," he said.

"What happened, Julian?"

"Don't know yet. I wanted to find her and get the diamond back—you really, *really* can't go keeping priceless jewels that are about to have a firestorm of publicity around them to yourself." He was trying for lighthearted, and not entirely succeeding. "I thought she'd get that, especially as she wants to have some fame around this discovery. So I went to her apartment."

"Where did she live?" I didn't even know that much about her.

"Up on the Plateau," he said. "Near the Yellow Door?"

I nodded, then realized that he couldn't see me over the telephone. "Yeah, of course, I know where that is. Noisy place to live."

"Graduate students don't always get to be choosy."

"The McGill Ghetto," I said, nodding again. I was referring to a neighborhood extending from University to Parc that had once been very affluent, then dropped in social status for reasons that were never clear—and where, lately, rents had begun to rise again. A few of the larger, unkempt apartment buildings are graying at the edges, while some of the four-story walk-ups have been renovated into condos. Victorian and Edwardian-style buildings feature dormer windows, spiral staircases, and Montréal's signature balconies, many of them decorated with ornate woodwork. Groups of students congregate there in the summertime. As ghettos go, not bad at all.

"So she was one of the cool kids."

"Not all that cool," Julian said. "Not now."

"What happened to her, Julian?"

"Like I said, I went to her place. I rang the bell but didn't get buzzed in, so I waited a while to see if she'd show. One of her neighbors arrived and I took the opportunity to slip in and see what was up. Her apartment door was unlocked." His voice sounded clinical: Julian the cop, reading a report. "She was there, all right. But dead."

I hated myself for asking, but I asked anyway. "And the diamond?"

"Nowhere that I could find, but I only did a cursory search in the apartment. The neighbor saw me go in, so I had to call in the cavalry."

"*Merde,*" I said and thought for a moment. "Do you know . . . ?"

"Nothing," said Julian. "But you can bet I'm going to find out. I'm staying on the case, because I have background and my boss thought that would be useful." Also, he was a Fletcher, a fact that continued to keep him employed with the city police. In this town, what the Fletchers wanted, the Fletchers got.

"I want to help."

"Martine, thanks, but honestly, no thanks. The last time you helped, you almost got killed."

"What, so you think I plan to make a habit of it?" First Ivan and now Julian worrying about poor little helpless me getting in trouble. It was nauseating. "Listen. I *knew* her, Julian. Not well, and I wasn't completely nice to her, but I knew her. And I'm involved in this, whether you like it or not."

"In other words, you're going to investigate on your own if you don't do it with me." He sounded resigned.

"That's one way of looking at it," I said. "I prefer to think that I am offering the police my knowledge of the victim and wide range of expertise and resources."

"Uh-huh," said Julian. "All right. I'll pick you up tomorrow."

I hesitated. "I don't want to be difficult, but—"

"If it's my driving, you can keep your thoughts to yourself."

"It's not. I have the kids, and Ivan's away. Not sure when he'll be back. And I promised Claudia the Underground City."

"So you're saying we're investigating with two children in tow."

"Kind of."

"Nothing surprises me about you, LeDuc. See you soon."

Now, as I sat in the basilica and felt the music from the tremendous pipe organ washing over me, I thought about that. Ivan would probably be aghast if the kids were to meet Julian, but I didn't see a way around it, and whatever was happening in Boston had to be pretty serious or he would have been back by now. Thus reminded, I said a quick prayer for Margery. And another for Patricia.

Patricia . . . I hadn't spent the time listening to her that I should have. I hadn't really gotten to know her, or tried to understand why she needed this so badly. I wondered if she'd started the dissertation. I wondered if I'd be allowed to read it.

I wondered if I had, somehow, failed her.

"Belle-Maman!" Claudia hissed, and I realized that everyone was standing but me. She passed me over the missalette, *Prions en Église,* with a whispered, "We're already, like, at the *prayers!*" Even in such a large church, where she was pretty much guaranteed to know nobody, Claudia didn't want to stand out.

I'd been exactly the same, at her age.

"*Désolée,*" I whispered back. Sorry.

She tossed her head and the blond hair whirled about her face for a moment, and for a second I saw glasses sliding down on a nose, a finger pushing them back up again. Patricia. Rest in peace, I thought, and turned the thought into a prayer. "Receive her, blessed Lord, among Your angels and saints. Let light perpetual shine upon her. May she enjoy the peace of Your everlasting kingdom. . . ."

And then it was time for the presentation of the gifts, and the organ again engulfed us in sound. And as I stood and sat and knelt in the rhythm of the Mass, I wondered exactly when it was decided that Patricia would have to die. Which meant figuring out who knew about the stolen diamond. Patricia hadn't been a threat to anybody until she'd taken it, and talked about it to Lev, and shown it to Avner.

Avner?

Somehow I didn't see it. I could see him being a little less than honest in declaring income tax, for example, or in bartering over some stones; but nothing about him indicated that he'd be willing to take a life.

His son, then, the lamentably still-unmarried Lev? He was probably in better shape than his father, physically—Avner looked for all the world like he was courting a heart attack—but simply being able to murder someone didn't mean that one would. Or had.

There was still too much missing here. By the time we left the church it felt like my mind had been going far too long on overtime. Usually we had a coffee and a croissant after Mass, but I was anxious to see if Ivan had returned, so over not-so-muted protests, we walked the couple of blocks to the apartment. Where, naturally, there was no trace of Ivan.

Julian, however, was sitting on the stone stairs, smoking a cigarette.

"Since when do you smoke?"

He stood up, gracefully, and put it out against the side of the building in one fluid gesture. "Good morning to you, Martine," he said, pocketing the cigarette butt and turning to the kids. "Lukas and Claudia, right?" Hand out to shake theirs. "*Détective-lieutenant* Julian Fletcher," he said.

"Wow!" Lukas was impressed. "A detective!"

"In the flesh," Julian said cheerfully, and winked at Claudia. She blushed, immediately, and turned away, but turned back just as quickly. "We're going to the Underground City," she told Julian. "Do you want to, like, come with us?"

"An invitation that's difficult to refuse," he acknowledged. "I was rather hoping for a coffee first."

Claudia glanced at me, hopeful. I sighed. "Coffee," I said, and her face lit up. Well, why not: Julian was extremely good-looking, and there's nothing wrong with a teenage crush. As long as it didn't actually *go* anyplace . . .

Lukas insisted on dragging Julian off to his room to see his model cars, and a few seconds later he was shrieking in delight at something Julian said to him. And then the coffee was done and Ivan was still nowhere to be found and we were sitting in the living area. "The *détective-lieutenant* says that I can go for a ride in his Audi TT sometime," Lukas informed me, eyes shining.

"Over my dead body," I said, conversationally, and then realized how malapropos the expression was. My eyes met Julian's. "Claudia," I said, "please go see if there are any rolls to go with the coffee."

"But, Belle-Maman . . ."

"*Now*, Claudia."

She got up with a flounce meant for me and a winning smile meant for Julian, and I added, "Lukas can help you."

"Belle-Maman!" Outrage from both of them, for completely different reasons.

"You heard me."

Julian watched them go. "Nice kids," he commented.

"Yes," I agreed.

"Their father?"

"He's in Boston. With their mother." His eyebrows went up. "No, nothing like that," I said quickly. "But I'm worried just the same." I felt vaguely guilty even saying it. Patricia Mason was lying in the morgue. Whatever problems I had were small by comparison. "Julian, exactly what are you doing here?"

"You wanted to investigate. We're going to investigate. We're having a coffee first."

Bisou wandered in, hopped up on the sofa, sniffed Julian, and curled up beside him. He petted the cat for a moment, then frowned at her and looked up. "Is this—?"

"Yes," I said. I'd adopted Bisou after her previous owner was murdered last summer, one of the killings I'd sort of investigated with Julian. Petting the cat of one murder victim while discussing another. Felt like we'd somehow come full circle.

Or were descending into one of them, anyway.

Julian was talking. "All right. I've been to see Lev Kaspi already. Their Sabbath not being our Sabbath, I found him hard at work, writing a program for sorting diamond futures."

"What are diamond futures?"

He shrugged. "Beats me. Seems to know his way around the trade. And around a computer."

"And what did he say about Patricia?"

"Liked her."

"Seriously, between you and Avner, you'd think Lev's love life was the only thing that counted in this whole story!"

"All right, all right. Let's take a step back and ask the question we ask anytime anyone is murdered. Something happened that made it necessary to kill Patricia yesterday, when it apparently wasn't necessary to kill her, say, last week. So what we have to do is look at what changed between last week and this week. We have to look at it from the point of view of the killer."

"If he's involved with the diamonds, everything changed." That much seemed obvious. "Okay. The first question is, did he know about the diamonds under the theater. If he did, he wanted them left there in peace . . . for whatever reason. If he didn't, then the obvious answer is that he didn't want Patricia digging any deeper."

"And she must have been going in that direction," said Julian. "Starting with stealing the one diamond and taking it to Avner."

"Who would Avner have told? His wife? She's got some kind of mental illness, I'll bet there's a lot he keeps from her."

He shrugged. "Probably he didn't tell anyone. But his son might have."

The rolls arrived and the kids with them, excited about their trip. Julian cleared his throat. "Your mother and I—"

"She's not our mother," said Claudia.

"Right. Your stepmother and I need to run a couple of errands."

Lukas pulled out his notebook. "Does that mean we're not going to the Underground City?" He clicked his pen in anticipation of a change in plans.

I looked at Julian helplessly. "No, of course not," I said. "We'll compromise. You can go for a while on your own and we'll meet you there. And by then maybe your dad will be back, too."

"We can go alone?" Claudia's eyes were dancing. She'd given up on thoughts of Julian pretty quickly, I thought.

"You can go alone," I said, "under *certain conditions*."

Claudia was still smiling. Her favorite place in the world, and without an embarrassing adult around? It didn't get better than that. "Yes, Belle-Maman?"

"You will stay together at all times. Nonnegotiable."

"Yes, Belle-Maman."

"You will call me every half hour," I went on, "and tell me exactly where you are. If I do not hear from you on the half hour, the *détective-lieutenant* here will send the police to your last known location. That will probably prove to be very embarrassing for all of us, so I'd advise you to avoid it."

"Yes, Belle-Maman."

"*Bon.* You both have money? You'll get something to eat?"

Two solemn nods. "Claudia, I mean it about staying together."

"We will."

I turned to Julian. "What do we do now?"

"City police are investigating," he said.

"Good for them," I said. "What do *we* do now?"

He looked up at me. "Find the diamond," he said.

Hans had developed a new habit: he loved going to the Hebrew delicatessen on the boulevard St.-Laurent.

He knew that it wouldn't endear him to anyone at home, of course, patronizing a Jewish restaurant; but he was alone in Montréal, merely waiting for whatever further orders might come through, and there was no one to see him.

And Schwartz's smoked meats were the best he'd ever tasted.

He was working in the area a lot: there were plenty of jobs for skilled workers, and he'd perfected his carpentry work. Who would have known that the hobby he'd shared with his father would ultimately earn him a living?

There was money from Germany, of course, which had gone

through banks somewhere else before arriving in small packets every month; but he had to become part of the scenery here, to fit in, and so he took a job. Several, in fact: there were few enough men around, and Hans was in demand.

He would have wanted to work, anyway. He couldn't just sit and wait for the invasion that was going to come, when the Reich would reach across the ocean and claim North America as its own. Life didn't get placed on hold just because the war wasn't yet over.

But he did have that extra little bit of money. He saved most of it. Some of it he used so that he could have lunch, every day, at the Hebrew delicatessen.

The war was raging on in Europe, the attempt to rid the planet of undesirables, and Hans was sitting at the counter at a Jewish establishment. From time to time, he enjoyed the irony of it all.

CHAPTER FOURTEEN

The Plateau is bordered more or less by Sherbrooke Street in the south and Little Italy in the north, and encompasses the beautiful and extensive Parc de Lafontaine as well as picturesque houses with the old curving outside staircases that were outlawed after 1962. I used to live on the Plateau; a lot of people did.

The apartment was on the Avenue Mont-Royal, busy and bustling and filled with light and laughter, especially this late September Sunday afternoon when everyone knew that the winter was just holding its breath, waiting to move in. It was impossible to not be infected by the feeling, and I found myself smiling in spite of everything. "We'll figure it out," I told Julian with assurance. "I know we will."

He had just maneuvered his TT into a very small parking space and was looking around for parking signs. "Relax, they're not going to tow you, you're a cop."

"You think cops never get towed?"

"Yeah, that's pretty much exactly what I think."

The apartment was up a narrow dusty set of stairs; more crime-scene tape at the top, but no one standing guard. Julian fitted a key into the lock and swung the door open.

Patricia Mason had lived a no-nonsense life. Either that, or she'd just moved in, or was just moving out. No pictures on the pale green walls. Cardboard boxes stacked in corners, filled with books and textiles of some sort. Minimal cooking gear in the kitchen. Only the area around the desk indicated life and personality: books stacked high on the floor around it, pages of manuscript, a large monitor, a decent lamp, pens at the ready. It looked as though she'd just stepped out.

As, in a real sense, she had.

I swung around to Julian. "Computer?"

"Down at the lab."

"Did you get a look?"

He shrugged. "Cursory. Nothing interesting. Lots of historical sites bookmarked in her browser, e-mail correspondence with other historians, notes for the dissertation. Didn't have time to read it all."

"Anything from Avner?"

"Not that I saw."

I continued my walk around her apartment. Bedroom, clothing all neatly on hangers, very much mix-and-match; her colors had been browns and tans, the occasional pale yellow. Julian had followed me in. "Mousy," he said.

"Understated." I turned around. "What are we missing? It's like a hotel room here. There's no personality, no sense of who she was, what she was doing. She was passionate, Julian. She was insane about what she had discovered. Why don't I feel anything here?"

"She must have kept that part of her someplace else."

"Right!" I snapped my fingers. "At school! Graduate students get their own carrels at the library, they can lock them. Anything important, she'd keep there. Round-the-clock monitoring!"

Julian looked bemused. "How do you know?"

"I did graduate studies once, too." I smiled. "And how do you think I met my husband? Graduate studies at McGill after he left Boston."

"All right, then: lead on, McDuff," said Julian, cheerfully misquoting Shakespeare.

I wasn't as sure of myself as I wanted him to think. "Do you think the diamond will be there?"

"No," he said. "I think it's long gone. But we're going to find it anyway. Doesn't matter who took it."

I sat down on Patricia's sofa; it felt sacrilegious, somehow. "Who else would know about it and want it, Julian? The audience is small."

"I keep coming back to what changed," he said. "That's what you always have to figure out: what it was that changed. For the killer. Something changed that made it necessary for him to kill Patricia. If we can figure out what that is, we're closer to finding him."

"What changed is a whole list of things," I said. I was feeling overwhelmed. My telephone rang: Claudia, checking in. "Where are you?"

"We're at Ailes de la Mode, Belle-Maman. We're fine."

"Has your father called you?"

"No." A note of puzzlement. "Why?"

"No reason," I said. "I just wondered."

And, as it turned out, would go on wondering for some time.

Julian dropped me off in front of the apartment. "Tomorrow," he promised, "we'll make some progress. You look tired. Have a bath, have a good meal and a good sleep."

It was probably going to take more than that, but I didn't say anything to him.

Ivan hadn't returned by 4:30—the witching hour at our house, when we have to leave for the airport or the kids will miss their commuter flight to Boston. Boston, where their father apparently still was.

Claudia and Lukas were in good spirits: the post-acquisition glow that teenagers get when they've spent all of their allowances—and done so without adult supervision and contrarian opinions. I walked them to the CATSA inspection station where their escort was waiting. "See you in two weeks, Belle-Maman!"

"Remember to call your father," I said.

"Okay. Bye!"

Lukas, at the last minute, tore away from the line of commuters waiting to have their luggage and selves scanned, and ran back to me for a hug. "I love you, Belle-Maman!"

"I love you, too, *mon chou*," I said automatically, mysteriously touched by the impetuous declaration of support. "Go on now."

I found myself scanning the faces of the people coming through the gate from the previous flight, as though magically Ivan would appear among them. I was getting seriously worried. He'd said he'd be back before the kids left, and Ivan was very good about delivering on his promises.

I drove home with my heart pounding. Who could I call? Margery? Probably not; whatever was going on there, I didn't want to sound like the jealous second wife, checking up on her. Ivan's mother had recently been admitted to an assisted-care facility as her Parkinson's was making daily living more and more difficult for her; I wasn't going to alarm her for nothing. Ivan's father? He didn't use telephones; found that the CIA could better monitor him through electronic devices. Yeah: Ivan's father was in a facility, too, though one somewhat different from his wife's. Who did that leave? Ivan's manager at the casino?

The police?

Calm down, Martine. You've left him messages. He will come back when he comes back.

And if he doesn't?

You'll deal with it then.

Julian had left me with a folder filled with photographs, and once I got home I poured myself a glass of wine and sat down on the sofa to look through them. Anything to keep my mind occupied. Anything to keep my mind off Ivan.

A lot of the photographs were of the sealed rooms below the theater: the crates, the hatbox, the bones, the diamonds. I thought about him, the man who had been lying there in the cold and the dark all these years. Who was he? A guard at the vault? Someone who'd *bribed* a guard at the vault? Was he stealing the jewels for himself, or had somebody sent him, paid him well, and then delivered the coup de grâce in the back of his head?

Wait; he had to know something was amiss. You don't swallow potentially dangerous sharp objects unless you feel that there's no other way.

Were the diamonds he'd swallowed the whole of what was stolen? Or were they just the ones he'd decided to keep for himself?

Who was he?

I sighed and flipped through the photos: the bones were stark in the light of the camera's flash attachment, framed by deep shadows. When I'd been down there, all I'd seen were the shadows.

For all that people seemed to be talking about the power inherent in the royal jewels, it seems they hadn't saved this man. But perhaps part of the power came from that, from death. No one said that power was ever only used for good. Maybe it was something dark that fed on all the deaths associated with the jewels through the centuries. Maybe that's why Hitler wanted them so much.

I sighed and thumbed through them again. "You might see something," Julian had said, offhand, when he gave me the folder. What was there to see?

Other than, of course, the memory ghost of Patricia, sharing her find, the lamp on her helmet making the shadows dance and move around us, her voice insisting that the credit was hers.

I shook it off, but the thought was still there. Had I not listened enough? Had I been too quick to summon the police? No: of course not. I worked in city government; I had an inkling, just an inkling, of the international storm that this was going to stir up. Of course I'd done what was right.

We were, I thought, being very rational about this whole thing. Well, why not: we lived in the twenty-first century in a developed country, of course we thought rationally. But from the start—and it was Patricia who had pointed it out—there was something profoundly irrational about the jewels. They were symbols, and symbols have nothing to do with logic and reasoning.

The answers were clearly somewhere else. Okay: let's say that it's 1938, and the decision's been taken to send the crown jewels along with the gold for Operation Fish to Canada. How many people knew?

I pulled out my notebook and pen and began a list. The people around Churchill. The people around the king. His daughters, for heaven's sake, and who knows how they might have chattered? The bankers, the people who amassed the securities and the gold, who escorted it on the *Emerald*. The Office for Strategic Services was in charge, and they passed it on to the folks at the Royal Navy. Whomever in the federal, provincial, and city government had been the contact here and made the agreement. Probably also the federal, provincial, and city police as well. The insurance officers at Sun-Life. Whoever escorted the jewels from Halifax to Montréal.

I sat back and looked at the list in dismay. Hundreds of people had known. Which brought us back to the beginning.

Think of it another way. Accept the magical properties of the jewels, the centuries of stored power, the opportunity to use them to accumulate more. They'd been stored away in Westminster, in

London, trotted out for coronations and other affairs of state, then returned to safekeeping. If you are in the market for esoteric relics— and Hitler clearly was—then you're out of luck.

Unless you hear that they're on the move, and it was more than possible that spies in London had passed along the word.

You may not know the specifics of how they're getting out of the country, and that's okay. And you may not be able to get at them in transit—sure, there were U-boats in the north Atlantic, but that would be risky business, you could sink the *Emerald* instead of capturing her.

Halifax? Better to wait and see where they end up: everyone's on edge when they're being transported. Montréal. A vault. An insurance company. That's when you'd make your move. Early on, mind: what if these jewels could influence the outcome of the war? So early on, you figure out a way to steal them.

What a headache, I thought. Someone in London was going to be tasked with seeing just how many of the jewels currently residing at the Tower of London had been made, instead, in the camp at Buchenwald. Someone in London was going to be very unhappy.

So either one of the Quebecker guards had been paid off, or blackmailed, or somehow co-opted . . . or those bones belonged to a Nazi. I didn't see a lot of other alternatives.

And it didn't get me any closer to figuring out who'd killed Patricia.

The town they were nearest, Elias was told, was Weimar.

Weimar. He'd heard of it, of course; who hadn't? Anyone interested in any kind of cultural life had heard of Weimar, nicht wahr? He could name the famous Germans who'd lived in Weimar: Goethe, Schiller, Franz Liszt, Bach.

And now, Elias Kaspi.

They had been separated almost immediately, him and Ruth, with her questions still ringing in his ears. "Why are they doing this to us? What did we do wrong?" There were no answers to her questions and he offered her no comfort, something that he thought about, long and hard, as time went by. Should God ever allow him to go back, he would hold his wife, he would kiss her, he would give her what strength he had.

But then? Then, he was too dazed to do anything. They'd pulled her away from him and herded her with other women onto a train. "Where are they going?" Elias asked the man standing next to him, who shrugged indifferently. Everyone was looking out for themselves, dazed and anxious to please, as odd as that seemed—they still had some hope, then, that good behavior could keep them safe. That what they did as individuals mattered. No voices raised in anger, no accusations, no challenges. Go this way, stop here, move quickly! And they did it all.

The train ride through the night was cold; Elias huddled inside his coat and thought about Ruth, thought about Antwerp, thought about his diamonds. There had been other options; at the very beginning, Jews were allowed to buy visas, to go away to America. The Germans were eager for them to leave, so their property could be seized. He could have bought visas, but he'd thought it wouldn't come to that.

Perhaps, after all, this would not last long. Perhaps he would go back, someday, and Ruth would be there and safe, and they could take up their lives again. Coffee with Smuel and Paulie down the street. Arguing over the cost of precious stones.

They walked the last few kilometers along a paved road just as the sky was turning gray. There were guards marching beside them, guards with big terrible snarling dogs, and Elias pressed himself into the center of the ragged line of men. They each carried a small suitcase, and he was wondering what Ruth had packed in his. It seemed heavier with every step.

Once, he permitted himself a question. "What is that smell?" But no one answered.

They arrived at what was called the Little Camp right at dawn. It was extraordinarily beautiful: roses and trees, a small zoo with a bear behind the fence who watched them with melancholy as they walked past.

Good, thought Elias; here we are, now we can sleep. No one had slept on the train. Here there were no guards, just prisoners with armbands, big men, yelling. Here they were to be quarantined, their bodies dipped and scrubbed, their heads shaved.

Here, there was no rest.

Elias did what they told him to do. He put on the uniform. He placed his suitcase on the bunk assigned to him. He listened to everything the kapos said, and he followed their directions.

"You will join the rest of the prisoners when we are clear that you are not diseased," said the camp commandant, Karl Koch, striding up and down in front of the ragged line they made outside the barracks. He was dressed in black and looked smart and elegant in the morning sunlight. "You will be treated well if you do as you are told. Here you will work. We have a quarry, and we have a factory. We are working for the Reich, and it is an honor and a privilege for you to do so."

Elias felt neither. At night, they whispered together in the dark. "Could be worse, I've heard there's far worse than this place."

Worse than this place? It was difficult to imagine.

CHAPTER FIFTEEN

The sound of the door closing woke me.

Fuzzy and disoriented, I realized I'd fallen asleep on the sofa, the photographs of the crime scene scattered around me, my notebook on the floor. I'd been dreaming of tunnels and endless corridors and someone calling my name. . . .

"Martine." This voice was familiar, and I blinked in the light and looked up at Ivan. "Sorry. Didn't mean to wake you."

"What time is it?" As though that made a difference.

"Almost midnight. I thought you'd be in bed."

I struggled to sit up. "I thought you'd be back this afternoon."

He sat down on the sofa, and a sudden wave of comfort engulfed me: Ivan's smell, Ivan's presence. Easy to forget all the anxiety and the fear: he was here now. "I know, babe. Sorry. I got delayed."

"I don't understand." I rubbed my eyes; it didn't help. "I kept calling you."

"I know." He sighed. "Didn't bring my charger, and there was a lot going on."

My mouth felt like I'd been eating wet wool. "What is it?" I asked. "What's happened to Margery?"

He looked around the large loft space as though seeing it for the first time. "Wouldn't you rather talk in the morning? I think we're both exhausted."

"Ivan, tell me."

"Margery's all right. So's Peter. But she's feeling—I don't know. I've been talking with her about it for a day now and I still can't describe it. Like she's not doing what she thinks she should be."

I blinked. "What are you talking about?"

"Back to the beginning," he said. "Peter works for Doctors Without Borders."

"I know that." And that he was away a lot of the time; the kids complained of it.

"And he's out there doing good in the world. And she's living in a white-bread upper-middle-class suburb."

I was starting to get the picture. "She wants to go with him."

"Pretty much, yeah. She's been getting back into clinical work herself." Margery had been a pediatrician back when she and Ivan were married. "She wants to make a difference. She's been depressed—"

"I know."

"—and there's the African thing. She thinks this is the solution. For her, anyway."

"What does Peter think?" I was avoiding the real issue here. Better to chat about how other people were doing, what they were thinking.

"He's all for it. He never wanted her to give up her clinical work."

"I see."

There was a long silence. We both knew what was coming next, and neither of us wanted to be the one to say it. "She wanted to know if the kids could come live with us," Ivan said finally.

There it was. "And neither of you felt it was appropriate to involve me in this conversation?"

"It was premature. She wanted to talk with me first."

"What, so you could make a preliminary decision? So the two of you could resolve whatever needs to be resolved and then report back to me?"

"They're our kids, Martine."

I'd heard the expression before: seeing red. Who thought that it was literal? I never actually did it until that night: but there it was in front of me, pulsing and angry. Red, red, red. "*Your* kids? They're *your* kids now? After years of parenting them together? After years of not being able to make plans every other weekend, not being able to do anything in the summer that didn't involve them, not being able to afford things—don't say you don't remember that, it's exactly what was happening when we were first married—because of paying child support and transportation and braces and . . ." I was having trouble breathing, and running out of English. I do fury much better in French, possibly the only thing I have in common with my boss. I took a deep breath, tried to regroup. "After all that, suddenly, they're your kids? I'm good enough to cook and care and transport and pay, but not good enough to make decisions affecting their lives—oh, yes, and incidentally, my life, too?"

"You know that's not what I meant."

"That's exactly what you meant! That's absolutely *precisely* what you meant! You don't give me any warning that it's what you're thinking about, you go off and don't answer your phone and leave me alone to deal with them and let me think all sorts of horrible things, that you were maybe even dead somewhere, and it's bad enough I have to deal with a murder here—"

"Wait," he interrupted. "What murder?"

"Don't even go there! Don't you *dare* go there! That has nothing to do with you!" I was shouting and crying at the same time, and I had to stop, I really couldn't breathe.

"Listen to me." Ivan grasped my hands in his. "Listen to me. I didn't know that's what it was about. Margery called me and asked me to come. She didn't say why, only that she didn't want the kids around for the conversation. So I thought that she was probably going to tell me she was sick. There was that hospitalization last year, and I know she's had some tests done at Mass General . . . anyway, I thought it was bad news, bad news about her health, which, yeah, might have led ultimately to the same thing, the kids coming to live here, but I didn't think that far. I thought I should honor what she wanted, they were okay here with you, we could have a conversation and that would be that."

"And she told you to keep this whole thing secret from me?"

He expelled breath in something like a splutter. "Of course not. But after they told me on the phone—well, you remember, we were with the kids all day, Martine. I didn't want to make a big deal of it in front of them. I thought I'd call you from Boston, talk with you then."

"But you didn't."

"No, and I'm sorry about that. I really am. First it was Margery—you know how she is, she feels guilt anytime she isn't the world's most perfect mother, and she was still going back and forth over the decision. And then I got a call from the casino—"

I could feel the hysteria rising again. "You took calls from the casino but not from me!"

"—and it was an emergency." "Emergency" is one of the words we respect in each other's lives. We both work with the public in highly visible positions. We both have jobs that aren't expected to end at the close of the day. We both acknowledge and accept that, and "emergency" is a word we don't use lightly. Normally, I would have completely accepted and respected his need to deal with an emergency rather than calling me. But this wasn't a normal night. "I don't care if the *foutu* casino was burning to the ground! I had a right to know! To not worry! I thought you might be dead, and instead you and Margery were talking about your lives, and . . ." I ran out of steam. The tears that had been vying with my shouting were too overwhelming.

"I'm sorry, Martine," Ivan said gently. "I should have involved you."

"Yes," I sobbed.

"And we're going to have to talk about it, but not now."

"No," I sobbed.

That's the problem with people, isn't it? That they will disappoint you. That even Ivan—who by and large is one of the best human beings I've ever met—is sometimes stupid, selfish, and completely unaware. I had an inkling that I wasn't completely easy to get along with all the time, either. But marriage is where you acknowledge that your partner isn't exactly who or what you want them to be, and you love them anyway. That they can disappoint and you can move on. I knew that, even as I crawled miserably into bed, to nurse the hiccups following in the wake of my meltdown. I knew that we would make it all right.

I just wasn't yet seeing quite how.

Monday morning, and the sun was far too bright. I felt as though I'd been up partying all night. I winced at the smallest sound.

And, worse luck, I had to go to work.

Hard to believe everything that had happened over the weekend: it was Thursday when I'd been called in to a meeting and heard Patricia Mason's story for the first time. I felt as though I'd been living it forever.

Richard was already in and looking disgustingly cheerful. He took one look at me and signaled to Chantal, who kept an espresso machine in the outer office. "*Ça n'va pas?*" he asked. "What is the matter?"

"An argument with my husband." I left it at that.

He followed me into my office. "I heard about the murder," he said. "It was in the newspapers yesterday."

Of course it would be. We'd gone from a PR coup to being a city in which young women students got killed: that was exactly the way that Jean-Luc would see—and articulate—the situation. And, somehow, it was going to be my fault.

"They're investigating it," I said, sitting down.

"And the jewels?"

"It's been passed on to a pay grade way over our heads," I told him. "All the way to Ottawa."

"*C'est dommage*," Richard commented. He sat down in one of the chairs facing my desk, elegantly crossing one leg over the other. "You won't hear from *monsieur le maire*, though, that's one good thing."

"What?" A glimmer of light in a very dark mood. "Why not?" I'd been expecting the summons to already be on my desk.

"He's in Québec City," Richard said. "The conference. He left Saturday, will not return until tomorrow or Wednesday."

"So maybe he doesn't know?"

Richard sighed and, reaching over, riffled through the piles of paper on my desk. He extracted a copy of the *Gazette* and held it up for me to see. I sighed. "Okay, so he knows."

"He knows," Richard agreed, tossing the paper back on the pile. "But you can be sure that it is not going to ruin his stay at the Château Frontenac."

The one thing we could count on: the mayor taking care of himself first and foremost. He was probably enjoying a massage at the Payot Institute spa even as we spoke. On the taxpayers' dollar, of course.

"No," I agreed. "Nothing could ruin that." I took a deep breath. "Okay. We need to send out a press release about the murder. Can you get a quote from the city police about how the investigation is going?" It was going nowhere, of course, but they'd find a way to say otherwise. No one wanted the people of—or the visitors to—Montréal thinking there was a mad killer on the loose.

If only they knew that they were perfectly safe in their beds. This particular killer was only interested in one thing. But what? I watched Richard leave and pull the door shut quietly behind him and still I couldn't move. What did the killer gain by eliminating Patricia?

I picked up my smartphone and snapped at the robotic voice to call Julian. "There had to be something she wasn't telling us," I said when he answered.

"Good morning to you, too."

"It just occurred to me. Sometimes people don't say everything that they should, they assume there will be time later to do it, but maybe in her case there wasn't. So maybe that's what we have to find out."

"Sounds like you're talking from personal experience."

"Did that occur to you?"

He sounded like he was talking to an old person. "Yes, Martine. That did occur to me."

"Oh." I felt deflated. "So, have you?"

"Have I what?"

"Found out what it was?"

A long sigh. "Not yet, Martine."

"Will you tell me when you do?"

There was a long pause. "This is a criminal investigation, not a cold case. An active criminal investigation. *I'm* even on the periphery, for God's sake."

"You work best on the periphery," I reminded him. Julian had somewhat rejected the life his family name and money could have allowed him—or at least put it on hold—yet was never really accepted into the rank and file of city police. Never really one of them.

And probably driven to show results more than anyone else on the force because of it.

"Julian," I said. "The only thing we have going for us is that we know her. Knew her, I mean." I remembered his energy, the last time the police had shoved him aside, his willingness to follow his own ideas, his own instincts, and where it had led. I wanted that Julian back again. "We should figure out who was following her." I had, of course, no idea how one might do such a thing.

"I've been assigned to pulling her history." He sounded glum.

"That should take you about five minutes."

He sighed. "I give up. All right. That guy she saw, that I saw, he may have just caught that bus because it was available and he knew I was onto him."

"Or he may have caught it because it was familiar, one he usually takes," I said, nodding, even though he couldn't see me. "It's a place to start."

"Yeah, okay." His voice was resigned, but I didn't care. He'd get enthused once we started making some progress.

"I have work to do here," I said. "What about lunch?"

"You're just looking for an invitation." That was better; that was more like Julian.

"Invariably," I said and laughed.

"All right. One o'clock . . . at Café Pavé?"

"*Parfait.*" I was even smiling as I hung up the phone. We were going to get somewhere with this clue; I was sure of it.

I had no idea how wrong I could be.

She was sitting at the counter at the Hebrew Delicatessen, just three seats down from him. He'd been reading the Gazette, *only looked up because the man beside him had knocked his arm standing and reaching into his pocket to pay. So Hans glanced up, reflexively, and his eyes met hers.*

In that first sharp brilliant moment, he had to remind himself to breathe.

She smiled, even, a quick, tentative smile, and he didn't have the courage to return it. But as he ate his smoked-meat sandwich he kept looking at her, his glances surreptitious, drinking in that beauty with each one. The dark hair, the dark eyes, the oval face. The dimple. She was the most beautiful thing he'd ever seen, in his entire life. Dark hair in waves that she let tumble down her back. Large gray eyes under dark eyebrows. A small waist and lovely hips and breasts . . . Hans looked away, shocked at his own thoughts. How could he disrespect such a woman? She was an angel. She was perfection.

On Tuesday, his heart was pounding when he arrived. "The usual?" Bernie asked him, and Hans nodded distractedly. He tried to pay attention to his lunch, to his newspaper, but every time the door opened he looked up, hoping to see the girl, afraid of seeing the girl.

By the time he went back to work, he was exhausted. That night, he sat on the edge of his bed and practiced clever things to say. I haven't seen you in here before. . . . No, I would have noticed, someone as beautiful as you . . . I wonder if you might be free on Friday, there's this movie. . . . None of them was particularly clever, he realized. How did you talk to a girl like that?

On Wednesday, he pushed the door open and saw two things at once: the girl was there, and the seat at the counter next to her was empty.

Hans took a deep breath and headed over. This was his chance. This was his opportunity. A girl like this only came around once in a lifetime. He'd manage to find something to say. He'd—"Excuse me!" The woman with the three packages had bumped ahead of him and was putting her bag down on the seat. His seat. She glared at him and Hans backed off, but the girl looked up and saw Hans and this time, when she smiled, he had the good sense to smile back.

CHAPTER SIXTEEN

Avner was on the telephone.

Chantal stuck her head into my office. "I cannot understand him," she said. "He doesn't speak very good French, and he is speaking too quickly."

"Who is it?"

"I cannot get his name. Something German, it sounds like. He keeps saying, Martine LeDuc, Martine LeDuc. Do you want the call?"

"Why not?"

A few clicks, then a voice. "Ah, so finally it is you on the telephone, I only have to wait to get to the right person. There are layers of people I must speak to first."

"And *bonjour* to you, too, Avner."

"Ah, well, at least she knows my name. The other girl, I think she couldn't hear so good."

"The other girl," I said, "hears perfectly well. She's francophone. And she *doesn't* know your name. What can I do for you?"

"You can tell me maybe why it is that I am sitting in my parlor instead of going to minyan like I should do, every day of my adult life.

Every day I go to the shul, no matter how cold, no matter if there is snow, if I wake up, I go. But not today. You can maybe help me with that."

"Because you don't have a car?"

A snort of derision. "You think, a car, this is what I need? No. What do I need a car for? I take a bus. Everywhere in Montréal, I take a bus. I can afford a car, yes, I can afford many cars if I want them. But do I want them? Do I want to be in the traffic with a car? There is no need of a car. What I need, I will tell you this: what I need is a nice Jewish daughter-in-law. What I need is mine wife to get better in her head. What I need, is right now a nice bagel from Viatur, and don't let nobody tell you that Fairmont it's just as good, that's a lie. What I need, is to go to minyan."

"Avner, what's wrong?"

"Ah, now it is she asks the right questions. What is wrong is why I call you. What is wrong is I think maybe Montréal, it's not as tolerant as I think. What is wrong is I get the death threat."

I think I gasped. I know it wasn't what I was expecting. "What happened, Avner?"

"Tell me this first, Martine. Is this still all right, that I call you Martine?"

"Yes," I said distractedly. "Go on, Avner."

"So, yes, Martine, tell me this. She has been killed, the girl with the diamond, the diamond that my father make a replica of in the death camp of Buchenwald?"

I drew in a breath. "Yes. She's been killed."

"This is what I think. I don't look so much at the newspapers, you know, but on the bus, you see all sorts of things. I think I see she is dead. And now at my house I am having my coffee, because my doctor he says, one cup of coffee in the morning, this is all I am permitted now—"

"Avner," I said.

"Yes, yes. So I am having my coffee and mine Naomi, she comes in, and she has in her hand this thing, it is an envelope, and she says it was in the door. I don't know how long it's in the door, me. We don't go out always by the front door, even though the park, it's close by, it's a nice walk, but not every day do we go to the park."

I was getting dizzy. "What happened?"

"So the envelope, mine wife Naomi, she says it is in the door. With mine name, Kaspi, on it. Just mine name, that is all, but on the back of the envelope, there it is, the Star of David. Just like that."

"What was inside the envelope? What did it say?"

"Inside this envelope with mine family name on it, inside this envelope with the Star of David on it, here is the note. It says—here, I read it to you, it is right here in my hand—it says, 'you are next, death is waiting for you.' And underneath that, there is another drawing, too.

"Another Star of David?"

"No, Martine, this time, you do not guess so smart. This drawing inside, it is the swastika."

I suppose I should have seen it coming.

"Stay where you are," I said to Avner. "I have to call Julian—*détective-lieutenant* Fletcher—but we're on our way."

"Yes, but with this plan, I see a problem."

"What is it?" I was already reaching for my sweater.

"You do not know my address. Perhaps I can give it to you now?"

Avner, you're going to be the death of me. "Go ahead."

I scribbled it on the paper that was topmost in one of the piles on my desk—Hutchinson Street, in Outremont, not in but not far from the Hasidic enclave—and hung up. Quickly I pressed Julian's digits. "Lunch is off. We're going to see Avner."

"Why?"

"He's had a death threat. And you're going to just love who it's from."

"A swastika."

Julian was standing in a cavernous living room in a very large house on a street where you could probably eat off the pavement if you were so inclined. There were paintings on the walls that were probably originals, and probably valuable; the Kaspis clearly lived extremely well. Avner might take the bus, but I'd spotted a Mercedes under the porte-cochère.

Avner's wife was sitting on a sofa, her face white. Avner surrendered the paper and envelope and then went to sit next to her. "It will be all right," he said, taking her hand in his.

She shook her head. "It is not all right. Avner, I told you not to involve these people. They will make it worse. They will get us all killed."

"This is mine wife, Naomi," Avner said to us. "She is upset by this."

"Anyone would be," I responded. "It's very upsetting. I'm very sorry, Mrs. Kaspi."

Julian looked at the paper and turned to me. "This may change things," he said. "About Patricia."

"That she was killed by neo-Nazis instead of diamond thieves?"

"That she may have been killed by diamond thieves who are neo-Nazis."

Avner looked back and forth between us anxiously. "This means what? This means that they know about the replacement diamonds?"

Julian frowned, sliding the card carefully into a plastic bag. "We'll see what we can get for fingerprints," he said, and then turned to Avner. "Are you familiar with any neo-Nazi groups operating in the area?"

"You ask me this because I am Jewish? What, every Jew knows this? Because I am Jewish, I should spend my time looking under rocks for crazies?"

"Someone will know," I said. "They keep records of these people somewhere." Offhand, I couldn't think of where. The Holocaust Museum? "If that's even what we're looking at. This whole thing could be just a prank."

"A prank that we're going to take seriously until proven otherwise," said Julian.

Avner had more practical considerations in mind. "So I should not leave my house? No work? No minyan? What about mine Naomi?"

Naomi had an answer for that. "I have to do the shopping," she said. "Every day, I do the shopping. I have to go out and do the shopping."

"Can't you arrange for someone to guard them?" I asked Julian.

"On our budget? You've got to be kidding." A beat, then, "I'll see what I can do." He looked at Avner. "I think we need to take this threat seriously. Is there somewhere else you and your family can stay?"

"For how long? I am not anxious to begin living mine life in fear of the crazies. I have not for many years. I will not start now."

Naomi clearly had other ideas. "And what, then? You want they should kill us in our beds? It's not funny, Avner. You know it's not supposed to be funny. We've seen this before."

Avner put his arm around her shoulder. "Mine wife, the rabbi's daughter," he said. "We cannot leave this neighborhood," he said. "This is our home. Your policeman, he can guard us here."

I understood his reluctance. Literally and figuratively, Montréal is a series of villages, and people tend to be fiercely loyal to their own *quartier*. Living somewhere else is like living in another city altogether. I'd made the switch from the Plateau to the old city, but it had taken some time to really feel at home in my new neighborhood. Now, of course, I couldn't imagine living anywhere else. "I'd like to see you somewhere else," said Julian.

Avner considered it. "Mordecai Kaufman, he rents out rooms," he said.

"That would be good," I told Avner.

Naomi clearly didn't agree. "A room? You want us to stay in a room, now? Like refugees? This is what we have come to?"

"We'll come back," he said, but she shook her head. "We will stay at my father's home," she said firmly.

"Mine father-in-law," said Avner, in the same voice he'd use to say, "a snake."

"Your father-in-law, yes," Naomi told him. "There at least I can cook, I can see my mother, we'll be next door to the synagogue, what more do you want?"

"How about Lev? Can he go with you?" asked Julian. "Or maybe stay with a friend?"

"You think mine son, he is in danger also?"

Julian and I looked at each other. "I think," I said, "that we don't want to take any chances."

Avner shrugged. "So, he will come, too, to the rabbi's house, to his grandfather's house," he said resignedly. "I go now, make the arrangements, oh, we have so much to pack, so much to do!"

"Better than arranging for a headstone," I reminded him, and he grimaced. Naomi was already halfway up the stairs. "And you think that he will appreciate seeing those slippers you wear, my father? How many times have I said, those slippers, they have to go?"

Avner turned to us and shrugged. "Mine Naomi, she will take care of things," he said. "But I had better go now and pack these slippers of mine away before this wife of mine takes them." He paused. "It is maybe good for her, to be with her family. Lately she is not looking so good."

"I'm sorry," I said, a little helplessly. I didn't know much about mental illness.

"It is what God sends," said Avner philosophically. "She takes her medications, it is good. Mine wife is a beautiful woman, a beautiful mother, but I say to you it is maybe good that we go to the house of her father. I will go now and help her."

Alone in the cavernous room, I turned to Julian. "What are you thinking?"

"I'm thinking that we need to rethink everything," he said. "And that we need more information."

"Who knows about neo-Nazi activity in Montréal?"

He gave me a smile that bordered on irony. "We do." He pulled out his smartphone. "Let's see if I can get us an audience."

"Sounds like we're going to see the pope."

"Naw. That would be easier."

It was on a Monday that Hans had first noticed the girl. Once he'd seen her, of course, he couldn't understand how he'd ever missed her. Or could ever think of anything or anyone else.

And now she had smiled at him. And he had smiled back.

It turned out that Bernie knew all about her. "Livia? You talkin' about Livia?"

Livia. What a name. The most beautiful name he'd ever heard.

"The girl in the green sweater," he clarified, nodding.

"Yeah, that there's Livia. Nice girl."

"She's beautiful."

Bernie sized him up. "Like that, is it? Caught the love bug? You'll have a time of it, my boy."

"Why? Is she married?" If she is, he thought in desperation, I shall have to kill myself.

"Nope." Bernie shook his head, throwing his dishcloth over his shoulder. "Just quiet, like. Not much of a talker. An' you bein' a foreigner an' all . . . Well, like I said, you'll have a time of it. But, hey, best of luck to you."

"Wait!" Bernie was the conduit to Livia. "When does she come in, usually?"

"Can't say, really. Couple times a week, anyway. Works some-where near here."

"Where?"

"Slow down, Romeo." He wagged his finger at Hans. "You're a nice guy an' all, but she's special. She's a good girl, is Livia. I don't want you treatin' her badly. She's got it hard enough as it is."

"Why? What has happened to her?"

Bernie gave an exaggerated sigh. "Gonna get it all out of me, aren't you? All right, then. I'll tell you. Her mom died—oh, I'd have to ask Sadie, but I want to say 'bout ten years ago." He shook his head. "Tuberculosis, you know. Terrible thing. And no brothers nor sisters, so Livia's been on her own, you could say, ever since then."

"What about her father?"

"Ah, him. First Canadian Infantry Brigade." He saw that Hans wasn't making the connection. "Forget you're a foreigner, sometimes, I get so used to you. Nu, here's what happened there. Went over there to your neck of the woods, the First Canadian," he said. "Fighting in Belgium and France and whatnot. Damned Germans drove 'em back to the sea. Had to get pulled off the beach at Dunkirk." He shook his head. "Night from hell, from what I've heard. Fires from Calais so bright they could see 'em burning all the way over in England. And those Germans, killing boys on the beach, killing boys in the water, shooting them from the cliffs and out of airplanes . . ." He sighed. "Nu, that was the end of Livia's dad. Didn't never leave that beach."

Hans shook his head. "So she's all alone."

"She's all alone, and don't you be gettin' any ideas in your head about changin' that unless you're serious. Like I said, she's something special. Sadie an' me, we keep an eye on Livia, and I won't see any Johnny-come-lately breakin' her heart. She's a good girl and she don't deserve that."

"I won't break her heart," said Hans.

CHAPTER SEVENTEEN

We went to the main headquarters downtown where Julian supposedly had an office, though I'd never seen it. This was the Service de
Police de la Ville de Montréal, or SPVM, the city police.

Just to keep our lives interesting, we have three police forces that
can potentially all be working in Montréal at the same time. They
sometimes even actually acknowledge each other's existence.

There was the SPVM (the city police), the Sûreté de Québec—
police who cover all of the province—and the national Royal Canadian Mounted Police. Three levels of policing—city, province, and
federal—and they do not always play well together. The city police
resent it when the provincial police try to home in on anything in
the city; and they both resent the Mounties, who aren't all that popular anywhere in the province.

Here in Québec we often choose to forget that we are, after all,
part of Canada.

Julian parked blatantly in a clearly marked no-parking zone.
Fine: if he got towed, it wasn't my problem. Probably everyone knew
the TT by now anyway. Up the stairs, down a corridor, and then he
asked me to wait outside. "It might be tricky," he cautioned me.

"Tricky? Why?"

"He got divorced a couple of years ago."

"And that makes it tricky how, exactly?" I caught his look. "Oh, no. Julian. No, you didn't."

Yes, he had. "She was very attached to me," Julian said. "Wait here, okay?"

"All right."

I waited. Two young officers in camouflage pants and bulletproof vests walked by, glancing at me curiously, and my mind strayed for a moment. Weren't camouflage pants supposed to— camouflage? As in fit in? No one but the police wore them.

A couple of people in an adjacent office had an argument. My watch ticked slowly. I thought about calling Richard and seeing what was happening at the office. I waited some more.

Finally the door opened and Julian signaled me in. "He'll talk to us," he said. He didn't look very happy about the whole thing.

Whoever this guy was, he had one hell of a view, out over the rooftops looking west, the Place des Arts and the Museum of Contemporary Art. I noticed it—framed in a vast expanse of plate-glass window—before I noticed him.

The man behind the desk was dressed in civilian clothes, and probably could have used a little help in that department. I'm no fashion plate myself, but even I know that there's a way of putting together different prints for an overall effect, and this wasn't it.

Still, it was the scowl that really finished off the picture. Bushy gray eyebrows, dark recessed eyes, and that scowl.

"This," said Julian diffidently, "is Capitaine Levigne. Captain, Madame Martine LeDuc."

"*Parle français*," the captain said to him, irritably, and then turned to me. "*Bonjour, madame.*" Oddly, he didn't stand up to shake my hand, and then I saw with some surprise that he was in a wheelchair.

I inclined my head. "*Mon capitaine.*"

"Marcus," Julian said to me in French, "is an expert on Nazism, neo-Nazism, skinheads, you name it. Anything right-wing that goes on in this city, he knows about."

"It must be," I said, "a challenging job."

"But a necessary one," he acknowledged, and the tension in the room lifted. He invited us to sit around a low table on the other side of the room, right up against the windows and the view, and wheeled himself over to join us. "How can I help?"

Julian pulled out the plastic bag with the envelope and note inside. "This was sent to a Jewish diamond merchant in Outremont," he said. "As I told you, it may connect to the case the murder squad's working on, the graduate student from McGill, because the diamond merchant himself is involved."

The other man took the bag. "This is interesting," he said after a moment.

"Interesting?" I echoed. "Seems like straightforward skinhead nonsense to me."

He shook his head, still peering at the envelope. "But you are wrong, madame."

"Call me Martine. How am I wrong?"

He indicated the swastika. "This is highly stylized, as you can see," he said, his finger tracing the contours of the symbol, which actually, now that I was really noticing it, looked like interlocking S shapes. I hadn't taken that in before.

"What does it mean?" Julian asked.

"That there is more to this than simple fanatical racism and hatred," Marcus said.

"Such as?"

He passed the bag back to Julian. "You're going to try and lift fingerprints?"

"As soon as we leave."

"Let's do it now. You may be here a while." He turned the wheel-chair and moved smoothly over to his desk, where he pressed some buttons on his phone. "Jean-Pierre? Can you send someone up to my office? I have a specimen for you. Very well."

"Why do you say we may be here a while, *capitaine*?" I asked.

"You may call me Marcus," he said absently. "How much do you know about Nazism and the occult?"

Julian and I exchanged startled glances. I'd thought he was go-ing to talk about angry young white men, or suburban gangs with heavy-duty tattoos, or even crosses burning on front lawns. What-ever I'd been expecting, this wasn't it.

"I think I heard that Hitler was very much interested in it," I said slowly. "I can't remember where I read that, though, or really any-thing else about it. Didn't he have an astrologer on staff, something like that?"

Before Marcus could answer, there was a discreet knock at the door. He wheeled himself over and opened it. "Ah, there you are. The *détective-lieutenant* will sign for the chain of evidence, yes?"

"Yes," Julian said grimly and did so. The person in the corridor muttered something I didn't hear as Julian came back and sat down. Marcus closed the door and wheeled himself back to where we were sitting. "So: Hitler and the occult. You're partially correct, Martine. It does seem that everyone has a vague association there," he said. "So I'll give you the story."

"Maybe in condensed form?" suggested Julian.

That earned him a scowl. "The story is what the story is," the captain said and turned back to me. "As soon as World War Two ended, there was a rush to connect Nazis with every imaginable conspiracy theory available. Everything from extraterrestrial visi-tors to madmen in caves. No doubt a way of psychologically dealing with the horrors they were still discovering. " He shrugged. "Some journalists published exaggerated accounts of occult groups in the

Third Reich. What really happened, of course, was that some marginal atavistic ideas influenced Nazi policy. And thus, of course, the destiny of modern Europe."

I tried to sort out something useful but was stuck on the "marginal atavistic ideas." He had to have been an academic before joining the police force. A twinge of pain as I thought, automatically, Patricia would really get along with this guy.

Not now, she can't.

"So all the wild speculation about Hitler and the occult?" asked Julian, clearly not plagued as I was by the ghost of a different scholar in the room. "That's all it is, wild speculation?"

"Occultism generally becomes popular when there are political and social upheavals," said Marcus, still in professor mode. "It's a way of coping, of assigning some sort of new meaning, when the old structures of meaning fail."

I got it. "Like wondering why God would allow the Holocaust," I said.

Marcus nodded briskly. "The nineteenth century saw another revival of occultism in Europe with the industrial revolution and the abrupt displacement of traditional ways of life." He glanced at me. "And of course the connection between occultism and racism. *That* started long before the Nazis."

"Hitler just latched on to it," Julian said, nodding despite himself.

"But Hitler wasn't the real occultist. That would be Himmler, the head of the SS, who actually retained a self-proclaimed Aryan mystic as part of his personal staff, didn't make decisions without consulting him."

"Like Rasputin in the Russian court," I said.

Julian was watching us. "And what does this have to do," he asked, "with the swastika on the note?"

"You are a man with little patience," observed Marcus, looking at him with what could only be described as distaste. "A little man."

"Tell me," I urged, eager to avoid the situation getting personal again. Seriously: I'd have thought that Julian knew better than to sleep with married women.

Marcus cleared his throat importantly. "I draw your attention to one Karl Maria Wiligut, who claimed to be the last descendant of an Aryan priesthood that could trace its origins back to god-like creatures who once inhabited Germany," he said. "He suggested to Himmler that the SS expropriate a castle in Westphalia. Wiligut prophesied that the castle would become a Nazi stronghold against invading barbarians from the East. Himmler used the place as an indoctrination center."

"It seems to me that organization was their strong suit," I murmured.

"Occultism," said Marcus, ignoring me, "is a symptom of alienation from society, but it is also a symptom of alienation from reality itself. As the Nazis clearly demonstrated."

"But what has that to do with a murder that happened last week?" I wanted to know. This was all interesting, but it didn't answer the fundamental questions of who had killed Patricia and who had sent the stylized swastika threat to Avner.

Marcus looked at me thoughtfully and with, I sensed, a little disappointment. "Ideas such as these do not die simply because the men who believe in them do," he said.

"So someone else is linking Nazism and the occult in Montréal," said Julian briskly. He wanted to get to the point and get out of there, too. "They know about the diamonds—somehow—and they know that Avner is involved. They killed Patricia Mason, probably to steal the diamond she'd stolen."

"They didn't get the diamond," I said. Both men looked at me.

"Otherwise they wouldn't be going to Avner, threatening him," I said.

"I think," said Marcus heavily, "that it's time you spoke to someone." He wheeled his chair over to his desk and wrote something on a piece of paper. Old-school: I'd have used my smartphone to send it to ours. Or maybe this was something he didn't want on the Internet. He turned back, wheeled himself over, and handed me the paper. "She may be more likely to talk to you than she is to the *police*," he said, indicating Julian.

It was a name, a telephone number. I looked up again. "Who is it?"

"Someone," said Marcus, "who knows firsthand about these things. Talk to her."

Julian nodded to me and I stood up reluctantly. "But—"

"*Écoute,*" said Marcus. "You find out anything, I can probably point you to the right group, to the people who are most likely involved. Believe it or not, even with all this talk of history, my real expertise is with groups currently active in Québec and Canada. You just need the background in order to narrow it down: there are enough neo-Nazis in North America to fill another stadium, and they all have some sort of philosophy, even if it's badly thought through. So you have to start with the beliefs rather than the corpse. This is something that my brothers in the police department appear to have a problem understanding. They think that you begin with the violence. I say that you begin with the reason for the violence." His eyes were on Julian.

"We came to you, didn't we?" Julian asked; but he sounded defensive.

"*En tout cas,*" Marcus said, looking back at me, "you won't be able to do that without this background. It's a lot more complex than you're willing to take on board right now. And you need to understand some things before you decide to take it any further." He caught my expression and sighed. "Martine. Most of the far-right groups in this country are innocuous. Sure, they throw stones, they write grammatically impossible diatribes on the Internet, they start fights in bars. They're young and they're angry and disenfranchised, and it's an outlet. But what you're talking about here—it's not innocuous. It's not innocent."

"So why can't you explain it?"

"Because you need to hear it from someone who believes it. Or believed it; I don't know what she thinks now. I haven't spoken to her in some time, and disillusionment happens to everyone, *n'est-ce pas*, at some time or another? I'm just an observer. Go and talk to her."

Julian shrugged. "Thank you for your time," I said to Marcus.

"Come back," he said, "when you're ready."

They moved him from the Little Camp into the main facility after a week.

The officer in charge, very correct, very elegant you'd almost say in his polished black boots and black uniform, glanced up. "We're not taking Jews in Buchenwald," he said, and turned to the soldier next to him. "Why has this man been sent here? He belongs at Auschwitz."

The soldier handed him a file.

Elias waited. He knew—how could he not know?—that whatever was decided here was deciding him, too. His future.

Or lack thereof.

The officer looked up from the papers. "Why didn't you say so before?" he demanded, irritation in his voice. "This is irregular. I should have been notified when he arrived."

"Yes, Oberleutnant."

He looked at Elias and shook his head, then gestured to one of the kapos standing by. "Take this man to Commandant Koch."

Elias was grabbed by the neck of his striped cotton uniform and pushed roughly toward the gatehouse. "This way," the kapo snarled.

The commandant's office was open and airy, with light flooding in from a long series of windows. It didn't escape the smell of smoke; there was nowhere Elias had been yet where one could escape the smell of smoke. But it was as far removed as could possibly be from the Little Camp.

The commandant himself was in his thirties, wearing the inevitable black uniform with the death's head insignia. "Elias Kaspi," he said, standing up behind his desk and, unbelievably, smiling. "Welcome to Buchenwald."

And that was the beginning.

CHAPTER EIGHTEEN

I wasn't going to call anyone with a background in esoteric Aryan thought without some preparation first. "I have to go back to my office," I told Julian, who nodded, preoccupied. "I'll take the Métro, it'll clear my head. I'll call you later."

"Are you going to go see that woman?" He gestured toward my handbag, where I'd tucked Marcus's paper.

"Not right now. You'll want to go with me, won't you?"

"Maybe."

I stopped. "What is it, Julian? You've been completely in your own world since this morning."

"Just thinking about something." He caught my expression and smiled. "Nothing to worry about. I'll let you know if it pans out."

I'm the one who should be preoccupied, I found myself thinking; but Julian wasn't going to tell me until he was good and ready. "I'll see you later, then," I said. "*A plus tard.*"

He grunted, which I took to mean *back at you*, and I headed over to catch the subway at the Maisonneuve station.

Chantal was hovering. "Monsieur Petrinko has called twice, and stopped in about an hour ago," she said. "He said it was not urgent, but he did not look well."

"Thank you, Chantal. Is Richard around?"

She shook her head. "At a meeting."

"Okay." I grabbed my message slips and headed into my office. Ivan had indeed called. I sighed, kicked off my shoes, and swiveled around to look out the window.

There was sun out there, white clouds in a crystal-clear blue sky. Everything out there seemed simple, beautiful, easy.

Real life? That was something else altogether.

I was so angry about my apparent place in Ivan's priorities that I hadn't really paused to think about the actual content of what we were arguing about: Claudia and Lukas not being every-other-weekend houseguests, but rather full-time responsibilities. Enrolling them in school here. Having dinner with them every night. Encouraging Lukas to be more assertive and Claudia to be less dramatic. Was I ready for that? Was it what I wanted?

My mother and I'd had a relationship that could best be termed problematic. We were pretty much alone: I had no siblings, and my father was a researcher with an obsession far greater than his love for his family.

His death was the stuff of my own nightmares: while my mother had died slowly of a cancer that ate her up from inside, my father's demise—like everything about him, really—was rather more dramatic, bigger than life. In fact, in a not-so-literal way, he was a victim of a mythical dark nightmare monster, the Kraken: *Papa* was a marine biologist whose obsession with the deep-ocean-dwelling giant squid was far more important to him than his family back in Montréal, an attitude that added to my mother's increasing bitterness at life in general and impatience with me in particular.

He hadn't lived long enough to see the extraordinary films of the real giant squid that emerged out of the American scientist Edith

Widder's research; and the fact that I even *know* about that research shows perhaps that I'm still a little obsessed myself. Or maybe I just want to know what this creature was, why it had lured him so completely away from us, and left me alone for all those years with an increasingly resentful, restless woman. What it had that I didn't have.

The squid wasn't what killed him; he died when his research ship out of the University of Québec at Rimouski miscalculated the path and ferocity of an August hurricane. There was barely enough funding for the trip; there was nothing left over for recovery.

I was sixteen years old.

I secretly thought it was appropriate, him staying forever in the deep cold waters that had so fascinated him in life, but I did campaign to have a stone placed up at the cemetery of Notre-Dame-des-Neiges, where my mother would eventually be buried, even if it didn't cover his remains, even if it was nothing but symbolic. *Maman* would have none of it. Her anger and bitterness kept her from really grieving, really mourning, really feeling. And then the moment when she could have done it was gone and life moved on.

I'm not complaining, not really; I had the great good fortune to have attended a convent school all the way up to university, sometimes as a day student, a few years as a boarder when my mother and I were really not doing well together; and the nuns, the *bonnes soeurs* as we called them, more than made up in love and caring and examples for any lack of parenting elsewhere in my life. Last year I'd had occasion to question that love, when the evidence that another group of nuns in Montréal had behaved quite differently—and quite horribly—to the children in their charge.

But me? I had nothing of which to complain.

Still, it's not the sort of background that teaches one about how to be a good parent in turn. My mother was never physically abusive, but she was an unhappy woman and I was a target for the amorphous bitterness and disappointment that her own life had brought her. And my father made clear by his absence from it his level of involvement in my life as I grew up.

Did I know how mothers were supposed to behave? Not especially.

I'd always felt that the saving grace in my current family life was the very fact of its irregular nature. Nothing that I could do to these kids was irreparable or even, in the final analysis, important. At the end of the weekend, at the end of the vacation, they always went back to Margery.

Until now. Could I deal with having full-time kids in my home? If so, it wouldn't really be *my* home, would it? It would be theirs as well.

And if I couldn't, what did that do to my marriage? Would Ivan resent me forever for saying no? Would he leave me, deciding—quite rightly—that his children's welfare had to come first?

My head was starting to hurt. And I wasn't the smallest bit closer to understanding my own feelings.

Okay, Martine. Think about something else. You don't have to make that decision now. Often I found that stepping away from a problem offered a solution. Or perhaps that was just something I told myself to justify my procrastination over dealing with difficult issues.

I swung back to the desk and pulled Marcus's paper out of my purse. Ignoring all the other messages waiting for me, I smoothed it out and read the name for the first time: Gabrielle Brand. A number over on the west part of town, the anglophone side. I took a deep breath. In for a penny, in for a pound, I thought, and pressed the digits on my desk phone. I knew that "City Hall" would come up on the caller identification, and hoped that wouldn't be a deterrent.

For many people, surprisingly, it seems to be.

The telephone was answered on the third ring. "Hello?" Definitely anglophone.

"Hello, this is Martine LeDuc calling. May I please speak with Gabrielle Brand?"

A long pause. "Who did you say you were?" A faint accent that I couldn't place.

"My name's Martine LeDuc. I work for City Hall. I was given your name by Marcus Levigne." Leaving out his occupation and rank.

"I see." A pause. "I am Gabrielle Brand."

Okay. I took a deep breath. "Ms. Brand, I'd very much appreciate being able to meet with you. Today, if possible."

Another silence, this one so long that I wondered if she'd put the phone down and walked away. And then she said, "Yes. I really think it will have to be today."

She hadn't asked what it was about, which seemed the obvious response. Okay. As Claudia would say, whatever. "That's great," I said heartily, as though countering her reluctance to speak with too much enthusiasm might even things out. "When can—"

"I am taking my grandchildren up to the park," she interrupted. "You can meet me there."

"Great," I said again. Up to the park probably meant the big one, the one covering part of the mountain that the city was named for, but I had to be sure. "Which—"

"We're going to Beaver Lake," she said. "I do not want to see you there. I do not want to involve my grandchildren." A German accent? I wondered. "On our way back, we always stop at the lookout, the one on Remembrance. You can meet us there. My daughter will pick up the children, and you and I will have this conversation that we must have."

For someone who had initially sounded so tentative, she was certainly on top of planning. "All right," I said faintly. "What time?"

"Three o'clock. And, Mrs. LeDuc—"

"Yes?"

"It is best, I think, if you come alone."

That was all that was missing, I thought, to make this a thoroughly clichéd experience. "Why is that, Mrs. Brand?"

"I'll see you at three, at the overlook."

Okay. Nothing mysterious there. And an hour and a half to kill before I could leave for the meeting. I glanced through my e-mails, returned a couple of quick calls that seemed urgent, drank three coffees in quick succession, and finally called Ivan's mobile, still with no idea what I was going to say.

There was casino noise behind him. "Martine."

"Is this a bad time? It's only that I just got in."

"No, no. Not at all. Let me just get someplace more private. Can I call you right back?"

"Sure." Click.

I picked at a hangnail and considered whether I should get a manicure. I decided that the painting of Marguerite Bourgeoys, our local saint, should probably be moved to another wall of the office as it was fading in the sunlight. I went back to my laptop and keyed in Gabrielle Brand's name and got a lot of returns that featured one or the other of her names, but not the two in conjunction; this was going to take more than just Google. I thought about whether or not my car might need an oil change. Anything to not think about the conversation we were about to—

The phone rang. "*Âllo?*"

"Okay," said Ivan. "Quieter now. Sorry about that. How are you doing?"

"I'm okay. We need to talk about this, Ivan. All the things we need to consider. Schools, and friends, and . . ."

"I know," he said, as my voice trailed off. I really didn't even *know* what all the things were that we needed to consider.

"I mean, you and me," I said. "You're right, at the end of the day, they're your children, not mine. But this is our life we're talking about changing. My life, too. I need to be part of this decision. If I can't be part of this decision, then there's no sense in my being part of *any* decision. Do you understand what I'm saying?"

A short pause. "I was wrong not to have you be a part of it from the start," he said. "God, as soon as those words were out of my mouth I realized what I was saying, and that I really didn't want to be saying it. I—it's not an excuse, mind you, but I just felt that as long as the conversation stayed in Boston, it stayed academic. Like it wasn't really affecting us at all."

I swallowed. "If there's an us, Ivan . . ."

"Of course there's an us," he said. "Good Christ, Martine, this is big, but it's not bigger than us. And I think we can—"

"No specifics," I interrupted him. "I can't put my head around specifics right now. I just need to know that this is as much about you and me as it is about Margery, or Doctors Without Borders, or even Claudia and Lukas."

"I'm not making the same mistake twice," Ivan said.

"All right, then." I didn't know what else to say. "Will you be home for dinner?"

"I'll make it a point to be. Want me to cook?"

"I don't want to spend the whole night washing dishes," I said.

"That's why we have a dishwasher."

"Uh-huh," I said, unconvinced. "Let's take a page from the kids' book and I'll pick up a chicken dinner at Saint Hubert. Rotisserie chicken, cole slaw, French fries . . ."

"Sold," he said promptly. "With a Nuits Saint Georges."

"But of course," I said, and we were both laughing when we hung up. It wasn't real laughter, not yet; but it was a step in the right direction.

And then suddenly, it seemed, it was time to leave for the

lookout and whatever was awaiting me there. After all that had happened, I couldn't say I was looking forward to it.

The next week, Bernie set the smoked-meat sandwich in front of Hans and said, without preamble, "Livia's coming in for lunch tomorrow. I'll introduce you to her, if that's still what's on your mind."

"I have not been able to think of anything else," Hans said frankly.

"Nu, I will do it. But you be careful with this girl, or you'll have me to answer to, you hear? I don't want her getting hurt. She's the real deal. She's special."

That was the one thing that Hans already knew about her.

Livia was wearing a blue sweater the next day. She laughed when Bernie told her that Hans talked funny, "on account of him bein' from Holland."

"It's all right," she said. "Everyone I know talks funny in one way or another. Sit down, please?"

"Thank you." Hans sat on the swivel seat beside her. It all seemed so inelegant for such a goddess. "Bernie speaks quite highly of you," he said.

She laughed again. "Bernie is like an uncle to me. He thinks I'm the most amazing human being God ever put on earth. It's all very complimentary, but a little silly, don't you think?"

"No," said Hans. "I think so, too."

"Then you're silly, too."

But she let him buy her lunch, and hold the door for her, and talk with her about his work. "Are you very homesick for Holland?" she asked as they emerged into the sunlight together. "You must be terribly worried about your family."

"I have no family," said Hans. It sounded abrupt and she looked away from him. He hadn't meant to do that, to be rude or insensitive. He didn't know how to talk to her. "There was an accident when I was young," he said quickly. "They all died."

She was instantly sympathetic. "Oh, no! I'm so very sorry. Is that why you came to Canada? To get away from the memories?"

It was as good a reason as any. "I like it here," he said. "I like Montréal. Though I still don't speak any French."

"That's all right," she said and laughed. "Mine is terrible, too." She stopped. "This is me, then."

He looked at the storefront. "You—make dresses?"

"I work for someone who does. Thanks awfully for lunch, and for the walk."

"I wonder," said Hans, "if I can see you again. I enjoy very much talking with you."

Livia smiled. "You can take me to the cinema on Thursday night," she said.

He didn't think to ask why she didn't choose the weekend. It didn't matter; he would go anywhere on any day with her. He was late back to work, and didn't even mind the foreman's reprimands.

He was in love.

CHAPTER NINETEEN

Richard was coming in just as I headed out. "There is a problem?" he asked.

"Do I look that bad?"

A delicate shrug. "You look worried."

"I am, but it's nothing to do with the office." Well, not quite true, but I didn't have time to explain. "Richard, do me a favor. Find out what's happening with these diamonds on the political front. Is Ottawa talking to London? It would be good to know."

He inclined his head gracefully. "Of course. Something else?"

"No. I have a meeting—probably won't be back in the office today. Can you hold down the fort?"

Another *bien sûr*. I sighed. "Richard, I'm sorry. You probably think I'm totally scattered and not pulling my weight around here these days—"

He put up a hand to stop me. "It is always," he said gravely, "easy to work with you. You work harder than anyone I have ever known. If there are things you need to deal with, then you must go and deal with them. We will be fine." A mischievous gleam. "Beside, while the mayor is away . . ."

"I wish this mouse were playing!" I said and laughed. "Thanks, Richard. I don't deserve you."

"It is nothing," he said, and I remembered how, last year, I'd covered for him. We took care of each other. I really was lucky in the team I'd assembled.

A brisk walk down a few streets to the garage where we kept the car. It started right away—a very good sign—and I headed out. It's easy to get to Mount Royal from anywhere in the city: just find a hill and go up it. Eventually you'll reach the "mountain"—part of a range of long-extinct volcanoes—that gave Montréal its name.

It's home to a whole lot of life. There's the park itself, the city's largest green space, where we all flock summer and winters alike. Saint Joseph's Oratory, Canada's largest church, is here, as well as two cemeteries; my mother lives in one of them, a beautiful and incredibly peaceful place. We take the kids there most Sundays they're in town. . . . I stopped my thought there. No reason to start stressing about more than one thing at a time.

The overlook was crowded; it nearly always is, in good weather and bad, tourists gawping at the view, Montréalers taking the walking paths that branch off from the lookout. I was early, so parked the car and got out, even though the day was clouding over. I had no idea how I would know who Gabrielle Brand was. I could only hope that she'd found me online and knew who to look for.

She had, and she did.

The woman who approached me was just past a certain age; I'd peg her in her early seventies, but a very healthy early seventies. She was dressed in the remnants of the sixties, not hers but the world's: a long print skirt with warm woolen socks and clogs under it; several layers of brightly colored sweaters and a dazzling pink scarf at her neck. "Mrs. LeDuc?"

I pushed myself off the car and held out my hand. "Martine. I'm glad to meet you, Mrs. Brand."

"Perhaps you won't be." But she took my hand anyway.

"So," I said, conversationally, "your grandchildren are gone?"

She looked startled at first, then relaxed. "Their mother has come for them," she said. "There is a path down here, and a bench. Would you care to walk?"

She clearly cared to, and so I nodded, grabbing my keys and my jacket. Up here, it was brisk, with an edge to the air indicating winter wasn't all that far off. We took the trail that led down through a thicket and at once it was as though we were alone on the mountain. As was, no doubt, her intention. "I am going to tell you some things," she said, her eyes on the path, not even glancing at me. "I knew when Marcus told me about you, when you called, that it was time to say something. I've been waiting with it inside me for too long."

I didn't want to prompt her; the reality was I had no idea what she was going to say, and assuming anything could get us off on the wrong foot altogether. She seemed to be waiting for some response, though, so I said, "Thank you for trusting me."

That earned me a quick sideways glance. "Perhaps," she said. I could hear it again, the echo of an accent in her voice, something from the east. German, Polish, Eastern European? I couldn't tell.

We walked for a moment in silence. I was scuffing the leaves that had already started falling and were crunching under my feet. Usually I found that to be delightful; today, it felt like a presage of something dark and ominous. There were clouds moving in from the south, and the wind was rising.

Gabrielle seemed to be preparing herself for something. "First I must tell you some history," she said, and the accent was stronger now. "It is important, so that you understand what is happening now."

She seemed to be waiting for a rejoinder, so I nodded. "I'm happy to hear whatever you have to tell me, Mrs. Brand." But I was hearing an awful lot of history lately, I thought. Everyone seemed to have something from the past that was resurfacing.

"Mrs. Brand," she echoed and laughed, but there was no pleasure in it. "You will hear about that, too." She indicated a bench ahead of us. "Come, and sit, and listen."

Here there was a break in the bushes and the view off the mountain was again spread out before us. It was dramatic and intense and, I thought, by no means accidental.

And the wind seemed to have disappeared, even though we were in a less protected area.

Gabrielle Brand was looking out, impassive, over the city below. "There is some history you must know, to start," she said. "Back in 1912, several German occultists with radical anti-Semitic inclinations decided to form a magic lodge. They named it the Order of Teutons." Her voice was almost conversational. Almost. "The Order of Teutons was organized along the lines of the Freemasons or the Rosicrucians, with differing degrees of initiation, different levels of belonging, *ja*? Only those people who could fully document that they were of pure Aryan ancestry were allowed to join."

I thought, 1912? Yes, we were indeed starting at the beginning.

"Later, many of those who had belonged to the Order of Teutons joined another group called the Thule Society." She paused. "The German Workers Party, which I know you will have heard of, was only one of many associations founded and controlled by the Thule Society, and eventually Hitler became the most prominent personality in the party as well as being very high up in the society itself."

So that was where it had started. The link between politics and magic began inside Hitler himself.

She was still talking. "He filled key positions with his own friends from the Thule Society and the army. During the summer of 1920, upon his suggestion, the party was renamed the National Socialist

German Workers' Party. The new name was intended to equally attract nationalists and proletarians. To go along with the new name, his mass movement also required a flag with a powerful symbol. Among many designs under consideration, Hitler picked a red cloth with a white circle in the middle containing a black swastika. So the mystical and the political were closely allied from the beginning."

I didn't want to interrupt her flow, but she seemed to be waiting for a comment. "Did people on the political side know about the mystical one?"

"Some did. Most did not." She still hadn't looked at me. "Thule was supposedly a legendary island in the far north, similar to Atlantis. It was destroyed, but its secrets were guarded by ancient, highly intelligent beings, and the initiated could establish contact with these beings by means of mystical rituals."

It sounded like the B movies on television on Saturday afternoons. I didn't say anything, and she continued. "The initiated would be given supernatural strength and energy. With that energy they would create a race of Aryan supermen to exterminate other, inferior races. The symbol of the Thule Society was a swastika with a dagger enclosed in laurel leaves."

None of this sounded particularly new to me; it sounded like cards taken at random from the Nazi recipe file: eugenics, racism, genocide. Nothing particularly wholesome, but nothing that should be causing havoc in the twenty-first century, either.

"And you must understand, there were a great many intellectual— well, undercurrents, as we might call them. During Hitler's years there, Vienna was a vortex of modern thinking. Think of what was happening then, think of who was sitting in the cafés and strolling in the parks." She glanced at me. "Freud was in practice at Berggasse. Ludwig Wittgenstein was in residence pondering avant-garde philosophy and metaphysics. Gustav Mahler had returned home to die and to name his protégé, Arnold Schönberg." She sighed. "Under different auspices, it could have been a good time, a creative time. But that was not to be. In contrast with this creative thought there persisted the deep anti-Semitic currents that had caused Mahler to convert to Catholicism, that forced Freud eventually to flee to London, and that informed the ancient pan-German folkloric nostalgia espoused by Guido von List. Von List substituted the swastika for the cross in perversion and practiced magic. He even looked like a wizard, in a floppy cap and long white beard."

Somewhere from close behind us, a crow cawed and I jumped. The cold was settling into me.

"Another player came onto the scene about then," Gabrielle continued. "It was called the Luminous Lodge, and *its* objective was to explore the origins of the Aryan race and to perform exercises in concentration. Aleister Crowley was one of them."

There was a name I'd heard: Crowley, the English occultist and magician. Satanist, also, I thought. "And Hitler was a participant?"

She nodded. "Hitler's unusual powers of suggestion become more understandable if one keeps in mind that he had access to the secret psychological techniques of these esoteric lodges. That is how in a remarkably short period of time he was able to move an obscure workers' party from the beer hall to a mass movement."

The clouds were still moving out in front of us, over the city. I shivered.

"Throughout the Nazi régime," Gabrielle Brand said, "these lodges exercised almost limitless power over the politics and policies of the Third Reich. Because they combined old rituals with new people performing them."

"Can't that be said of all religions?" I asked mildly.

She inclined her head. "But the rituals in mainstream religion are fixed," she said. "They weren't, not for these people. Listen, when you create something new, you're free to put whatever you'd like into the mix. You can look at what works, what has worked, for other belief systems, and incorporate those elements into your own."

"Religion à la carte," I said.

"Precisely. And in that regard, though the term was not used until decades later, we can say that it was the beginning of the use of chaos magic." She glanced at me. "In chaos magic, you take what you need for your purpose. What you use depends on what you are trying to do. And you can take it from any tradition, create customized rituals that don't have the inconvenience of elements you don't want, that aren't useful, within it."

I didn't say anything. She sighed. "Do you follow a religion, Mrs. LeDuc?"

"Martine," I said again, automatically. "Yes. I'm Catholic."

She nodded as though I'd just confirmed something in her mind. "You are an intelligent, thinking person. And you are a Catholic. There are things about your religion that trouble you intellectually, yes?"

Well, that or the way some people chose to practice it. "Yes," I said.

"When you attend Mass, there are parts of it that aren't quite right for you. But you're stuck with them. They're part of the whole. In chaos magic, that never happens. Everything is customized. There are no parts of any ritual that are uncomfortable for the participants, because they've taken what they need from all sorts of different traditions and fused them into something new—and, potentially, extremely powerful. They've gathered the magic, if you will allow the term, of every tradition from which they have borrowed something, then reduced it all as you would reduce a sauce on the stove. Making it more concentrated. Making it more powerful."

"But the point of ritual," I objected, "is that it's handed down through the ages—"

"The point of ritual," she interrupted crisply, "is to find something that *works*. That is all. The beauty, if there is any, is window dressing. Organically, ritual is utilitarian."

I shifted uncomfortably. "Maybe if you're talking about magic," I said. "But religion is different."

"Is it? So you do not pray to be given anything? You never ask your god for anything?"

"Of course I do. But I don't believe in God because of what he can do for me."

"Of course you do," she said. "You believe that he created the world, and gave you life. You believe that his son died a terrible death to free you from sin. You don't have to ask for a new Porsche to see that, already, before you even said your first prayer, you loved this God because of what he's done for you." She shook her head. "Humans are utilitarian beings. We want to get things done. Some see religion as one way to do it."

"While others see magic," I said. I wasn't sure I bought her argument, but I didn't want to stop her.

"Magic is far more simple than you think," said Gabrielle. "All it is, is training yourself to exercise your willpower and to harness energy. That is all. It is not creating something that has not already been there. It is capturing the wild and wanton energy of the planet and making it work for you."

That phrase—wild and wanton—sounded like she was quoting something. But I didn't know what.

"The other component of chaos magic—and remember, please, that no one was using that term in the forties—is that it can easily become extremely violent. If ritual is customized, then nothing is forbidden. Indeed, taboos are seen as the efforts of a society to keep the wild energies in check; violating the taboos will release the energy. And it is all about energy."

I turned in my seat and stared at her. "That means—"

She nodded. "Oh, yes. The more taboos you can violate, the

closer you will become to the source of the energy, and the more you will take it into yourself. The perverse has an energy all its own. They weren't Satanists, Mrs. LeDuc. To believe in Satan, you must first believe in God. But evil? Yes: this, I think, is where you will find the root of evil."

I was already way ahead of her.

Once they got him the sapphires to work with, it all went smoothly enough. Oh, they weren't perfect replicas, no, but they were respectable. "They don't need to be exact," the commandant said, "they have to be close."

And they were very close indeed.

Life settled into a routine. Every morning they assembled in the Appellplatz, the roll-call square, standing in lines and staring straight ahead. Kapos—the high-ranking prisoners, most of them Communists—were quick to beat anyone who stepped or fell out of line, and there were dogs.

Elias was mostly afraid of the dogs.

After everyone had been counted, the prison orchestra assembled itself and began playing music—Viennese waltzes, someone had told Elias they were. Such light music, such happy music. It accompanied the prisoners as they were marched off to their work details, either in the quarry or in the factory making munitions for the German war effort. But the music, Elias learned, was good; it allowed them to talk freely to each other.

Some of the prisoners stayed behind. Several of them had been assigned office work; there were cleaners; and there was Elias.

They gave him everything that he needed. They gave him two surly assistants. They gave him plenty of raw materials to experiment with. And he wasn't just to imitate the crown jewels; there were other uses for precious stone substitutes. But the most important were the three he was doing on Berlin's orders.

Food was distributed twice a day. Weak coffee, weaker potato soup, a hunk of bread. The bread was the consistency of clay, and the coffee made from acorns. Prisoners, Elias noted, were rarely mistreated, and when it happened, it was only at the kapos' hands. "Why?" he asked Franz, his German bunk mate.

"No wanton cruelty, that's the Nazi policy," said Franz.

Elias stared at him. "Now you're making no sense."

The other man lifted his shoulders. "Policy is policy," he said. "Reality, that is something else." He scratched his head, hard. "Look, we are here to work. We cannot work if we are injured. If they want us dead, they just stop giving us food. It is simple. No gas chambers at Buchenwald."

"Gas chambers?" Elias didn't know what he was talking about.

"Ja. Other camps, they kill people with gas." He glanced at Elias. "Jews, mostly. Then they burn their bodies."

"They do that here," Elias said. It hadn't taken him long to understand the meaning of the smoke that seemed to hang over the camp all the time, whether the crematorium was working or not.

Franz shrugged. "Prisoners here die every day," he said. "But they are not executed."

"Why not?"

The other man looked at him. "Bullets are expensive," he said. "Starvation is cheap."

CHAPTER TWENTY

"If you can harness energy, like that, then you can transcend limits, boundaries," I said. "You're compelled to."

Gabrielle Brand looked at me as she might an approving tutor. "Precisely," she said. "And you can transcend natural limits as well as societal ones. Space, for example. Or time."

I shivered. I didn't want to go there. "And that's what happened with Hitler?" I asked instead. "This magic?"

"Look. By all societal reckoning, Hitler should never have existed, *ja*?" Her German afterthought was oddly like the Canadian way of ending sentences with *eh*—both seemed to invite agreement. "Everyone knows this. He was neither particularly brilliant nor particularly well educated. His political platform lacked subtlety. He seemed to those around him at best odd—and at worst, insane. And yes, there were serious sociological and cultural reasons for his rise to power. But they cannot explain it in total. They alone would not have been enough."

"Enter black magic," I said flippantly.

That earned me a sharp glance. "You are the one who asked to see me."

"I know. I'm sorry." I shifted uncomfortably on the bench. "It's just so—fantastic. So far removed from anything we normally experience. And so long ago."

"So far removed from a murder in Montréal last Thursday?"

Point to you, I thought, and wondered if that was what we were doing, playing a game of chess, accumulating points against each other. To what end? And what would the winner receive? Looking at her face, one word came to mind.

Redemption.

"You're involved with all this, aren't you?" I asked. "You're too young to have been part of it during the war, but somewhere along the line, you've been involved."

She nodded. "I have been involved."

We sat for some time in silence. I didn't know what questions to ask, and I wasn't even sure whether, if I could, I'd want them answered. The story was shot through with too many veins, the taboos Gabrielle had alluded to, the atavistic fears that we usually keep well under our beds, monsters we don't ever have to look at in the light of day but whose breath curls round our nightmares and whose voices haunt our dreams. But I still couldn't see how the threads connected. Or even if they did.

"So what happened?" I asked, quietly, gently.

She cleared her throat; she'd been waiting for me to ask the question. "So, as you see, Hitler was fully engaged with what we now call chaos magic throughout his dictatorship."

"And yet in the end it failed him."

She lifted her shoulders. "Who can say where the failure came from? It is not relevant to what I am going to tell you."

Perhaps not, but I imagined the last days of the Third Reich, the underground bunker, the despair, killing the children, finally the stream of suicides that were the last proof that the magic hadn't worked. It would have been very difficult to believe at that point. "What is relevant, then?"

"One of the secret societies, one of the lodges, was called the Order of the Black Sun," she said. "And after the war, the Black Sun became a cherished symbol within the far right of several countries, including the Ukraine, which has a Black Sun Battalion. But that is not our business. Our business is the New Order of the Black Sun, begun after the turmoil of 1970."

"Nineteen seventy—so you're talking about here, in Québec." It was coming home a lot faster than I'd anticipated. "The October Crisis."

"Yes. It was felt by some that the government's response to the crisis was inadequate."

"Inadequate?" I was incredulous. "You've got to be kidding. The government invoked the War Measures Act, for heaven's sake! Most people now think it was an *over*reaction, not an inadequate one."

"We are not," she said calmly, "dealing with *most people* here."

Nor were we then. Québec's October Crisis began with the kidnapping of James Cross, the British trade commissioner in Montréal, by members of the Front de Libération du Québec. It rapidly devolved into the most serious terrorist act carried out on Canadian soil after another official, Minister of Immigration and Labor Pierre Laporte, was kidnapped and killed by another leftist faction. The crisis shook the career of recently elected Liberal Premier Robert Bourassa, who solicited federal help along with Montréal Mayor Jean Drapeau. The FLQ wanted a separate Québec and saw itself as a colonial state rising against foreign imperialism.

Montréal was, then as now, divided as to whether this would be a good thing to do. "There were soldiers in the streets," I said to Gabrielle. "Sounds like it would have been right up their alley."

"Not far enough," she said. "A group of disaffected and extremely disenfranchised young men, all of them right-wing, were unimpressed with the handling of the situation. They were, oddly enough, also in favor of a separate Québec, but only because that might ensure racial purity and keep immigrants away. They began meeting, and eventually one of the more intelligent among them, a young man whose parents had emigrated from Germany right after the war, who was named Heinrich Marke, this man was very attracted to the concept of secret knowledge that no one but them could possess, and to the idea that they could make change, not necessarily through overt violence, but through the manipulation of the natural world. Under his guidance, they began calling themselves the New Order of the Black Sun."

I had the sense to stay silent. Something was happening here.

Another deep breath. "Heinrich Marke," said Gabrielle, "was my husband."

The wind kicked up again, as though the mountain itself had been holding its breath, waiting for that revelation. "He translated his name into English so as to simplify things," Gabrielle said. "Heinrich Marke became Henry Brand, and that was what he was called when I met him. Of course I knew he was German; so was I. And I was so attracted to him, his strength, his utter and complete certainty about things. I was feeling lost and lonely, and he filled all the corners of my life."

What could I say to that? "Tell me about the New Order of the Black Sun," I said finally. Her personal life was her personal life. Women have approached monsters before, have touched the smoke and mirrors, have dared themselves to do the unthinkable, and all in the name of love.

"The New Order of the Black Sun," Gabrielle said, "was first about recapturing the past. These boys—they felt that they had missed out, somehow, on not having been born earlier, on not having been part of the Third Reich. So at first it was all about secret meetings in basements, secret handshakes, Nazi salutes, flags with swastikas on them. Terrible, of course, but dangerous only to themselves. But as time passed, and they grew more angry—the decade was one of change, and they were being left behind by it—they started acting. Rocks through windshields. Defacing people's homes. Once, they knocked out an old Jewish man on the street." She shook her head. "For Henry, this was all secondary. He accused them of playacting when they could do the real thing, *be* the real thing. So finally they listened to him."

"Were you—married to him then?"

"We were married in 1980. I was much younger than Henry. I believed in him. I wanted something or someone to believe in, and I believed in him. Slowly he introduced me to the order, he indoctrinated me." She made a gesture of finality with her hands. "I do not say that to excuse myself. I embraced everything that he offered me, wholeheartedly. I wanted to believe, and I believed."

"In what?"

"This is why you must understand about magic," Gabrielle said. "Like Hitler, Henry was a man who could play both with the elements and with people's minds. Ultimately, of course, he failed. Those around him did not want magic, they wanted action. They did not understand that magic could have delivered far, far more than their acts of vandalism ever could. Our friends drifted apart; some moved away. In the west, in Ontario and British Columbia, there were active skinhead groups far more to their liking."

"And what happened to Henry?"

"It is really quite disappointing," Gabrielle said. "He wanted drama so much, and yet he died so prosaically, of cancer. Such a suburban disease."

This wasn't all there was to it, I thought. Something urgent had compelled her to tell me this story. Something that wasn't part of the past, or of this particular past.

Finally she spoke. "You asked what became of the New Order of the Black Sun," she said. "It has been resuscitated, and by people who know what they are doing. People who understand focus. People who understand visualization."

There was so much pain in her voice that it could only point to one thing. "Someone close to Henry is bringing it back."

She looked at me, her eyes filled with tears. She didn't bother to brush them away. "Our son," she said. "Aleister."

There was a special showing of a Hitchcock movie at His Majesty's Theatre on Guy Street, which made a change from the opera and play performances that were usually on the marquee. Suspicion, it was called.

Probably, he thought later, not a perfect choice.

He met Livia at the dressmaker's, waiting as she turned off the lights, locked the doors, taking pleasure in just watching her simple movements. Tonight she was wearing a soft yellow dress; her hair was dark and lush against it.

They walked to the theater together, close on the sidewalk but carefully not touching. Once her sleeve brushed against his and he felt an electric jolt run all the way up his arm.

"We used to go to the cinema quite often when my mother was alive," Livia told him. "This is such a treat; I have not been in years."

"What were your favorite films?"

"Trouble in Paradise," she replied at once. "And All Quiet on the Western Front. Oh, and Grand Hotel."

"Grand Hotel? I know this one. It was originally German. I saw the play—" He stopped himself in time. "The play came to Amsterdam, where I used to live," he finished.

She didn't seem to notice his flushed face. "They're wonderful, aren't they?" she asked and sighed. "Films, plays. They take you away from your regular life, from your problems, from your worries. You don't think of anything at all. You just are."

They were seated in one of the boxes above the stage and Hans pulled a flask from his pocket. She looked a little shocked when he offered it to her, but accepted readily enough; and halfway through the movie he reached over, slowly, a very little at a time, and took her hand.

She didn't move hers away.

Hans tried to concentrate on the movie. Joan Fontaine was becoming more and more convinced that her husband was going to try to kill her. Lie after lie piled up between them, and even with the warmth of Livia's hand in his own, Hans felt more and more panicked. Lies echoing lies, he thought. His situation was untenable. What would happen if Livia ever found out his secret, saw behind his lies? He barely knew her and knew, already, that he couldn't live without her.

He was a German. A soldier in the Third Reich. A spy in an enemy country.

She could never know.

CHAPTER TWENTY-ONE

"Named after Aleister Crowley, no doubt," I said. I couldn't think of anything else to say.

She nodded. "Henry's idea."

"Of course."

"It did not really become—problematic—for many years," she said. "Aleister was in college, and he had ideas—well, everyone has ideas in college, don't they? But he seemed all right. He started working, as a journalist."

"Which newspaper?"

"Freelance," she replied. "He said it gave him more freedom to write what he wanted. He went out to the west coast, spent three years in Vancouver, and then went to Berlin for a time, a year, I believe. He said he needed to find his roots. When he returned to Montréal, he was very angry."

"About what?"

"Me, primarily. How I had not honored his father enough. How I had failed to carry on his mission. That sort of thing. I can only guess at who he was associating with. You will remember than many of his father's associates went west, to British Columbia. No doubt he saw them there. No doubt the rhetoric was still in place. And in Berlin . . ." She lifted her shoulders. "Not everyone in the New Germany carries guilt. Not everyone believes that it should never have happened."

I could just imagine. The remnants of fascism, licking its wounds. "And when he came back? What happened then?"

"He bought a building in Saint-Jean-sur-Richelieu," she said, referring to a city just south of Montréal, twenty minutes away by car. "Right on the canal. Have you seen it, the canal? So pretty, I thought. A new life for him." She sighed. "And it was, I suppose. First it was boarders—he rented out rooms, you see, it was an old warehouse. Or mill. Something of the sort. He said it helped him pay the mortgage. But all the people he rented to, they seemed the same as him. Very correct. Very clean, very articulate. Not like his father's friends at all."

"The new face of fascism," I said.

"Yes, I think it is so," she said. "And more and more, he wanted me to be part of it. I was, I think, a link to his father—and, through him, to the rest of the past. For a time I stayed there. There was an appeal. You have no idea, Martine, of the energy of the perverse."

"Perhaps I do," I said, thinking of what had happened to me last year, of a lonely and deprived boy who had grown into a monster. Who was trained to become one. Evil was everywhere.

Gabrielle was talking. "All magic works through focus, through a harnessing of energy. When one person can do it, it is powerful. When more than one person does it, together, it becomes stronger, concentrated . . . dominant."

"So he's gathered . . . what? A coven?"

"The New Order of the Black Sun," she said soberly. "A group of people, with an identical focus, working with perfect synchronicity in a sympathetic environment—that produces amazing results."

"So they're doing what, exactly? Manipulating elections?" If so, my boss was going to want a piece of that.

"Nothing so small." She batted the idea away as she might an annoying fly. "You were close to it before, Mrs. LeDuc. Do not let your fear blind you."

"When? What did I say?"

"When you spoke of transcending boundaries," she said. "It was well known that Hitler and Himmler both could project themselves, for very brief periods, into a different space, a different dimension. It is not uncommon for people to be able to do it today, or so I understand."

I blinked and didn't say anything.

"They had only really begun to explore it when everything came crashing down in 1945." She caught my glance. "It is true that I have not told you everything," she said. "Hitler's inner circle—they have been called the Devil's disciples, but as I said, Satanism only works if you believe that there is a God, and none of them believed such a thing. But they were involved in the rituals with him." She sighed. "So. My mother was Hermann Göring's maid when he stayed in Bavaria. She was very frightened of him, and when she found she was pregnant, she ran away, to relatives who lived in Stuttgart. It was there that I was born. But even modern cities have long memories, and I preferred to emigrate to Canada. I did not understand, then, that you can never completely run away from the past."

"But not your past, surely," I said. "Just because Göring was your—father—that has nothing to do with you." But even as I spoke, I knew I was wrong. How could it not?

"Unless you believe that it is in the blood," she said soberly. "Henry believed that it was; it is why he married me. And Aleister believes it as well. He sees it as a magical connection, a connection between himself and his grandfather, between the past and the present. And he wants to connect them."

"How, exactly?"

Gabrielle looked directly at me. "The New Order of the Black Sun in Saint-Jean-sur-Richelieu," she said, "is planning to use the remaining crown jewels in order to summon Hitler—back from the dead."

I waited until Gabrielle had left before starting up the path to the lookout myself. The clouds had moved on and the sun was painting the sky pink over in the west. Innocent, as though nothing had happened.

I wasn't ready to get back in my car and go home. I wasn't sure what I was ready for. My hands were shaking and I pushed them deep into my jacket pockets. Everything here was pleasant, ordinary. Tourists chattering together in a plethora of languages. The city, sparkling like a jewel—

A jewel. That was why she'd agreed to talk to me. I realized that even as I watched her move slowly up the path, her gypsy garb swirling around her, just another aging hippie. She thought I could get the diamonds back.

So what was I going to do?

I was standing looking out over the miles of Québec spread out before me when a voice at my elbow said, "So, you're a little late getting the rest of the tour in, eh?"

I looked up and into the eyes of François, my Gray Line tour guide. Of course; the overlook was a popular stopping spot for all the tours, and I could see his bus behind us. I laughed out loud, relief washing over me. François, so normal, so part of a different life. "I'm sorry I had to leave early, before," I said. "It was my work."

He nodded without speaking and we stood shoulder to shoulder, looking out, companionably. "It never gets old, this view, eh?" he said.

I smiled, allowing myself to be distracted, my dark fears to be pushed away. "You love the city."

"With all its political corruption, its problems, its new buildings that are taking over . . . *eh oui*, even with all that, I love this city, eh?"

"François," I said suddenly, "how did you know about the British crown jewels being stored in the Sun-Life Building during the Second World War? I'd always heard that to be a rumor."

He looked at me curiously. "You have the advantage of me, madame," he said.

"Oh, sorry!" I wasn't going to last much longer at my job if this was the best I could do in terms of *politesse*. "I'm Martine LeDuc," I said, automatically putting out a hand to shake his. "I'm the—"

"—*directrice de publicité*," he said, nodding. "I thought it might be so, eh?"

"So when you said that the jewels were being stored . . ."

"It is the narrative," he said. "We're all trained with the narrative. We can say other things, yes, of course. You would be surprised at some of the questions I get." He caught my eye. "Well, perhaps you wouldn't, but it is always entertaining. But as to your question, it is from the tourism center that the narrative comes. Are you saying it isn't true?"

"No," I said and sighed. "I think you can rest assured that that part is very true indeed."

They all had the same thin cotton clothing: striped shirts over work-pants, shoes that might or might not fit. But there were ways to get more. A thriving black market flourished at Buchenwald, kapos and prisoners—and even the guards—all participating. The camp had its own currency and there were things you could buy—chocolate, an extra undershirt, or even a jacket, boots, or oranges.

Mostly the money was used to bribe kapos for better assignments. The quarry was the worst place to work; men didn't last there very long, even the youngest, even the strongest: it broke everyone. Most of the bodies hauled into the crematorium came from the quarry.

The factory was better: the work was indoors, and even though the building wasn't heated, it was better than being out in the wind. The only ones there who had problems were the Jehovah's Witnesses, who refused to do any munitions work, and their refusals earned many of them the quarry.

But the best assignments were in the camp itself, which required scores of people to keep it running. Cooking, serving, washing dishes in the canteen all fell to prisoners; so did working the laundry and cleaning the offices. All of the officers had servants who were prisoners: cooks, cleaners, chauffeurs. Even personal prostitutes, the youngest, the best-looking men.

There were unpleasant assignments, too. The infirmary didn't deal much with people who were sick; at Buchenwald, it was simple: if you got sick, you died. But there were doctors all the same, doctors working, Elias was told proudly by the camp commandant, to perfect a typhus vaccine. Mostly they used the criminal prisoners, the ones who were there for killing or stealing or who were generally deemed antisocial, for experimentation; they died quickly, too. And then the crematorium detail took over, gathering the bodies and taking them to the ovens and adding to the smoke that lay over the camp like a haze.

Some days, the crematorium didn't run, and the smoke wasn't so bad.

The day ended as it had begun, with roll call at the Appellplatz, lit up at night with strong searchlights. Elias wondered why they bothered: everyone was so exhausted that it was difficult to think of escape.

He was wrong, of course.

CHAPTER TWENTY-TWO

I called Julian on the way home. "We don't have to go see your friend Marcus again," I said. "Or if we do, it's for us to give him information, not the other way around."

"What's up?"

"We may have a bigger problem than we thought. Depending on what you believe, of course."

"Tell me."

So I told him, about the inner circle and Gabrielle's connection to it, about Crowley and the manipulation of elements and energy. I told him about the secret societies and the New Order of the Black Sun. "Christ," Julian said. "Now we've got to involve the Saint-Jean-sur-Richelieu police, too?"

"Not yet. Nothing's happened yet."

"They took the diamond from Patricia, didn't they? And they meant to silence Avner?"

"It's their logo on the envelope, all right," I said. I was suddenly exhausted. "She seems to think they don't have all the elements in place yet to conduct this—"

"—séance?" suggested Julian.

"Whatever it is," I said.

"Whatever it is, it's probably not a police matter." He paused. "Unless the diamond is there."

"She seems to think they need it for focus," I agreed.

"Okay, let me get this straight. Hitler and his cronies dabbled in the black arts and it helped them come to power. Something happened and they lost it, and so lost the war. But people believe that somehow, somewhere out there, Hitler's allegedly still lurking as this mass of pissed-off energy and all it takes are the British crown jewels and a group of skinheads in a basement somewhere to bring him back. And then what? He hangs out and drinks beer with them? Runs for prime minister? What?"

"I don't know," I said wearily. "I don't know what the plan is. But it's bad energy, Julian."

"Okay." A long pause. "Actually, I've not been sitting around twirling my thumbs while you've been off having tea and crumpets with Himmler's daughter."

"Göring's daughter."

"Whatever. Let's compare notes. You want to get together?" He sounded energized, finally, and I was pleased to hear it. Julian defeated wasn't a Julian I recognized.

"Not tonight," I said. "I have to see Ivan."

"Aha. Trouble in paradise?"

"Not as much as you're in, sleeping with officers' wives. What were you *thinking*?"

"I was *thinking* that she had nice—"

"Never mind." I cut him off. "I get it, I get it. Tomorrow?"

"Breakfast at Chez Cora?"

"Have a heart, I live in the Old City now."

"Relax, there's one on Drummond. Eight o'clock?"

"Yeah, okay," I said and disconnected. It felt bizarre to shift gears. I felt overwhelmed by this whole esoteric thing that I really didn't understand. I needed a long walk, or a session on the massage table, to process it, get it out of my system. Instead I was working my way through Montréal's evening traffic, on my way to what could only be an uncomfortable conversation with my husband about the course our lives were going to take for the next ten years or so. Small potatoes.

I left the car in the garage where we rented a space and made my way to the apartment. The evening was warmer here than it had been on the mountain, and I moved among couples and groups of tourists intent on finding just the right outdoor seat at just the right restaurant so that they could look so much more hip than all the others milling about, buying postcards and tins of maple syrup. "Henry!" yelled a woman near me, and I nearly jumped out of my skin. Her Midwestern accent did nothing to quiet my heart rate: what were the chances of her husband being called Henry? "Henry, over here! Jack and Lois are already inside!"

Ivan was wearing his evening uniform of sweatpants and T-shirt, this one proclaiming his allegiance to Boston College. He looked at me suspiciously. "Where's my chicken?"

"Chicken?" I was baffled, and then it came back to me. "Oh, *merde*, that's right. I was going to stop at a Saint Hubert."

He came over and put his arms around me. "That's okay, I prefer you, my little chicken."

I squirmed away. "I'm starving," I said. I wasn't ready to be held. I wasn't sure exactly what I was ready for. "I can't believe I forgot it."

"It's nothing," he said lightly, moving away from me, but not before I saw the hurt at my rejection flit across his face. "I'll put on some decent clothes, we can go out."

"You're sure you want to have this conversation out?"

"Don't *have* to have it over dinner," he said, heading up the stairs and into the bedroom. "It can be a postprandial discussion."

I had to smile in spite of myself. Who can resist someone who works "postprandial" into his daily vocabulary?

He reappeared wearing khakis, a sweater, and a jacket, with his fedora tipped dangerously over one eye. "How about Brazilian?"

"Rodizio? Why not?" It meant having people coming by the table every few minutes to offer us more meat, but perhaps that was the point. We walked there in silence, but after a moment I reached out and took Ivan's hand, tentatively, and was reassured when he held mine.

The truth was I didn't know how I felt about the whole situation. Two caipirinhas and a full churrasco meal later, I still didn't know. But my heart rate was back to normal, the headache that had been threatening when I was driving through town had receded, and I'd even managed to talk about how I'd spent my day.

A little, anyway. I had a feeling that Ivan wasn't going to be thrilled with a lot of what I was uncovering.

Walking home, he said, almost diffidently, "Don't think I don't realize what I'm asking of you here. I do. I know how enormous this is."

We were like salmon swimming upriver: the flow of tourists down Saint-Paul was nearly overwhelming. Ivan grabbed my hand and we fled down a side street, ending up at the riverside, along Montréal's "beach," tonight lit up and filled with tables, people drinking and laughing, grabbing what they could of the last days of good weather. Ivan took a deep breath. "They're my children," he said. "I divorced my wife, not my kids. It would have been my dream to have them come and live with us from the beginning." He paused. "But I know that's my dream, not yours. And I know—I think I know—how much it's asking of you."

I stopped and turned to face him. "Actually, I don't think I'd *want* to be married to you if you were the sort of person who wouldn't create a home for his children, who would feel okay turning them away from his door just because his wife couldn't have them live with her."

Ivan started to say something then, but I cut across it. "That doesn't mean that I can do it, Ivan, and this isn't a decision I can make in a heartbeat, either. We're in completely different situations here. There's only one decision you can make, and for once you're lucky, your head and your heart say the same thing. It's a lot more complex than that for me. This is eight or ten years we're talking about. And you think I can do that overnight?"

"Yes," he said, finally. "Yes, actually, I do. You love Lukas and Claudia. You've told me so. I assumed that—"

"Of course I love them. It doesn't mean that I want to live with them permanently, deal with them every day, make sacrifices of time and energy and money for them. You don't understand this, do you? You *chose* to have children. You *chose* to make those sacrifices. You didn't have another person's children foisted on you." I took a breath, realizing how ragged it felt. "Whatever I decide, at some point, it's going to be the wrong decision. I know that. There's no right way to do this."

At home, we switched on the television as if by common accord: it was clearly time to back off each other. "I met a woman today," I said, trying to find something else to talk about, "who's Herman Göring's daughter."

"Really?" Ivan frowned. "Which one was Göring?"

I didn't like saying it, but I didn't really know, myself. "Didn't he commit suicide?" I asked uncertainly.

Ivan reached behind the sofa for his tablet. "Wikipedia will know," he said. "Wikipedia knows everything."

"Wikipedia is sometimes wrong."

"Shh! The gods of the Web will hear you. If it's on the Internet, it *must* be true." He settled the tablet on his lap and typed. "Hermann Göring," he read aloud. "He was a German politician, military leader, and leading member of the Nazi Party. A veteran of World War One, an ace fighter pilot. Hey, he flew in the Red Baron's squadron!"

"Hey, watch out there, Snoopy," I said.

"Let's see . . . the second most powerful man in Germany. He founded the Gestapo but later handed it off to Heinrich Himmler when he became head of the air force. By 1940, he was at the peak of his power and influence. In 1941 Hitler designated him as his successor and deputy in all his offices."

I was wondering about the maid. He sounded like someone who would take whatever he wanted, consent or no. Had Gabrielle been the product of rape?

"Looks like once the war turned, things went downhill fast. Hitler blamed him for the Luftwaffe's failures, and when he heard that Hitler was going to commit suicide, Göring wrote to him and said *he* would then take command of the Reich." He glanced up. "Seems a stupid thing to say to a dictator."

"Suicidal," I agreed.

"Hitler called it treason and told people to arrest him, named someone else as successor, and then killed himself. Göring surrendered to the Americans after that, and was tried and found guilty at Nuremberg, but—hey, you're right, he committed suicide with cyanide before he could hang."

"I used to do pub quizzes," I offered by way of explanation.

"Not an altogether attractive person," said Ivan.

"No, I'd say creating the Gestapo and ordering the killings of millions isn't exactly going to make one the sexiest man of the year."

"I meant physically. Fat," said Ivan, who worked out every day.

"I wonder how he got the cyanide," I said.

Ivan shrugged. "Wow. Listen to the verdict," he said, and read it out loud. "Göring was often, indeed almost always, the moving force, second only to his leader. He was the leading war aggressor, both as political and as military leader; he was the director of the slave labor program and the creator of the oppressive program against the Jews and other races, at home and abroad. All of these crimes he has frankly admitted."

I didn't say anything for a moment. I was still wondering where he'd got the cyanide. My mind specializes in minutiae. Last summer, when Julian and I were trying to find out who had killed several women in Montréal, I'd obsessed on the cat that had belonged to one of the victims—the same cat who now went by the name of Bisou, had insinuated herself between Ivan and me, and was purring loudly. Sometimes minutiae is important.

It was to Bisou, anyway.

Probably someone had smuggled it in to him. Christ, Martine, I thought: you'd be terrible at this business of enacting magic, you can't even focus on a topic, much less visualize and call something into being.

Ivan was talking. "So his daughter—she lives in Montréal? Or was she visiting?"

I gaped at him. Right. My husband hadn't been traveling with me inside my head, contrary to what I sometimes assumed. "She lives here," I said. "He didn't know about her. Apparently he got a sixteen-year-old maid pregnant and she went home to have the baby."

"Tough situation," said Ivan with compassion. Tough indeed. Another tough situation with a child one hadn't planned on having come into one's life. Gabrielle's mother had done her best, but she'd given up something for the child. A marriage; other, legitimate children. Things she might have preferred. Things she might have dreamed of. And here I was, complaining because these two children might interrupt my life. . . .

Stop it. This is not even close to being a parallel situation.

But I wondered, all the same.

The phone rang shortly soon after that; it was Margery. "Listen, I know this is last-minute and all, but would it be okay for the kids and me to come up tomorrow? I can stay in a hotel if that's convenient."

"Let me put you on speakerphone," I said, gesturing to Ivan. "It's Margery. She wants to come up tomorrow with the kids."

Ivan frowned. "It's not really a good time," he said.

"I get that." Margery's voice sounded tinny out of the speaker. "But it's the only time I have, and I'd like to—well, at least see the place."

I could feel the longing in her voice. No matter what I was going through, Margery had to be hurting, too. You don't just make up your mind to move away from your children on a whim: whatever was driving her to Doctors Without Borders had to be pretty intense.

Ivan was talking. "Aren't the kids in school?"

"It's only a few days. They're both on top of their studies, you know that, Ivan. They don't even have to stay at your house if you don't want them to, I can take them to a hotel. It's just important that—"

I cut her off. "Don't be silly, Margery. Of course you should come, and of course you all should stay here. We have a guest room."

Ivan was looking at me like I'd suddenly started speaking Sanskrit. I made a silent palms-up gesture: *what can you do?* He cleared his throat. "We'll both be at work," he said. "The kids have keys. Just come in and make yourself at home."

"Really?" The relief was tangible. "I really appreciate this—Martine, thank you, thank you both."

"It'll be good to see you, Margery," I said. "Travel safely."

We disconnected. Ivan was still looking at me. "I didn't say I'd decided," I said, finally. "I just think she has a point. She needs to be able to shut her eyes and imagine where the kids are, what they're doing, where they hang out."

"Yes," said Ivan. "She does need all of those things." He was trying hard not to smile.

"Oh, stop it!" I said, and threw a cushion at him.

"Why don't," said Ivan carefully, "we go to bed?"

After that, it started feeling natural for Hans to spend time with Livia. Normal. They ate lunch together at the Hebrew Delicatessen; he walked her home from work several times a week; they went roller-skating and to more movies and to dinner.

It wasn't until Hans asked her to a Friday night dance that she told him. "Of course I can't, silly, it's Friday."

"Yes," said Hans. "I know it is Friday. That is when the dance is held, yes?"

She sighed. "I had a feeling you weren't practicing," she said. "I just had a feeling about you. Maybe you turned away from it when your family died." She looked sympathetic. "You know very well that Friday's Sabbath. Even though I live alone, I still keep the tradition. I have my mother's candlestick, and I light it at sundown." She smiled. "It's such an important gesture, isn't it? Doing the same thing with other Jews all over the world? Someday"—this with a quick glance at him upward through her lashes—"someday I'll have a family, and I'll say the Sabbath prayers with them."

They were sitting on a bench in the park, and Hans's arm was around her shoulders. He willed himself not to move it, not to betray himself. "Yes, of course," he heard himself saying, as though from a great distance.

Livia was still talking about traditions, but Hans wasn't listening anymore. How had he not known? It was the Hebrew Delicatessen, after all, it was Jewish food, and she—Livia, the embodiment of perfection—was a Jew, too.

He felt as if he couldn't breathe.

He'd been told all his life that Jews were filthy, conniving creatures, little better than vermin. He'd believed the stories about Jewish men raping innocent young Aryan girls, about Jews defrauding good

Germans, about their moral turpitude. He knew in his heart that these stories were true; they had to be.

And now this girl, this angel, this goddess, was telling him that she was a Jew. And assuming that he was one, too.

No. This couldn't be so.

Livia was still talking. ". . . and so of course I keep kosher as best I can, but it's not easy, in such a small space. That's why I eat at Bernie's so much." She paused. "And how I came to meet you. One of the happiest days of my life. You never told me, Hans, how you managed to escape."

"Escape?"

"From Holland, silly! We've heard terrible stories about what the Nazis do to Jews when they invade a country. You were so clever to get out before that happened to you, I thank God for that every day."

"Yes," he said, summoning breath and courage together. "Yes, it was difficult. But I decided on a new start in the New World."

She seemed to find that funny. "You have such a positive way of looking at things, Hans," she said, and snuggled closer to him. "That's one of the things I like so much about you. You never complain, no matter how bad things are."

"There's no sense in complaining," said Hans. What was he going to do now? He couldn't lose Livia, not now that he'd found her. And she had said that meeting him was one of the happiest days of her life, too! She loved him! It didn't really matter what she was: they were soul mates, that was all that mattered.

But what would Berlin say?

He didn't care. He couldn't care. As she lifted her face to his for a long kiss, Hans could feel his heart hammering wildly in his chest. He didn't even know if it was from fear—or exhilaration.

CHAPTER TWENTY-THREE

"I have an address," said Julian the next morning.

I peered at him over my shiny plastic menu. Chez Cora is a chain of breakfast-and-lunch joints throughout Canada that specializes in—well, just about everything. Cheerful in décor and waitstaff, the chain's food is decent and plentiful. And Julian apparently loves it here. "An address for what? Or whom?"

"I think I'll have the Cora's Special," he said.

"Your funeral," I responded, and when the waitress arrived I asked for the fruit plate. Julian stuck to his high-cholesterol choice. "And a bowl of café au lait," I added before she left. I was going to need more caffeine to keep up with Julian this morning: he seemed bursting with energy.

Which was a nice change.

"So what's the address?" I asked. "Or are you just playing with me?"

"I play not," he protested, but his eyes were twinkling. "Tell me, first, what you know about Saint-Jean-sur-Richelieu."

My stomach twisted. So that was where this was going. "I know about the hot-air balloon festival," I said. "That's really about all."

"It's a transportation hub," said Julian. "Railroads and the Chambly Canal."

"Fascinating," I said. "Any other tourist tidbits you'd like to share, or are you going to tell me what this is really about?" I knew what this was really about.

Julian said, "You know what this is really about."

"You found Aleister Brand."

He nodded. "I found Aleister Brand. And some other guys you probably wouldn't care to meet in a deserted alleyway on a dark night." He stopped as our *déjeuners* arrived, and waited until the server had left again. "And not all of them the people you'd think."

"What people would I think?" I sipped at the café au lait, my hands wrapped around the bowl for comfort.

He shrugged. "Well, skinheads, young angry guys. That's the stereotype, right? Don't get me wrong, they're there, and Mr. Brand himself isn't exactly a low-key figure. But it's not just them." He cleared his throat. "Do you know why Brand bought a place in Saint-Jean-sur-Richelieu?"

I shook my head. "His mother just said that he settled there when he got back from living overseas."

"Saint-Jean-sur-Richelieu," said Julian, "is home to the Area Support Unit of the Canadian Forces. That's where they do recruitment and officer training."

I put down the bowl and stared at him. "The *army* is involved?"

"Not as an entity. But some of them, yeah. Some of them hang with him." He shoveled some eggs into his mouth.

"Holy hell," I said. "This just keeps getting better and better."

"It's nothing new. There's always been this connection between the military and nontraditional religions. The Romans and their old mystery religions, Mithras and those guys, it's what built the empire. And everything you told me, all that stuff about directing energy, about absorbing power, well, that's pretty much right up the army's alley, isn't it? Who wouldn't want to use all the weapons they can lay their hands on?"

"The people in Hitler's lodges were mostly military men," I said slowly.

"There you go," said Julian comfortably, crunching his toast. "Have you talked to the local police?"

"Briefly," he said. "They thanked me and moved on. There was an army officer shot last week, it was on the news, remember? They're still looking to solve that one. I couldn't interest them in something dating back to the Second World War."

I sipped the coffee again. "What about the skinheads? Have the police had troubles with them in the past?"

"Not particularly," said Julian. "Model citizens, most of them. Your Aleister guy, he writes for the local rag, ghostwrote a book last year on the history of the military academy. Neighbors like him."

"Neighbors liked Paul Bernardo and Karla Homolka, too," I said, thinking of creepy people in history. "Probably liked Jack the Ripper."

"Let's not get carried away yet," Julian said. I'd never seen anyone eat like that, not even Ivan. Not even *Lukas*. "Brand hasn't killed anyone."

"That we know of," I said darkly.

"That we know of," he agreed. "So I thought, why not meet the guy?"

I stared at him. "You're going to go knock on his door and say, hello, we were wondering if we could get an invitation to your next satanic ritual?"

"That's what I like about you," said Julian. "You cut straight to the chase."

"You don't know what you're getting into, Julian," I objected. "These people—"

He waved a hand airily. "Oh, I know a lot about them. Neo-Nazis and skinheads, racists and the Aryan Nations and all sorts of off-shoots. I've been spending a lot of time getting acquainted with every racist homophobic misogynist thing that's ever crawled out from under a rock in this province." He shook his head. "I've been taking a lot of showers, too. We've been lucky here, actually, they don't seem to like the east coast. Out west, British Columbia and Saskatchewan and Alberta, those places, they've got it bad."

"Maybe they need space to practice in?"

He ignored my frivolity. "Don't get me wrong, Canada's got a far-right network. We're not on the level of the States yet, but we could get there. Depends on the economy: when it's bad, there's more of them, blaming it on everyone but the people who created it—ironically enough, white men."

He picked up his cup, took a swallow of coffee, set it down again. "You know about the Ku Klux Klan, right?"

"The KKK, sure. They're here?"

He nodded. "Out west. Not so much in Montréal, though nothing would surprise me." He smiled suddenly, vividly. "Know how they started?"

"I'm not sure I want to."

"Sure you do. You have to wait for me to finish my coffee, anyway."

"Tell me," I said, resigned. Julian loved telling stories.

"Right after the American Civil War ended, the South was defeated, and—wait for it—the economy crashed. Mass violence is always about the economy, one way or another."

"So what happened?"

"Well, small town in Tennessee, these six young bucks, just out of the Confederate army and looking for something to do. Lawyers, I think, most of them were. Bored out of their skulls. So Christmas Eve they decide to start a social club."

"A social club? Like the Knights of Columbus?"

"More like a secret society, but with the only goal being to have fun. All the fancy northern colleges had secret societies, why shouldn't they? They'd play pranks, wreak mild havoc, and have a good time of it. One of them wanted to call the group the Merry Six."

That was a long way from cross burning and lynching. "Sounds like Robin Hood."

"Ah, but there wasn't anything altruistic about this group," said Julian. "None of that taking from the rich to give to the poor. These guys were just about having fun. One of them knew a little Greek and thought they should call the group *kuklos*, which means circle, and someone else added the word clan. The name got a little massacred after a lot of bourbon, but eventually became Ku Klux Klan. All as a prank. And there you go."

I waited while he ate some more. "What about the white robes?"

"Well, see, that's the thing: this was all meant as a *joke*. They decided first to give each other titles, the more ridiculous, the better. The Grand Cyclops. The Grand Magi. The Grand Turk. They'd attract members and call them Ghouls."

"Hence the ghostly outfits," I said.

He nodded. "Right on. They put sheets over themselves, with masks and pointed hats, got on their horses, and rode through town one night, screeching and generally creating mayhem. Then back to the bourbon."

"I can see where that would be frightening, even if they didn't do anything really bad," I said.

"Depends on your definition of bad. The American South at the time was not a nice place to be. Too much fear—and fear always stokes violence."

"I thought the economy was what stoked violence."

"*Any* economy. The money economy, sure. But there's also the security economy—will you be able to live out your life the way you want to? Fear of losing what you have." He shook his head. "The Ku Klux Klan grew—there was a lot of unemployment and a lot of former soldiers, young men with anger and nothing to do. And slowly the founders' intent, to have fun and make mischief, got lost. The emancipation of slaves freaked them right out. So the organization started targeting black people and they went from threats to injury to lynching. And they grew and grew and grew. But it's ironic, isn't it, that it just started out as a boys' club?"

It was ironic that fear could be manipulated to the point they had. But hatred always did, I thought. Fear of the "other," fear of loss. Julian was right about that, anyway.

"Didn't happen right away," said Julian, signaling for the check. "They were formed in the 1800s down in the States, and they reached Montréal in 1921. They targeted Catholic institutions in Québec, burning them down. Then they headed west, burned Université de Saint-Boniface in Winnipeg, killed some students. And except for a little activity here around 1980, they've pretty much stayed in the west."

"So what do they have to do with Aleister Brand?"

"Nature," said Julian, "abhors a vacuum. So do people attracted to hate groups."

"So anyone here who would have otherwise joined the Klan—"

"—could well find themselves in sympathy with neo-Nazis. The hatred's the same. The fear's the same. The need for violence is the same."

I thought about it. "I don't know. From what Gabrielle said, I'm thinking that the violence is a little different here. That it's not violence for the sake of violence."

"What, then?"

"That it's used to transcend. That the cruelty is somehow necessary in order to get past normal accepted decent human boundaries." I remembered about chaos magic and how it decimated taboos.

"I don't know that people who want violence care about taboos."

"Brand cares," I said. "He may have recruited people who don't. If he did, then he'd have to indoctrinate them. This is sophisticated stuff, Julian. This isn't about galloping through a village wreaking havoc, or even stringing someone up from a tree. This is about concentrated evil."

"All the more reason to pay him a visit."

"And do what?" I asked again. "Walk up to his house, introduce ourselves? Hi, we think that you're doing something bad, and we'd like you to please stop it? Isn't that a bit more information than he needs about us?"

"If he's the magician you seem to think he is," said Julian, "then he already knows."

He'd been wrong about the escapes. There'd been quite a few, most of them successful, and all carried out by the same group of people.

They met in the cellar under the canteen.

Elias had been sensing an undercurrent ever since he'd been brought out of the quarantine of the Little Camp, a sense of some of the prisoners being closer than others, having some sort of shared secret. He ignored it, by and large: his plan was to do what he was supposed to do and stay alive. Some days, that alone felt like a tall order. The workshop, the daily report to the camp commandant, the hours spent standing still in the Appellplatz; they were all taking a toll on him. Elias had no interest in joining any groups, or factions, though he was well aware of their presence.

But if he'd been ignoring them, they weren't ignoring him.

He was awakened one night, a rough hand shaking his shoulder, a light shining in his eyes. "Come on, Kaspi."

"What? What is it?"

"Come with us."

It wasn't even all that secret, he thought as they marched him across the square; now that they were out in the blinding spotlights he recognized several of the kapos, the high-ranking prisoners, the ones who really ran the camp. No guards were in sight. "What have I done?"

"Shut up! Come on!"

Under the canteen the cellar was oddly cozy. A stovepipe extended from the chimney, and a wood-burning stove offered welcome warmth. There were chairs, and tables, and lamps hanging from the low ceiling.

About twenty men were in the room.

Elias was forced into a chair and the others grouped themselves around him. One of the kapos, a Russian called Vladimir, was directly facing him. "So, the Diamond Man," said Vladimir.

"Yes," said Elias nervously, his eyes darting around at the men. "I don't want any trouble."

"You hear that?" Vladimir demanded of the room. "He doesn't want any trouble!"

They laughed as though at a joke.

"No trouble, Diamond Man," said Vladimir, holding up his hand for them to stop. "No trouble. Do you know who we are?"

Elias shook his head.

"We're the ones who will liberate this camp someday," said Vladimir. "We're your comrades. Do you get it now?"

"Communists," Elias said. There was no secret of their presence in the camp; at least a third of the inmates were Communists. Some said the guards were afraid of them.

Vladimir nodded. "We're the resistance," he said. "We're the ones who make life better for you here, by not letting those sons of bitches get away with what they do in other camps. We're organized. We have a printing press. We have a wireless."

"Why are you telling me this?" It couldn't be good, he was thinking.

"Because you're one of us. You're a worker, like we are. You're exploited, like we are. And you can help us, Diamond Man."

"How?"

Vladimir nodded as if Elias had just confirmed something for him. "You meet with Commandant Koch every day," he said. "You are in his office. He trusts you."

"I don't think he trusts anybody."

"All right, all right. See that? Did you all hear that? I told you!" Vladimir cried to the other men. "Diamond Man is smart! All right, he does not trust you. But he needs you, and that is even better."

"What do you need me to do?" Elias asked.

He knew already that he would say yes.

CHAPTER TWENTY-FOUR

We deferred the trip out of town when Julian got a call from head-quarters. "Marcus has something to show me."

"I thought Marcus wanted you off the face of the earth."

"We cops," said Julian airily, "can separate out our personal feel-ings from our professional work."

"Uh-huh."

What Marcus had, in point of fact, was a slideshow. "You got me interested," he said to me, wheeling over to the table where the lap-top was connected to the projector. "So I did a little digging."

"Into what?"

"The New Order of the Black Sun."

I exchanged a quick glance with Julian. I was reasonably sure we hadn't talked to Marcus about that—in fact, I hadn't heard about it until Gabrielle told me about it, up on the mountain.

Marcus was still talking. "Very interesting, how they've man-aged to stay under the radar," he said. "We usually get wind of any activity . . . there's an echo. I'm a little like a spider, you see," he added, looking at me, winking as he shifted metaphors. "I sit here at the center of the web, and I can usually tell when something hits one of the lines I have out there—it sets up a vibration, you might say. And I feel it. I check into it. I look and see who might have been setting it up." He shrugged. "Didn't get a feel for this one right away."

"When did you first hear about the New Order of the Black Sun?" Julian asked.

Marcus got it, then. "Gabrielle Brand told me," he said easily. "She's one of my best contacts for the neo-Nazi world. Having had some experience of the former one, don't you know."

"But she didn't," I said. "Her father didn't even know she existed."

"Beside the point," Marcus replied. "Allow me to show you what I have." He turned on the projector and an image came up on the wall, a large imposing building with water behind it. "This is Aleister Brand's headquarters," Marcus said. "In—"

"—Saint-Jean-sur-Richelieu," Julian finished for him. "We're heading out there ourselves."

"Are you? Good, then." He touched the laptop and a new image appeared. "Photo taken last year, in Calgary, the center of Canada's neo-Nazi movement. That's not the term they use, by the way: they prefer to call themselves nationalists. Here's Aleister Brand with Kyle McKee, Calgary's leading nationalist. Look to be on friendly terms."

It was my first look at Gabrielle's son, and the contrast between the two men was stark. While McKee looked the stereotypical skinhead—dressed in black, covered in tattoos, his head shaved— Aleister Brand was wearing a button-down shirt and khakis. Kyle McKee looked like he belonged in the streets; Aleister Brand looked like he belonged in the boardroom.

Marcus had more images. A march in some large western city, could have been Calgary, could have been Edmonton, Aleister discreetly visible on the sidelines. A rally, with Aleister present but not on the podium: standing beside it. Then a photograph taken from behind, of an unidentifiable person wearing a cape. The stylized swastika of the Order of the Black Sun was front and center on the cape.

"When did you find these?" asked Julian. He was frowning.

"I collect them," said Marcus, turning off the projector light and wheeling around to face us. "You forget my job. I keep an eye out on all the right-wing groups in Canada."

"The spider image," I said helpfully.

"Indeed." Marcus's gaze was benevolent. Nothing to see here, folks, move along. "You would be surprised at what tidbits come my way."

"And yet," said Julian, "you didn't mention any of it the last time we were here."

Marcus was unfazed. "I thought it better for you to speak to Gabrielle first," he said blandly. "I wasn't positive there was even a connection to your—case." He made it sound questionable. "But I think that your researcher, Miss Mason, was onto Brand."

"Onto Brand in what way, exactly?" asked Julian.

"Well, it stands to reason that there was some connection," said Marcus. "He wanted the missing diamond; she had the missing diamond. The moment she had someone valuate it, people would start talking, he'd find out about it. Montréal's a small town in a great many ways, and no doubt Aleister Brand has his own sources of information."

"His own spiderweb," I suggested. Why was Marcus throwing Aleister at us? He couldn't be any clearer about accusing him of murder.

"As you say." He smiled. "I must do my investigations online, alas, as I find my lack of mobility to be an obstacle in getting around to question suspects. You have no such limitations." He beamed at us. "I wish you luck."

His door had no sooner closed behind us than I rounded on Julian. "And what was that about?"

He was jiggling keys and change in his pants pocket. "Not exactly subtle, was he?"

"He might have been clearer if he'd put watercress around the platter he's serving Aleister up on, but only a little," I said. "If he's so desperate about it, why didn't he tell us about Aleister before? Why wait?"

"Something changed," Julian said. It appeared to be his mantra. "Let's find out what."

I told Julian about Ivan and Margery and Claudia and Lukas on our way down to Saint-Jean-sur-Richelieu. "I feel like if I say yes, then a huge chunk of my life is going to get subsumed, and I don't know if I have the energy," I said, closing my eyes briefly as we passed a slower-moving car with inches to spare. "On the other hand, if I say no, then that pretty much makes me the Wicked Witch of the West. *And* I lose my marriage."

"Why?" He looked startled. "Ivan would leave you?"

We were advancing quite quickly on a stationary car and my right foot automatically sought the brake. Hard. Deep breath. "Yeah, he has to say yes. They're his kids. He loves them. The worst part of the divorce, for him, was losing the kids. Of course he wants them to live with him. And if I don't . . ." I let my voice trail off.

"I see," said Julian.

I glanced across at him, suddenly curious. He was probably about eight years younger than me, handsome in a way that comes from generations of good breeding and a whole lot of money. And he was, after all, one of the Westmount Fletchers. "Why aren't *you* married, Julian? Seems to me you'd be quite a catch."

He surprised me. "I was, once."

"Really? What happened?" I prepared myself for a tale of dramatic woe and expensive alimony.

"She died," he said shortly.

There was nothing constructive to say to that. "I'm so sorry, Julian," I said, inadequately, and he didn't answer. We crossed the Jacques-Cartier Bridge in silence. After a moment, Julian said, "Sorry. Didn't mean to be so abrupt."

"That's all right. It was my fault. I didn't mean to pry."

"You had a right," he said, and I could feel his shrug next to me. "So here it is. Her name was Elizabeth. She wanted to go to law school, but she wanted a baby first. Her mother was forty-two when Liz was born, and she always said she didn't want to be an old mother, too. So she got pregnant almost as soon as we were married."

"How old were you?"

He frowned at the road. "Where's— Oh, there's the turnoff." He negotiated the turn, managing to keep all four tires on the road. "I was twenty-one," he said. "She was a year older, twenty-two. Anyway, long story short, things went wrong, she had to have a caesarian long before the baby was due, and she died."

She died. No intruders in that thought; I didn't intrude. I let the silence go on for a few heartbeats before asking the question. "And your baby?"

"He lived for ten days," Julian said. "I spent all of them in the hospital with him. Ten days, ten nights." A pause. "So tiny, so incredibly tiny. In an incubator, you know, but I could touch him, they let me touch him. I sang to him, sometimes, when we were alone, during the night. Beatles songs, mostly. I don't know where those came from."

I shivered. I could see Julian, a younger version of Julian, wearing jeans and a cashmere pullover and perhaps awash in the realization that this was the first disaster his family's money and influence couldn't fix. Touching the tiny feet, the tiny hands. Singing in the night. "I'm sorry," I said inadequately.

"No problem," he said, his voice light. "I don't talk about it much. And haven't really seen the point, since then, of getting involved."

"Unless the woman's already married," I said.

"Yeah, there's that."

"Explains a lot."

Time to change the subject. We were driving along the Chambly Canal now, the water serene and unruffled. Trees here had burst into a brilliant symphony of color, reds and yellows and oranges, garish and gorgeous. "Is he dangerous, do you think?" I asked suddenly.

"Who?"

"Aleister."

"Dangerous in what way? Is he likely to whip out his grand-father's Luger and shoot us? I think not. Is he involved with Patricia Mason's murder? Quite possibly. Does he preside over satanic ritu-als? Who cares?"

"I think we should care."

"Why?"

"Don't you think," I said diffidently, "that there are things be-yond simple policing which make a difference?"

He glanced at me. "I have no idea what you're talking about."

"I mean," I said, trying to articulate something I was feeling intensely and didn't know how to communicate, "I mean that evil is at the root of criminal activity anyway, isn't it? So any time you have the opportunity to stop something evil . . ." I let my voice trail off.

He seemed to think about it. "Okay. I don't always even know the motives behind crimes, you know what I mean? Much less looking through those motives for something as abstract as evil." He braked at a stop sign. "I really need to get myself a GPS device," he said.

"But evil—"

He interrupted me. "I get what you're saying. And, sure, we see a lot of what you'd call evil. But it's not something you can define, or bottle, or do a blood test for. Lacking all that, I'm still after the motive, the opportunity, the weapon . . . you know, boring police business."

I felt like I was losing some sort of argument, and didn't even understand what it was supposed to be. "But if you could stop something evil before it manifested, wouldn't you want to do it? *Before* it became police business?"

"Then it wouldn't be police business." He glanced at me, exasperated. "I know what you're saying, Martine. But *thinking* something bad isn't against the law. I wish crime didn't exist, but at least once a crime has been committed, the right path is clear. You catch them, you take them to trial and, with a little luck, you punish them. For something they *did*, not something they *thought*."

"Magic rituals are more than a thought," I said.

"And they're not against the law." He scowled at the road. "That's the canal."

"But there's law, and then there's morality," I objected. "Would you kill Hitler if you could time travel and go back to his days in Vienna and shoot him before he ever got started? Of course you would."

"Moral dilemmas are, fortunately, out of my purview," said Julian. "Do I wish I could have done that? Sure. I'd take him out without a second thought. Does that mean it's legal? Not for one second."

I started to say something else, and he cut across my words. "Listen, Martine. We're not dealing with Hitler here. We're not dealing with hindsight here. We may just be looking at a bunch of socially inadequate people who get their identities through chanting and burning incense. Which isn't all that far off from *your* religious tradition, if I recall rightly."

"Catholic monks and nuns," I said tightly, "do not try to bring back the dead to wreak havoc on the world."

We rolled quietly up to the building we'd just seen at Marcus's office. It was clearly meant to be a warehouse, sitting right on the canal, probably for ease in offloading onto barges some of the textiles for which the city had once been famous. There was some faded paint high up on the wall that looked like a company name, but I couldn't make out the letters. No number on the side, of course. Doors closed, windows blank.

That didn't matter. As soon as I got out of the car it hit me: someone watching. I scanned the windows but couldn't see anyone there. "Someone's here," I told Julian.

He nodded, unconcerned. "That's the hope, isn't it?"

The door was rusted in places but had once been a rather cheery orange. There was no bell, no nameplate, no mail slot. And there was something about the door, about the whole building in fact, that reminded me somehow of a creaking old sailing vessel—or a freighter: that was it. An abandoned freighter left to haunt the seas, its crew mysteriously disappeared, its appearance a harbinger of misfortune. A ghost ship.

Well, we'd started with treasure ships. Perhaps we were coming full circle.

Julian, plagued by no such fantasies, pounded on the door and immediately pulled his hand away. "Fuck me!"

"What is it?"

"*You* try knocking. That thing is solid."

Before I could say anything, the door opened.

I don't know what I expected, really. Despite having seen him in casual khakis in the photos, the warehouse itself built up tension. Aleister Brand was anticlimactic in almost every way: he was about Julian's height, clean shaven, with blue eyes (of course) and brown hair that had just started to recede. "*Oui?*"

Julian said, in English, "Are you Aleister Brand?"

"Who is inquiring?" His voice was lightly accented but not, I thought, from French.

Julian pulled out his identification. "*Détective-lieutenant* Fletcher," he said.

The man looked at the ID and lifted his eyes to Julian's face, as though assuring himself that it was the same person. "From the Montréal police," he said. "How interesting. Are you not away from your jurisdiction here?"

"I am," said Julian, unruffled. "But I'm only here for a conversation." He paused. "For now."

"I see." He crossed his arms over his chest and leaned against the doorjamb. "A conversation about what?"

"Let's start with you," Julian suggested. "Are you Aleister Brand?"

The light eyes rested on him, briefly, then moved back to me. "I am," he agreed. "I have not yet met the young lady."

Odd way to refer to me, I thought. I was clearly older than Julian, probably close to Brand's own age. "I'm Martine LeDuc," I said, wondering why it felt as though I were handing him something precious, something significant, in giving him my name. "I work for the city, also."

"I see." There was a hint of amusement in his voice now. "And what would you like to talk about?"

"Can we come inside?" Julian asked.

"I think not. It's a lovely day, and there's no reason for me to invite you in."

Julian started to say something, but I interrupted. "I met your mother," I said, hoping to surprise him, catch him off guard.

Nothing. If I was rattling him at all, he hid it well. "Yes?" he said politely, as I'd paused.

"She told me that she worries about you."

A lift of the eyebrows. "And?"

"And I thought you might be concerned about her," I said, floundering. He wasn't giving me anything to work with here.

Julian asked, "Where were you last Thursday afternoon between two and six?"

Aleister transferred his gaze, lazily, to Julian. "My," he said. "That sounds like you're asking me for an alibi, detective."

"Something like that," Julian agreed.

"You know that I don't have to give you anything of the sort," he said pleasantly. "But because you have come all this way, I will. On Thursday I spent the afternoon and evening here at my home."

"And a cozy one," Julian commented, looking at the forbidding windows.

"Thank you."

Julian's eyes came back to Aleister. "Anyone confirm that?" he asked, almost conversationally.

"Any number of my friends," he said. "We were having a little— get-together, I think you'd call it."

"What would *you* call it?" I asked.

That limpid blue gaze again. "An evening with friends," he said.

"And you wouldn't mind supplying their names?" Julian had taken out his notebook. I could feel his discomfort. He wanted to be in the place, looking around. He wanted to find something he could sink his teeth into. Drugs lying out in the open. A stolen diamond in the center of a circle. A law being broken. Anything. I wanted to tell him to stop visualizing: if I could pick up on his thoughts, then what did he expect from Aleister Brand, celebrated mind reader?

"I would be very happy to supply you with my friends' names once I am legally compelled to do so," Aleister answered. "Other- wise, I think we shall respect their privacy. I don't believe that I have broken any laws, Detective." A flash of a glance my way, amuse- ment. "Accuse me of something if you'd like, or let me get back to my work."

"And what work would that be?"

"I am a journalist, Detective. As I'm sure my mother told

Mrs. LeDuc." He stepped back into the shadows and began to close the door.

"We'll be back," Julian said, clearly running out of things to say.

"I shall look forward to it." The door was partway closed. "Oh, and Martine?"

A sharp thrill of cold running down my spine at the casual use of my name. "What?"

"You can say yes to the children." And then it shut for good.

I turned to Julian, fear coursing through my body like adrenaline. "Did you hear that?"

"Come on, let's get out of here." He was already halfway to the TT.

"Julian, did you *hear* that?"

For someone who didn't believe in magic, he was moving very quickly. Already in the car. Already starting the engine. "Come on, Martine."

I slipped in beside him, my heart pounding. "He knows about Lukas and Claudia. How does he know about Lukas and Claudia? Are they in danger? Oh, my God, Julian. What have I done?"

"Nothing." We nosed our way out of the driveway. "You haven't done anything, Martine." He sounded irritable. "His mother may have called him, and he looked you up. Maybe he keeps files on people anyway. And he's obviously good at reading people; he saw your tells. That's all. There's no magic there."

I'm not married to a casino director for nothing. "I don't have tells," I said. I was lying to myself, of course. Everybody has tells.

"Everybody has tells," Julian said, unaware of echoing my thought. "Don't let him get under your skin, is all I'm saying."

I looked at him. "Seems like he got under yours."

He did look shaken, and I wasn't sure that I understood why. What else had he expected? For Aleister Brand to say, yes, you're right, I shot her? "Let's get something to eat," I said impulsively. It had been three hours since Chez Cora, so chances were good that

Julian would have his appetite back, and I needed to sit somewhere where I didn't feel my life was in danger. Julian's TT—with Julian driving—didn't qualify.

We were driving along the canal toward the highway and he abruptly turned in to a parking lot. "Okay," he said.

The restaurant had clearly just opened for lunch, but already there were tables occupied, a good sign in terms of the food. I didn't care; I was still trying to recover. Should I tell Ivan? Should I keep the kids away from Montréal until this business was sorted?

We were seated and I blinked at the menu. "This place is called Le Capitaine Pouf?"

"Apparently so." He was scanning the drinks offerings. "I need a beer."

"Or four," I agreed, and we put in those orders right away. Only French-speaking, I noted; Saint-Jean-sur-Richelieu didn't seem to have Montréal's tendency to bilingualism. "How did you come by the name?" I asked the server in French.

"A long story," she said, not unkindly. "What will you have to eat? Our specialty is fish and chips." We both ordered it, and she left.

The man at the table next to ours leaned over. "I can tell you about the name, if you wish," he said.

I was about to decline, politely, when Julian roused himself. "Yes, tell us," he said, and cut me a glance. Something going on here.

He seemed pleased to be asked. "It's a popular drinking game," he said. "Well, at least, popular among students. It goes like this. One person is chosen to be Capitaine Pouf. The others buy the drinks for as long as he plays without making a mistake."

Sounded like a deal to me.

He glanced around and, needing refreshment, took a swig of his own beer before resuming. "He is given a glass of beer, and says, '*Le capitaine Pouf prend sa première verre de la soirée.*'" I glanced at

Julian, but he seemed to have understood about the captain drinking the evening's first glass. Probably had played it many times himself.

"He grabs the glass between the thumb and forefinger of one hand, drinks the beer down in one draught, wipes the beer off his upper lip or moustache with one forefinger, once for the left side and once for the right, wipes the beer from that finger, once on his left knee and once on his right, gives one satisfied sigh (or belch, if he can), and raises his posterior from the chair once in order to fart (although he need not necessarily do so), the last action in the sequence supplying the 'pouf' part of the name."

It was an exhausting narrative; he had to refresh himself again. I thought that if I was doing any serious drinking I'd never remember all those rules. Julian, with a glance at the man's glass, signaled the server for a refill. "*Merci,*" our new friend said in acknowledgment. He wasn't finished. "Then the second glass of beer arrives. He repeats exactly the same sequence of actions, in exactly the same order, but this time he says, '*le capitaine Pouf prend sa deuxième verre de la soirée,*' grasps the glass with his thumb and two fingers, drinks the glass off in two draughts, wipes his lip twice on each side with two fingers, which he then wipes twice on each knee, belches and rises to fart twice. If he hasn't made a mistake, it's on to *la troisième verre*, three fingers, three gulps, and so on. As soon as he makes a mistake—any mistake—he is out, and it's somebody else's turn to be Capitaine Pouf." He looked at us with pleasure. "It's fun," he said.

"It's a great way to get free drinks if you have a capacity for beer," said Julian.

"That, too," he said as his new glass of beer arrived. "But," he added mournfully, "you really do have to be young."

"Apparently," I said. I was still unclear what we were doing here.

Our friend wasn't finished. He leaned in confidentially and I was quite sure he was ready to fulfill the belching part of the game. "The owner of the restaurant was once a real captain in the merchant marine," he informed us. "He dresses as a pirate with a three-cornered hat, eye patch, horizontally striped black-and-white shirt when he's on the premises."

"We'll watch for him," promised Julian, and the man nodded and returned to his lunch.

Somewhere in the narrative the fish had arrived, and everyone was right: it was amazing, crisply fried but tender and flaky inside. I didn't think I'd ever eaten anything that good. "What was that all about?" I asked Julian.

"What do you mean?"

"You're interested in stories about drinking games now?"

"I'm interested in giving my thoughts time to settle," he said, taking a long swallow of his beer.

"And have they?"

"I wasn't," he said, "taking your black magic stuff very seriously. I'm sorry, Martine, but like I said, for me it's all about facts."

"And now?"

"And now, I'm not so sure. He's the one."

"The one what? Who killed Patricia?" He didn't say anything, and I rushed on. "For God's sake, Julian, talk to me. He's behind the whole thing? He's dangerous?" Another pause and I reached across the table and put my hand on top of his. "Julian," I said urgently, "he knows about my children. Are they in danger?"

His eyes met mine. "To tell you the truth," Julian said, "I have no idea."

In the end, it wasn't that difficult after all. All he had to do was put the old images out of his mind, replace them with new ones. Jews were not snarling dogs, they were not rapacious old men, they were music and laughter and sunlight. If Livia was a Jew, then being a Jew was a wonderful thing.

And yet he still didn't tell her the truth about himself. She asked questions—the woman could ask questions!—but he was evasive, made up stories, told her about the life of someone who didn't exist. There was too much at stake. He had to remember who he worked for. He had to remember what could happen to him if he betrayed them.

And not just to him. Now, he had someone else to worry about.

"I do not pay attention to religion," he told her, and she laughed. "Sometime Bernie will take you to shul, you'll see," she predicted. "You'll end up the most observant of us all!"

He laughed it off with her, but he was becoming more and more fearful. They went everywhere together these days; he'd even moved rooming houses to be closer to her. What if someone saw him with her? He had no doubt but that there were other spies like him in the city; there was no reason to think otherwise. He could say it was for better cover of Hans the Dutchman, but the thought of answering those questions made him feel cold all over.

And then there was Maurice.

Hans continued to keep an eye on the police corporal, making sure that he was still indulging his wildly active libido, making sure that Maurice knew he knew. No one told him anything, but he knew that there was interest in what was in that vault he'd installed—two years ago, now?—under the Sun-Life Building. He knew that there was going to be more to the story.

He knew that he'd have another visit from New York.

One week, without having planned it at all, without meaning to say anything, he heard himself speaking: "Can I share Sabbath with you? I don't know how to do it anymore, but you can remind me."

Livia's eyes widened. "That," she said, "is the best thing in the world you could have asked!"

And that was the beginning.

CHAPTER TWENTY-FIVE

He was the one.

I knew it. Julian knew it. Gabrielle knew it. No doubt Aleister Brand himself knew it.

So what were we going to do about it?

We didn't say much of anything on the drive back to Montréal. The wind had picked up again and was whirling dead leaves all around us; late October weather. It was too early for that.

"How can we connect him?" I asked suddenly into the silence.

"Pardon me?"

"The New Order of the Black Sun," I said impatiently. "Aleister Brand's outfit. How are we going to connect them to the missing diamond? That's what you need to do, isn't it? To get your evidence? Find the diamond?"

"That would help," Julian conceded. He seemed to be oceans away from me, to be pulling himself back with some effort from some other foreign place. I wondered what he had been thinking.

"I mean," I went on doggedly, "at the end of the day it doesn't matter that he's related to Göring. And it doesn't matter, at some level, what kind of rituals he plans to preside over. What matters to you is that diamond."

"It would be helpful," Julian said carefully. "Whoever has the diamond is probably whoever killed Patricia."

"And you need something concrete so you can arrest him."

I could feel his glance in my direction, sharp and focused. "Why this sudden interest in his arrest?"

"Because," I said, "I don't really understand much, but I do know that he can't enact any rituals from the inside of a prison cell. And that's what matters to me, stopping him."

"Doesn't it matter to you that he killed her? Or that he ordered someone to kill her?"

I flipped my hand impatiently. "Of course it does. I'm only separating it out for your benefit. You're the one who doesn't want to talk about evil, you want to talk about crime. So I'm talking about crime. But it's all intertwined, all of it. The crime and the evil. The past and . . . what they want to do to the future."

"So if you're so sure that this famous ritual is about to take place, what do you plan to do about it?" He sounded impatient.

That was, of course, the million-dollar question. What could we do? How could we stop it? The New Order of the Black Sun had been planning it for . . . oh, for God only knew how long. Waiting for the right artifact to surface.

"We can't exactly stake out the warehouse," Julian was saying. "Even if it was within my jurisdiction, I couldn't do it. And you and me alone? Don't make me laugh. There's no way to keep him under surveillance."

"So there has to be another way to stop him," I said urgently.

"Listen, LeDuc, his own *mother* doesn't know how to stop him," he said. "She wouldn't have come to Marcus and you if she could handle it. She wants to just hang out with her grandkids and let you take care of defusing her Satanist spawn."

"What if she's right, Julian?"

"Is that what you believe?"

"I don't know what I believe," I said slowly. "I think there's a lot going on here that I can't begin to understand. That maybe nobody could understand." I took a deep breath. "But I'd feel a lot safer if we could disband this group. Stop whatever it is that they're planning. Arrest Aleister Brand."

"We're back to that. He has to break a law before we can arrest him," Julian said prosaically. "All right, he gives me the creeps, too. There's something about him, it's not even in what he said, it's in my gut reaction to him. It's bad, I'll grant you that. Maybe even what you're calling evil. But I still don't see what can be done."

We'd crossed the bridge and were back in the city now, everything gray and oddly austere. Gotham City, North. "I want him gone now," I said urgently. "If he's in prison, he can't hurt anyone." I took a deep breath. "I don't care about eventually," I said. "If he's in prison he can't get to my kids."

There was a long silence. "Well, well. Don't look now," said Julian finally, "but I think you just got your answer."

"About what?"

"Lukas and Claudia." He smiled, his eyes on the traffic ahead of us. "Anyone who's about to leave their father and cancel them out of her life isn't going to take on the devil for their well-being, is she?"

"It's not the devil," I said, but my heart wasn't in it. He was right. I had my answer.

Julian dropped me off at City Hall and I walked up the stairs to my office in a daze.

Chantal was frantic. "The mayor has called from Québec," she said, "twice. He wants to know what is going on around Mademoiselle Mason's death."

"He should call the police," I said. "They're the ones who investigate crime in this city." I knew how absurd that sounded the moment the words were out of my mouth. My boss would be well within his rights to chastise me for trying to do the police's job. Martine LeDuc, Amateur Crimefighter.

"And Richard has been dealing with the trade delegation from Japan. They're very upset."

"Richard's good at that," I said. "Chantal, did anyone named Gabrielle Brand call, by any chance?"

She looked doubtful. "No—I think not. It is not a name that I recognize."

"It would have been too much to hope for," I said, heading for my office.

"But wait," said Chantal. "Madame Maréchal called."

That stopped me in my tracks. "Élodie? From Ottawa? When?"

"Twice, also. First thing this morning, and again"—she checked her computer monitor—"about half an hour ago."

"*Merde,*" I said with feeling, and this time made it into my office. Closed the door. Took great breaths of air. It all seemed, suddenly, like too much. There were black clouds gathering in my heart.

I'd met Élodie Maréchal in graduate school. She was my closest friend back then; we went on the occasional vacation together, drank coffee daily, and told each other everything. For a while we shared an apartment up on the Plateau; I remember the old lady downstairs complaining that we were too clean, that we ran the vacuum cleaner every morning, and us laughing about it—it was our coffee-bean grinder she'd been hearing.

So much to remember . . . Late nights and long talks, borrowing each other's clothes, vetting each other's boyfriends. Drinking too much and giggling together on our way home from a club or a café, debating each other in political science classes, deciding in the middle of the semester that what we really wanted to do was emigrate to the Yukon and study caribou and to hell with humanity (that last one was usually accompanied by shots of brandy). Being the closest of friends, holding each other when a romance ended, lying for each other to cover a late night or a missed class. We'd been so close, once.

After we each got our degrees, though, we'd gone our separate ways: I to city government—or at least a reasonable facsimile thereof—in Montréal, Élodie to join the big cheeses, the feds, in Ottawa.

We'd both gotten married; I had an instant family with Lukas and Claudia while Élodie decided to have her child the old-fashioned way, with her husband taking time off for paternity leave while Élodie continued to work. I can't imagine him ever considering doing anything else: one simply doesn't say no to Élodie.

She worked for the Deputy Minister of National Defense. I'd never been sure exactly *what* it was that she did, but she had whole departments reporting to her at the National Defense headquarters in the Major-General George R. Pearkes Building on Colonel By Drive in Ottawa; even the names echoed with stiff military bearing. Élodie wasn't in the military herself but that didn't seem to matter much; she had the authority she deserved and didn't much care what people thought about her beyond that.

I'd had occasion, last year, to turn to her for help; had even made the drive to the capital to meet with her, and she'd responded in spades. We'd e-mailed from time to time since then, feeling mutual joy at the renewal of our friendship, however far apart we'd drifted; but Élodie never contacted me at work.

This couldn't be good news.

I buzzed Chantal. "Can you get Madame Maréchal on the phone for me?" I waited for the call to go through, looking out the window at the port and wondering why the sun seemed so bright.

Élodie didn't waste time. "What the hell have you been doing?"

"I'm well, thank you very much for asking, and how are you?"

An exasperated sigh. "I don't expect to see *your* name cross my desk, you know," she said.

"Believe me," I said fervently, "I didn't mean for it to."

"Okay." She was fiddling with something, some sort of wrapper. "Sorry. Nicotine gum."

"Does it help?"

"Not particularly. If they'd let us go on smoking in public buildings, I wouldn't need the damned stuff. Seriously, Martine, what's going on there?"

I swiveled my chair around to look at the view again. "How much do you know?" I asked.

"I've heard that we may have some bad news to break to our cousins across the pond. Report from the police in Montréal. That's enough to be going on with."

I sighed. "Tip of the iceberg, but it's probably the most important from your point of view, I suppose. The thing is, I don't even know if it's true. I mean, yeah, we found the diamonds with the remains of whoever stole them from the vault back during the Second World War."

"Dear God," whispered Élodie.

"And then probably Patricia Mason took one of the ones that were there, and then that one probably got stolen from her when she was shot. Presumably by whomever shot her."

"This just gets better and better."

"But the thing is, really, we're only going on her word, in a way. In the research she did, in what she says happened. It's entirely possible that those diamonds aren't actually from the crown jewels." Yeah, possible also that pigs will someday fly. I seriously doubted that Aleister Brand would waste time on paste. Or Marcus Levigne. I was starting to get a funny feeling about Marcus, too. "They've been authenticated locally. The police are handling that. But I think that Avner knew from the beginning that they would be."

"Avner?"

"Avner Kaspi. He's a diamond expert. Patricia—she's the researcher who started this whole thing, she's the one who stole one of the diamonds—"

"—which were already stolen—"

"Yeah, yeah," I said. "She took her diamond to him. To Avner."

"Why?"

I took a deep breath. "I think she found out about his past. Who he is." I passed a hand over my forehead. "Sorry. I'm explaining this poorly. Avner Kaspi says when his father was in a concentration camp early in the 1940s he was forced to create some artificial stones. Stones that are, apparently, just like ones in a certain crown, part of the cache of British jewels. That seems to be too much of a coincidence to not believe that something's going on."

"Yeah, I was afraid you were going to say something like that." A silence, stretching out taut between us, filled with unanswered questions. "Where are they now?"

"The two diamonds? The city police still have them. I can find out for sure." Julian would know. "The other one—well, we have an idea, but no proof."

"You mean the one that the Mason woman stole?"

"Right." A nagging thought was intruding. If the New Order of the Black Sun needed the diamond so desperately, why kill Patricia Mason at all? Why not just follow her and take it then? The police weren't officially involved until after she was shot, and certainly they didn't have the diamonds in custody until then. Wouldn't it have been easier to just follow her into the underground tunnels? Had one of them been doing that the day at the museum when Julian chased him off?

"Martine? Are you there?"

I snapped back to my office; my mind had been wandering down too many dark tunnels that all ended in despair. "I'm here, Élodie."

She seemed to sense my unease. "Okay. This is a big deal. I'm convinced. How about I fly out there tonight and take a look at the diamonds myself? I can talk to your expert, I can decide what to tell the people here who are asking the questions. Will that work?"

Gratitude washed over me. "Absolutely. Yes. Please."

I was feeling much more cheerful. Élodie, aside from being a good friend, was also one of the smartest women—no, people—I knew. And sensitive. If anyone could help me piece all of this together, she could. And she knew people in Montréal that even my boss didn't know. "Let me know your flight information, I'll meet you at the airport."

"I'll text it to you. Gotta get some things done here first." A pause. "Don't worry, we'll get it sorted."

I smiled. "I know we will. Thanks, Élodie."

"I'm not doing you a favor. This is a pretty big deal, no matter which way the pieces fall. It's going to end up involving more people, but I think that may be a little premature. Maybe we can figure something out together before it comes to that."

Maybe we could. I was smiling like an idiot. Aleister Brand had infected me with his darkness; Élodie was all light. We'd sort it, she'd said. Élodie did that kind of thing to you, made you believe.

The phone rang under my hand and I jumped. Deep breath, Martine, you're turning into a nervous wreck. "Martine LeDuc," I said crisply.

It was Julian. "Saddle up," he said grimly.

"Why?"

"Avner's gone missing. Slipped his police protection, so it's not your friend Brand after him this time. And I have a feeling I know where he went."

It had been three years since Elias had made the first imitations of the royal jewels, and he'd been working all this time, perfecting the technique, getting the sapphires to glow with the brilliant light of the gems he knew and loved.

And it had been one year since he'd started working with the Communist resistance movement in the camp.

"You have privileges," Vladimir told him. "You need to use them for the good of the many."

And so Elias had made dazzling stones for Ilse, the commandant's wife, to wear, putting the stones shyly on the commandant's desk and waiting to be invited to stay for a schnapps, which he almost always was. He pressed for more privileges for the inmates and, to his surprise, many were granted: the camp built a movie theater and a library, organized an art show.

The few Jews at Buchenwald were confined to Block 17, and Elias spoke for them as well. "We work as hard as all the others," he'd said. "We always get the last servings at meals, the last showers when there's no longer hot water." And the commandant acquiesced, because Elias kept bringing him stones, and Ilse became soft when he gave her jewelry.

He drew the line at the camp brothel, though. "No Jews can have sex with the German prostitutes," he said. "They'd have my head if I gave in to that one!"

The resistance was well-informed. It knew that the commandant was embezzling money from the prisoners' accounts and from the camp itself. It knew that the commandant's wife was sleeping with the guards.

And it knew, well ahead of time, when Hermann Göring was coming to visit.

Göring had been one of the architects of the camps, but had largely left the role of running them to Heinrich Himmler and the Shutz-staffel, who'd been in charge ever since. Himmler had visited Buchenwald more than once, and the prisoners had learned to stay well away from him when he visited, despite his tradition of ordering the release of one prisoner every time he came. If he was in a bad mood, bad things could happen. The Nazi policy may well have been to eschew wanton violence; it was possible that Himmler had not read the policy.

But Göring? No one knew what that was about.

CHAPTER TWENTY-SIX

The young officer was nearly incoherent with distress. "There was nothing out of the ordinary," he said. "Really, sir, there wasn't. The family does the same thing every day. They get up, they have breakfast, early—around six o'clock. Then the son leaves, and about five minutes later the subject leaves, to the synagogue. After that, to work, diamond shop on Sainte-Catherine. He comes back from work. Sometimes he goes to the synagogue again. Him and his wife have dinner together. Sometimes the son's there, sometimes not. Mostly he's in bed by nine."

Julian nodded. He wasn't going to offer any comfort; the kid had to learn. "So what happened?"

"He went into the synagogue this morning, like he always does," the officer said. "I don't go in after him, sir. I always wait outside. Watching the street, like." He drew a breath. "Seems disrespectful, somehow, to go in when they're all praying." He was one of the new politically correct cops, I thought. They'd been a long time coming. "So the prayer service breaks up and they come out. All men, always. Sometimes just a few, sometimes more, depends on the day."

"What about today?" asked Julian.

The cop consulted his notes. "Fourteen, sir. Sometimes they all come out together, that's when it's mostly old men, gray beards, some of them go down the street to the coffee shop afterward. When it's the younger ones, they're in a hurry to get away, they come out pretty much one at a time. I figure the older guys, they're retired, they have all day. The younger ones, they're fitting this in before going to work."

"Probably true," said Julian. "And Kaspi?"

"The subject went in at his usual time, sir, and I took up station outside as usual." Thankless job, I thought, but at least he had the weather on his side. Late September was still glorious . . . and comfortable for hanging out on street corners. "Today it was mostly old guys. Well, the subject's pretty old, too, he knows them all, but he still goes to work. Well, not *every* day, and not necessarily for long. I'd say he's semiretired. Sure t'be."

"Yes?" asked Julian. He was fast losing patience.

"So these other guys, they come out. Nice morning, sunshine, they stand out there in a clump and talk. Funny sort of language they have, not French or English, I never can really understand them."

"Yiddish," I said.

"And then I noticed that the subject wasn't there, wasn't chatting with them like he usually does. But I saw him go in. So I went over to them and asked if they knew where he'd gone, if they'd seen him after the prayer service."

I could well imagine that one, the young officer trying to interrupt the flow of words as politely as possible, the inquiring looks, the thoughtful shaking of the heads. If Avner had ducked out voluntarily, then these guys weren't going to give him up.

"I got nowhere, sir," the kid said, apology coloring his voice. "They all started talking at once, where they'd seen the subject, when they'd seen the subject, what he might be doing. At the end of it I just went into the synagogue myself."

That would have been interesting.

"I got inside the door, and—well, sir, I don't know anything about their traditions, do I?"

"I don't know," said Julian. "Do you?"

"I don't, but I thought that maybe I should take my shoes off," the boy said. "I mean, my brother, he goes to a mosque, they take their shoes off there. It's a sign of respect. So I took my shoes off, and I'm walking around, and this other old guy came up and asked me what I was doing, and I said I was looking for the subject, I was his police detail, there to protect him." It was boots the kid had taken off, and he'd probably felt awkward in his camouflage pants and socks. "He wanted me to put the shoes back on," he said. "He said it's not part of Jewish tradition. And so I said I was sorry, I said that I was trying to show respect, and he started talking about shoes and how maybe it really was a good idea to take off your shoes and how God told Moses to take off his shoes and perhaps Jews should try it but perhaps not because it really wasn't what they do traditionally."

He paused for breath and I glanced at his notebook. He'd actually written all that down. "So," he resumed, with a quick glance at Julian, "I said how I really needed to find the subject and he said, oh, you're looking for old Avner, are you, and I said yes, sir, I am, and he said he'd left right after something called minyan. I think that's what they call that prayer service, sir."

Julian was gritting his teeth.

"So I said, no, he couldn't, because I was outside all the time. And he said yes, you know, I, too, was surprised that he would use the kitchen door to leave, he hasn't ever left by the kitchen door in the thirty years he's been a member of the congregation. And then he asked me if I wanted to talk for a while, he was happy to talk with me if I was interested in the religion."

"Like I said," Julian turned to me, "Avner skipped out."

"He'd never gone that way before, sir."

"You couldn't watch both doors," I said soothingly. And probably the city police couldn't spare two officers, though that was mildly surprising: we take hate crimes very seriously here. The figured swastika on the envelope glowed in front of my eyes. "Where do you think he went?" I asked Julian.

"Report back to your unit," said Julian to the kid. "We'll let your commander know when we've found him."

"Yes, sir. I'm sorry, sir."

"Where do you think he went?" I asked again.

Julian turned to me. "I think," he said grimly, "that Avner is being seriously stupid. Come on." He paused. "Loïc?"

"Sir?"

"This is the rabbi's house, yeah?"

"Yes, sir."

"Okay, you can go."

The rabbi's house was far less imposing than the Kaspis' mansion; but I gathered that the rabbi himself made up for it. I was not unaware of him: not Hasidic, but radical in other ways, an ardent Zionist and intense anti-Nazi. Oddly enough, from what I'd read— and I do keep an eye on everyone in the city who has that kind of stature—he echoed some of the Nazi principles of racial purity, though his rants had to do with Jews keeping to their own communities. I'd always found that mildly ironic.

Naomi was inside the house, looking frightened. "They took him," she said, her voice accusing.

"Who took him?" asked Julian.

"Them! Whoever they are, sent us that swastika! Who do you

think? Nazis, there are Nazis everywhere!" She was biting her fingernails and I could see they were down to the quick. As she spoke, she paced restlessly, fast, back and forth in front of us.

Julian was unruffled. "Let's sit down, Mrs. Kaspi," he said gently. "Would you like a glass of water?"

"No. I do not want a glass of water. What I want is, my husband back, this is what I want."

"And that's what we're going to do." I could feel his impatience humming in the air, but his voice was slow, soothing. "Did he say anything to you before he left this morning?"

"Say anything? Why should my Avner say anything to me? Thirty-eight years we've been married, thirty-eight years he leaves every morning for shul, what should he say to me?"

Yeah, but this morning, he didn't come out. I managed not to share the thought.

"Okay," said Julian. "I'm going to have an officer come and stay with you, Mrs. Kaspi. Here's my card. If your husband contacts you, I want you to call me right away."

"So you can keep him thinking about murders and missing diamonds, when he has his family to think about, his business?"

"We want to keep him safe, Mrs. Kaspi, that's all."

She started pacing again before we'd even left the room. Julian didn't say anything until we were back in the car. "Avner," he said, "is unhappy with us."

"Why?"

A quick glance. "Not happy to be on the periphery of the investigation. He's been making Loïc crazy with questions."

"Loïc?"

"Officer in charge back there who lost him."

"Oh, right." I thought for a moment. We'd taken a left on Saint-Laurent and were starting to pick up downtown traffic. "He *must* be scared," I said. "He gets a credible death threat and gets assigned a kid to babysit him and has no idea how close or far we are from making him safe again."

"First of all," said Julian, "that kid is a crack shot. He's young, and maybe he's not too articulate, but he's good. We gave Avner the absolute best we had to offer. We're taking this very seriously. And you know that Marcus's been working round the clock."

"Marcus," I said. "We keep coming back to Marcus."

He leveled a glance at me. "What are you saying?"

"I don't know." I shrugged. "No, don't look at me like that. I still think it's Aleister Brand who killed Patricia, who took the diamond. I *think* so. But Marcus . . . there's something going on with Marcus."

"Brand's alibi checks out," Julian said, his voice neutral.

"So what is it you're saying now?" I demanded.

He shrugged. "Maybe we're not casting a wide enough net, is all," he said. "But, sure, his guys would give him an alibi in a second, so we're probably right."

"Marcus is in a wheelchair," I said.

"And he's a decorated police officer," Julian agreed.

I didn't like where this was going. "What about Avner?" I asked.

"Yeah," he said thoughtfully. "What about Avner?"

We pulled up and did what Ivan calls movie parking—that is, finding an empty space directly in front of wherever one is going—in front of the Notre-Dame-de-Bon-Secours chapel, part of the city's patrimony that we're always talking about. Or, at least, that my office is always talking about. The chapel, these days, houses a museum dedicated to Marguerite Bourgeoys, our own French missionary saint; but it's also long been known as the sailors' chapel where mariners expressed their thanks to Our Lady of Good Hope for seeing them through another perilous journey. She was Leonard Cohen's "lady of the harbor" in his song about Suzanne.

Julian was, surprisingly, heading into the church. "Where are you going?"

"Patricia wasn't the only one who knew her way around underground," he said cheerfully. "Come on, LeDuc. I want to show you something."

I followed.

He flipped his badge at the woman selling tickets and included me with a sweep of his arm, and I trailed obediently along in his wake. Part of this museum was underground, accessible through the crypt (of course), and the carefully placed lights threw dramatic shadows up over the roughly excavated walls, making it feel a little like a stage set. It's an ongoing archaeological site where the remains of Marguerite's first church can be seen as well as a First Nations settlement that dates back 2,400 years, one of the oldest in the city.

I informed Julian of all this. He seemed unimpressed. "Come on," he said impatiently.

Through a door hidden behind a statue. And down some stairs into a lower section still, with a dark archway gaping black. "Used to be one of the tributaries of the Little Saint-Marie River," he told me.

Another one of them. "You've been doing your homework."

"Turns out there's a veritable warren of tunnels crisscrossing the city," Julian said.

"I knew that," I said. "Not sure why *you* do."

He was opening a wooden storage crate bolted to the wall. "Put these on. It's wet down here." He pulled out some rubber boots, putting a pair on over his own expensive shoes. "I never really got it myself," he confessed. "All this digging around. Even all the urban exploration that you said Patricia was into. I know people who do it, sure, it's actually pretty hip, but it all seemed like a kid's pastime, and I had important things to think about. You know, this case, how to catch her killer, all that. But yesterday I got one of the city engineers to take me through the architectural drawings of the tunnels, the maps, and what's inside them . . . and, well, you can't help but get excited. This is the real city, Martine."

"You're feeling okay, right?" I took the massive flashlight he handed me.

"Of course I am." He moved his own flashlight around the tunnel entrance. "I never realized it, most people don't even think about what's under their feet unless they see repairs going on . . . but everything that makes the city actually run is underground. Everything's down here. The energy. The sewage. The ways that we connect with each other. The whole infrastructure is buzzing along under the streets and the buildings all the time and we don't know anything about it."

"Julian, what has this to do with—"

He reached for my hand and helped me up onto the lip of the passageway. "Come on," he said gently. "You'll see."

We dropped down a couple of levels—Julian jumped first and helped me down, I had no idea how we were going to get back up— and then we were in a stone-walled tunnel, this one higher and broader than the ones I'd traversed with Patricia. The thought of her, not so long ago, suddenly brought a lump to my throat. She should have written her dissertation, got the recognition she'd worked so hard for. She should still be living and breathing and . . . "How did Aleister know where she lived?" I asked suddenly.

Julian stopped and I bumped into his back. "What's that?"

"How did he find her? You said it yourself, the apartment isn't even in her name. For that matter, how did he know she had the diamond? How did he know she even existed?" Something skittered off to my right, something high up, and I swung around to look. Bats? *Really*?

"It wouldn't have been that difficult to find the apartment, all you'd need was a contact at McGill," said Julian. "One of his group could be there, could have contacts. Marcus isn't the only one who sees himself at the center of a spider web."

"And the diamond?"

"Secrets are never secrets," he responded. "Listen, back during the war, someone found out about the jewels, right? And then Patricia found out, she brought a stolen one to Avner; who knows who he told? That's juicy information to sit on. Aleister could have found out easily enough."

"Marcus knew," I said.

There was a silence, water dripping dramatically in the background. "Marcus is a cop," said Julian.

"Yes."

"Marcus is in a wheelchair."

"Yes."

"Marcus hasn't got a motive, damn it!" He was visibly upset; Marcus was, after all, a fellow officer.

"No," I conceded. "Probably not." But isn't greed one of the major motivators for murder? I thought I'd read that somewhere.

"I still think it's Brand. I think you really think so, too. Listen to me." He turned and his Maglite swept across me. "Whoever pulled the trigger on Patricia, that isn't the guy we want. The police'll find him, all right: they're actually very good at what they do. And when they do find him, what are they going to find? Some kid. Some skinhead kid who will say he did it as a rite of initiation into a skinhead club and will go off to prison and join the Aryan Nation there or some such group and sublimate his anger and hatred there. He's not the one who matters."

I stood still, waiting for it.

"You know who matters," Julian said. "They're getting the kid. If I have anything to say about it, *we're* taking down the New Order of the Black Sun."

"And Aleister Brand," I said.

"And Aleister Brand. In fact, most especially Aleister Brand."

"I wondered what was going on there," I confessed, "with all your talk about him not having broken any laws. It sounded like you weren't interested in going after him at all."

"We just," said Julian, "need to go after him in a different way. Now—is it okay for us to move on? It's cold down here."

He was right about that. It was a damp cold, the kind that we'd be experiencing soon enough on the surface, the kind that seeps into you and makes you feel that you'll never really be warm again. I pulled my light jacket closer around myself. "Where are we going?"

"Wait and see."

I was grateful for the cold and the damp, actually. Last year I'd spent some very tense moments underground, in the dry air of steam tunnels under an old asylum with someone who wished me very ill indeed, and it wasn't a feeling I was eager to get back anytime soon. I'd been suffering from mild claustrophobia ever since, and had been rather surprised I'd been able to tolerate my adventure with Patricia last week.

But this was different: damp, actually dripping in places, water inching down the walls, with a smell I couldn't identify but somehow—fancifully, no doubt—associated with the grave.

Well, and why not? For all of Julian's steampunk excitement about the inner workings of the city underground, these tunnels, the rooms they opened into or closed off, were no doubt the final resting place for hundreds of Montréalers, some marked, most unmarked.

I shivered and looked at Julian's rapidly retreating back. "Wait for me!"

Once Hans had decided what to do, there was no turning back.

He stood in Livia's cramped room with the table in front of him spread with fresh white linen, and watched her as she lit two candles and spoke words in a language he had never heard before.

She was curious about his lack of experience. "But surely, when you were small, your parents observed the shabbat! Your father must have taught you the prayer over the wine, over the challah?"

"I cannot remember," Hans said. "I think—so much of my childhood was filled with grief, there is much I cannot remember of it. I think I have forgotten everything that was important."

She took his hand. "Then I will help you," she said softly. "I will help you to remember."

Now, when he went alone to the Hebrew Delicatessen, Bernie was all smiles. "Well, you are a man of your word, I will say that for you."

"Why? What are you talking about?"

"Livia Rosen," he replied. "In all the years I have known her—and I have known her for many, many years!—I have never seen her happy like this. She is a new woman." He tossed the dishrag over his shoulder, planted his elbows on the counter, and leaned in to Hans. "So when is it you will be popping the question?"

"The question?" Hans looked at him blankly.

Bernie guffawed. "To marry her, of course! It is what people do when they are in love, no? So when is this going to happen?"

"There's a war on," Hans reminded him.

"There is always a war, somewhere. That is why you do it! You take your happiness while you can! You start your family!"

He was right, of course. If things had been different ... Hans slowed his thoughts down. Not if things had been different: if he had been different. Not a German soldier. Not a member of the Nazi Party. Not a spy.

"We will see," he told Bernie, put some coins on the counter, and left.

CHAPTER TWENTY-SEVEN

After that, the tunnels were, surprisingly, lighted. And, apparently, used: we passed large pieces of equipment whose use was mysterious, large looming metal artifacts that just increased the whole steampunk feeling. I almost expected a Dr. Who impersonator in a top hat to step out in front of us at any moment.

Julian had been here before: that was clear. He didn't hesitate, striding past forks in the way, large inviting passageways that were better lit and bigger than the one we were in. "What are these places?" I asked.

He glanced at me. "Was going to be part of the Métro system," he said. "Private company's exploring the option of running tours down here. You know, like the sewer tours of Paris. Could be pretty fantastic, actually, can you imagine? Rats and all . . ."

"Why don't I know about that?"

He grinned, suddenly, vividly. "Probably because I just made it up," he said. "But hell, it *would* be a great idea, wouldn't it?"

It would. Just not at this precise moment. I cleared my throat. "Part of the old Métro?"

"Following a river course," he said. "That's what all the under-ground network is about, anyway: they just dropped the waterways."

"Some of them are still running," I said, vaguely remembering Patricia's voice in the mayor's office, talking about the hidden un-derground metropolis, the one that shoppers and commuters in the interior city never saw. It felt like it had been months ago, not less than a week, that conversation. A sense of inexpressible sadness closed around me. "The waterways, I mean."

"A whole network, crisscrossing the city," Julian said. He hadn't lost his enthusiasm for his new urban exploration discoveries. "Waterways, sunken streets, even buildings down here. And all out of view. Every Montréaler thinks they know the underground, and they don't know anything."

"Don't get too smug," I said. "You'll trip over your ego. How do you know where you're going?"

"There's a map," he said, surprised. "Who knew? Some of it's a grid, like the Métro tunnels, and some of it just meanders, all criss-crossing each other at different levels, different depths, and not knowing that right behind a wall there's another set of tunnels."

"You sound like a kid at Christmas."

"It's extraordinary," he said. "Come on, it's this way."

I'd been feeling the gradient rising slowly beneath our feet as we walked, and now, after a left twist, it started going up sharply. Julian took it in stride. We're all good with hills; Montréal is, after all, a moun-tain itself, and the cyclists who crisscross the city daily, many of them on the rental bicycles available everywhere, have the best leg muscles around. But this was unexpected, and my calves were burning.

"You okay?"

"I'm wondering," I said, "whether I should join a gym."

He laughed. Damn him for having the breath to do it.

"Are we almost there?"

"You sound like one of your kids," he said. "Soon."

One of my kids.

"Patricia had these maps in her apartment," Julian was saying. "That's where I got the idea. She's apparently been down here a lot over the past six months. She was really careful, really organized. Worked out everything on a grid. Every time she learned something new, she marked the maps. I don't know where she learned that the jewels were down here, but she sure went looking for them."

I remembered the Google maps that she always left open on her computer, just in case. She had anticipated getting lost, getting trapped, getting delayed.

She hadn't considered getting *shot.* "Where are we?"

"Close to where you started," he said.

"Which is?"

He pointed. "About four hundred meters that way are the new excavations at the Pointe-à-Callière museum," he said. "We're going this way. Remember reading about the cave drawings at Lascaux?"

"Of course." Now closed because of the damage wreaked by pollution, the caves in southwest France were the beginning of humanity's obsession with art. "What—?"

"Wait," he said, his Maglite searching the wall. An indentation, the sort of semicircle where Catholics are always throwing statues of Mary or the Infant of Prague or something like that. "There it is."

"There what is?" Maybe I was starting to need glasses.

"Look," Julian said impatiently, drawing me closer. And then the image emerged from the darkness. The black sun. The stylized swastikas.

"They were here," I whispered.

"They were here," Julian agreed.

I took a deep breath. "What is it? A warning?"

"I don't know," he said. "He was down here looking, maybe he got the wrong coordinates, maybe he didn't realize that the vault was under the Exchange."

"Maybe Patricia had a gun to her head and told him the wrong place and he shot her anyway," I said.

Somehow, the tunnels were suddenly feeling a lot more scary.

Élodie arrived at Montréal-Trudeau Airport at seven o'clock.

I'd already called Ivan. "May be home late tonight," I said. "Élodie's coming in, I don't know whether she'll want to get to work tonight or not." I hesitated. "I'm sorry," I said. "I don't mean to leave you alone with Margery and the kids."

"It's not a problem." Ivan sounded cheerful. "I took off early from work, we're planning Margery's stay." Some noise from the background. "Everyone says hi," said Ivan.

"Tell them hi from me," I said faintly, an absurd picture forming in my mind of the four of them sitting around the table together. I had enough on my plate. I would *not* feel jealous.

"We're thinking of taking your Gray Line tour tomorrow," Ivan said. "I'll go along if I can get away from work. You want to come?"

"I wish I could." And in that moment I did. I wanted to go back to not knowing everything I knew, to not having met Patricia Mason, to be able to just deal with the usual headaches of my job and then go and spend time with my family. It was tempting. "I have too much to do right now, I'm afraid. But tell Margery I'll definitely take some time off before she leaves."

"Okay, babe." He paused as Claudia squealed in the background. "See you when I see you."

"See you when I see you," I echoed. All I wanted to do was go home. Instead, I got in the car and headed out to the airport.

Part of being a grown-up, I have learned, is doing the thing you're supposed to do when there's something else that you'd really *rather* be doing.

Élodie looked great. She's always looked smart, even when we were back in school together; but her authority gave her an edge that hadn't been there back in the day. Neat autumn-weight coat, her hair styled into a careful-casual knot, the scarf a brilliant blue at her throat. Glasses, I noticed, which I'd never seen her wear before. "Nice librarian look," I commented.

"Haven't you heard? Librarians are the new *in* thing," she said, kissing my cheeks. "You look tired."

"You mean I look old. When people say you look tired, they mean you look old."

She looked at me sharply. "Where did that come from? Are you all right?"

"Not particularly," I said. "Do you have luggage?"

She hefted the carry-on slung across her shoulder. "Traveling light. I have a reservation at the Queen Elizabeth."

"You could have stayed with me," I complained, then remembered that the guest room was taken. Well, there was always the couch.

"Sounds like you have enough on your plate," she said, reading my mind. "Speaking of which, let's get something to eat. We need to talk."

"We can eat at your hotel," I said. She knew that; Élodie always stayed at the Fairmount Queen Elizabeth when she came to Montréal, and she nearly always ate there, at the Le Montréalais Bistrot-Bar, for dinner, brunch, afternoon tea . . . not a great one for exploring, Élodie.

"Good," she said, as though just learning of the restaurant's existence. She wasn't wasting any time, though. As soon as we were in the car, she turned to me. "Update," she said.

"Avner Kaspi's disappeared," I said, my eyes on the lights of the traffic around us. "We don't know where he is, or why he slipped his police guard, but I don't think it can be good." I took a breath, braking at a red light. "The diamond that Patricia stole still hasn't surfaced. I guess the police are waiting to hear from your people about what to do with the other two."

"They've been authenticated? You were going to check on that."

I nodded, switching into first gear and moving through the intersection. Richard had been following that process for me, being careful to keep anything he learned just between us. Our boss, up at his conference in Québec, was happy with the bland noninformative e-mails Richard sent him. "And before you ask, yeah, sworn to secrecy."

But how secret could it really be? Like the existence of the treasure ships themselves: the more people knew, the more potential there was for the information spreading, getting into the wrong hands.

Not that it wasn't there already.

Élodie sighed. "What a mess," she said.

"More than a mess," I said with some asperity. "One person's been threatened and is missing, another's dead. That's a little more than just an international kerfuffle."

I could feel her eyes on me. "You're taking this personally," she said, her voice neutral.

"Yes," I agreed. "I totally am."

"Hmm." She settled back in her seat after that and contented herself with watching the city go past. We pulled up in front of the hotel and I let the valet take the car; I wasn't in the mood to look for a parking place. "Go check in, Élodie. I'll meet you in the restaurant."

I hadn't realized how tired I was until I got to the restaurant and sat down and tried to relax. A waiter materialized and I ordered a cocktail. I was halfway through it when Élodie joined me, her coat gone, her blue dress a statement against the restaurant's beige-and-brown color scheme. "Drinking already, I see."

"That kind of day," I said.

She'd already spoken to the waiter on her way in; Élodie doesn't waste time. Now he delivered her gin and tonic. "*Voilà, madame.* Would *mesdames* like me to tell you about today's additions to the menu?"

"Not yet." She waved imperiously and he disappeared quickly; the staff here was used to visitors behaving in all sorts of different bizarre manners. She took a gulp of the g-and-t and then commanded, "Tell me who's worrying you. And don't say there's nobody: I know you too well for that."

She did, too. "His name is Aleister Brand. He lives down in Saint-Jean-sur-Richelieu, in this old warehouse. He's some kind of journalist." Deep breath. "And he's a neo-Nazi. I met his mother a couple of days ago, and she's concerned that he may be using some kind of dark magic to—to cause things to happen. I know that's vague, but it all really does come back to the crown jewels. Eventually, anyway." I took a sip of my own drink. "Brand is Göring's grandson—you know, Göring, Hitler's right-hand man?—and he's convinced that he's got this special blood in him, that his heritage is a sign somehow."

The waiter approached the table again and Élodie put up her hand to wave him off without looking at him, as though he were a recalcitrant sheepdog. "How do the jewels fit in? With this guy Brand, I mean?"

"There's this current of thought that they possess a certain energy," I said. "I got that from his mother. She believes that after centuries of connection to royalty, of being the symbol of royalty, there's power in them."

To my surprise, Élodie nodded. "That makes sense," she said.

"It does? It didn't make sense to me."

"Why shouldn't there be? There are places that are haunted, aren't there? If that kind of energy can inhabit a place, why couldn't it inhabit an object?"

I was staring at her. This wasn't my prosaic and practical friend speaking. "What are you talking about?"

"Okay. I've been reading since we last spoke." She sighed. "Apparently, energy doesn't dissipate, not when it's been built up through time, or intensity, or both," she said. "Look: it's a documented fact that churches are traditionally built on top of earlier, pagan centers, to provide continuity, to tap into the holiness of the place. You've heard of ley lines, haven't you?"

She was speaking in a language that wasn't part of my repertoire. "What are ley lines?"

"Back in the 1920s, somebody in England noticed there were these lines that crisscrossed parts of the country, and that they connected locations that were significant. He said you could draw a straight line between, say, a church and a circle of standing stones and a spring, that sort of thing: that these holy places were all in alignment with each other. This is going back to the Iron Age, mind: the Christian churches came later and just insinuated themselves into the landscape that had already been marked by the lines."

I was staring at Élodie, but all I was seeing was Julian's map, the grid of crisscrossing tunnels and waterways underneath the city. A power network. Ley lines.

She took a sip of her cocktail. "No one knows what the leys were used for, but of course there are theories, everything from the scholarly to the crackpot. They may have been spirit paths, letting the dead travel through the countryside. Or fairies. Or something."

"How on earth do you know this?" I asked.

She looked surprised. "James," she said.

"Your *husband*?"

"Well, yeah. He thinks the concept of ley lines is rubbish, of course, but really it's not whether it's true or not that's the issue, it's if people believe it to be true."

I was still a beat behind. "James works for the government," I said. "What does that have to do with this?"

"It's not his *job*," she said, impatient. "It's his *brother*. Don't you remember? James spends enough of his life rescuing Philip one way or another that it sometimes feels like we've got a social services office in our house." She paused. "Philip lives in England, in Glastonbury—where the music festival is?—and that's supposedly Power Central when it comes to ley lines and site energy, and Philip is way into it, as you can imagine."

I'd met Philip only once, but he'd been wearing a black cape fastened at the shoulder with a large dragon brooch. Not an image you were likely to forget anytime soon. Yeah, I could imagine.

"So anyway, I know about all this, because it's all he ever talks about. Earth energies and fairy paths and sacred springs. And who's to say that some of it isn't real? I mean, if you have a lot of people in one place believing the same thing, really passionately believing it, I guess that something can happen. Just because we don't understand it doesn't mean that it doesn't exist. Some people think of it as magic. Some people think that it's just because we haven't developed the knowledge to understand the science of it yet."

"But there aren't ley lines here," I said. "We're talking about jewels, not Stonehenge."

She stared at me. "You're kidding, right? We're practically sitting on one of the most significant ley lines in North America. It's the Trois-Rivières line. And there's a network of smaller leys connecting various sites in Montréal itself. I can't remember them all, but I know that one goes from the oratory down through a couple of small churches and hits the basilica, and there's another that intersects with Pointe-à-Callières."

All roads—or ley lines—seemed to connect back to Pointe-à-Callières. It was where Patricia had done much of her research, and it was the director who'd made her go to the mayor in the first place.

I remembered him sitting in Jean-Luc's office, his bland approval of the project.

The power grid, in many more ways than one, holding the city together. The tunnels followed the waterways and the waterways followed the leys; the network was one and the same. "Oh, *merde*," I said suddenly.

"What is it?"

"Saint-Jean-sur-Richelieu," I said with some desperation. "Is it on a line?"

The camp commandant was terrified.

He had reason to be, of course. Anyone who wasn't afraid of Reichsmarschall Hermann Göring was a fool, and probably a dead one at that. And there was no reason for him to come to Buchenwald.

Ilse, his wife, was frightened, too, but she showed it in different ways. She worked the horses in her private indoor ring harder than ever, and then ordered prisoners—randomly, it seemed to her husband—to be strung up from the trees.

Elias stayed in his workshop. This was not the time for baubles for Ilse, or for schnapps with the commandant. This was the time to be very, very quiet. Göring was less anti-Semitic than most of the others, but that meant nothing: like Ilse's, his spurts of anger and cruelty could be random, and no one wanted to be in his path when that happened.

As it turned out, Elias had no choice. Early afternoon a kapo— not one of the resistance men—came for him. "Commandant's office," he said, jerking his head toward the door. "Now."

"Me? What does he want with me?"

"Did I say you could speak? Move quickly, or I'll see that you can't move at all!"

Elias stumbled up and out, trotting across the square to the gatehouse, staying as far ahead of the kapo's baton as he could. He'd only ever seen the Reichsmarschall in photographs, but there was

no mistaking him, portly and self-satisfied and downing the commandant's schnapps at an impressive clip. "This is the man?"

"Yes, Herr Reichsmarschall," said Karl. "He has been creating
beautiful things here. We can show you a selection—"

Göring waved the suggestion away. "You know which pieces I need,"
he said, still looking at Elias with something not unlike curiosity.

"Of course, Herr Reichsmarschall. They're here, in the safe."

Elias watched as the commandant fumbled with the combination,
twice, before finally getting it right. He moved quickly to shield the
view of the interior, and Elias remembered the camp gossip about him
lining his pockets. He brought out a case; inside, carefully wrapped in
cloth, were the stones, the ones crafted to look like the small tiara, part
of the British royal jewels.

Göring looked at them. He brought out a jeweler's loupe and ex-
amined them. He ran his chubby hands over them. And, finally, he
looked up and smiled.

"You are to be congratulated," he said to Elias. "What they all say
about you is true."

What they all said about him? Elias looked at the camp commandant, but Karl was busy avoiding his eyes. "You may speak," Göring
said, his voice encouraging.

"Thank you," Elias said. What did the man expect of him? "It is
about the cut. If you cut stones correctly, they are—beautiful." He
didn't know what else to say.

Karl waved a hand. "You may go," he said.

Behind him, Elias heard the two men talking. "I will take these to
Berlin at once."

"Yes, Herr Reichsmarschall."

"Good. The Führer will be pleased."

"It is all I ask, Herr Reichsmarschall."

CHAPTER TWENTY-EIGHT

By the time the conversation got around to the political issues involved, I realized that I was becoming increasingly and thoroughly frightened. I only half believed all the information I seemed to be amassing, but as Élodie said, perhaps it didn't really matter what was real and what wasn't. The energy of belief was what was important.

Élodie had her mind on other things. She solved problems. Ancient secrets or New Age concerns were interesting to her, but only for a while. Over a dinner that I did little but move around on my plate, she came back to her own dilemma. "I'm not convinced that the best route is to tell London," she said.

"Let them keep the paste? Sort of like, let them eat cake?"

She smiled. "Must be damned good paste, to have fooled people for this long."

Damned good paste, I thought. Crystal forgeries hammered in the dark distillery of a death-camp workshop. "Shouldn't you wait until we have them all, anyway?" I asked. "Julian's determined to find the missing diamond."

"Possibly." She thought for a moment, swirling her wine around in its glass. "I know somebody at MI6," she said suddenly. "Spies are usually the best bet for moving information. And they work for the Home Office, that's pretty much where we'd have to start anyway."

I was staring at the fish on my plate. It was really good halibut, but tonight it tasted like cardboard. "Fine," I muttered. "*D'accord.*"

"It's important to get this right, Martine."

I looked at her. "You don't think I know that?" I took a deep breath, ticking items off on my fingers. "We have Aleister Brand who wants, at the very least, to resurrect the Nazi Party. We have Patricia Mason, who finds missing crown jewels and keeps one and shows it to Avner Kaspi, and now she's dead and he's missing. We have a police captain who spends his time tracking down neo-Nazis but is more interested in the missing diamond than he should be. I have an interesting family situation where I should be centering my attention, not to mention on my *job*, and instead I have to figure out if Aleister Brand really did kill Patricia and take the diamond and is planning to use it for black magic, which if you're right could work because so many people believe it will *and* it's happening on one of the most powerful ley lines in North America. Do you really think I don't want to get this right?"

"Martine," she said, "think about it. You have these guys—they're all guys, right? Aleister Brand's mates?"

I nodded. "I think so."

"Okay. Young, testosterone-driven, neo-Nazis, probably full of anger and resentment that they're not rich and famous. You get a charismatic leader to step in and he shows them a few magic tricks and *pouf!* you've got a circle. Probably need about nine or ten, right?"

Nine or ten. Just like the minyan. We still had to find Avner. "Right," I said.

"Okay. And let's say for the sake of argument that it all works just right. That the place—you said it was a warehouse, right?—is right on the ley line. That they have the diamond, and it's retained its power separated from the other jewels, which isn't even necessarily a given, but for the sake of argument again, let's say it does. And let's say that they have the wherewithal to focus the kind of energy this would take. Let's say that it all comes together and that it works. What happens then?"

"What do you mean?"

She sighed. "Adolf Hitler in Montréal. What's he going to do, Martine? Find another beer hall? We're not even in the same century anymore."

Julian, I thought, had asked almost exactly the same thing, but I was getting irritated. "You think it couldn't happen again? You haven't seen a drift toward the right everywhere—in the U.S., in Europe, here in Canada? *Merde*, Élodie, you work in Ottawa, you know what's happening. We're about eighteen goose steps to the right of center, and marching merrily along toward fascism, everyone's doing it, and yeah, I think it could happen again. The middle class is disappearing, the poor are starving, literally, and if that isn't the best possible backdrop for someone to come along and rally them behind a swastika, I don't know what is."

I stopped and took a deep breath, held it, released it. Calm down, Martine. "I don't know what it would look like, Élodie. I don't know if he'd get summoned and be a little man with a Chaplin mustache . . . or be a nice white conservative member of parliament. I don't have to know the specifics to know that we *can't let it happen*." I sighed. "I think I have to talk with his mother again. And maybe with Marcus Levigne."

"Who's that?"

"Captain with the city police. And he—Oh, I don't know, maybe I'm just tired, but I'm getting a feeling about him, Élodie. I think he's involved in this somewhere, and not in a good way. But for now—he's an expert on hate groups, especially neo-Nazis." I thought for a moment. "He's the one, actually, who sent me to talk to Gabrielle Brand in the first place."

"Your magician's mother."

"Not *my* magician," I said. "But yeah, that's Gabrielle. Marcus gave me her name."

"Sounds helpful," Élodie said, her voice distracted. She wasn't with me anymore: she was already thinking about what to say to her contact in London. You didn't have to be a mind reader to deduce that.

"We'll see," I said. "What's your plan now?"

"I'll call Jeremy tonight," she said, glancing at her watch. "Wake him up. See what he says. I'd like to meet with the police tomorrow and see where they are with recovering that diamond."

Probably not very far at all, I thought, but I didn't say it. "You can talk to Julian," I said. "He's more likely to tell you what's really going on than the higher-ups are."

"Courtesy call," she said absently. "I can't be in town and not see them. But, yeah, let me talk to Julian, too." The waiter reappeared, and Élodie signed the check with her room number. "You haven't talked about Ivan," she reminded me when the waiter was gone.

I sighed. "Margery—Ivan's ex—wants to go work abroad with Doctors Without Borders. She's really amazingly brave, ready to confront Ebola, anything. And that's great, that's impressive—but it means the kids moving in with us. Full-time. Maybe even permanently."

"I see." She looked at me thoughtfully.

"I know what I'll say. I just need to be able to say it—wholeheartedly, you know? I'm still digesting the idea, all the changes it means." I paused. "They're in town now, actually. The kids wanted to show Margery around Montréal."

She lifted her eyebrows. "Now?"

"She didn't know I'd be investigating a murder," I said, trying for humor and not coming even close to bringing it off. "Well, one problem at a time." I stood up and she followed, slowly, reluctantly. "I'll call you in the morning, let you know when Julian's free," I said. We did the usual kissing of each cheek, and then, on impulse, I hugged her. "Thanks, Élodie."

I came home to the smell of popcorn and the sounds of an uproarious game of Pictionary taking place on the living room floor.

Lukas saw me first. "Belle-Maman!" He scrambled to his feet and ran to hug me. "Mom and I are winning!"

"Good for you," I said. "Hey, Margery."

She, too, had stood up. Claudia already looks just like her mother: wavy blond hair, perfectly symmetrical face, Margery could have stepped out of the pages of *Vogue*. I always felt a trifle unkempt around her. We hugged, a little awkwardly, and I bent over to kiss Ivan. "Good game?"

"Mom and Lukas cheat," Claudia informed me.

"Then cheat right back at them," I said cheerfully, wondering what to do next. Pictionary doesn't allow for a fifth player, and anyway, the truth was, I was exhausted.

Ivan said, "Why don't we call it a draw for now, since Belle-Maman's home?"

Lukas howled in protest. "No, don't," I said quickly. "Listen, I've had a really tiring day, and all I can think of is a hot bath and bed. You guys finish your game. Margery, I'm sorry, would you mind terribly?"

"Of course not," she said. Our eyes met over Claudia's head and she acknowledged what I was doing with a grateful smile. "We can catch up tomorrow."

"Absolutely," I said.

I didn't even make it to the bath. I looked up a couple of things on the laptop, dutifully, still not really believing everything Élodie had said. Then, halfway through undressing, I leaned back into the bed, and that was, as they say, all she wrote.

Ivan and Lukas were already in the kitchen when I woke up—late—and wandered in sleepily in search of coffee. Ivan was sitting at the table with his tablet in front of him, consuming the morning news along with his croissants and orange juice, and Lukas was enthusiastically scribbling in his notebook. "Belle-Maman! We're taking a bus tour today!"

"So I heard," I said, kissing first Ivan and then the top of Lukas's head, which was pretty much all he allowed me. "It's a great tour; you're going to love it."

"*We* already know all about Montréal," he said. "It's for Mom's benefit, really."

"I see." I exchanged smiles with Ivan and sat down. "Good heavens, these are warm!"

"We got them specially this morning," Lukas informed me. "It was on my schedule." He turned the notebook to face me.

"I see that it was. No, thanks, just coffee first." I reached for the French press and poured. "Is everybody else still asleep?"

"Not a chance," said Ivan. "They're already out and about. There was a great deal of talk about dresses and jewelry. They're going to meet us at one for the tour." He glanced up. "Margery says she's sorry to miss you, but we'll all have dinner tonight."

"Of course," I agreed.

"We're going, too," said Lukas. "Dad's taking me to work with him."

"Just for two hours," said Ivan. He grimaced. "Couldn't get out of it," he said to me.

"Lukas is going to become a cardsharp before he's twenty," I said.

"Yes, I am!" He was delighted for a split second, then, "Belle-Maman, what's a cardsharp?"

I made my way through a second cup of coffee and watched them gather themselves and get out the door. It took two this morning to clear the cobwebs: the bad dreams I'd had were still clinging stubbornly to my brain.

Finally I called Julian. "Élodie Maréchal's in town," I told him.

"So Ottawa's going sub rosa," he said, and whistled. "They'd have sent the deputy prime minister if they were going to go public."

"At least for now," I agreed. "She knows someone in MI6, she's doing all those cool spy things and getting in touch with him."

"Cool spy things? Like what, decoder rings?"

"And invisible writing, no doubt," I said. "She wants to know where things stand with the diamonds."

"Wouldn't we all," he said. "Mum's the word, and that's straight down from the rarefied air of the upper echelons. Rumor is the feds want to get involved, and the border people, and we're bracing for an all-out turf war."

"As opposed to doing any actual, you know, policing?"

"Yeah, something like that."

"And Avner? Any news on him?"

"Well, funny you should ask that. I think Avner's doing a little sleuthing of his own."

"Oh?" I reached across the table and picked up Ivan's unfinished croissant, balanced my smartphone while I buttered it and took a bite.

"Had a word with his son Lev last night," Julian said.

"Lev, the one who needs to find a nice Jewish girl and settle down?"

"The very same. And I checked up on him, too. It seems that Lev might not be what we'd call a model citizen."

"Oh really."

"Oh really indeed. A whiz with computers, apparently, I'll grant him that, but he gets bored easily and likes to go places he's not supposed to go. Online, I mean."

"A hacker," I said.

"A hacker," he agreed. "He knew Patricia, by the way. In fact, he's the reason she got started with all this. He hacked into the museum's archives. Digitized archives."

"Well, yeah, of course they're digitized, it's a computer—" I stopped myself. "Digitized? As in, old records digitized?"

"The very same. And we've got paperwork about the gold, and paperwork about the jewels. The whole treasure-ship manifest. He passed on all that info, and I'd guess told her about his father being a diamond expert. Maybe even told her about the diamond substitutions—that's my guess, anyway. He must have liked her."

"Pity she wasn't a nice Jewish girl." I sat and thought about it for a moment, eating the croissant without thinking about it, without tasting anything.

"Well, there's that and then there's that matter of being dead, not exactly Avner's dream daughter-in-law."

"Funny man. What did Lev tell his father?"

"Apparently the captain isn't the only one to know about the New Order of the Black Sun," Julian said.

"Christ, Julian!" I jumped up, sending my chair spinning away. "He's gone to Saint-Jean-sur-Richelieu!"

"That would be my guess, too."

"They'll kill him! Julian!"

"If they haven't already, they're probably not going to. Yet, anyway. And stop panicking, I've got some people out there, watching the warehouse."

"It might not be enough." I took a deep breath. "I don't know how to condense this, but Élodie has this hippie brother-in-law who lives in Glastonbury."

"You don't know how to condense telling me that Élodie has a hippie brother-in-law?"

"No, no. Just listen. The important part of that sentence was that he lives in Glastonbury."

"That in Saskatchewan?"

"You're *such* a funny man. Anyway, it's because of him that she knows all this."

"Knows all what?"

"Shut up and I'll tell you." I ran a hand through my hair, trying to organize my thoughts. They felt feather-light, ready to disappear in the smallest puff of air, clear at the time and becoming more amorphous the further I drifted from them. "Okay. In a nutshell, this energy thing we've been talking about, you know? It's apparently particularly potent, I guess you'd say, in Saint-Jean-sur-Richelieu. The city's sitting at a crossroads of two ley lines—"

"Two *what*?"

"Ley lines," I said impatiently. "Spirit paths. Energy tracks. Take your pick. It's some kind of liminal space where anything can happen, like the Bermuda Triangle, maybe, but the point is that energy is attracted there in a big way. It's why Aleister Brand chose to live there instead of Montréal: it's got stronger vibes." I paused and visualized his expression of disbelief: I didn't need a Skype video session. Maybe I was getting more psychic.

Or maybe I just understood how strange the things were I was talking about.

"Listen, Julian, these lines, I looked at them again last night. Remember your map, the one of all the tunnel networks under the city? The gas lines, the sewers, the electricity, the rivers, all that? The lines that Élodie told me about, these energy lines, they correspond almost exactly to the network of tunnels you showed me, the secret underground city. Do you see what that means? All the city's infrastructure was built on these other, these older lines." I took a deep breath. "The infrastructure's tapping into Psychic Central."

I realized that my hands were shaking. When we took the kids to the amusement park, Claudia screamed the loudest on the rides, and I asked her once if she was frightened, if she'd rather not go on them. "Oh, no, Belle-Maman!" she explained. They're scary, but they're scary-*fun*."

This was definitely not scary-fun.

"And here's the thing, Julian—maybe this is just me overthinking it, and maybe this whole thing is making me crazy, but—well, here it is, if something bad happens in Saint-Jean-sur-Richelieu, it's going to go seismic. Go fizzing all up the line to Montréal, and then around the network, like some sort of supernatural Roman candle. Completely out of control. Chaos magic for real." I stopped for a moment. "It can't happen. We can't let it happen."

There was a moment of silence before he spoke again. "Okay," he said. "I'm gonna take your word for all this, because honestly, I have no idea what you're talking about. But let's make sure it doesn't come to that. Like I said, I've got guys watching him. Do you think you can rope the mother in? Would he be likely to listen to her?"

"I have no idea," I confessed. "I don't think they've spoken in years."

"Worth a try, though, wouldn't you say?"

I shrugged, then remembered he couldn't see me. "Worth a try," I agreed.

"Okay. You call her. I'm checking in with the guys I have out around her son's place."

"They're watching for Avner?" Absurdly, I was more concerned in that moment about him than I was about anything else. I really, really wanted Avner to be all right.

"Yeah. He's not there, LeDuc, okay? Wherever he is, you don't have to worry, he's not with Brand. I would've heard."

"Okay." But I was feeling uneasy all the same. Something was teasing the edge of my consciousness, something dark, like the feeling you have when you know you've forgotten something important—but can't reach deep enough to find what it is. Something about his house, perhaps? Something was nagging at me, and I had no idea what it was.

And somehow I didn't think that Julian's recruits out at Saint-Jean-sur-Richelieu were going to be much help.

Do something, Martine. I paged through the recent calls on my smartphone and pressed Gabrielle's name. Voice mail, the same German-accented French I remembered from the conversation on the mountain—which also felt as though it had happened a long time ago. "Hello, Madame Brand, this is Martine LeDuc. I wanted to ask you a couple of questions about—well, about what we were talking about, before. Please call me back as soon as you can."

I thought about calling Marcus, but decided to check in at the office first instead. "Hey, Richard."

"*Bonjour*, Martine. Are you all right?"

I frowned. "Why wouldn't I be?"

He cleared his throat. "I have received a telephone call," he said. "Just three minutes ago, in fact. It came from a blocked number. A male voice. Very sure of himself, very smooth. He said—well, it was not a threat, not exactly, but when he heard that you were not here, he said that it was very important that you come into the office today. Immediately, he said. He was very forceful."

Something cold gripped my stomach. "Richard," I said.

Oblivious, he went on. "He seemed to know that you have been working outside and—"

"Richard," I interrupted. "Get out of there. Now."

"What? But—"

"Leave," I said urgently. "Oh, Christ, we have to evacuate the building. Richard, pull the fire alarm, and get the hell out of there. Now!"

I disconnected before he could say anything else and pressed Julian's telephone-number icon. "Someone just called my office and said that it was important I go into work right away," I said without preamble. "I'm getting City Hall evacuated."

"I'll call you back." No small talk. I liked that about Julian: he might well have been skeptical about my offering of ley lines and dark magic, but when it came down to it, he didn't question me, or my motives, or my judgment.

I looked around the apartment but suddenly didn't want to be there. I wanted to be sure I'd been right. If it turned out that Richard's call was just about someone really, really needing to see me on another matter, I was going to have a hell of a lot of explaining to do when Jean-Luc got back in town.

At least it was another gorgeous fall day.

I walk-trotted the five blocks to City Hall, half enjoying the sun on my face and half dreading what I was going to find there. It was clear even from a distance that Richard had taken me seriously: people were leaving the building, a steady stream of them, and already the first fire truck was on the scene along with two police cruisers. A couple of officers, their camouflage pants standing out in the crowd of office workers, were moving people back from City Hall and putting up tape. The inevitable gaggle of tourists was madly taking photos and asking what had happened in several different languages.

I found Chantal, though not Richard, in the crowd. "What's happening?"

"Monsieur Rousseau said there might be a bomb," she said, her voice low.

"He's not *saying* that?"

She shook her head. "No, no, just to me. He told Amélie down the hall that he smelled smoke."

"Is he in there now? With the fire department?" Dear God, if it went off now . . .

"No," she said. "He is conferring. The fire department is on its way. There will be the bomb-disposal unit from the police coming soon. They are doing the routine fire drill, managers making sure that everyone from their departments are out. But the police, they are suspicious. Privately. Someone from the detective unit told them it could be a bomb."

Good for Julian. I knew how much of a risk he was taking, professionally, believing I was right about this. Maybe risking something that even being a Westmount Fletcher couldn't get him out of. I sucked in air and realized that I'd been holding my breath. "Are you okay?" I asked Chantal.

"Yes, yes, of course." She was wrapping her cardigan closely around her. "It is a thought that brings no comfort," she said.

"I know."

"Was it meant for you, Martine?" she asked.

"We're getting ahead of ourselves here. We don't even know for sure." But I did.

The bomb-disposal unit was unmarked, just a big black van, and people made way for it, citizens disgruntled that their business in City Hall had been interrupted, secretaries pleased at the change in their routines, everyone more or less good-natured. That was because of the weather. If it had been February, it would have been a different story.

The men who emerged from the van, on the other hand, were anything but ordinary. Kevlar and then some. They strode past us and as they did I felt a tap on my shoulder. "LeDuc?"

It was Julian. "Thanks for coming," I said. Even I could hear the relief in my voice.

"They'll need to talk to Richard," he said, watching the police, hands in his pockets. Just another office worker.

"I know," I said.

"Okay," said Julian. "Keep your eyes out." And he headed over to talk with one of the men from the black van.

"Who are we looking for?" asked Chantal. I'd forgotten she was there.

"Someone that the *détective-lieutenant* is interested in talking to," I said. "Never mind. Chantal, don't say anything to anyone about a bomb, all right?"

She shook her head solemnly, and I squeezed her arm. "Good," I said. "I'll tell you about it later, okay?"

"Of course."

I smiled and squeezed her arm again and made my way through the crowd. As I got closer in, more and more of them were people I knew, and we exchanged suitably shocked and curious remarks. Julian caught up with me at the edge of the police tape. "Come on, time to go," he said, grabbing my elbow.

"But I wanted to see—"

He pulled me close against him so that his lips were by my ear. "There's at least one device in the building. They haven't finished going through it yet. You want to risk someone with binoculars and a remote detonator? We're getting out of here, *now*."

I allowed him to lead me through the people and away from the building, off onto a side street, the Champs de Mars. We were alone. "That's better," said Julian.

My hands were shaking. "Then there really was . . ."

"Someone," Julian said, looking at me consideringly, "wishes you a great deal of harm indeed."

"*Merde, alors,*" I said, and sat down, hard, on the curb. The only other time in my life when someone had wished me this kind of harm was very personal; he was a hands-on sort of person. But exploding a bomb in a public building? We were entering a whole new level of craziness here.

Still, why not? If Aleister Brand really did want to bring Hitler back from the dead, why would a little thing like killing dozens of people at City Hall bother him in the least? "He was in the military," I said to Julian.

"What?" He squatted down beside me. "What did you say?"

"He was in the military," I repeated. "Aleister Brand. Gabrielle told me. Maybe he was in ordnance. Maybe he learned this there."

Julian said, "Let's let them figure out who did this, and why, okay?"

I looked at him. "We know who did this," I said. "We know why he did this."

"Maybe," he said.

"What aren't you telling me?"

Julian sighed. "I just found out myself," he said. "Marcus Levigne has, as of this morning, also gone missing."

I stared at him, trying to figure out what that meant. "He's in a wheelchair," I said slowly. I felt like we'd had this conversation before.

"Not at the moment. He left it in his office."

"He left it in his office?" I absorbed what that meant. Was that the thought that had been following me—had I picked up on it, somehow, when we were together? Did Marcus Levigne have a tell I'd copped to without even being conscious of it? "What's his angle?" I asked.

He shrugged. "Money? A diamond like that . . . the price would be incalculable." He sat down on the curb next to me. "Maybe we've been looking at this wrong, Martine," he said. "Your magician . . . maybe he's just in it for the money, too. Skinheads, splinter groups, they can always use funding."

"We're assuming that whoever killed Patricia has the diamond," I said. "But they can't both have it—Aleister Brand and Marcus Levigne."

"So we need to find out who does."

I shook my head. "I have to talk to Gabrielle."

"Then I'll take you."

I looked at him. "You really don't have to babysit me, you know. I'm perfectly fine."

"Sure. You always sit down in the middle of the street."

"It's not the middle of the street."

"Listen, LeDuc." He sounded thoroughly exasperated. "Someone just tried to kill you. Spectacularly, with a whole lot of collateral damage. What do you think he's going to do when he learns it didn't go off as planned? Call it a day? You're stuck with me, or with somebody I choose, until this is over."

I was beginning to think it would never be over. Had it really been less than a week since I'd jumped on François's sightseeing tour? And what was he going to say in his narrative, today, when he drove past City Hall? In fact, with Ivan and Margery and the kids on his tour, or someone like him . . . "Oh, *hell*," I said suddenly.

"What?"

I was fumbling for my phone. "I have to tell Ivan I'm all right."

"It just looks like a fire drill," Julian reminded me.

"I can tell you're not married," I said, then stopped, stricken. "Oh, Julian, I'm sorry. I didn't think—"

"It's okay," he said. "I didn't get much practice at it, anyway. Call away." He stood up and dusted off the seat of his pants.

I got voice mail. "Just checking in to see how your morning's going," I said cheerfully. "We had some excitement at City Hall, but it was all a false alarm. I'll tell you about it later. Have a great tour."

"You good now?"

"Okay," I said, pushing myself up off the curb. Julian grabbed my arm and helped me the rest of the way up. "I'm going to see Gabrielle. You're welcome to come along."

"I think that's an excellent plan," said Julian.

"We'll see if *she* does."

The next day, Maurice had news for Hans.

"They're moving the contents of the vault," he said, puffing nervously on a cigarette.

"Why?"

A lift of the shoulders. "Who knows? Who cares? They don't con-sult me on these things, eh?"

Hans thought about it. "Where are they going?"

"Another vault. The gold and the hatboxes."

"Hatboxes?"

"With the jewels. They're what you're interested in, right?"

"Who told you I was interested in them?"

Maurice actually looked frightened. "No one! No one, boss, sorry!"

"Don't talk about this to anyone," hissed Hans. He had to think. "When are they moving?"

"Don't know. Listening at keyholes, that's how I knew, eh?"

"You have to find out," Hans said. "I need to know exactly when, and where." He got up close to the other man. "I don't need to tell you what will happen if I'm disappointed," he said. "Don't disappoint me."

"But—"

"It's not just your wife, you see," said Hans. "You'll lose your ca-reer. Your home. It's a bad time to be looking for a job. And you're not exactly qualified, are you?"

"But—"

"Do it," said Hans, and watched him scuttle away.

So it was coming to this. He went slowly to the telegraph office, to send word to Kurt; with his handler coming up from New York—as he was bound to do—then he was going to have to do something about Livia.

He wished to God he knew what.

CHAPTER TWENTY-NINE

She didn't.

She lived in one of the newer high-rises downtown: glass and steel, parking garage under the building, all the modern conveniences. When I buzzed her apartment and told her who I was, a disembodied voice that sounded remotely like hers was clear. "I do not wish to talk to you."

Julian sighed and buzzed again. "Madame, this is *détective-lieutenant* Fletcher, Montréal city police department. Please allow us in to talk to you."

The door clicked and opened. "Fourteenth floor," the voice said coldly, and there was another firm click as the glass door closed behind us. "She'll warm up to me," Julian assured me in the elevator. "People always do."

"Really? Then why haven't I?"

"You're just playing hard to get."

Gabrielle Brand stood framed in the doorway to her apartment. Still the aging flower-child look: if I wasn't mistaken, she was wearing Birkenstocks. "I thought I would not have to speak to you again," she said to me.

"Madame Gabrielle Brand, *détective-lieutenant* Julian Fletcher," I said.

"Madame." Julian proffered his hand. After a moment's hesitation, she shook it. "May we come in and speak to you, please?"

She shot me a look, but stood back and allowed us to enter. The apartment was spacious, with brilliant views of the city; but entering it was a little like going back in time. Oriental rugs on the floor, some thin, clearly valuable. Subtly patterned wallpaper; mirrors with gilt edging; oil paintings in still more gilded frames; heavy dark furniture. She'd brought her old-world sensibilities with her to the new world.

We sat awkwardly on a small sofa behind a marble-topped coffee table. She didn't offer us any refreshment, and it was that, more than anything else, that communicated best her displeasure at our appearance. "So," she said.

"So," Julian echoed. "We've paid a visit to your son."

An expression flitted across her face, impossible to read, banned as soon as it appeared. "Yes," she said.

I glanced at him and then said, smoothly, "When we met before, madame, you were kind enough to share some history with me. The beginnings of Hitler's involvement with—magic. The esoteric lodges and his ability to—to manipulate energy. You spoke of chaos magic."

The eyes were flat now. "Yes," she said, displeased.

"And you expressed some concerns to me about your son Aleister," I said. "I do not want to cause you any more pain, madame, but we believe that your concerns were correct. We visited him out at Saint-Jean-sur-Richelieu. He—it seems that he may have chosen to live there on purpose. That it's a place that might be—sympathetic— to the kind of focused energy you believe that he means to create." I was floundering a little.

"The crossroads," she said.

"You knew?" I asked, startled. "About the ley lines? Why didn't you say something before?"

"What would it have changed?" she asked. "I was giving you a warning, Mrs. LeDuc. I told you everything I felt that you should know. About how this happened, how he happened. I hoped you would know what to do with that warning."

"She did," Julian said. "And it doesn't matter. We're very grateful to you. And we know how difficult it must have been to—to point the finger at Aleister. We appreciate that. But things are becoming more and more serious. He placed a bomb in City Hall this morning."

"That's impossible." The voice was haughty and very sure of itself.

I looked at her with a mixture of amazement and pity. Of course she'd have to say that—it may be one thing to believe your son might practice black magic, but it's another to admit that he'd be willing to blow a public building filled with people sky-high. So infinitely difficult to believe anything that bad of someone you knew. It was unimaginable. An image of Lukas passed in front of me, briefly.

"It would be easy for me to blame myself," Gabrielle said. "The parents are always the ones held responsible. I understand that when there are—terrible events, inexplicable events—always, they look to see how the person was raised. They look to the parents, to what the parents have taught the child." She shook her head. "They look for logic where there is none. But it still happens. I have read of these things. Parents of teenagers who shot people have had to resettle, to start new lives, because they were blamed for what their children did. Society must find something: a reason, an individual, something concrete and real to reassure people that what happened is an aberration, and that it can never happen again." She smiled frostily. "But it always does. Always, it happens again."

"We're not blaming you," Julian said, leaning forward, trying to connect. "And you shouldn't blame yourself. People do what they do for many reasons."

She looked at him frostily. "This is what I am saying. I am not blaming myself."

He cleared his throat. "And you did the right thing, talking to Captain Levigne."

"Who is Captain Levigne?"

Julian and I exchanged glances again. "He is a police officer," I said. "He—he studies hate groups, he keeps track of who might belong to which ones." The polite expression hadn't left her face. "You have to know him," I said. "He was the one who gave me your telephone number, who told me about you, who said that we should talk."

Gabrielle was shaking her head. "I know of no such person. You must understand, with my background, I am not likely to approach the police myself."

"Perhaps he approached you? And you forgot?"

"Young man," she said icily, "I may be older than you are, but that does not make me stupid. My memory is perfectly functional. I have never heard that name before."

I started to say something, but Julian stopped me, his hand brushing my wrist. "No doubt he got your contact information from someone else," he said smoothly. "It doesn't really matter. What matters, now, is your son. We believe him to be a very dangerous man."

"Yes," she said, nodding. "That must be the priority. Stopping him."

"Before he puts a bomb somewhere else," said Julian, and at the same time, I said, "Before he summons the New Order of the Black Sun to do—what you told me they will do." I couldn't make my mouth form the words. "Mrs. Brand—do you have an idea *when* he's planning to do it? Is there something special he's waiting for? A phase of the moon? An anniversary?" I couldn't think of any other milestone off the top of my head. The only thing I was sure of was that it had to be soon: he wouldn't risk the investigation that would surely follow a bomb explosion at City Hall unless he was very close to his endgame. "Anything could help."

"'A phase of the moon'?" Now there was no mistaking the expression: pity. "How disappointing, Mrs. LeDuc. I thought that you understood, that you had taken my warning seriously. A phase of the moon?" She made it sound like I'd suggested a child's birthday party. "That would not help."

"What *would* help," said Julian, "would be for you to talk to him."

The china-blue eyes were bland. "And how do you think that would work, *détective-lieutenant*?"

"He's your son. He might listen to you."

"Listen to me saying what, exactly?"

"It would be good," said Julian, "if he could turn himself in. That way, no one has to get hurt."

"Turn himself in to the police?" She was politely incredulous. "What an interesting idea. How do you see that improving the situation?"

"He won't be able to hurt anyone. Detonate bombs." He glanced at me and backed down. "Conduct black-magic rituals."

"Chaos-magic rituals," she corrected automatically. "And it will not matter. You do not understand." She sighed. "Yes, of course Saint-Jean-sur-Richelieu is an excellent location for what he does, for what he plans to do. You are correct about the power building up there, at the crossroads. You are correct that he selected that city, that canal, that warehouse on purpose. But really, the truth is that it does not matter, *ja*?"

"How can it not matter?" I was feeling a little lost, feeling my way slowly through a thick bright fog to find her, to understand what she was saying. It had all seemed clearer, somehow, up on Mont Royal.

"The place amplifies the focus. It does not provide it. If you arrest Aleister, if you put him in a jail cell, if you lock him away underground, it will not matter. He will find a way."

What I was feeling was slightly sick. "You mean he can reach out from wherever he is."

"And that he can also be reached. Roads do not go only one way, not ever. Do you not think that there is an intelligence behind the magic?"

Julian was looking a little wild. Metaphysics clearly wasn't his cup of tea. "If he's behind bars," he said, obviously trying to get a grip back on the practical aspects of the conversation, "then he can't set off bombs. He can't hurt innocent people. That's my priority. This is my city. I'm not letting him take it away from me."

"It is not yours to be taken," she said quietly. "I thought that perhaps it could be stopped. I thought that perhaps you would stop it."

"But he *can* be stopped," said Julian with a sort of desperate energy, a child who's just been told there's no Santa Claus. "*You* could talk to him. Make him see that it's the only way. Otherwise—it's only going to get worse from here on in."

She was responding to Julian. "In what way will it get worse?" she asked, politely, showing the same amount of interest she might if he'd offered to show her photographs of his favorite dog. Why wasn't she feeling this more? She had to still love Aleister at some level, why wasn't she mad with concern?

"If we go and talk to him, if you talk to him and he comes with me, no one will need to get hurt. Including Aleister." He paused. "He put a bomb in a public building. You have to understand this, madame. He's reached a whole new level of interest. The provincial police are going to get involved now. The RCMP are going to get involved now. And, believe me, those boys play rough. When we're talking a potential crime such as this one—well, they're likely to shoot first and figure out what they should have done instead later.

Aleister has a better chance at survival if he lets me take him in. He's upped the ante too far here for there to be a good outcome. That's the best offer he's going to get."

"The ante," she murmured. "The ante? Is that how you see it? This is not one of Monsieur Petrinko's casino games, *détective-lieutenant*."

I froze. How did she know who Ivan was? Did everybody know who Ivan was?

Gabrielle was talking; she hadn't even glanced my way when she brought Ivan's name into it. "Let me be absolutely clear. You must disabuse yourself of the notion that I can effect any change in my son's thoughts or behavior," she said. "It has been many years since he last felt that I had anything to say to him. He believes that I have disgraced the bloodline, that I have not lived up to my heritage."

"As Göring's daughter," I said.

She nodded. "To Aleister, that connection is everything. I have not spoken to him in years. And then there is the futility of it all. Believe me when I tell you, all that the warehouse does for him is make it easier, faster. The diamond as well. He can do it anywhere. He will do it anywhere."

"When?"

"I don't know!" The words burst from her and for the first time I felt she was being completely truthful, completely cooperative. "*Ich weiße nicht!* There are too many reasons to do it at one time or another. It will be soon: I've felt it coming closer. It will be soon. But I do not know when. As *Gott* is my witness, I do not know when!" She pulled her arm away from my hand and hugged herself, looking all of her seventy-odd years. "I do not know," she repeated, more calmly, and I looked at Julian.

"I believe her."

"Yeah," he said. "I do, too. Which leaves us exactly nowhere."

"Maybe not," I said, and turned to Gabrielle. "Please don't worry about it," I said. "We'll figure it out. You were right to give me the warning. You were right to see us today and to explain it to us. It's going to be all right. You can rest now. We'll make sure it doesn't happen." Like talking to a child.

Julian wasn't happy, but even he realized that he wasn't going to badger information that she didn't have out of her. "If you can think of anything that might help us," he said, standing up, buttoning his suit jacket, "then please give me a call." He proffered a business card that, after a moment's hesitation, she took. "I don't have to stress how important—"

"No," I cut in, "you don't. Good-bye, madame. We're sorry to have bothered you."

She saw us to the door, the same haunted expression on her face. She didn't say anything and, after a moment, I stepped into the hallway, Julian right after me. The door closed with a definitive click behind us.

"So are you going to tell me what that was about?" he demanded as we waited for the elevator. "Nothing to see here, everyone move along? What's the story?"

"She's terrified," I said. "And she really doesn't believe that Aleister tried to blow up City Hall."

"Well, she wouldn't," he said reasonably. The elevator doors opened and we stepped in. "It would be awful to face the fact that anybody you love could do anything like that."

I shook my head. "She's facing worse than that," I said and turned to face him. "I just finally got it in there, Julian. The bomb? It's inconsequential to her. She doesn't believe he'd do it, not because it's so dreadful, but because it's not dreadful enough."

He reached over and pushed the stop button; the elevator juddered and then stood still. "What are you talking about?"

I took a deep breath. "Put away what *you* think and what *you* believe for a minute, and try and see it from her point of view. She believes in evil. She believes that there's something bad that's been passed down through the Göring bloodline to her son. She believes that he's able to summon a great deal of destructive power. He wants the whole Nazi régime back, everything, the racial cleansing, the camps, the experimentation." I drew a shaky breath: after last summer, we both knew a little too much about medical experimentation. "Next to that, what's blowing up a building? So what? So a few hundred people are killed? That's *nothing* compared to what he wants to have happen. She's scared of the right things, and you're just annoying her, pushing on about the damned bomb."

"The damned bomb is how we're going to get him," said Julian. "We can't arrest him for trying to bring someone back from the dead. We can't stop that. We have to do it within the law."

He was back to that recording, and I was getting fed up. "Then he'll win. He'll win because he doesn't give a toss about the law. He doesn't give a toss about anything but this." A thought was glimmering suddenly, somewhere, and I felt Gabrielle's energy behind it. "He has to make it up to Hitler," I said suddenly.

"Make what up? What are you talking about?"

I was feeling sick. "Göring was Hitler's chosen successor, his right-hand man, the most important man in the Reich after Hitler himself," I said. "But they had a falling-out at the end. So Hitler was in Berlin and the Russians were surrounding him, he went down into the bunkhouse and got a telegram from Göring saying essentially that he was taking over as chancellor of the Reich. Hitler was all about loyalty and he saw that as the ultimate betrayal. He went ballistic and ordered the SS after Göring. If the Americans hadn't gotten Göring, the SS would have killed him for sure."

"Okay, but . . ."

"Don't you see?" I felt impatient. "Aleister is Göring's *blood*. He wants to make up for Göring's betrayal. This is how he's doing it." I stabbed the Down button and the elevator shook and started descending again. "And that's going to tell us when," I said.

Julian found my wavelength with a click. "On an anniversary."

"We just have to figure out which one."

It felt, in those last weeks, that everything was moving far too quickly.

"*I have to go away for a while,*" *Hans told Livia. It was a special night; he'd managed to get hold of some champagne.* "*I wish that I did not, but there is work I have to do, work away from here.*"

"*Where?*"

He said the first place that came into his head. "*Toronto.*"

"*Oh! For how long?*" *She looked like she was about to cry. He had to do it. He had to keep her safe. Kurt couldn't know that she existed.*

"*For a week, perhaps longer, I do not know,*" *Hans said.*

"*You are leaving me,*" *she said.* "*I knew it could not last. I knew that no one is allowed to be this happy. I knew you would find, after all, that you don't love me. You should just tell me. You don't have to go all the way to Toronto.*"

"*That is not true,*" *Hans protested.* "*I do have to go. And then I am going to come back.*"

"*You're just looking for a way to break things off. You're not going to Toronto.*"

"*Listen to me. I must go to Toronto,*" *said Hans.* "*But there is something I very much want to ask you before I go.*"

She was crying now. "*What is it?*"

They were in her room, sitting next to each other on the bed. He got down on one knee, awkwardly. "*I need to ask you,*" *he said carefully,* "*if, when I return, you will marry me.*"

Her eyes widened. "*I cannot believe you asked me that!*" *But she was smiling through the tears.*

"*You have not yet given me an answer.*"

She flung her arms around him. "*Yes! Yes! Of course I'll marry you!*"

He rose, dusted off his knees, and sat down again next to her.

"*Why could you not believe I would ask? I love you, you know that I love you.*"

"*I thought,*" she said, wiping her cheeks with her hand, "*that you were making up the trip to Toronto so that you could break up with me.*"

He stared. "*But—*"

"*No, no!*" Livia interrupted him. "*It's all right. It really is.*" She put her arms around him, leaning back as she did, onto the bed, with him on top of her. "*I love you, Hans,*" she murmured. And then they did not speak again for a very long time.

Kurt was waiting for him, the next morning, at the train station. "*You're late.*"

Hans was euphoric and trying to hide it. He couldn't see Livia; he couldn't even think of Livia, not until Kurt was safely on his way back to New York City. "*I am here now,*" he said. "*What is it?*"

"*Berlin got your message,*" Kurt said, opening a newspaper and keeping it in front of his mouth. "*It's the moment we've been waiting for. When they move the jewels, you're to be there.*"

"*And steal them?*" It was amazing how calm he felt.

"*Of course. But replace them. Here,*" and he pressed a small package into Hans's hand. "*Substitute these. There's a photo in there so you'll know which ones.*"

"*And the real ones?*"

"*I'll take them.*"

"*And how will I know how to find you?*"

Kurt smiled. It wasn't a pleasant smile. "*Oh, you'll know,*" he said. "*I'm staying with you.*"

There was only one thing he could do, Hans decided.

Tell the truth. And—not tell the truth.

He had served the Reich, but he owed it nothing. And Canada was vast. Livia needed her people; fine. There were sure to be Jews out west.

Out west, where he would take her. With the money they'd get from the diamonds.

Maurice had come up trumps. Tuesday. In the morning. The vault's contents would be transported to the Securities and Exchange Building in a baker's truck, and brought to the vault there. "There's a leak, see, in the one at Sun-Life," Maurice said, having gleaned that information at keyholes. "And there's papers involved. That's why they're moving it all, eh?"

"You will make sure I am there," said Hans.

Maurice nodded. "I knew you'd ask me," he said. "An' I got that covered, see? We'll dump the contents in the new vault, an' I've signed on for first shift guarding it. I'll get you in, all right." He paused. "But you got to do something for me. They'll know I'm the one let you in, so you got to cut me in, so I have something, so I can get away."

"They will not know that I was there," said Hans.

"No? An' how you going to arrange that?"

"I am replacing them," said Hans. "That is the point. No one is to know at all."

"I see." *There was something in his voice, something that Hans couldn't put his finger on, but which bothered him. He didn't know what it was.* "Tuesday," he said.

"Tuesday," Maurice affirmed.

Monday night, then, thought Hans. Monday night he'd tell her to pack. Monday night he'd tell her the truth.

CHAPTER THIRTY

The anniversary wasn't all that difficult to find. We stopped at the nearest Second Cup coffeehouse and I pulled my laptop from my tote bag. "Here's a timeline," I announced.

Julian put the two cappuccinos he'd ordered on the table. "What's it say?"

I frowned. "Most of it happened in the spring," I said. "Here, look. The first rift is here, back in the spring of 1941. Göring's head of the Luftwaffe, and Hitler blames him for not wiping out the Soviet air force."

"Not enough," said Julian. He had a thin mustache from the frothy milk.

"Right. So then it's spring of 1943 when he loses it over the Allied bombing of the Ruhr, all the industrial targets they were hitting. He blames Göring again."

"Sounds like a long decline."

"I think Göring lost interest in the Luftwaffe. He was behind the final solution." Neither here nor there, I told myself. "Anyway, here it is: April 1945, Hitler's cut off and Göring's in Austria, and Göring sends that telegram. Hitler flips out, but then kills himself. Göring thinks he can have some sort of role in the new Germany and gives himself up to American troops, thinking that he's going to consult with the Americans." I sighed. "But that's in May. No dice."

Julian had read ahead of me. "There it is," he said, his finger on the screen.

And there it was. October 1, 1945: the judges of the International Military Tribunal at Nuremberg sentence Göring to death by hanging. He'd cheated them, of course, swallowing a cyanide pill in his cell the night before his scheduled execution. But the sentencing date was there, and it was the only date in the fall.

Julian and I looked at each other. "What's the date today?" I asked. It didn't matter, I already knew.

"September 30," said Julian.

"We have one day," I said faintly.

Jean-Luc Boulanger, my intrepid boss, had managed to tear himself away from the delights of an all-paid vacation—oops, I mean, *conference*—in Québec City, and was finally on his way back to Montréal. This I learned from Chantal when I got back to City Hall; the building had been swept for additional explosive devices, and people allowed to return to their business.

Even Jean-Luc couldn't justify not being around when his office became a possible terrorist target. Although I suspected that he'd tried.

Richard was on the telephone talking to news outlets. "He's been doing that since we got back," said Chantal. There was something in her voice that wasn't quite an accusation, and it was clear she thought my deputy was doing my job. I let it go. If this really happened, dealing with the press was going to be the least of the city's PR problems. "The mayor will be here by one thirty," she said.

"I'm happy for him."

"Is there anything you want me to be doing?"

I glanced up at her. She was twisting her hands together and looking a lot more nervous than I'd ever seen her. "Are you all right, Chantal?"

A quick nod. "It's just . . . the bomb."

"Of course. Anyone would be shaken," I said.

"It's not that," she said. "The police interviewed us, and Martine, I swear I didn't want to tell them, but they asked the questions and I didn't want to lie, so I finally told them . . ."

"Told them what?" Her hand-wringing routine was getting on my nerves.

"That you knew about it ahead of time." Her voice caught on a sob. "I'm sorry, I'm so very sorry, I couldn't think of anything else to say when they asked, you called Richard and you told him to evacuate the building, how could you have known, I wondered, but you know all sorts of things and I just couldn't think fast enough to make anything up. . . ." She was running out of steam. "And so if you want me to resign, of course I will, it's the least that I can do after betraying you like that, I will totally take the blame for it."

I put up my hand. "Chantal, stop it. Of course you had to tell them the truth. Of course I don't want your resignation. What I would like, very much, is a coffee." Well, not really, since I'd just had one at Second Cup, but I wanted to be nice to her, make her feel useful. "Why don't you get that for me, and then we'll talk some more. But you should never, ever feel that you need to lie to protect me. That has never been part of your job description."

She swallowed. "Thank you, Martine, thank you. Of course I'll get the coffee, thank you, I never want to betray you in any way, and if I do—"

"Chantal," I interrupted. "The coffee?"

"Yes, yes, of course, Martine." Blessedly, she left.

I just had to make sure I didn't become a bombing suspect. *That* would play havoc with the city's PR. I sank into my chair with a sigh and looked at the piles on my desk. Clippings of any mention of Montréal in French and English-language publications—all available online, but Jean-Luc didn't believe anything unless he could touch it. Letters that had to be answered, requests and comments and heads-up about everything from foreign dignitaries in town to school tours of City Hall.

And all of it, one could argue, important. All of it worthy of my attention. All of it part of my job. And the worst part, I knew, was that Richard had already picked up the most urgent messages, without a word, without a complaint, leaving me free to traipse around the city doing he knew not what.

If we all survived this, I was going to have to do something very, *very* special for Richard.

In the meantime, there was Jean-Luc to deal with. I picked up the telephone and hit the speed dial for Ivan's phone. "I was just thinking about you," he said.

"Glad to hear it. How's your day?"

"Great. You should see the kids, you'd think they were born and raised here, the way they're showing off the city. They actually listened to you from time to time, it would seem."

"Will miracles never cease," I said. "Listen, Ivan, I just have a quick question."

"Shoot."

I winced at the word. "Do you know someone named Gabrielle Brand?"

A pause; I could imagine him searching his mental data banks. "Doesn't sound familiar. Any context in particular?"

"I'm not sure." I twirled my chair around so I was looking out the window. "She's an older woman who lives downtown. Emigrated here from Germany, I don't know, decades ago."

"She comes to the casino?"

"No. Well, I don't know, but I don't think so." I paused. "I only ask because she knows your name, knows you're my husband, and that just seemed—odd. You're right, you don't have a context together, there's no way she should normally know that."

"On the other hand," said Ivan diffidently, "it's not exactly a secret. You'd be surprised, the number of people who know I'm married to you—well, married to the PR director. We're public figures, babe."

"I know," I said.

"But there's more to it than that, isn't there?" he asked. "Something about this woman. She's special?"

"Not in a particularly good way," I said. "But, yeah, she's— important, I guess." I wasn't sure how much I was comfortable sharing with Ivan. I was dealing with people who had some sort of sixth sense in regards to my thoughts, and I didn't want to put him out there any more than was absolutely necessary. "Never mind, babe. I'll figure it out."

"You said the name was Gabrielle Brand, right?" Ivan asked. "If anything comes up, I'll let you know."

"Yeah," I said. "But—don't go looking for anything, Ivan, okay? Only if you hear something."

There was a sound and then muffled voices, and I could picture him with his hand over the receiver before he came back on. "What's going on, Martine? Are you all right?"

His voice, calm and gentle, felt like soft, sheltering love, miles away from the coldness of that morning. I wanted to cry. I wanted to say no, please come get me, hold me, protect me. Help me forget everything that I've learned in the past five days.

I drew in a breath that I hoped didn't sound too shaky. "I'm okay," I said. "Just tired. I'll talk to you later."

"And I'll let you know if I remember anything about your Gabrielle Brand."

I was already regretting having spoken her name. "See you when I see you," I said.

"See you when I see you."

I sat for a few moments looking at the telephone and wondering if I'd just made a very bad mistake.

One day, and time running out.

I sent a quick e-mail to Richard—the tip of the iceberg about what I wanted and needed to say, but there was no way that I could stay still at my desk all afternoon—and drank Chantal's coffee in three swallows. "I have to go out again," I told her.

"Of course, Martine." She was cooperation itself.

"I'm on my mobile if there's an emergency."

She nodded. "Richard is here."

"Right." Richard was clearly getting Chantal's vote for Boss of the Year. I sighed. When I was in college, at the Université de Québec à Montréal—UQAM—there was a guy I knew who would disappear from time to time, and when he returned, he kept talking about how he'd been off saving the world on some astral plane. It was probably a combination of some mild mental illness and some of the drugs that were always floating around campus, but he seemed quite convinced that we'd all been going about our lives and business without any knowledge that the earth had been in grave danger and that he alone had pulled it through. Yves: that was his name.

I looked at Chantal now and couldn't help but think of Yves as I prepared to go out and do some sort of battle with some sort of unseen forces that were possibly threatening the planet, and nobody else had any clue what was going on.

Just trying to keep things in perspective.

No word from Julian. He really was the one saving the day, I thought: he would have to go through official channels to mobilize the police out at Saint-Jean-sur-Richelieu to stop whatever was going to happen at the warehouse. He was doing the heavy lifting; but I still was concerned about Avner, and thought it might be useful to find out where the hell he'd gone when he'd decided to ditch his police minder.

I called Élodie. "What are you doing?"

"In a meeting," she said, her voice muffled. "I can meet you later."

"What kind of meeting?"

"The kind I can't tell you about in a room full of people," she whispered into the receiver. "I'll call you when I'm done."

So that was that. No Julian, no Marcus, no Avner, no Élodie. I thought briefly of Avner's wife, but she'd have called if she'd heard from him. Or so I fervently hoped. It was high time, I decided, to meet the mysteriously still-single Lev Kaspi.

I ran him down in an almost-empty computer lab at McGill's McConnell Engineering Building, sitting in front of what looked suspiciously like a video game on the screen. I sat down in the seat next to him. "For someone whose father is missing, you seem pretty carefree," I said.

He spared me a quick glance. "You must be Martine LeDuc."

"I must be," I agreed.

Bushy eyebrows over dark, intelligent eyes. "Give me a moment," he said.

I watched as several alien-looking individuals were vaporized on his screen before scores flashed across it and then it went dark, and Lev turned to me. "I've been expecting you," he said.

He was large, far larger than his father, with pasty white skin that probably came from too many hours in this room, with its lack of windows and flickering florescent lights. Curly dark hair and a blue embroidered yarmulke. I wondered if Naomi had embroidered it for him.

There was a gentleness about Lev, though, and clear intelligence in the dark eyes, and . . . something else, a strange feeling of peace that seemed to emanate from him. This was someone totally at ease with himself, who either didn't have any shadows or had banished them a long time ago. I felt as though I knew him already, had known him for years, forever. "Well," I said, "I wouldn't want to disappoint you."

"You're looking for my father." It wasn't a question.

"When the police go to the trouble of arranging protection for someone, it seems bad manners to slip out the back way," I said. "And it's funny, but your father didn't strike me as a man with bad manners."

"You're perceptive," Lev said and glanced around the room. "Would you care for a coffee, Mrs. LeDuc?"

At my current rate of caffeine consumption, I was going to be awake for the next month. At least. "Why not?"

We went to the aptly named and recently renovated E-Café and Lev bought me coffee; the food court was large and filled with students, but we were there between meals and Lev found us a table by the window. "So," I said encouragingly.

"So," he echoed, stirring his coffee. He looked up at me suddenly. "You think that my father was frightened by that swastika," he said.

"I don't know. It seemed like a credible threat," I said cautiously.

He shook his head. "Credible threat," he repeated. "Do you really think that's anything that's new to my family? Do you think it's the first swastika we've ever seen?"

I sipped the coffee: too hot. I put the cup back down. "I'm sure it's not," I said. "But it's the first one that we could do anything about." I paused. "What happened, Lev? Where's your father gone? Wherever he is, he'd be safer with us, you know that."

He sighed. "My father has felt all his life that he arrived too late to do anything useful," he said. "Oh, he had the business, of course, for years and years he's run the business, and made a success of it.

Well, you saw where we live, you saw what we can afford. He's done well for himself, and for us, carrying on a family tradition, making enough money to help others. For a lot of people, that would be enough."

"More than enough," I agreed. "It sounds like a good life."

"It is a good life. It was a good life. He's got money. He's got stature in the community—both through his own trade and through my grandfather, who's a pretty influential rabbi." He glanced at me. "His name wouldn't mean anything to you, but believe me, he's very important in our community, and it was considered an honor for my father to marry into his family. A big honor. But that's not necessarily enough." He looked at me speculatively. "I don't know if you know much about the dynamics of being a child of the Holocaust," he said.

I shook my head. "I don't know anything about it."

He nodded. "I don't want to lecture you," he said diffidently. "But it may help you to understand."

I spread my hands. "Lecture away."

He nodded again, seemingly gathering his thoughts. "The children of Holocaust victims and survivors, the second generation, my father's generation, have been studied at length," he said. "His father survived the camps, he was at Buchenwald, he worked for the SS there."

"Yes," I said, nodding. "Avner told me. He manufactured copies of the crown jewel diamonds out of—"

"White sapphires," finished Lev. I shut up; it was, after all, his story. Not to mention his family's business. "The way that his parents lived, the way that they raised him, all had a tremendous impact on who he was and who he became."

I nodded. "That makes sense."

Lev sipped his coffee. "So. Studies of this generation have shown that they assume the role of victim and survivor themselves. Even though they weren't the ones *in* the camps, they dream *of* the camps, and the experience is as real to them as if it had happened. It's an ongoing sense of guilt, both guilt that it was allowed to happen, and guilt that they weren't themselves the ones to suffer."

"It sounds complicated," I said.

He nodded. "It is. At first glance, the concept of transmission is difficult to grasp. It is like saying that someone's headache is caused by the fact that his father was hit on *his* head by a stone some fifty years ago. But psychologists have long said that it makes sense . . . that emotions which couldn't be consciously experienced by the first generation are given over to the second generation. So my father was brought up in an atmosphere of anxiety, tension, and fear. He did not hear the stories of his parents' lives until he was in his teens. No one wanted to speak of it, but it was there behind everything, every remark, every thought."

I could imagine it: the elephant in the room, hiding in the shadows of every dinner table, looking over everyone's shoulders. "What about you?" I asked suddenly. "How are you affected by it?"

He smiled. "I am third generation," he said. "There was a study done—actually, it was done here, in Montréal, about us. It found that we function extremely well."

We sat with that thought for a moment. "So," I said finally, "I appreciate the history lesson, Lev, but I'm still totally in the dark about what all that means for your father here and now."

He rolled his cup in small circles on the table. "He feels guilt," he said finally. "So this is something that he can *do*, you see. At long last, here is something that he can do something about. But he was not going to be able to do anything with the police watching him all the time."

I gazed at him in horror. "Lev—what is your father doing?"

He looked uncomfortable. "You have to understand," he said, "I only wanted to make him feel more involved. It was all he ever talked about, the moment that he met you, all he wanted to talk about was this—situation. The diamonds. His father, the journal. How it all seemed to lead back to him. He wanted to know more, he wanted to feel involved."

"And so you . . . ?"

"And so," he said, "I hacked into a couple of e-mail accounts. I know that the police—Captain Levigne, I believe—follow the activities of local skinhead groups and neo-Nazis, but some of the rest of us, civilians, we do as well."

"It sounds like you're doing more than just following their activities," I said.

He shrugged. "It is best to know," he said. "And I can do things that the police cannot."

"Because they're illegal."

He was unperturbed. "Because they're illegal," he said, nodding. "Listen, it's not the activity—because to be frank, most of Montréal wouldn't stand for overt anti-Semitism, not now. But the undercurrents, the writings . . . they're still alive and well, and it's important to understand what is happening. There have been a lot of publications, starting in the 1930s and continuing today, talking about a worldwide Jewish conspiracy—blaming us for everything from UFOs to global warming. We keep an eye on things, what new groups are forming, where the next leader is coming from."

There was a moment of silence. "And then you came across Aleister Brand," I said.

He nodded.

"And you told your father about him."

He nodded again. "He assured me that he would be discreet. He wants the diamond back. The one that his father copied. He feels connected to it." He smiled. "And, of course, to bring an anti-Semite to justice."

"Discreet?" I echoed in dismay. "Discreet? Lev, your father will stand out like a—a—flamingo at a Quaker meeting, out there. He won't get within a kilometer of the warehouse before they'll be onto him. And if they think he'll get in their way—"

"I know," he said. "I know. But my father, he's not easy to stop."

"The timing's awful," I said, pulling out my smartphone and hitting Julian's contact button. Voice mail. "Listen, Julian, it looks like you were right, Avner's gone out to Saint-Jean-sur-Richelieu. I don't know where, exactly, but Lev Kaspi says that's where his father was heading." I looked up. "How? Does he have a car?"

He shook his head. "Public transport. The bus, probably."

"Oh, God. Julian, he's gone out on the bus, which means he's going to be wandering around, and he's wandering around with a target on his back, for all we know. I think we should go find him. We can't wait until tomorrow. Call me back."

I clicked End and met Lev's eyes. "What is happening tomorrow?" he asked calmly.

"Nothing, if we have anything to do with it," I said, standing up. "Thanks for telling me this, Lev. I have to go. If you hear from your father, please get in touch with me or *détective-lieutenant* Fletcher, okay?"

"Yes," he said. He still seemed so unaware of the danger, I wanted to shake him. "We'll get him back," I said.

He nodded. "Yes," he said again, but his mind was clearly elsewhere.

As I needed to be.

It should have gone smoothly.

He'd practiced it enough in his head, lying on the extra mattress on the floor since Kurt had taken his bed. Practiced what he would say, and how he would say it.

He had no idea how it had gone so incredibly wrong.

Livia caught sight of him through the plate glass of the dressmaker's, and gestured excitedly for him to come in. Good, he thought; he'd made sure he wasn't being followed, but best not to tempt fate, stay off the street. Kurt was at the cinema. Or supposed to be, anyway.

"You're back!" She threw herself into his arms. "I missed you so much! I am so happy! So very happy, my darling!"

Hans kissed her. And then again. "I couldn't wait to see you," he said.

"Me, too!" Her eyes were shining. She was the most beautiful woman in the world.

"I have to talk to you, my love," he said finally. "Are we alone here?"

"Yes, yes, of course, but we can go to my room—"

"Later," Hans said. "You know what happens when we go to your room."

"Yes," she said, and giggled. "This is why I want to go to my room."

"Later," he said again, taking her hand, leading her to the small fainting couch where by day women sat and looked at different dresses for sale. "Livia, you know that I love you—"

She kissed him. "I love you, too, my darling."

He pulled away. "I have to ask you how much. How much do you love me?"

"What a silly question! With all my heart!"

"Would you," he asked carefully, "do anything for me? Anything that I asked of you?"

Her smile faded. "What is it, Hans?"

He cleared his throat. "Livia. Tomorrow I want you to stay home from work. I want you to pack a suitcase—anything that is important to you, that you cannot leave behind. Like your mother's candlesticks." He smiled. "We are going away to start our life together. We are going away tomorrow."

"I cannot go tomorrow! There is the dress for Mrs. Goldstein—"

"It does not matter. Mrs. Goldstein does not matter. This is our life."

She looked disturbed. As well she should be, all things considered.
"But why, Hans? Why so suddenly? Is this about your trip to Toronto?"

He inclined his head. "A little, perhaps."

"And how will we live? We have saved no money! We are not even
yet married!"

"We will have plenty of money. And we will get married, I
promise you that, my love." *He stroked her hand for a moment, then
looked up into her face. She was troubled, and he would have given
anything not to say what he was going to tell her.* "My love, my
Livia . . . you have always thought that I am from Holland, and that
I am Jewish."

She nodded. "Yes. Yes, this is what you are, this is what you've
told me."

"It was not the entire truth. I said it—I said it because I wanted
you to love me."

"But of course I love you!" *Now she wasn't looking anxious; now
she was looking frightened.* "This is what you are, Hans!"

He shook his head. "No, it is not. But you have to know, I came
here for my work, and I am giving it up. I am giving it all up, because
of you."

"What are you saying to me?"

"I did not tell you the truth. I did not know that I'd fall in love
with you."

*She pulled her hand away from his, hunching her shoulders, de-
fensive.* "Tell me."

He took a deep breath, let it out. "I am German," *he said.* "I am a
soldier in the German army, and I have been sent to Montréal to work
for the army."

She was staring at him; her hand went to her throat. "No."

"Ja. I told people I was from Holland; no one knew the difference.
And there is more—I am not Jewish. I was taught that Jews are
evil, but I know now that is not true. I am not Jewish, my love, but

for you, I will be. I will convert. I will do whatever is necessary to make you happy."

He reached for her again, and she recoiled. "Do not touch me! If this thing is true about you, then I don't know you!"

"Of course you do. I am the same person I was a few minutes ago, Livia."

"Don't say my name!" She was on her feet. "You are a Nazi!"

The words were meaningless. Nazi was meaningless. She alone held meaning for him now. "I am a member of the Party, ja. But that does not matter. It is nothing."

"It's not nothing to me!" Her eyes grew rounder. "Oh, my God. You are a Nazi, and I went to bed with you!"

"You love me, Livia," Hans said, trying to sound reasonable. How could she not see? How could she not understand that love like theirs cancelled out everything else? His face was flushed, his anxiety almost overwhelming. He stood up, his hands out in supplication. "We love each other. Do you not see? I am giving it all up for you. Everything. It is only you that matters now. I will love you forever." The words felt stiff, his mouth dry with fear. He couldn't lose her now.

"Get out." He felt the slap before her hand even connected with his cheek. "Do you think I am that stupid? I know what your people think of Jews! I know what they do to Jews! And you think—you want me to—it is unthinkable!"

"But it is not me!" cried Hans. "That is not me! Livia, listen—"

"Get out! Get out, or I will start screaming, and they will arrest you and shoot you as a spy! Get out now!"

He moved unwillingly toward the front of the shop. "Livia, think of what you are doing. We could be so happy together. We could—"

She strode past him and opened the door, leaning on it. "Get out," she said again, and her voice was trembling. When he reached the doorway, she said, without looking at him, "Do you know why I am *sparing your life? Why I'm not screaming for them to come and get you?"*

Miserable, Hans turned to her. "Why?"

"Because," she said, and wiped her tears quickly with her sleeve, "because I had news for you today as well. Because whatever I do in my life, whatever happens, I cannot cause the death of my child's father. Now, go!"

CHAPTER THIRTY-ONE

There was a text from Élodie.

MEET ME AT THE HOTEL. NOW.

Grand. Possibly the worst place in the city to find a parking place, and my budget didn't stretch to valets all the time. I opted for the Métro instead and was calling her mobile as I came out at Victoria Square. "Meet me in the lobby?"

She was starched and official-looking, in a dark blue skirt suit and white blouse, her briefcase in her hand, her eyes on her watch. "You look awful," she pronounced when she saw me.

"Thanks. Always happy to have a compliment," I said.

"*De rien.* Have a seat. I have a story to tell you."

Why did everyone, it seemed, have some sort of story to tell me? I felt the pressure of the minutes ticking away, closer and closer to whatever was going to happen out at the warehouse. Avner might already be out there. We were wasting time. "What is it?"

"Well," she said, arranging herself on the sofa, "the first thing you need to know is that they know."

"Who knows?"

She looked surprised. "The English, of course. At only the highest levels. They'd already made the decision to keep it private. The substituted diamonds are part of a piece that isn't usually on display in the tower, and certainly when it is, none of the tourists gaping at it would know the difference, anyway. And it's not like that's never been done before. In fact, apparently it used to be quite usual for the regalia to be set with jewels hired for the coronation only. Afterwards, the stones were returned to the jewelers and the regalia reset with crystals or paste and put in the jewel house for display." Élodie shrugged. "So, in some ways, it's not as big a deal as we thought it might be."

"But there's more to the story."

A quicksilver smile. "There's always more to the story," she said. "So listen up. You've been thinking about this for a while, you know the stories, that King John lost them in some quicksand someplace—"

"—at the Wash River," I supplied. "Hence the phrase of something getting lost in the wash."

That didn't even rate a smile in passing. "Right. And then when they abolished the monarchy, nearly all the jewels were destroyed by Cromwell, who thought that everything to do with kings or queens was detestable—his word, by the way, not mine."

"Yes," I said. "Hurry up, Élodie."

"Well, there was one thing that was saved. Hidden in an abbey somewhere godforsaken like Northumberland. Saved because it was more than just a crown."

"Here it comes," I said.

She nodded. "Your diamonds come from a circlet that was probably forged in the thirteenth century in France," she said. "By the Templars."

"No," I said. "No. Not *The Da Vinci Code*. Not Dan Brown. Please, anything but that."

"Dan Brown didn't actually *invent* the Templars, you know," Élodie chided me. "They were very real. Warrior monks who got way too rich. The king of France got the Templars suppressed so that he could claim their wealth. And *that* included a number of jewels that they'd—well, not to put too fine a point on it, *stolen*—from the Holy Land when they were out there busily hacking off heads and plucking the riches of the infidels. Jewels that had belonged to a caliph, so the story goes. Centuries of being in courts of richness and power."

"We're sensing a theme, here," I said.

"You said it. The king stole them and had them made into a circlet for the queen. But once they were suppressed, the Templars who *hadn't* been killed went underground, and a few of them more than dabbled in black arts. Suddenly the queen found that she couldn't wear the circlet anymore; she claimed that it burned her."

Right. The famous curse.

"The king's daughter Isabelle was married off to Edward II of England, and the circlet went with her. But it was gone by the time Cromwell seized the jewels, and reappeared once the monarchy was restored. Like magic. But no one seems to have ever been very comfortable with it, and it's never been worn at any state occasion that I can find any record of. Or that my assistant can find any record of; he's been snooping around for me. The next people to really handle it at all? Princesses Margaret and Elizabeth. In 1938 they dismantled all the jewels, put them in hatboxes, probably a big joke to them at the time, they were kids, and shipped them off to Canada, and you know all about *that* story."

"So you're saying that they've always carried a curse. And that no one in London really even wants them back."

"That's the unofficial line," Élodie agreed. She stood up.

I blinked at her. "Where are you going?"

"Back to Ottawa. My work here is done. We've successfully averted an international incident. Champagne all around."

"An international incident," I said, "may be the least of our problems."

"*Your* problems, *chérie*," said Élodie. "Sorry, and all that, but officially speaking, there isn't a problem here."

And if Élodie said there was no problem, there was no problem.

Except that there was.

By the time I got home, my nerves were frayed. Too much was happening too quickly. A month ago I'd sat in my office one afternoon contemplating how bored I was. I'd give a lot for that boredom now.

The afternoon had been successful, apparently, and Margery looked relaxed and contented. I wondered if the trip wasn't partly to ascertain that she could in fact leave the children here in good conscience. Apparently their attachment to Montréal was winning her over.

Ivan and Claudia were already in the kitchen cooking dinner when I got in. Lukas was enduring a time-out in his room ("he's tired," said Ivan when he told me, "and called Claudia some nasty names"), and Margery was leafing through a copy of the *Gazette* in the living room. I brought a bottle of Médoc and two glasses in with me. "Wine?"

She glanced up and smiled. "Lovely, thanks."

I poured and sat down next to her. "So you enjoyed the tour?"

"It was spectacular. I haven't had that much fun in a very long time." She sipped her wine reflectively. "The kids seem to like it here."

"I think so," I said cautiously. "Listen, Margery—"

She interrupted me. "Don't think I don't know what we're asking of you," she said. "We do. Well, *I* do. I know it will mean changing your whole life. I've been struggling with—this—for over a year. I didn't know if you'd be willing to take it on."

"I wish you'd told me," I said. "It's just, the suddenness of it . . ."

"I know." She nodded. "I couldn't come to terms with it myself. Feeling so frustrated, every day, but reminding myself that I'd made my choices and I should see them through. Then last year, when I was in the hospital—well, I had to face up to it all. So it was a slow process. I'd have talked about it sooner if I'd been sure."

"And you're sure now?"

"Oh, yes," she said, and her whole face lightened. "I kept thinking it made me a bad mother, allowing someone else to raise my kids. But this is the best place for them right now. I've been seriously unhappy, and it's made them unhappy, too, and that can't be a good thing. Well, they're both insecure, and they didn't used to be like that."

I thought of Lukas and his obsessive lists and calendars. "They're finding ways of coping," I said.

"Maybe." She drank some wine, looking away from me, someplace that wasn't happy. "Claudia may be cutting herself," she said suddenly.

"What?" I put my glass down on the coffee table. "Why? Did you see it?"

"No. And I made her show me her arms last week."

I thought of the oversized sweaters, of the sleeves that Claudia kept pulling down over her knuckles. I'd thought it was a grunge fashion statement. "Should she see a therapist?"

"She is, already." I hadn't known that. "She should probably keep seeing someone, too. What happened is, one of her friends texted another of her friends, who—thankfully—told her mother, who called me. The girls say they don't know for sure, but they thought she might be. I didn't see any evidence—nothing recent, no scars—but it brought it home to me, what I've been putting them through."

It had been so far off my radar to worry about something like that, that I was shocked into silence. Loud, assertive, combative Claudia? I associated cutting with Ophelia-type girls, not someone as *present* as my stepdaughter. I clearly had a lot to learn about this parenting thing.

Better learn it fast, LeDuc.

Dinner was boisterous, to say the least, but it suddenly felt fine. Lukas came out of his sulks and told some hilarious story he'd cribbed from the tour guide. Claudia was permitted a half glass of wine and took selfies all night with various adults in the pictures with her. Over their heads, Ivan and I smiled at each other. And Margery talked about us all planning a vacation together next summer.

I loved where I was. Being part of this circle of people. Seeing them all relaxed and enjoying each other. It balanced out the darkness, somehow.

Julian called me while the kids were still arguing over who had to clear the plates and who had to fill the dishwasher. The police in Saint-Jean-sur-Richelieu were on the lookout for Avner, but he hadn't yet turned up. "I think we just need to be there," he said. "I don't know what it is exactly that we're trying to stop, but we can't do it from here, whatever it is."

"The jewel is exactly what we thought it was," I said, taking my phone upstairs and into the bedroom for privacy. "It's got stored vibes from centuries of magical goings-on, and is cursed on top of it, by the Templars of all people. It's perfect for Aleister."

"Okay." I could tell that Julian was skeptical about the magical goings-on, but he at least understood that we had to stop whatever it was. And, of course, find Avner. "They're keeping an eye on the warehouse, checking it on the overnight tours. I'm gonna owe them for this."

"If it comes off, they'll be owing you," I said. "Tomorrow?"

"Yeah," he said resignedly. "Pick you up at ten. Maybe by then we'll have some news. Magicians work at night, right?"

"How do I know?"

"Well, who knows. If I hear anything overnight I'll give you a call. Pray they don't start it at midnight tonight when all we'll have out there is a couple of constables on a graveyard tour."

"There's that," I agreed. But somehow I thought we were looking at tomorrow. The sentencing at Nuremberg was during the day; they'd want to replicate that.

Probably. We hoped. Unless it was Nuremberg time, which made it . . . I couldn't do the math. What time zone was Nuremberg in?

There were just too many variables, and every time I tried to catch at one of them it disappeared, a will-o'-the-wisp, tantalizingly out of my grasp. Too much to think about. But the one thing was that they had to be stopped. All of us—Gabrielle, Marcus, Avner, Julian, even Élodie in her own way—seemed to be in agreement at least about that.

Julian sounded cheerful. "Anyway, I got us some new recruits," he said. "Been talking with the RMCP."

"Really." None of the police forces were particularly known for their easy entente.

"They're joining us tomorrow," Julian said. "Seems they're hot to get this last diamond back. They're the ones who got them stolen in the first place."

"The Royal Canadian Mounted Police were guarding the vault?"

"Yes indeedy. And probably one of their own—long gone now, of course—was responsible for the hatboxes moving down to the other vault, where Patricia found them."

"Wow," I said. "Talk about needing to make up for something." I hesitated. "But I thought all you guys didn't play that well together."

"LeDuc, I'm still not even close to being sure that any laws are going to be broken tomorrow. Not sure who's getting arrested for what. If we can get any kind of clarity from anybody, I'm open to it."

"Okay," I said. But I was envisioning a full-blown raid, American-style, and I had a feeling that Aleister Brand was too smart to allow something like that to happen.

And just as I was falling asleep, something was tickling the edge of my consciousness and pulled me back from the brink. Something that knotted my stomach and jarred me wide-awake. But I still had no idea what it was.

It was unthinkable. It was impossible.

Numb, Hans walked down the street, through the park, by the bench they'd called theirs, laughing and silly together. There was too much loss to assimilate. Too much . . . too many . . . he couldn't even tell how he felt. The world had shifted impossibly in an instant, and people passed him by, acting as though nothing had changed, oblivious to the darkness pressing in on all sides. Without her, without Livia, there would be no point. In anything.

And now not just Livia. Livia and their—child. The concept so new he couldn't articulate it.

But surely she couldn't mean it. She was a young woman alone, alone and pregnant. She could not survive as an unwed mother. She needed help; she must know that she needed help. She had to change her mind. She had to realize how much he loved her, her— and their unborn child.

She would realize. She would come.

He would do what he had to do at the vault, and then he would take the jewels and wait for her in her room. He would pack the candlesticks. She would change her mind; he knew she would change her mind.

And he was right.

He stepped out his front entrance the next morning and a shadow detached itself from the bagel shop next door. "Hans."

"Livia!" He looked around, desperate that Kurt wasn't coming down after him, shaken at the thought that he might. Livia in danger was unthinkable. "What are you doing here?"

Her smile was a little shaky and, he thought, very brave. "I am ready," she said. "I am ready to go wherever you want to go. You are right; you are the one I know, you are the one I love. The past does not matter. What matters is our future."

"Come with me." Quickly, now, quickly, around the corner; Kurt could come downstairs at any moment. "Listen to me, darling. Go to the bus station," he said. "Here are the tickets. Wait for me there. I will be there, my love, I promise."

She was crying again, but smiling through the tears. "And where are we going?"

He put his arms around her. "Ottawa, to start. And then west, as far west as we can go. Someplace where they will never find us."

"Hans. I love you."

"I love you." He kissed her. "Now go quickly. Do you have a bag packed?" She nodded. "Then go. I will be there before three o'clock. Yes?"

She nodded again. "Yes."

And, just like that, the world was right again.

Maurice was waiting at the side door. "Come on," he said. "You're late, eh?"

Hans grinned. "No," he said; "I'm right on time."

"Come on." In through a narrow passageway, and then down the stairs, two flights of them, deep underground.

The vault was a huge dark creature, lurking, waiting. "Stay here," Hans instructed Maurice, taking the flashlight from him. Kurt had gotten the vault combination, God only knew how; Hans concentrated on it, turning the tumblers slowly. Every nerve told him to hurry; his brain counseled caution.

It was fast; it had to be fast—Livia was waiting. He grabbed the hatbox and pulled out the diamonds, slipping the substitutes Kurt had given him inside. He'd give the real ones to Kurt, but keep just enough out to pay for their new life. Three ought to do it, he thought, looking at their size, and held on to them tightly, sharp against his palm.

Kurt was going to be waiting outside; that was the plan. There wasn't time for much subterfuge. "There," he said to himself, backing out and closing the vault, the diamonds in his hand.

"This way," Maurice hissed, pulling him away from the passageway they'd come in through. "This is the way out."

It was a locked room with a steel door—some other kind of vault, looked like—and as Hans stepped into the doorway, Maurice said, "That will do."

Hans turned and his flashlight picked up the gun in Maurice's hand.

No. No, this wasn't happening. Not when everything was going to work out. Not when . . . He held the bag out to Maurice. "Take them," he said, and with the other man's eyes on the bag and dazzled by the flashlight, he slipped the three diamonds into his mouth, swallowed hard. "Take the diamonds, and we're even," he said.

"Drop the bag," said Maurice, "and turn around."

Hans obeyed. Maurice would take the jewels and leave him, and then all he'd have to do was get away, away from Maurice, away from Kurt, on to the bus station and his new life. To Livia, and their new life together.

He never even heard the shot.

CHAPTER THIRTY-TWO

October 1.

Fitting, in a way: October is, after all, an important month in Québec's history. If Gabrielle Brand was correct, the October Crisis had been the start of Aleister's disenfranchisement. And now perhaps he wanted to end it altogether.

Or perhaps it had started earlier, decades earlier, when a rotund man with deep-set eyes sat in an international court and heard the judges pronounce that he should die.

There was a note on the kitchen table from Ivan.

Have to run out to the casino for a few hours. Be back by noon at the latest. Claudia and Lukas, why don't you show your mom the Underground City?

No one else in the house seemed to be up. It was unfortunate: I could use a shot of ordinary life this morning.

Stop it, Martine. The world wasn't going to blow up. None of this "high-on-drugs astral-planing I just saved the universe" stuff. It was a police matter.

Right.

I dressed without thinking about my clothes: jeans, a pullover sweater, a warm scarf knotted around my neck, boots. Jean-Luc and his dress code could go to hell.

I called Richard while waiting for my coffee to steep in the French press. "I won't be in today," I said.

"*Bien.*" He was never ruffled, my deputy. I could have said, I'm taking the shuttle to Mars today, and he'd just give me that same "very well" and carry on beautifully without me. "Jean-Luc will not be happy," I predicted, "but you can tell him—"

"Yes?"

I took a deep breath. "Tell him that I am working on something, something that will help solve who planted the bombs at City Hall." Best to leave it at that. Though I knew already who had planted the bombs, I wasn't about to go into that now. Not until we had him in custody, under whatever pretext we could manage.

"He will be pleased to hear it. He will be *very* pleased that it was not you."

"He thinks it was me?" Momentarily distracted at the idea, I frowned. There were probably days when he wanted it to be me. Focus, Martine. "I'll—I'll call you later, Richard. And—Richard?"

"*Oui?*"

"Thank you. Thanks for thinking so quickly the other day. Thanks for—well, for everything."

He sounded surprised. "It is nothing. It is my job."

"Yes, well, thank you for that. I'll call you later."

I would, too, I promised myself. No more taking Richard for granted. Or, I added as I took a last look at my husband's note, Ivan, either.

I pulled on my jacket, grabbed my bag, and five minutes later was risking my life yet another time in Julian's TT. He had the radio on and was tapping the steering wheel in time to it; nervous energy. "Is the RCMP there?"

He nodded. "And Saint-Jean-sur-Richelieu local police, too. And," he glanced at me to catch my reaction, "we've got military backup, too."

"You're kidding."

"Not a bit of it. Remember, there's a military barracks at Saint-Jean-sur-Richelieu. And the military school's back there? Seems JTF East wants to make sure there's no spillover from what's happening at the warehouse."

"Aren't they stationed in Montréal?" He was talking about the military's Joint Task Force, Canadian Armed Forces' response to any request for military intervention to provide emergency assistance or support in critical incidents. I wondered if part of Aleister's plan was to take over the military school and barracks. "We should've thought of that."

"We did; who do you think called them in?" He sounded irritated.

"Okay, sorry." I looked out the window; we were crossing the Jacques-Cartier Bridge now, massive over the St. Lawrence Seaway.

"No, it's me. Nerves."

As we got closer, the atmosphere changed tangibly; I glanced across at Julian and saw that I wasn't imagining it. The barometer had to be plummeting. Air thick and somehow contaminated, a faint ringing in my ears.

Approaching the epicenter.

"It's going to happen," said Julian. I didn't think that he really believed it until that moment. "It's going to happen."

"Yes." I wondered if we should have been better prepared: brought a Bible, or holy water, or—an exorcist. I thought back to my convent-school days, searching for the right prayer, I must have heard it sometime. But there was only cotton-ball opaqueness: something clogging the channels.

Two blocks from the warehouse, Julian pulled the TT over and cut the engine. "Here we are," he said unnecessarily.

"Yes." What did soldiers say when preparing for battle? What did the dying say when they saw the stairway of light? "Do you have a gun?" I asked.

"Yes." He wasn't looking at me, his eyes moving restlessly around the car, the sidewalk, the street, cops' eyes are never still. I'd forgotten that about him. "Did you bring anything?"

Like what, I wanted to ask. Lukas's confiscated water pistol, the one I'd never gotten rid of even though I'd taken it from him nearly four years ago? "Only my wits," I said, a lame attempt at humor.

It fell on stony ground, all right. "Stay behind me," said Julian.

"Fine with me."

The building itself looked no different from the last time we'd been there, two days and a lifetime ago. No *Ghostbusters* green slime emanating from it, no spaceship hovering overhead. Cars parked nearby. "Where's all your police presence?"

"Here somewhere," he said.

We were at an angle to the orange door, on the canal side of the building. A car engine was running someplace close; Julian caught it. "Wait here," he said, and scurried off to talk to the guy who'd just driven up. There was a van behind him.

Breathe, I reminded myself. Best if you breathe.

Julian was back in a moment. "You're not going to believe this," he said, and he wasn't keeping his voice down anymore.

"What?"

"Come on." He marched across to the door. This wasn't the approach I'd envisioned, but what the hell; I stayed close behind him. "What *is* it?" I hissed.

The door was ajar; he pushed it the rest of the way open. Down the corridor there was light. Voices. "They're doing it!" I exclaimed.

"Not what you think," Julian said.

I followed him down and into the doorway of a large space—the main warehouse floor, no doubt. Big, echoing area, perfect for drama. The place where the ritual was to take place, where the skinhead magicians were practicing chaos magic, were summoning Hitler back from the dead.

Except that the body lying in the middle of the floor surrounded by people wearing protective clothing wasn't Hitler's.

It was Aleister Brand.

"Not the same gun used on Patricia," said Julian.

I was staring out at the canal. "Do you think it was Marcus?" I asked.

"It was a larger caliber than the other." He sounded tired, and he wasn't answering my question.

I was feeling completely disoriented. It had never occurred to me that I could be wrong. Everything had pointed to Aleister being the one. Even his *mother* had pointed to him being the one. "Where's everyone else?" I asked.

"Who?"

"The boys in the band," I said flippantly. "All those testosterone-driven skinheads who were going to play séance with Aleister. Where'd they go?"

"Would you stick around if you found a body and you're part of a group known for violence?" Now he was being flippant. We were both dealing with a severe case of anticlimax.

"I don't suppose they killed him," I said.

"Can't rule it out."

"Probably not, though."

"Probably not," he agreed. "You okay here? I have to go do the liaison thing for a while, then we can head back into the city."

"Yes, of course." I was still looking at the canal ten minutes later when my phone rang. I glanced at the screen: Ivan. "Hey, babe."

"Hey, Martine. Listen, are the kids and Margery with you?"

"Who? The—kids?" It was so unexpected, I found myself stammering. "No—no, of course not. Weren't they all going to the Underground City?"

"Thought so, but Margery's not been answering her cell for a while. Neither are the kids."

"Well," I said, "it might not be anything, you know reception isn't always great down there." I know I sounded lame—I'm not so advanced at this detective thing yet that seeing a dead body isn't upsetting, and I realized that my hand on my smartphone was shaking. I wasn't ready to talk about something as ordinary as losing cell-phone reception.

"Could be," said Ivan, "but we were supposed to meet out at the casino, spend the afternoon at the Ronde."

I felt my stomach lurch. Maybe this wasn't ordinary, after all. "There has to be an explanation," I said. "Have you called the police?"

"Not yet. I wanted to check with you first. I'll keep calling them." He sounded worried.

"I'll check with Julian," I said, feeling my heart start to race. This was way too coincidental for me. "I'll call you back, Ivan."

I tracked Julian down by the warehouse, where Aleister's body was being loaded onto a gurney. I wondered, fleetingly, how Gabrielle would take the news. He turned to me. "What's up?"

"The kids and Margery." I took a deep breath. "They're missing."

"They probably—"

"No," I said, cutting him off. "They're missing. For real. No one's answering their phones, and those kids live with their phones glued to their bodies." I looked at the big building behind us. "What if he took them? And then someone killed him? Maybe they killed the kids, too? Or maybe he hid them so we'll never find them?" I was sounding a little hysterical. I tried to get by Julian. "Maybe they're in here, somewhere, tied up or—"

"Stop." He grabbed me. "This isn't helping."

"Someone has my kids," I said, the panic rising until I felt I was going to be sick. Everything about the day suddenly crystallized, clear and sharp, the canal, the impossibly blue sky above it, the people in uniform still moving about the property. The barometer was still playing with the pressure inside my head. I suddenly realized that my chest was hurting, that I couldn't breathe. "Julian, Julian—"

"Okay." He was already on his cell phone. "And somebody get me a paper bag, *now!*"

A constable came trotting up with a bag and Julian stabbed me on the shoulder with his forefinger. "Sit down, LeDuc, and breathe into the bag."

I grabbed it like it was a lifeline and a moment later, my head down, stopped hyperventilating. Lukas and Claudia. The kids I saw as a charming—or, sometimes, not-so-charming—interruption to my real life, my important life, my chosen life. How long had I been treating them as symbols instead of people? Claudia, pretending indifference, ostentatiously filing her nails and drawling affectedly in an effort to look and sound sophisticated and maybe even cutting herself when she was alone and scared. Lukas, organized and having OCD, but eager to please, eager to try new things, go new places, filled with an energy that I'd always allowed to sap my own.

Lukas and Claudia.

I pulled the bag away from my face. Julian was still on the phone. "Yes. Yeah, okay. I want reports every five minutes, you got that?"

"Julian," I said. He held up a finger, signaling me to wait. "Yeah,

that's what I said. Then do it now," he said into the phone and clicked
off. "Are you all right?"

I shook my head.

"Stupid question," he agreed and reached his hand down to help
me up. "Come on."

"Where?"

"Montréal." He sounded grim. "Seems we just got a call from
Lev. Your kids aren't the only ones gone missing."

"Who?" Avner was already gone.

"Naomi Kaspi. Mrs. Avner. And Lev sounds in worse shape
than you."

The Americans came in and liberated the camp.

*Their voices hearty, a never-ending supply of cigarettes in their
pockets. And food—even the black-market food in the camp couldn't
compare to this. Inmates were pushing it down their gullets as fast as
they could, diarrhea coming out the moment the food went in, their
bodies unable to assimilate it.*

*The camp guards had fled; Karl and Ilse had fled; there was no
one there but the prisoners and the kapos. The camp resistance created huge signs to put up, and everyone had their own message: the
politicos created one that read* THE GERMAN POLITICAL PRISONERS
WELCOME THEIR AMERICAN FRIENDS, *while the Communists coun-
tered with a poem—well, something that rhymed, anyway—that
read,* WE ANTI-FASCISTS WANT TO GO HOME TO ERADICATE NAZI
CRIMINALS.

*Elias tried to feel elation, but all he really felt was tired. A GI
stopped him as he trudged from the commandant's office to his barracks. "Hey, buddy!"*

*"Yes, sir?" He'd spent too many years saying "sir" to anyone in
uniform.*

The soldier liked that. "Hey, Stoney, get that? He called me sir!"

"He don't know you too well, then."

The soldier turned back to Elias. "Where you goin' when this is over, buddy? You got a girl back home?"

"I did, once," Elias said. "I do not know if she is still alive."

The boy—and he was a boy, probably younger than Elias himself—looked genuinely distressed. "I sure hope she is, buddy," he said.

"Yes," said Elias. "I am sure she is."

But he knew in his heart that he was wrong.

CHAPTER THIRTY-THREE

Julian put the siren on and slapped a blue light on top of the TT. I'd never seen either before. He caught my look. "LeDuc, don't worry. We have three separate police forces looking for them. We'll find them."

"Yes," I managed to say, and even to my own ears my voice sounded dead and cold. "Yes, I'm sure we will."

He was on the telephone all the way back. "Who's coordinating? Who? Okay, yeah, I know him. Yeah, I know he did. Okay." A quick glance at me. "Listen, handle it how you normally would, but I have some additional information that you need. They're Martine LeDuc's stepchildren and their mother. Yeah, I know, and that's a decent line of inquiry, too, but you have to hear me. She's been working with me on this jewel heist . . . yeah . . . I'm just throwing it out there, it could be a connection. . . ."

I bit my lip and turned away from him, looking out the window instead. Big-box stores, cinemas, hotels, all looking ridiculously normal. How could people go shopping for appliances? How could everyone behave as though the ground weren't crumbling beneath our very feet? And then we were sweeping onto the bridge and the traffic was snarled and we worked our way through the maze of vehicles, curious glances, wondering what desperate mission we were on, what tragedy we were racing to face. I'd done it myself, sent a small prayer aloft at the sight of active ambulances, fire trucks, police cars.

My stomach was so tight it was nearly unbearable.

I punched Ivan's icon on my smartphone. "Have you heard anything?"

"No." His voice was rough and I could hear, behind it, the shimmer of fear, the spiderweb gossamer thread holding him a millimeter away from screaming, from losing it. "The police are on it," I said.

"Yeah, I know, they're here with me now."

I glanced at Julian, holding up my phone, and he nodded. "I'm putting you on speakerphone, Ivan," I said, pressing buttons. "Julian's here with me."

"Ivan," Julian said, calm and clear. "Are you at the casino?"

"Yeah. They said I should stay—"

"They're right. Stay put. Who's there with you?"

Some blurred voices, and then a louder one. "This is Commander Harrison, RMCP. With whom am I speaking?"

"*Détective-lieutenant* Fletcher, city police," Julian said. "Are you coordinating from there?"

"We've set up headquarters downtown, at City Hall," the voice said. "I'm staying with Mr. Petrinko in case a call comes through."

"Has anyone been to the house to check?" Julian asked.

Ivan said, "No. But I tried the house phone, too. No one's answering anywhere."

"That's okay," said Julian. "We'll head over there now, just to be sure." He reached over to my phone to click off the connection and said, "Okay, so what changed? Why did Aleister have to die?"

"I know you're trying to get my mind off things, but I can't—"

"They're related. It's all related, and you know it," he said. "Focus."

"Okay." I swallowed hard. "Avner disappears, then . . ."

"Wait. Before that. Let's start at the beginning. Lev Kaspi and Patricia Mason are connected. Right? Through McGill?"

"Yeah. He's the one who tells her about the treasure ships, and the jewels under the Sun-Life Building. He's the one who found out they got moved, too." I was fighting hard to stay in control.

"So he knew about all that, but he never talked about it until she came along. And she was around because the excavations at the museum had opened up some of the sealed underground tunnels. So she sees her opportunity and the museum, whose director was with her when she first opened the room, makes her get *you* involved. And now the circle of people who know about the sealed room where she found the diamonds is getting bigger."

"Right," I said. I couldn't see where this was heading.

"Think," urged Julian. "What if we've been too focused on the diamonds? Was there anything else in that room?"

"Papers," I said. "Documents. But probably all of it just duplicates of what was already digitized. Lev told me he had the *Emerald*'s manifests, he had lists of securities, he had the diary kept by the guy from the Bank of England, for heaven's sake."

"Still," said Julian, "what would be more precious than a diamond? Information?"

"Don't see what it could be," I said stubbornly.

"I don't either," he confessed. "But I'm starting to think that's what this is about."

We pulled onto my street and I had the door open before the TT had even come to a full stop. "LeDuc! Wait for me! You don't know—"

I didn't listen. There was a clue there, somewhere, a clue in the apartment that would tell me where he'd taken them. I didn't even know who the "he" was—Aleister, before he was killed? Marcus? Someone outside of our radar? Someone who'd now taken Naomi Kaspi, as well.

All I had to do was find the clue.

I had the key out and ready before I even reached the door, before I heard Julian in the entryway behind me, swearing as the street-level door closed on him. It didn't matter. There would be a clue here.

There were three people sitting in my living room. Margery was perched on the edge of the armchair. Claudia and Lukas were together on the sofa. No one was doing anything; they were frozen in a tableau.

I walked through the door and it closed behind me. Margery said, in an anguished voice, "No!"

And then Naomi Kaspi said, "It is time you finally get home." And showed me her gun.

I never saw it coming.

I looked at the kids. "Are you all right?" They both nodded. They were holding hands, which had to be a first. When we got out of this, I'd remind them of it.

When we got out of this.

Avner's wife looked terrible. There were red splotches on her face and neck, and her hair was disheveled. But it wasn't her face or hair that worried me: it was the steadiness of her hand.

The one with the gun.

"What do you want?" I asked her. "If it's me you're waiting for, then here I am. I'll do whatever you want me to do. And so you can let them go, right?"

"Let them go? You think that I can do that, yes? So they can get the police here?"

"The police are already here," I said. "I came with the police. Didn't you hear the siren?"

"We heard the siren," said Margery, her eyes on Naomi.

"So if you let them go, we can have a conversation," I said. "You can tell me why you wanted me here."

"I can tell you right now. They don't have to go nowhere."

"Okay," I said. "So tell me what the problem is, Mrs. Kaspi."

"The problem is you. Before, not so much, but now the problem is you. Before, the problem was other people, but now the problem is you."

Alice through the looking glass, I thought: I could hear the words, but they weren't making any sense. This wasn't getting us anywhere. And I didn't even know where to begin trying to make it make sense. "Is this about the swastika?" I asked. "The death threat to Avner?"

"You think that was for Avner? Everyone thinks that was for Avner!" She shook her head. "That was for me. That man, he knew we have money. We are in the diamond business, *nu*? Of course we have money. He wanted payments. Lots of payments. That note? That was to remind me. To remind me to keep paying."

"Someone was blackmailing you?" Somewhere in here there had to be a sane thread of conversation that I could catch hold of. Somewhere.

"Was it Aleister Brand?" It was a decent guess, since the swastika was from the New Order of the Black Sun.

"That man," she said, nodding. "He would ruin everything, he would. Everything it is good until he finds out about that girl and that diamond." She changed tack. "It was her fault. Really. Her fault."

"Patricia Mason," I said. "What did she do, Naomi?"

She didn't seem to mind my use of her first name. "Him, and her, and now you," she said vigorously. "But we have all been through too much. We have survived too much. We have survived worse than you. You are not going to ruin our lives now, now that we have them back."

I had absolutely no idea what she was talking about. It was becoming pretty clear that she was off whatever meds Avner had mentioned she took. "Tell me, Naomi," I said. "Tell me what happened. Tell me what went wrong." Even if I wasn't going to be able to follow her disjointed logic, the more time she spent talking, the less time she was spending putting bullets into my family.

The landline rang then, suddenly and shrilly. Margery jumped; it was on the table next to her. "Don't touch that!" hissed Naomi.

"It's the police," I said. "They're here to help." It kept ringing. "They want to talk with you, Naomi. They want to help you solve this problem."

"You are the problem," she said. This was a woman with focus. The telephone was loud and getting on my nerves; I couldn't imagine what it was doing to hers. "Then tell me how *I* can help," I said, a little desperately, not daring to look at the kids.

"Lev should never have met that girl, that shiksa," said Naomi. "I told him she was bad for him. He should stay with his own kind."

"I don't think they were romantically involved," I said gently. "He was just helping her—"

"He should stay with his own kind," she interrupted. "This would never have happened. That was the start of the troubles. Everyone should stay with their own kind. My father is right. It is important not to mix with other people."

The ringing stopped as suddenly as it had begun.

She had to be getting tired, and I didn't want that gun going off accidentally. "Naomi," I said, "why don't we sit down? It will be so much easier to chat that way."

"You sit."

"Okay." I eased my way gently into the stiff-backed chair near the door, the one that had once been my mother's. Odd, the thoughts one has. "Okay, I'm sitting now. You can put the gun down."

"No. You will not trick me that way." But she lowered it, all the same.

I took a deep breath. "So tell me what happened, Naomi," I said.

"It was all right," she said. "Avner never knew, and that was all right. My father never knew, and that was all right. That was better. It was the way it should be. We were happy. We were all so happy."

I couldn't decide which fork to take, which of the two obvious questions to ask. I could hear Julian's mantra in my head, and I followed it. "What changed, Naomi? What happened to make you unhappy?"

"They found out! You don't understand; you don't come from our community. It is not right. The new Jews in the city, for them it is fine, all this tolerance. These new Jews, they do not know better. But it is not fine. It is *not* fine."

"No," I agreed, completely in the dark. "It couldn't have been fine."

"You see!" She nodded vigorously with something approaching a smile. "You see. Something had to be done. My father—no, he could not know. He could never know. No one could ever know, could ever think less of him for it. It would have shamed him. It is unimaginable. A million times over, it would have shamed him. He has a place in the community. He has stature."

"Rabbi Kahn," I said cautiously.

"He is not just a rabbi," she said. A flash of pride. "He is important. He writes—significant things. Many books. Learned books. Books that tell us how we must live." She drew in a deep breath. "He tells us that we cannot trust them, the goyim, people like you. That we have to stay inside our community. If we do not, we betray our people. We betray their history, their sacrifices."

What was she talking about? I glanced at Margery and she met my eyes, lifting her shoulders slightly: she had no idea. Was it Lev and Patricia? But Lev had said they were just friends.

Fortunately Naomi didn't need to be prodded. "So he could not know. He could not know. We would all have been shamed. Our lives would not be worth living." She shook her head. "What I did was what was right for all of us," she said.

"Naomi," I said suddenly, fearing the worst, "where's Avner?"

"He's here," she said. "I made him come here." She lowered her voice. "He does not understand, but he will."

Lukas said, suddenly, "He's in your bedroom, Belle-Maman. She made him go in there when he got here. He has rope on his hands."

"You be quiet!" She rounded on him, and Margery and I cried out together. "Then, fine! You want Avner? You want to shame my husband? Fine, fine!" She gestured to Lukas. "Go and get him!"

Lukas looked at me and I nodded, and he went up the stairs. There was an extension of the landline in the bedroom; I hoped he was using it.

Avner appeared at the top of the stairs. He looked definitely the worse for wear, but he didn't seem to be actually hurt. He was rubbing his wrists and I could see that they were raw; he'd probably been trying to get away the whole time we'd been there.

Naomi watched him with detachment, and didn't say anything when he got down to our level and sat on the loveseat adjacent to the sofa. Lukas came down the stairs, slowly, and she waved him over to the sofa again. "So now you know," she said to Avner.

He shook his head. "I know nothing," he said, "but that mine Naomi needs help."

"All I want," she said, "is to go back to being fine."

There was a short silence. I tried to catch Lukas's eye, but he was examining Avner. "Are you all right?" he asked him finally, anxiously.

Avner smiled. "You are a good boy to ask," he said. "Fine, I am not, but okay for now, yes. You are a good boy, and a lucky one, to have two mothers. Thank you for asking." He turned to his wife. "And so I want to know what is happening," he said. "You use a gun. This is not right. It is not righteous. We are Jews. We are righteous. We do not threaten people with guns. So this you must tell me, what is wrong here."

"*You* are righteous," she said. "My father the rabbi is righteous. Not every Jew is righteous."

"This, what you say, this is true. Not every Jew. But our family, Naomi, we are."

"*Your* family, Avner," she said, and there was a mixture of sadness and bitterness in her voice. "Your family, yes. Your father, he was a survivor. He survived the camps. He lived a good life, a strong life. And you are good like that, and strong." She started to cry, tears running soundlessly down her cheeks.

"What has happened to you, Naomi?"

"Don't," she said, as he started to rise. "Stay where you are. We will be together again, but only once the problem is gone."

"People are dead. This did not solve your problem?"

"He was the problem, but now he is not." She looked at him. "Do you not remember, Avner? Do you not remember when our son Lev came to us and told us about this shiksa?"

Avner's face reflected horror for one split second before the love flooded in again. "Mine dear wife—" he began.

She waved the gun at him. "He should never have done that," she said. "The past should stay buried."

"No," said Avner. "This is not true. If we have learned anything, it is the opposite. We must always remember. We must never forget."

"That is simple for you!" she burst out. "Your father, he was a survivor, he was a hero! Easy that you should say never forget! Well, me, I have to forget!"

"I do not understand," said Avner. "Your father is a great rabbi—"

"My father was a *Nazi*!"

Margery gasped. The rest of us stayed where we were, staring at her, riveted. She must be mad, I thought. Delusional. Where did that come from?

Avner was staring at her. "No," he said quietly. "You are confused, it is understandable, so much has happened here. You are confused, Naomi. We can call your father, yes? Have him come here and be with us?"

"No!" There was definite hysteria in her voice now. "He's not my father. Not my real father." She stopped speaking and looked down at the gun in her hands. Steadying herself. "My mother was with a Nazi in the war," she said, getting a grip on the hysteria that even she must have heard in her voice. "Here in Montréal. She went away to have the baby—to have me. She invented a husband who died. She married the rabbi as a widow, and he adopted me."

I said, "That doesn't make any difference, Naomi, who your father—"

Avner put up his hand. "Please, Martine," he said quietly. "Do not speak of this. We know different, Naomi and me." Nothing but sorrow in his voice. "The rabbi who has adopted her, Rabbi Samuel Kahn, my father-in-law who makes me move to Montréal, this man he would never accept the child of a Nazi. This man, he wants to keep our community pure. Separate from the rest of the world. Perhaps too separate; perhaps it is not right. But it is what he does. It is what he stands for."

It sounded a lot like Nazism in reverse to me, but maybe there was something here I wasn't understanding.

Naomi was nodding. "Shame," she said. "Shame for his name, shame for the community. This I cannot allow." She looked at Avner. "This is why that swastika comes to our house," she said. "This man, he has learned of my secret, he will tell everyone unless I give him money."

Avner shook his head. "And all this time, you cannot trust me? To tell me this? All these years when you are mine wife? Am I so difficult to talk to? Have I ever been so difficult to talk to?"

She looked at him and her whole expression softened; I saw a glimmer of the girl she'd once been. "Not even you could I tell, Avner," she said. "I was too ashamed."

"How did this happen, that your mother—"

I cut him off. The longer she stood there with a gun in her hand, the longer my children were in danger. There would be time for the whole story eventually. "Naomi, what matters is how you act now, not how your parents acted in the past," I said. "Whatever's happened, whatever you've done, whatever anybody's done, there's a way out. Taking hostages like this, it isn't the way. Let the children go. They have nothing to do with this. They're innocent. Let them go."

Avner pulled himself together and nodded. "You cannot hurt the children, mine wife," he said softly. "No matter what else has passed, you cannot do this."

"No," she agreed suddenly. Her face looked gray. I wondered if telling Avner had taken the last ounce of strength she'd had. She looked at me. "They can go. That woman, too. You stay."

Avner began, "Why—" but I was already standing up. Reaching across to the kids. "Come on," I said. "Quickly. Just go down to the street. They'll take care of you."

Lukas said, "Dad's down there."

So that was the call he'd made. "Good," I said. "You go down, and tell him I'll be there as soon as I can." I looked at Margery. "Take care of them."

"Of course," she said. She walked cautiously across Naomi's line of fire and opened the door. "Quickly," she told them. Claudia gave me a quick scared smile as she went through, and then the door closed, and the three of us were alone.

"So, Naomi," I said, "What do you want?"

She looked at me blankly. "What do I want?"

I nodded. "Now. What would make this turn out all right for you?"

She looked at Avner, helpless. "I thought I could make it right," she said. "I thought, if this woman dies, then our Lev, he stops talking silly talk of treasure and jewels and papers. But she dies, and he doesn't stop, this talk."

"Lev wanted to know about his past, his *mishpocha*," said Avner. "This is normal."

"His past, it is not normal," she said. "I am not normal! I am a monster! And I have hidden it! I have hidden it since I first knew of it, when my mother died and told me, that she was this German's whore, and I think then that I must kill myself for shame. But suicide is shame, too. So I live with it and I keep it secret, always such a secret, from my father and my husband and my son, but now because of Lev and that shiksa and the swastika, now everything is known. I may as well have killed myself." She looked at him, her eyes wild. "I *have* killed now, mine husband. I have killed."

"Yes," said Avner quietly. "But you can stop now."

"Can I?"

Avner said, "It is not for us to say what happens, mine Naomi. But what we can do, we can do what is right at every turn. You can do what is right now."

"You are not angry with me?"

Nothing but sorrow in his face. "I think you have a sickness," he said. "I think you're *fermisht*. I think you need some help. But angry? How can I be angry with mine wife of thirty-eight years? This, this does not happen."

"Naomi," I said suddenly, "do you have the diamond?"

She shook her head. "It is cursed. I am sorry, my Avner, I know that it reminds you of your father, but this diamond, it has brought our *mishpocha* nothing but terrible luck. I gave it away."

"To whom?" I couldn't resist the question.

"To the man in the wheelchair, of course," she said. And then she handed Avner the gun.

For the second time that day, anticlimax set in. There was a long silence in the room, and then Avner nodded at me. "We will go," he said.

"Yes," I agreed.

We all three trooped down to the street where the police took Naomi off in a car right away, and Avner with her. He wouldn't let go of her hand.

I looked around me, blinking: it felt like hours since I'd run into the house. My street was cordoned off, with onlookers and tourists craning their necks at either end to catch a glimpse of what was happening. But all I saw, after that first glance around, was Ivan. Ivan, and Claudia, and Lukas, and I was already moving past Julian, toward them.

And I knew I was home.

The war was over.

Everywhere there were victory dances, victory parades. She even ran into one of them as she walked hesitantly up the hill, back into her old neighborhood, pushing the stroller.

Bernie was standing in front of his delicatessen, just as she remembered him, his belly vast despite the war's privations, his apron starched and white, watching the parade. "Livia Rosen, as I live and breathe! Now there's a sight for sore eyes! You've been missed, you have." His eyes lighted on the stroller. "Hello, and who's this?"

"This is my daughter," she said. "Say hello, Naomi."

"Cute little thing." Bernie and the little girl peered at each other. "Where's Hans, then? Don't tell me you are moving back to the neighborhood? That's almost as good news as the parade! I've missed you both. No one liked my smoked meat like Hans did."

She took a deep breath, trying out the story for the first time. "He couldn't stand not helping with the war, Bernie," she said. "He was that brave. He went in on Juno Beach." She sniffed. "They buried him over there, in France."

Bernie nodded, unsurprised, his face grave. "Country's full of young widows, just like you," he said. "Don't be sad, Livia. You and this little girl, you'll still have a good life. We'll take care of you; the neighborhood'll take care of you. Come on in, I'll get you and little Naomi something to eat. Smoked meat, just the way you like it, extra pickles." He laughed. "Everything is going to be fine. You'll see: we can start thinking about the future again. Now that I think of it, there's a fellow here for you to meet, someone who could use a wife like you. Just starting to get a reputation in the community. Building quite a following. We're going to hear a lot from him, mark my words."

"Why?" asked Livia. "Is he a politician?"

Bernie grinned. "Oh, much better than that," he said. "He's a rabbi."

EPILOGUE

The diamonds—the two that were left—were returned to London. Discreetly. They never found the third one—and never found Marcus Levigne, either, who oddly enough sent me a letter months later. "The *détective-lieutenant* thinks it was all about wealth," he wrote. "But imagine yourself, Martine, spending your whole career looking at the worst of all possible specimens of humanity. I made it my life's work to know about them, to understand their inner workings, to be at one with them, and after a time I came to the only possible conclusion: that there is no hope for the human race. We are petty, cruel, stupid self-serving individuals. So better to be a wealthy one than an impoverished one."

The story of Livia and Hans emerged finally, and, sadly, Naomi was right: her adoptive father distanced himself from her as completely as possible once it became news.

When Patricia brought the stolen diamond to Avner for appraisal, she set in motion a string of events that no one could have anticipated. It became the worst-kept secret in the city: Avner couldn't resist talking about it. Gabrielle found out; Marcus found out; Aleister found out.

Naomi didn't care about the diamond. She cared about the secret that Patricia now knew, and she killed Patricia to silence her—even though Patricia couldn't have cared less about it; for Naomi, it was the only thing that mattered. Lev was the one stunned to learn of his real parentage, but again, absorbed it and moved on; he was that sort of person.

Aleister, thinking that the Kaspis had the diamond, and party by now to the information about Naomi's real father, intended to frighten the couple with a death threat that he'd then follow up with blackmail. While Avner was ducking around town playing amateur sleuth, Naomi met Aleister in a park and gave him the diamond. She meant to kill him, but Marcus beat her to it, having access to a car and having, like us, circled the October date on his calendar.

Avner wasn't quite as innocent about Naomi's mental illness as he pretended to be, but certainly he'd no idea that she'd be able to hurt anyone.

Lukas and Claudia had ten kinds of hissy fits each before they were officially moved into our loft apartment in the Old City, and even more once they started school—in French. And after they went to bed at night Ivan and I toasted them with wine and laughed a lot together. Margery went off with Doctors Without Borders and sent regular letters to the kids, who started—maybe—seeing that she hadn't rejected them so much as having said yes to something new and important.

Jean-Luc Boulanger didn't fire me. He took full responsibility for the outcome at my apartment, and as my role in it couldn't be eliminated, he made sure that the newspapers all knew I was working at his instigation at the time. As Claudia would say, "whatever."

Naomi was judged incompetent to stand trial and was hospitalized; Avner went to see her every day. "What can I do?" he asked me over smoked-meat sandwiches at the delicatessen now known as Schwartz's, sitting perhaps at the same counter where Livia and

Hans had met. "She's my *bubbela*. You don't turn your back on people you love."

"Rabbi Kahn did," I reminded him.

"Ha. He's no mensch, that one. Better rid of him." It was a refreshing point of view.

Lev stood next to me at Patricia's memorial service at McGill. "There's only one thing to do now."

"What's that?"

He shook his head sorrowfully. "I have to get married. It's the only thing that will make my father happy."

Élodie sent me a package from Ottawa. "Thought you'd like to see this," she wrote. It was a declassified shipping manifest from Liverpool, England: the manifest for the treasure ships. On a soft spring day I went up to the cemetery at Notre-Dame-des-Neiges— where my own mother is buried—and sat down next to Patricia Mason's grave, now beginning to blend in with the rest of them. "They're writing it up, now," I told her. "Your name will be associated with it forever."

She'd stolen one of the diamonds, and died because of it; but I still thought that it was an impulse, maybe even one that she later regretted. Her priority was the priority of every academic, from my father grappling with his sea monsters to the young woman lying under this headstone: the truth.

Perhaps, like him, she'd finally found it.

AUTHOR'S NOTE

Depending on your source, either the British crown jewels were absolutely, positively stored under the Sun-Life Building in Montréal during the war—or, just as absolutely and positively, were not. You pays your money and you takes your pick, as the saying goes. I think it's probable that they *were* in Montréal: the most popular alternate "undisclosed location" is in Wales, and if Great Britain had been invaded and occupied, as Patricia pointed out, the jewels would have been as unsafe there as they'd been in London.

Wherever the jewels were eventually stored, they were first disassembled by the king and his daughters (who apparently found the process uproarious fun) and placed in—yes—hatboxes for transport.

To the best of my knowledge, there is no Templar connection to any of the current crown jewels, and nor is there a curse on them. It is true that Cromwell destroyed all of the jewels then in existence, so what's now included in the collection is of relatively recent vintage.

The passage, storage, and use of the gold and securities on the HMS *Emerald* and via Operation Fish is extremely well documented: it kept convoys moving across the dangerous North Atlantic and supplying an island nation that would have otherwise been cut off from survival throughout the war. Patricia was right about that, too: it was the largest physical movement of wealth in history. Alexander Craig was indeed the Bank of England official who went across on the *Emerald*—and did apparently enjoy the irony of his wife worrying about him having enough money with him—and Francis Cyril Flynn was her captain.

Where I deviated from the truth is in not respecting what is perhaps the most extraordinary aspect of Operation Fish: its complete secrecy. The needs of my novel dictated leaks, stolen jewels, and rumors; in fact there were none. This and other successful British naval operations, undertaken with unspeakable courage in the face of appalling odds, are documented in Alfred Draper's *Operation Fish* as well as in Robert Switky's *Wealth of an Empire: The Treasure Shipments that Saved Britain and the World*, and it is with complete respect and amazement that I write about them here. *No one knew.* There were no leaks. There were no rumors. They did this extraordinary thing and they kept it secret and it saved Great Britain from German occupation.

The story of Dunkirk and the famous evacuation known as Operation Dynamo—including the heroic role of the "little ships"—occurred between May 27 and June 4, 1940. Dunkirk has been referred to as both a miracle and a myth, and I invite you to explore both analyses of the operation. What is true is that 700 private boats took part and helped rescue more than 338,000 trapped British and French soldiers. A river ferry, the *Royal Daffodil*, alone rescued 7,461 service personnel; the paddle steamer *Medway Queen* made seven round trips under heavy fire; the yacht *Sundowner* (owned and captained by *Titanic* survivor and second officer Charles Lightolier) nearly capsized before getting 130 men to safety. The smallest craft, the *Tamzine*, was only fifteen feet long. Some small craft took men across the Channel; others ferried them off the beaches and onto waiting Royal Navy ships. The operation inspired Churchill's famous "we shall fight on the beaches" speech.

The relationship between the Gestapo and the occult is fairly well documented, even if some of the work veers into the conspiracy-theory arena. There *is* a distinct line to be drawn connecting racial-purity theorizing about the beginning of the world with several strains of occult belief and practice, and Himmler believed that the SS were the twentieth century's answer to the Teutonic Knights. He held ceremonies at night in castles lit by flaming torches, used a King Arthur–type roundtable for meetings, and believed himself to be the reincarnation of Heinrich I of Saxony.

It's true that there is, blessedly for the city, less neo-Nazi activity in Montréal than elsewhere in the country: western Canada seems to be the unfortunate host to a number of ever-shifting Aryan groups. Kyle McKee is a real person and as of this writing one of the leaders of the "Nationalist" movement, sometimes known as Calgary's "micro-führer." If you're interested in learning more, read Warren Kinsella's scary book, *Web of Hate: Inside Canada's Far Right Network*, which is where I also found the story about the founding of the Ku Klux Klan.

The Pointe-à-Callière archaeological and anthropological museum does exist in Montréal, and it is in fact opening up some of the underground tunnels and buried rivers as part of an ambitious expansion program; but its director is not named Pierre LaTour, and he is not meant to resemble anyone connected with the museum. Visit Pointe-à-Callière next time you're in Montréal: it has some amazing collections.

If you're interested in urban exploration, watch this fascinating TED Talk on the subject by a passionate practitioner: www.youtube .com/watch?v=TS1kuG-Z78g.

Lev was right about the studies made of second- and third-generation survivors of the concentration camps; the *Israel Journal of Psychiatry and Related Sciences*, doctoral work by Melissa Kahane-Nissenbaum and Perella Perlstein, the Conference on Jewish Material Claims Against Germany, and the Anti-Defamation League, the Hidden Child Foundation, and others continue to engage in understanding the lasting effects of this particular trauma.

The rest of the book is fiction. I hope that you enjoyed reading it.